MORNING KISSES

"Good morning," Elizabeth whispered as Cole entered the room.

He turned, disappointed to find her fully clothed, and smiled suggestively. "Although you look utterly charming, I must confess I like you better with a few less clothes on."

Feeling a blush spread over her cheeks, Elizabeth smiled shyly. "I thought you were anxious to make an early start this morning."

Circling her waist with his hands, Cole drew her close against his chest. "I've had a change of plan. . . ."

Goose bumps broke out over Elizabeth's arms. Her eyes opened wide. "You can't mean you want to—"

Cole nodded, drawing her closer into his embrace.

"But it's broad daylight!"

"So?"

Elizabeth opened her mouth to protest, but Cole silenced her with a kiss. . . .

MILLIE CRISWELL
CALIFORNIA TEMPTRESS

ZEBRA BOOKS
KENSINGTON PUBLISHING CORP.

To
Jen, my first editor,
my favorite daughter,
my harshest critic . . .
and to
Matt, my son,
who doesn't read romances
but is definitely hero material.
I love you both.

ZEBRA BOOKS

are published by

Kensington Publishing Corp.
475 Park Avenue South
New York, NY 10016

First printing: June, 1991

Printed in the United States of America

Chapter One

"What the devil do you think you are doing, Elizabeth?" Josiah Worthington's voice reverberated off the lemon-colored walls of his granddaughter's bedroom. Even the patter of the rain against the mullioned windows of the mansion did not muffle the harshness of his tone.

Elizabeth Forrester gave her grandfather only the briefest of glances before continuing with her packing. "I should think that would be rather obvious," she replied. "I am leaving!"

Straightening his imposing six foot one inch frame, Josiah crossed the threshold into Elizabeth's room. "Don't be absurd. You'll do no such thing! I'll not allow it." He crossed his arms over his chest, a pose he often used to intimidate his adversaries.

Elizabeth brushed back the riotous strands of blond hair that threatened to obscure her vision. Her own unusually tall stature gave her the advantage of being able to stare directly into her grandfather's implacable features. She had always hated her statuesque build,

5

except when doing battle with her grandfather.

"You do not own me, Grandfather. You may own half the people in the city of New York, but you do not own me. What you have done is unforgivable . . . detestable. I am traveling to California to find my father, with or without your blessing."

Observing the mottled rage on her grandfather's face, Elizabeth drew a deep breath. Few people dared to defy "The Lion of Wall Street," as he was referred to by the newspapers. Josiah Worthington was still a formidable opponent despite his seventy years. Time had turned his blond hair white and his stomach soft, but his will was as strong as ever.

Bearding "The Lion" took courage. Elizabeth was determined that this time she would not give in to her grandfather's demands. For twenty years, she had acquiesced to his wishes, striving to be the dutiful, loving granddaughter, basking in his approval and endeavoring to win the love he was reluctant to give. But not this time.

"You do not understand my motives, Elizabeth. What I did was for your own good. I sought to protect you."

Elizabeth's blue eyes narrowed, becoming as hard as the sapphire orbs she stared into. "Protect me! How? By telling me lies about my father? Leading me to believe he had abandoned me? That he no longer loved me? Here is the proof of your lies, Grandfather. The letter you tried to hide from me. One of hundreds my father has written me over the past twenty years. How could you be so cruel?" She held the letter up, daring him to deny his treachery.

Grabbing her shoulders, Josiah noted the look of bitterness on her face. "What do you know of cruelty?" he shouted. "What about my Kathryn . . . your mother? It

6

was your father who cruelly took my only daughter away from me to search for gold and glory. I had provided for them . . . gave them everything they wanted. But that wasn't good enough for Jonathan Forrester. He had to be his own man . . . make his own way in the world. He convinced Kathryn to accompany him on his trek to California . . . to leave you here with me because you were too young and would not survive the arduous journey. But instead, it was Kathryn who did not survive. He killed my Kathryn just as surely as if he had placed a gun to her head and pulled the trigger." Dropping his hands to his sides, his shoulders slumped slightly forward, he turned to stare out the window.

The rain had finally stopped, replaced by the remnants of a setting sun that had become an orange glow, growing smaller and less distinct as it disappeared into the horizon.

The beauty of the grounds before him did little to gladden his heart as it once had. At one time, the lush green of the lawns and towering oaks had stirred a great sense of pride within him. Pride of his accomplishments. Pride that he had been able to provide a life of grandeur and ease for his Kathryn. But Kathryn was dead.

It had been twenty years and still the thought of his beautiful daughter's death brought a dull ache deep inside his chest. Kathryn. His darling girl. He had tried to warn her about Jonathan, had told her he was nothing but an adventurer, but she wouldn't listen.

Placing her hand on her grandfather's arm, Elizabeth tried to reason with him. "My mother died of cholera. You can't blame my father for her death." She noted the mask of hatred on his face and could see her words had little effect.

7

"I can and I do. I will hate Jonathan Forrester until the day I am buried alongside the grave of my daughter. You were my revenge, Elizabeth. Jonathan took my only daughter, I took his."

Elizabeth brushed at the tears streaming down her face as she watched her grandfather stalk from the room. He suddenly looked old, not quite so intimidating. She stared at the door, unable to comprehend the events the last few hours had wrought.

Up until today, her life had been orderly, uncomplicated. She had only to decide what gown to wear or what suitor she would choose to bestow her brilliant smile upon. She had plenty of both. Her wardrobes were crammed full of expensive Worth gowns and imported French creations. Men lined up to court and woo her. She never lacked for their attentions, although none had sparked the least amount of interest within her breast.

Sighing, she sat down on the ivory-colored counterpane that covered the four-poster mahogany bed, caressing the smooth satin beneath her fingertips. For the past twenty years, she'd been led to believe that she had been unwanted . . . unloved by her father who had left shortly after her birth to make his fortune in the gold fields of California. Now she knew differently. The letter she had found was proof of that.

Staring at the letter she had tossed carelessly on the bed, Elizabeth picked it up. It must have been fate that had sent the envelope floating to the floor at her feet, she thought, thinking back to this morning's event.

Stevens, the butler, had just entered the hall with the day's mail. She had been arranging a lovely bouquet of red roses and white baby's breath in the huge Meissen vase that rested on the walnut table in the hallway. As

Stevens passed by her, the letter slipped unnoticed out of his hands. Bending over to retrieve it, she was just about to call out to him, when she discovered that the envelope was addressed to her.

Studying the handwriting on the envelope, Elizabeth tried to envision what the man whose broad strokes filled the paper would look like. Was he fair and blond like her? Or dark and swarthy in appearance? She would never know if she did not venture to California to meet him.

Did she dare travel alone to a city as wild and corrupt as San Francisco in search of her father? She had read stories about the "Paris of the West," as San Francisco was often called. New York had its share of gambling, vice, and corruption, but it was supposedly nothing compared to what existed in its western counterpart.

Reaching up, she absently toyed with the perfectly matched set of pearls resting against her throat. They had been a gift from her grandfather on the occasion of her sixteenth birthday. She heaved a sigh. Grandfather had been good to her. One had only to glance about the opulently furnished bedroom to realize that.

The furnishings were exquisite handcrafted pieces of mahogany; the bed, dresser, and wardrobe had all been imported from England. The floor was covered in an expensive carpet of French design, the shelves of her etagere lined with porcelain dolls and figurines that her grandfather had given her over the years.

Everything money could buy had been hers for the asking. But she would have given it all away just for the chance to have lived in a normal family with a mother, father, and siblings to play with.

She knew she was being unfair, even disloyal to her grandfather. He had raised her and loved her in his fashion, but Josiah Worthington was not an easy man to live with. He could be as stubborn as a head of wet tangled hair when he chose to be. She had overheard the housekeeper, Mrs. Baxter, remark on several occasions that she, Elizabeth, was just like him. Perhaps they were too much alike. Lord knows they butted heads often enough.

She thought of the disagreement they'd had about her father. She hated arguing with her grandfather. Why did he have to be belligerent and hateful where Jonathan Forrester was concerned?

Jumping up, she paced across the blue and gold Aubusson carpet. Could she really defy her grandfather's wishes and travel to California in search of her father? she asked herself. Mountains of uncertainty rose up before her. She knew it would be an uphill battle to make her grandfather change his mind about letting her go. Staring at the letter clutched in her hand, she suddenly knew the answer.

If her father truly cared for her, truly loved her, then surely she owed it to herself, as well as to him, to try and establish a relationship between them.

Crossing to the elegant rosewood escritoire, Elizabeth retrieved a sheet of cream-colored stationery. Picking up her pen, she proceeded to write the letter that could alter her life forever.

Chapter Two

Every chug and hiss of the steam engine brought Elizabeth closer to her destination and to her father. She and her companion, Mrs. Baxter, had been traveling for what seemed like forever. A seemingly endless ride of starts and stops over miles of vast prairies and seedy cow towns. She really should be grateful, she supposed. If the transcontinental railroad had not been completed the year before, in 1869, Lord knows how long it would have taken her to reach the west coast.

Venturing a peek at her companion beneath lowered lashes, she observed Mrs. Baxter's restful posture. She had worked for Josiah Worthington for as long as Elizabeth could remember. She was competent and efficient, an employee who knew her station in life and never attempted to rise above it.

Elizabeth had never known her grandmother, Sarah Worthington, who had died before she was born. Nor did she have any memory of her mother, Kathryn. There had only been Mrs. Baxter to rely upon when she was growing up. She was kind and caring, but not a woman given to displays of affection or emotion. To a small child, Mrs. Baxter had been as intimidating as a nightmare, but to a woman grown, she was merely a widow whose disposition, although vinegary, could be sweetened with an occasional hug of appreciation.

Elizabeth thought Violet Baxter would actually be a handsome woman if her brown hair wasn't stretched so taut against her scalp. It came to rest in an unattractive bun that hugged the nape of her neck; there was only the slightest sprinkling of gray at her temples, but the severity of the style gave her a continually pinched look. She definitely needed to smile more, Elizabeth concluded.

Reclining her head back against the red velvet cushion of the Pullman car, Elizabeth stared absently out the window, reflecting on her hard won battle to take the trip. Her grandfather had finally agreed, provided that she was accompanied by Mrs. Baxter and they traveled in the Worthington private railcar.

He had not been easily won over. But Elizabeth, who knew how to cajole most anything she wanted out of him, had finally been able to bring him around and was relieved that they had been able to part on friendly, if somewhat strained terms.

Sighing, she glanced about the opulently furnished passenger car. She guessed she was destined to live forever in a gilded cage. The newspapers even referred to her as "'The Gilded Lily,' whose hair glimmered as yellow as Josiah Worthington's gold." She smiled at the memory of that quote. The newspapers had written such gross exaggerations about the extent of her wealth and her exploits with the eligible bachelors who had squired her around town. If they only knew the truth about her so-called experiences—or should she say, lack of experience.

She was twenty years old and had yet to experience anything that could even be remotely described as passion. The kisses she received were all very chaste and proper pecks on the cheek. No man of her social standing would dare take liberties with the granddaughter of Josiah Worthington. Not if they desired to remain in New York City.

She had dreamed of meeting a dashing hero, like those written about in the romance novels she liked to read. But at twenty years old, her prospects were decidedly dim. Most women her age were considered "on the shelf" if they were not married. The only thing keeping her from being labeled a spinster was her grandfather's money. Money that had enabled her to live her life amidst luxury and splendor.

As heir to Josiah Worthington's millions, she was the darling of the society set, never lacking for invitations or male companions, although she often wondered if her suitors weren't more interested in her money than herself.

Grandfather had been correct in warning her about the dangers of men . . . about their faithlessness and greed. Hadn't he been correct about Reginald Winthrop? Dear, dishonest Reggie, who had sworn his undying love, only to be bought off by her grandfather's money. She hadn't really been in love with Reggie, only infatuated with his good looks and easy manner; she realized that now.

She shook her head. What if her grandfather's warnings about her father turned out to be correct? What if he turned out to be the self-centered, money-hungry adven-

13

turer Josiah had warned her about?

"Elizabeth, whatever is the matter? You look positively ghastly."

Looking up, Elizabeth found Mrs. Baxter's searching gaze upon her. "Do I? I guess I'm just weary of traveling on this train."

"It has been a dreadfully long trip, dear, but it will soon be over. Tomorrow you will see your father, and we can get off this smelly contraption."

Elizabeth smiled. It wasn't often that Violet Baxter was given to such loquaciousness. Being a New Englander, she seldom strung more than three words together at a time. "It was kind of you to accompany me on this trip, Mrs. Baxter. I know my grandfather would never have allowed me to go if you had not volunteered to go with me."

"One doesn't have much choice, my dear, when one is faced with the likes of Josiah Worthington. You either volunteer or you lose your job."

Elizabeth felt a blush steal over her cheeks. "I see. I'm sorry; I had no idea."

Violet's smile softened her features, making her look younger than her fifty-five years. "Don't worry yourself over it, Elizabeth. I came because I wanted to. It's high time I had an adventure or two before I die, and besides, it will give me the opportunity to visit my sister in Sacramento. I haven't seen Pansy in over thirty years."

Elizabeth's eyes widened. "I never realized you had any family."

"I daresay, there is quite a bit about me that neither you nor your grandfather know," she said, closing her eyes and resting her head back against the cushion, effectively halting the conversation.

Staring at the older woman in stunned silence, Elizabeth pondered her cryptic words. What could Mrs. Baxter have meant by her comment? she wondered. And what about her grandfather's allegations concerning her father? Leaning her head back against the cushion once more, she closed her eyes. Tomorrow she would have some answers . . . tomorrow.

"Cole! Cole! You'll never guess what's happened," Jonathan Forrester shouted, bursting through the door that adjoined his law office to that of Cole MacAlister's.

Looking up from the pile of papers scattered over his battered oak desk, the concerned expression on Cole's face soon turned to one of annoyance when he saw the wide smile plastered on Jonathan's face. "What the hell happened? Why are you shouting? And why do you have that stupid smile on your face?" Cole demanded.

Jonathan was much too happy to let Cole's dour mood spoil his joy. "I've just received a letter from Elizabeth. You know . . . my daughter, Elizabeth, the one I told you about."

Cole's eyes narrowed. He knew all right. Elizabeth Forrester. The daughter who had never answered any of Jonathan's letters. The daughter whose years of indifference had caused untold heartache to the man Cole loved as a father. "So . . . what does she have to say?" He shuffled the papers into neat little piles, trying to mask his annoyance at Jonathan's news.

Smiling, Jonathan perched himself on the edge of Cole's desk. The sun shining in through the large window behind the desk reflected off the silver at his temples. He was still a handsome man at forty-eight, Cole thought.

The gray in his hair only made him appear more distinguished.

"She's coming!" Jonathan announced. "Elizabeth has written to say that she is coming to visit."

"When does Miss New York society say she is arriving?" Cole asked, unable to keep the bitterness out of his voice. He had seen the articles about Elizabeth Forrester's exploits in the newspapers Jon subscribed to; he was not impressed.

Jonathan chose to ignore Cole's caustic comment. Cole's sarcasm and cutting remarks were a thing to be reckoned with in a court of law. It was easier to ignore Cole's criticism than to get him started on one of his tirades. "From the date on this letter, Elizabeth should be arriving any day now."

"And are we expected to welcome her with open arms and pretend the last twenty years didn't happen?"

Jonathan stood, walking around the desk to place his hand on Cole's shoulder. "Be happy for me, Cole. I know you have preconceived ideas about Elizabeth. Christ! I don't know what to expect myself after she's lived with that bastard Worthington all these years. But she's my daughter . . . Kathryn's daughter. I've never given up hope that one day she would want to see me."

"It's been twenty years, for God's sake, Jon. She never once wrote or acknowledged your existence. What about all those wasted trips you made to New York, only to find out she wouldn't see you?"

Staring out the window, his hands clenched behind his back, Jonathan observed the San Francisco skyline stretched out majestically before him. The fog had lifted, leaving the sun to glimmer off the gray stones and red bricks of the buildings below.

Rising from his chair, Cole draped his arms around Jonathan's shoulders. "I don't want to see you hurt any more than you've already been. Why not leave things as they are? You don't have to see her."

"Not see her! Are you crazy?" Jonathan shouted, turning about to face Cole. "I have waited twenty years to see her. It will be worth any amount of pain I may have to endure, and you can be certain I will find out why Elizabeth has rejected me for so long." His face masked with pain, he marched out of the room, pulling the door shut behind him.

Running his fingers through the black waves that fell across his brow, Cole resumed his seat. With his booted feet propped up before him on the windowsill and his head resting in the hands clenched behind his neck, he stared absently out the window, ruminating on his long association with Jonathan Forrester.

They had met in Independence, Missouri on a wagon train heading for California. Cole, traveling with his parents, William and Martha, and his sister, Abigail, had taken an instant liking to Jon Forrester and his pretty wife, Kathryn. The Forresters were filled with the same lust for adventure and excitement that had consumed his family and most of the other members of the wagon train. Gold fever had spread like a prairie fire, igniting passions that only the discovery of a bonanza could extinguish. The common dream was there for all: gold.

Cole had been ten, his sister Abigail fifteen, when the wagon train pulled out. The MacAlisters were leaving behind years of disappointment and frustration, along with a farm that never seemed to pay for itself. Pa had tried in those early years, but his experience had been in running a mercantile, not a farm. Cole smiled wistfully as

17

he thought of his parents, William and Martha.

They had been so determined to make a new start for themselves, to strike it rich and purchase another store that would see them through their old age. But their dreams had been dashed by the cholera epidemic that had swept through the Platte Valley and the wagon train, killing half of their members, including his parents and Jon's wife, Kathryn.

With the death of their parents, Cole and Abigail found themselves orphaned. If it had not been for a grief-stricken Jonathan, they might never have made it to California. It was Jonathan who suggested that Cole and Abigail throw in with him. He was lonely; they would be good for each other, he had said. And he was right. Cole had never regretted their decision.

Journeying to Sacramento, they had provisioned themselves and headed up to the hills east of the city in search of gold. For two years, in the sweltering heat of the summer and freezing cold of the winter, they labored in search of the elusive mineral.

Their efforts were finally rewarded when Abigail, who had been scrubbing clothes on the bank of the American River, spied a flash of color. That flash had been a nugget the size of a silver dollar. There had been more, lots more where that came from, and they suddenly found themselves rich beyond their wildest imaginings.

Cole and Abigail took up residence with Jonathan in his newly acquired Nob Hill mansion. They were sent to the finest schools to complete their education. Cole, following in Jon's footsteps, earned his law degree. Abigail was enrolled in Elvira Potter's School for Discriminating Women. Jonathan had been determined that Abigail would become a woman of breeding and refinement.

It was hard to believe, when one looked upon Abigail now, that she had ever groveled in the dirt like a common laborer. She was the epitome of goodness and graciousness . . . a real lady. Cole smiled at the thought of his older sister, wondering how she was faring on their ranch.

Rancho del Oro lay just south of San Francisco in the valley of Santa Clara. Abigail found the peaceful tranquility of the valley more suited to her temperament than the hustle and bustle of the big city. Cole would be the first to admit that he also preferred the ranch to life in San Francisco, but his thriving law practice demanded he spend his time here. "Once a farmer, always a farmer," Cole muttered to himself.

The knock on the door brought Cole abruptly out of his reverie. Swinging his legs about, he straightened himself at the desk. "Yes? What is it?"

Cole's secretary, Robert Perry, stuck his head in the office. He was a squat man with thick wire spectacles. "Sorry to disturb you, Mr. MacAlister, but Mrs. Truesdale has arrived for her appointment."

Cole grimaced. Hetty Truesdale. What a fitting ending to a perfectly miserable day. "Give me a few minutes, then send her in." He shook his head. Women! Why were they all such terrible pains in the ass? And Elizabeth Forrester. She would probably prove to be the biggest pain in the ass of all!

Chapter Three

"Why me? I don't even know the woman, for Christ's sake!" Cole shouted. The brandy glass he clutched tightly in his hand threatened to break under the force of his anger.

Jonathan crossed the short distance to where Cole was standing in front of the hearth. The fireplace in the library remained empty due to the warmth of the summer evening. "I'm asking you for a favor, Cole. Elizabeth will be here on the morning train. I received her telegram this afternoon. I have to be in court tomorrow. There's no one else but you."

Cole ran impatient fingers through his hair. Of all the damn luck! he thought. Having to play nursemaid to a spoiled brat. "I could try the case for you," he offered hopefully.

Jonathan shook his head. "That's not possible. I've been working on this litigation for months. It's very complicated. I have to present this one myself." Walking over to the desk, Cole glanced down at the engagement book lying open in front of him. No appointments were listed. Slamming the leather volume shut, he turned back to face Jon. "Very well. I'll do it, but only because I value our friendship."

Breathing a sigh of relief, Jonathan smiled at the mutinous expression on Cole's face, which at the moment reminded him of a recalcitrant schoolboy. "I knew I could count on you. Elizabeth is traveling with a companion . . . a Mrs. Baxter. Bring them back here and entertain them until I arrive."

"Now wait just a minute!" Cole shouted, but it was too late. Jonathan had closed the door, making his escape before the words were halfway out of Cole's mouth.

Snapping his gold pocket watch shut, Cole sighed in exasperation. Eleven-fifteen. He had been cooling his heels at the depot, pacing back and forth across the wooden planks of the sidewalk for the past thirty minutes. Damn! Where was that train? He had better things to do than to wait all day for some rich society bitch and her old lady guard dog.

Pushing the Stetson back on his head, he wiped his forehead with the back of his hand. It was hot, damned hot, and the weather matched his mood exactly. It was unusual for the weather to be this warm in June. The breeze from the ocean could usually be counted on to keep the temperature mild. But there were always exceptions, and today happened to be one of them.

The whistle of the engine drew Cole's immediate attention. Looking down the long length of steel track, he could see the black of the locomotive and the white smoke of its stack.

The depot soon became a flurry of excitement, as

passengers disembarked and were greeted by anxious friends and relatives. One by one the platform cleared, until all that remained was a willowy blonde whose regal stature and haughty demeanor could only be that of Elizabeth Forrester. Cole glanced at the shorter woman next to the blonde—Mrs. Baxter, no doubt. Probably a self-appointed protector of chastity, if the charming Miss Forrester still had that commodity. He snickered to himself.

Elizabeth looked anxiously about for some sign of her father. She knew he would be close to fifty years of age, but the only man left at the station was considerably younger than that. Judging from the way he was dressed, in blue jeans and a plaid shirt, she guessed him to be some type of baggage handler.

Walking forward, chin held high, Elizabeth approached the unfriendly-looking gentleman. "Excuse me," she said, her tone cool and crisp. "Would you please be so kind as to fetch our bags. We are waiting to be met by my father and are in need of some assistance."

Cole's gray eyes narrowed at the affrontery of the woman. Just because he had dressed in his work clothes so he could help Buck Henry install the new forge in his blacksmith shop was no reason for Miss "High and Mighty" Forrester to assume he was some damn lackey.

"Do I look like a porter, Miss Forrester? You *are* Elizabeth Forrester, I take it?"

Elizabeth was taken aback. She was not used to being spoken to in such a harsh manner. She stared into the silver eyes, which she now realized were part of a most handsome face. "Actually, I'm afraid that you do. And yes, I am Elizabeth Forrester. Please forgive me if I have offended you."

22

Cole was entranced by the delicate beauty of Elizabeth Forrester. Her face looked as if it had been sculpted out of fine porcelain. Her eyes were the color of cornflowers—blue, like the summer sky overhead. The bright yellow gown she wore accentuated the golden color of her hair, which hung in curls down her back. She was like a ray of sunshine. And like a man blinded by staring directly into the sun, Cole's eyes remained transfixed on the vision before him.

"You don't need to apologize to this riffraff, Elizabeth. He should recognize his betters when he sees them," Violet Baxter proclaimed, staring indignantly at the stranger.

The woman's comments broke the spell. Cole bit back a smile at the matron's remark. It seemed the old biddy was protective of her young chick. Glancing at Elizabeth's reddening features, Cole bestowed a smile on the mismatched pair and extended his hand. "Cole MacAlister at your service. I'm a friend and business associate of Jonathan Forrester."

Elizabeth was fascinated by the change a smile had wrought on Cole MacAlister's face. Where before he loomed dark and brooding, he now appeared almost pleasant. His smile was devastating. His teeth gleamed white against his deeply tanned skin. His rugged good looks were softened slightly by the appearance of two dimples on either side of his face.

"How do you do? I am Jonathan's daughter, Elizabeth." Elizabeth saw the stranger's eyes narrow a fraction at her announcement, but his smile remained affable. "May I inquire as to my father's whereabouts, Mr. MacAlister?"

"Jon's in court," he replied, clarifying his comment

when he noticed the puzzled expression on her face. "He's a lawyer, Miss Forrester. We both are." The surprise that registered on Elizabeth Forrester's face irritated the hell out of him. That she should think he was something common and beneath her sent a spurt of renewed anger surging through his veins.

"Some of us 'common folk' have to work for a living, Miss Forrester. We all weren't born with silver spoons in our mouths." With that remark, Cole stalked over to the pile of luggage on the platform, leaving a very flustered Elizabeth and a very angry Mrs. Baxter to stare after him.

"Well, of all the nerve!" Violet Baxter declared.

While she observed Cole loading their luggage onto the waiting carriage, Elizabeth couldn't help but notice how his muscles strained against the blue plaid of his shirt as he lifted the heavy bags with ease. The tight-fitting blue pants he wore were molded to his thighs, leaving nothing to the imagination. She had never seen anyone dressed quite as indecently before, and she felt her face warm.

"Are you ready to go, Elizabeth?" Mrs. Baxter inquired, startling Elizabeth out of her less-than-proper observations.

Nodding, Elizabeth approached the conveyance. Her stomach fluttered nervously when Cole gripped her arm to assist her up inside the carriage. Chancing a peek at his face as she boarded, she noted both contempt and disdain written there. The mysterious silver eyes burned with an intensity that both terrified and excited her.

Elizabeth was spared further contact with Cole when he chose to ride on top with the driver, rather than in the carriage with her. While Mrs. Baxter was absorbed in her study of the city, Elizabeth took the time to contemplate her unusual meeting with her father's business associate.

24

Why did he seem to dislike her so? She had apologized for mistaking him for a porter. Why then did Cole MacAlister seem to abhor her very presence? She shook her head. Maybe he just dislikes all women, she thought. Her grandfather had told her about men who preferred other men to women, but he'd never elaborated on what he meant. Perhaps Mr. MacAlister was one of those men her grandfather had spoken of. Perhaps, but somehow she just didn't think so.

Staring out the carriage window as it rumbled over the unevenly paved roads, Elizabeth noticed how busy and crowded the streets were. Newsboys stood on corners hawking their daily papers, while fashionably dressed ladies peered at the enticements displayed in the store-front windows. If she closed her eyes, she could well imagine she was traveling down Broadway back in New York rather than Market Street as the sign post indicated.

As the carriage pulled away from the downtown area onto California Street, Elizabeth's nervous apprehension increased. The houses were becoming more fashionable and ornate the farther up the hill they climbed, and she suspected that they were nearing her father's residence.

Taking a deep breath, Elizabeth decided she wasn't going to let the irascible mood of Cole MacAlister ruin her reunion with her father. She had waited twenty years for this moment, and she wasn't about to let some surly, ill-mannered cowboy spoil it for her. Lawyer my foot, she thought. If he was a lawyer, then she was the Queen of England.

The steady clip-clop of the horses' hooves as they plodded their way up the incline had a soothing effect on Elizabeth's nerves. She was just beginning to relax when the carriage came to an abrupt halt, jerking her forward. She nearly collided with Mrs. Baxter, whose sleep-induced body fell toward her at the sudden motion of the carriage.

"Oh, dear!" Violet exclaimed, wide awake and patting her hair with quick, nervous strokes. "We must have arrived."

Elizabeth smiled at the older woman's gesture, doubting if Mrs. Baxter had ever had a misplaced hair in the last fifty years.

Sticking her head out the window, Elizabeth's gaze fell upon the most enchanting house she had ever seen. It was not a huge house, not nearly as large as the Worth-ington mansion, but it was infinitely more inviting. Where the gray granite walls of her grandfather's home seemed cold and foreboding, this house was somehow comforting. It reminded her of the lovely gingerbread house their cook, Mrs. Thomas, had prepared for her one Christmas long ago. The cinnamon-colored brick was warm and welcoming, the ornately carved cornices and gables as white as confectioners' icing.

"We're here, Miss Forrester," the cold, clipped voice announced. Elizabeth suddenly found herself gazing into the hostile eyes of Cole MacAlister, who was staring back at her through the carriage window, blocking her view of the house.

Opening the door, Cole assisted Mrs. Baxter down first. Judging from her lethal gaze, Cole surmised that the woman was still furious with him for his earlier comments.

Extending his hand to Elizabeth, he watched as she tentatively placed her hand in his. Her hand felt cold through the glove she wore. He could sense her nervousness. She should be scared, he thought bitterly, after the miserable way she had treated her father all these years.

Staring into her eyes, which were wide and full of fright, Cole suddenly felt pity for the young woman before him. Patting her hand in a reassuring gesture, he smiled. "We don't bite, you know."

Elizabeth felt her cheeks warm at Cole's comment. She alighted from the carriage as gracefully as possible, smoothing the silk of her dress and adjusting her bustled skirts. She glanced over to find Mrs. Baxter giving last minute instructions to the driver concerning their luggage. Turning to face Cole, Elizabeth finally replied, "You could have fooled me, Mr. MacAlister. Your teeth may not have pierced my flesh, but your words have penetrated just the same."

Lifting her chin and her skirts simultaneously, she proceeded up the brick path toward the house, leaving a chagrined Cole MacAlister with an uncomfortably warm flush creeping up under the collar of his shirt.

The inside of the house was every bit as charming as the exterior. Elizabeth had been ushered into the parlor by an ageless little Oriental man who introduced himself as Ah Sing. She stood in the center of the room, taking in her surroundings.

The walls were papered in a cranberry and cream-colored floral print. Delicate lace curtains hung at the window, while an exquisite cranberry velvet settee made of rich dark walnut sat before it. Several elaborately carved chairs were placed in various positions about the large room, and a lovely oval rosewood table topped with marble sat in the center of it.

The whole room was enchanting, and Elizabeth wondered if perhaps her father had remarried. The house definitely showed evidence of a woman's touch. Staring pensively out the window, she chewed her lower lip, suddenly realizing that she had never considered that possibility.

"I sent your companion up to her room," Cole announced, walking into the room and closing the double doors behind him.

Elizabeth swung about at the sound of his voice.

"I see Ah Sing has already seen to your comfort," Cole said, noting the fresh pitcher of lemonade and glasses that rested on the table.

"Yes. He was very kind." She offered a small smile to mask her nervousness. Cole MacAlister set her on edge, making her feel like she was tiptoeing on eggshells whenever she was around him.

"And are you very kind, Miss Forrester?"

Elizabeth's mouth dropped open, but she quickly snapped it shut. Recovering her aplomb, she replied, "I try to be."

"Do you consider your treatment of Jonathan Forrester kind?" Cole asked, his voice dripping cold with contempt.

"That is really none of your business, Mr. MacAlister," she replied, pacing nervously about the room. Why was he interrogating her about her father? she wondered. What possible reasons could he have for his impertinent questions?

"I'm making it my business, Miss Forrester," Cole ground out, stalking after her like a cat with a mouse in its sight.

Fearful of the malevolent glare Cole was directing at her, Elizabeth swallowed her unease.

"Why did you come here, Miss Forrester?"

28

His question surprised her; she paused a moment before answering. "I came to see my father."

"Why now, after all these years?"

Elizabeth tried to keep her voice steady, unwilling to let Cole MacAlister know that he was provoking her ire. "I told you that is none of your affair."

Cole advanced on Elizabeth, clutching her arms in a bruising hold. "Tell me," he demanded.

Elizabeth was shocked that he would dare lay hands on her. Why, in the East, a gentleman would never have the audacity to put his hands upon a woman's flesh in anger. These westerners were no better than the savages she had read about in Mr. Beadle's dime novels.

"You had better leave, Mr. MacAlister," Elizabeth brazened out. "My father would not take kindly to your treatment of me."

"How do you know that, Elizabeth? Maybe he wouldn't give a damn. After all, you haven't seen him for twenty years."

Elizabeth's fear mixed with anger as she struggled to break free of Cole's hold. "Let me go. I am his daughter, his flesh and blood. You are merely an employee. Take care that you don't lose your job, Mr. MacAlister."

At Elizabeth's words, Cole's anger and jealousy rose to the forefront. He didn't want to be reminded that he was not really Jonathan's son, that he would soon be replaced by the woman he held none too gently in his arms. Pulling Elizabeth hard against him, he ground his lips down over hers in a kiss that was meant to terrify and punish.

Elizabeth was terrified, not because she was frightened of Cole, but because of her own body's reaction to his kiss. The touch of his lips sent waves of pleasure radiating throughout her entire body. Struggling wildly, she tried to break free of the viselike hold he had upon her, but Cole only increased the pressure on her lips, rendering her faint and light-headed.

Elizabeth's pitiful attempts at resistance were no match for the persuasive movements of Cole's lips. She ceased her wild thrashing and slowly gentled. Consumed by a liquid fire that ran through her veins, she made no protest when Cole's searching tongue found its way between her teeth. Her heart hammered so loudly in her chest that she was sure he could hear it. She had been kissed before, but never like this. She felt ravaged, consumed by an unknown entity that was threatening to devour her.

Sensing her surrender, Cole's grip on Elizabeth's arms loosened. He ran his hands over her back, finally dropping them down to cup her buttocks, forcing her up against the growing evidence of his attraction.

Elizabeth's hands came up of their own volition to circle about Cole's neck. She ran her fingers through the soft hair resting on the collar of his shirt. Her breasts were full and aching, the nipples hard with desire as they flattened against the hard planes of his chest.

Cole smiled inwardly at Elizabeth's response. She wasn't quite so prim and proper after all. No wonder she needed a guard dog. She was like a bitch in heat. Cole brought his hands up to cup her breasts, massaging the hardened points. He heard her moan softly in response.

It might be amusing to find out just how far the society bitch would go. It was always the pristine ones that couldn't get enough of what he had to offer. If he could expose her to Jon for what she really was, her father might not be so eager to be taken in by her sweet, unassuming act.

Cole pulled back, smiling sardonically into Elizabeth's flushed face.

At the sight of his mocking smile, Elizabeth came immediately to her senses. My God! What had she done? How could she have forgotten herself that way? She had acted no better than a common trollop. Wrenching herself free of his embrace, she drew her hand up and slapped the smile off his face. "How dare you!"

"How dare I what, Miss Forrester?" Cole replied, rubbing his cheek where she had hit him. For a gently reared woman, she certainly packed a wallop, he thought. "How dare I kiss you? Or how dare I laugh about it?"

Elizabeth choked back her response. Her fingers itched to rake her nails across his arrogant face, but instead she clenched her hands into fists, digging her nails into her own palms. Her grandfather had always taught her: Never let your opponent know your weaknesses. It was good advice. Her temper was definitely a weakness she had tried to control over the years. Perhaps it was a throwback to her Irish grandmother, but whatever the case, she would not act the shrew for Cole MacAlister's sake.

Elizabeth strode to the opposite side of the room, putting as much distance between herself and the despicable man as she could. She was careful to keep her back to him lest he see how much his kisses and his words had affected her. "I think you had better go home before my father arrives," she said.

The sound of Cole's infuriating laughter caused Elizabeth to twirl about. She faced him, hands on her hips, a baneful expression on her lips.

Cole thought she was the most enchanting creature he

had ever laid eyes upon. Under different circumstances, he might have been tempted to . . .

"I fail to see what is so amusing, Mr. MacAlister. Your ungentlemanly, boorish behavior is anything but funny."

Cole's laughter died on his lips, replaced by a mocking smile. "Are you denying that you enjoyed my kiss, Elizabeth? Ah, I can see by your expression that you are. But we know better . . . don't we? Shall I put it to the test?"

Elizabeth's eyes widened in fright. She would not let him touch her again. Unconsciously, she took two steps backward.

"Don't worry, Miss Forrester. I'm not about to kiss you again. I only wished to see how far you would go. Call it a test . . . which you failed miserably, I might add."

Elizabeth gasped. "How dare you!"

"I dare almost anything, Miss Forrester. It would be wise to remember that in the future."

"Leave this house at once, or I shall have you thrown out." Elizabeth knew the words were an empty threat as soon as she uttered them, but it was too late to call them back.

Cole threw back his head and roared. "By whom, Miss Forrester? Ah Sing? Or perhaps you care to try it yourself. Never mind. Since you are so determined to have me gone I will leave, but there is one minor detail I neglected to tell you."

Walking over to the glass doors, he placed his hand on the knob. He turned back to face Elizabeth, whose face was red with suppressed rage. "I won't be going too far, Elizabeth. You see, what I neglected to tell you is . . . I live here."

Elizabeth clutched her throat as Cole's words exploded

around her like a bombshell. She watched him leave, then fell upon the settee in a state of nervous exhaustion. My God! He lives here! Here . . . in this house. I will have to see him every day . . . bear his company, his unwelcome advances.

She blushed at the memory of her recent encounter. The truth was, his advances had not been all that unwelcome, and he knew it. What was she going to do? The perfect reunion she had imagined between herself and her father was going to be spoiled by the unwanted presence of one Cole MacAlister.

Elizabeth was having the most wonderful dream. A dark, handsome stranger with eyes the color of silver had whisked her away on a golden horse. He was just about to place his lips over hers when a voice intruded rudely into her fantasy.

"Elizabeth, wake up. The Chinaman said your father would be home any minute." Violet stared down at Elizabeth's sleeping form, giving her shoulder a little nudge. "Elizabeth," she called louder.

Both eyes popped open at once to find Mrs. Baxter hovering over the bed.

"Get up, Elizabeth. Your father is due to arrive home at any moment."

Reality came crashing down upon Elizabeth as she remembered where she was and in whose bed she lay. She looked frantically around the room, expecting to see Cole's mocking face peering out at her from every corner.

Ah Sing had shown her to Cole's room when she had requested a place to rest. She had protested vehemently, but the little man had shaken his head, insisting that this was the only room available at the moment.

"Whatever is the matter with you?" Violet questioned.

Sitting straight up, Elizabeth practically launched herself out of the bed, astonishing Mrs. Baxter with her agility. "Why, nothing is the matter," Elizabeth finally replied, her face growing warm. "I must have fallen asleep. I was so tired after the train ride."

"I'm sure you were," Violet replied, casting Elizabeth a searching look before she indicated the bath that had been prepared for her. "I've pressed your gown. It's there on the chair. Now hurry along."

Elizabeth breathed a sigh of relief when Mrs. Baxter exited the room. She wasn't about to confide her ridiculous fears to her. Gazing longingly at the tub and then nervously at the door, she decided she was just being fanciful. Surely Cole had left town. That was why Ah Sing had installed her in his room. Smiling at herself for being such a ninny, Elizabeth stripped off her gown and underclothes, then climbed into the tub of rose-scented water.

Relaxing against the back of the tub, she let the steamy water surround her. It felt wonderful, and Elizabeth permitted herself the luxury of soaking while she surveyed the room.

The oil lamps had been lit, bathing the room in a warm radiance. The room was decidedly masculine, just like Cole. The large black walnut bed had a handsomely carved footboard and headboard. The dresser, in the same design as the bed, was topped by a white piece of marble and a huge mirror that rose almost to the ceiling. A well-worn red leather arm chair sat near the fireplace, and a table with stacks of books and papers stood next to it. No signs of feminine frippery here.

Elizabeth stepped out of the tub, toweling herself dry. Picking up the chemise and stockings that rested on the chair near the tub, she proceeded to dress. She had just fastened the last button on her smart satin tasseled boots when she heard the door open. "I'm almost ready, Mrs. Baxter. I just have one more button . . . there."

Spinning around, the smile she wore on her face melted quickly, to be replaced by an expression of complete and utter mortification. "You!" she shrieked. Her eyes froze on the long, lanky form of Cole Mac-Alister, who was leaning casually against the door frame.

Stepping further into the room, Cole closed the door behind him. His breath caught in his throat at the sight of Elizabeth. She was even lovelier than he had imagined. And after the kiss they had shared earlier today, he had let his imagination run wild.

Her legs were incredibly long, smooth, and satiny. The damp cotton of her chemise rendered her breasts clearly visible through the thin material. He could see that they were full and perfectly formed.

"Well . . . well. You're the last person I would have expected to find in my room. Pity, I arrived too late to catch you in your bath." He grinned wickedly.

"Get out," Elizabeth hissed, groping for the green silk dress on the chair. She held it up in front of her, as if its mere presence could offer some protection against the lustful gaze of this man. Her reaction seemed to amuse him.

They stood staring at each other until the sound of footsteps in the hall propelled Cole into action. Walking over to the paneled wall on the right side of the bed, he pushed lightly against the wood molding until it

35

sprung open.

Elizabeth was barely able to control her gasp of surprise. She stared in astonishment as Cole entered the secret compartment. Shaking her head, her lips thinned in disgust. She should have known a disreputable rogue such as Cole MacAlister would have a way of secreting women in and out of his bedroom. She was just about to utter those very thoughts when Cole flashed her a heart-stopping smile, winking broadly.

"Regretfully, I must take my leave before the dragon lady enters. Take care you don't take a chill, Sunshine. I'll see you at dinner."

Elizabeth watched Cole disappear through the narrow opening. She stood there several moments staring dumbfounded at the wall. Cole MacAlister was the most infuriating, contemptible man she had ever met. He was certainly no gentleman, even if he did profess to being a lawyer. It was obvious that he had no respect for the female sex. He was rude and crude and had not an inkling of proper decorum. Why was he staying in her father's house? And why did she feel an undeniable attraction toward him?

Chapter Four

Elizabeth was the first to arrive downstairs for dinner. Ah Sing had once again escorted her into the parlor, apologizing profusely when he had to explain that Mista Jon and Mista Mac, as he referred to her father and Cole, were busy in the library. He had bowed repeatedly, until Elizabeth thought she would grow dizzy watching him.

Mrs. Baxter had become sidetracked as soon as she heard about the new cookstove that had just arrived from Europe. She begged Elizabeth's indulgence and had run off to take a look at it.

Glancing about the room, Elizabeth's attention was immediately drawn to the two portraits that hung in the gilt oval frames on either side of the window. Moving closer to get a better look, she immediately recognized the one on the left. It was a likeness of her mother. Grandfather had a much larger version of it displayed over the mantel in his drawing room.

The resemblance she bore to Kathryn Forrester was remarkable. It was almost as if she were looking into a mirror. As a child, she had spent countless hours staring up at the painting, endeavoring to get to know the woman in it.

As fascinated as she was by her mother's portrait, it was the one on the right that really captured her attention. It was the first time she had ever seen a likeness of her father. There was no mistaking her resemblance to the man in the painting. The blue eyes were the exact same shade as her own. She guessed he had been about twenty-five when the portrait was painted, and she could certainly understand why her mother had fallen in love with him. Jonathan Forrester was indeed a very handsome man.

"I hope you won't be disappointed by the real face, Elizabeth. I fear I don't look quite so young and dashing anymore."

Elizabeth's heart raced as she spun about to face her father for the first time. The smile that lit his face was all the encouragement she needed to propel her forward. With tears blurring her vision, she ran to the outstretched arms of Jonathan Forrester. "Father," Elizabeth choked out, barely able to speak.

Hugging Elizabeth to him tightly, Jonathan swallowed the tears of joy that overwhelmed him. "Elizabeth! Elizabeth! I've missed you so. You don't know how I've longed for this day. Your decision to come and visit has made me the happiest man on earth."

"I have also longed for this day, Father. I have so much to tell you," Elizabeth said, staring up into her father's tear-stained face. She could read the love reflected in the bright blue of his eyes; her heart burst with love as well. "I can't begin to—"

"What a charming reunion," Cole said, unable to mask the hostility in his voice. He couldn't help the feelings of jealousy stirring within his breast at the sight that greeted his eyes. His place in Jon's affections was being usurped by a conniving little piece of baggage.

At the sound of Cole's voice, Elizabeth spun around, startled by the resentment she detected in it. She started to pull out of her father's embrace, but Jon kept her close by his side, his arm wrapped firmly around her shoulder.

Ignoring Cole's angry glare, her gaze slid over his well-built physique, which the tight-fitting black trousers and jacket he wore did little to conceal. He looked very handsome, every inch the proper gentleman. The cowboy of this morning had disappeared, but despite Cole's polished exterior, there was still an underlying wildness reflected in his cold gray eyes.

She could feel the warmth of a blush stealing over her cheeks as Cole's eyes perused her own attire. The pale eyes were lit by an inner fire, making them sparkle like the diamonds she wore around her throat. The knowing smile on his lips told her that he hadn't forgotten their earlier encounter.

Cole's eyes raked over Elizabeth. Her body had been indelibly imprinted in his mind. He had memorized every delicious detail, every luscious curve, every inch of milk-white flesh that he had seen this afternoon. The beautiful green silk dress she wore could not disguise the charms he knew were hidden beneath it.

"Come in, Cole," Jon said. "I know you and Elizabeth have already met."

"Yes," Cole said, "Elizabeth's many charms have already been revealed to me." His gaze lingered insultingly over the white flesh of her bosom, bringing a flush to her cheeks.

The audacity of the man! Elizabeth thought angrily,

39

trying to mask her embarrassment. She shot a venomous look in his direction.

"Yes. Well, let's all sit down and have a drink to celebrate Elizabeth's arrival," Jon suggested.

Smiling up at her father, Elizabeth seated herself on the red velvet cushion of the settee. "That would be lovely."

Taking a seat next to her, Cole draped his arm around the back of the sofa, lightly brushing the back of her neck with his fingers. A sudden chill ran through Elizabeth's body, causing the tiny hairs on the nape of her neck to stand up on end.

"I'll have a brandy, Jon," Cole said, looking over at Elizabeth and smiling innocently. "What about you, Sunshine? Care for a sherry?"

"Yes . . . please," she replied, barely able to repress the hostility in her voice. The man was infuriating. How dare he embarrass her by alluding to their earlier encounter? My God! she thought. What if he mentioned it to her father? No. He wouldn't be that bold. If he had wanted them to be found out, he wouldn't have left through the secret passageway. Taking a sip of the sherry, she tried to bring her anxiety under control.

Jon took a seat opposite the two young people. He couldn't help but notice what a handsome couple they made, despite the fact that they seemed to dislike each other. The tension in the air had become palpable as soon as they had come together. There was definitely something going on between them; his lawyer's instincts told him that much.

"Now, Elizabeth," Jon said, facing his daughter, "tell me why you have chosen to come and visit. Has something happened to Worthington?"

Elizabeth looked first at her father and then at Cole, who had leaned forward in his seat in anticipation of her answer. Turning back to her father, she replied, "I would prefer to talk with you alone . . . if you don't mind." She smiled inwardly at the annoyed expression on Cole's face.

Jon's brows furrowed in confusion. "Of course, but you needn't worry about Cole; he's like a son to me. I trust him implicitly. Why, you might as well think of him like a brother."

Elizabeth choked on the sherry she had just swallowed. Reaching over, Cole gave her back a gentle pat. "Take care, little sister, you mustn't bite off more than you can chew." His eyes glittered with laughter at Elizabeth's look of outrage. He didn't know why she was reluctant to talk in front of him, but he would find out the truth; he had ways to make her talk.

"Are you all right, my dear?" Jon asked, rising out of his chair.

Elizabeth motioned him back down. "Yes. I'm fine. Please, don't get up. I just swallowed too much."

"Please forgive my tardiness," Violet Baxter said as she hurried into the room, self-consciously smoothing down the folds of her black bombazine dress. "I'm afraid that new contraption you have in your kitchen was just too much of a temptation for me, Mr. Forrester."

Elizabeth's sigh was almost audible. She had never been so happy to see anyone in her life. Mrs. Baxter's arrival had given her the reprieve she needed to collect her thoughts. After dinner, she would get her father alone and give him the answers he desired of her, but for now, she would let the inquisitive Mr. MacAlister stew in his own juices.

The time had come for Elizabeth to face her father with the truth about her grandfather's deceit. They sat staring at each other across the small distance that separated the two black leather chairs of the library. While Jon relaxed over a brandy and cigar, Elizabeth sipped thoughtfully on her glass of sherry.

The room was illuminated by the soft flicker of two oil lamps resting on the desk. Hundreds of aging calfskin books filled the shelves that lined the paneled walls. The room was quiet, save for the ticking of the grandfather clock that kept perfect time with the nervous beating of Elizabeth's heart.

The ordeal of dinner had blissfully ended a short time ago, and by some miraculous piece of luck, Cole had said his farewells and departed for his ranch. Cole. That was one subject Elizabeth was determined to broach this evening. But how? She didn't want her father to think she was prying into his private affairs. Yet, if Cole was merely a temporary houseguest . . .

"Elizabeth, dear, I don't want to put a damper on our reunion, but I really think that it's time we discuss our previous estrangement," Jon said.

Setting the glass of sherry down beside her, Elizabeth folded her hands primly in her lap. She had rehearsed what she was going to say over and over again in her mind, but now that the time was upon her, she felt oddly tongue-tied.

"I hate to be the cause of more hard feelings between you and grandfather, but I'm afraid what I have to tell you will do exactly that."

Reaching over, Jon patted Elizabeth's hand. "My dear, never blame yourself for what is between Josiah and myself. Our dislike for each other started long before you were born. Your grandfather never wanted Kathryn to marry me. He did everything he could to dissuade her. He even went so far as to bribe me with money, as if all the money in the world would have prevented me from marrying the woman I loved."

Elizabeth could well imagine her grandfather's high-handedness. She had been the victim of such interference, although in her case, Josiah Worthington had proven himself correct. If only she could find a love like the one her parents had shared, she thought wistfully.

"My mother was lucky to have found a man like you. I only hope someday to be as fortunate." Jon's smile touched her heart.

"Thank you, my dear. True love only comes along once in a lifetime. When it does, grab it, Elizabeth, and never let it go."

Elizabeth nodded, blinking back her tears.

"Please continue your story," Jonathan encouraged. "I'm afraid I have a terrible habit of going off on tangents. It's just the lawyer in me, I guess."

Taking a deep breath, Elizabeth related all the details of how she had come upon his letter and the subsequent argument with her grandfather. They discussed what her life had been like during the past twenty years.

Her father wanted to know everything: the details of her coming-out party, the schools she had attended, her childhood illnesses. She patiently recounted all the important events of her life, leaving little out, for she understood her father's need to recapture the parts of her life that he had missed. She, too, felt that same need about him.

She was shocked to learn that her father had made several visits to New York over the years to see her, only to be turned away by her grandfather.

"I should have realized Josiah was behind your refusals to see me," Jon lamented, shaking his head sadly. "I let that man rob me of twenty years of your life."

"Don't blame yourself," Elizabeth said. "Josiah Worthington is very adept at getting his own way. I love my grandfather, but I don't know if I can ever forgive him for what he has done."

"Kathryn's death made him bitter. It was I he meant to punish by his actions, not you. Josiah may be a cantankerous old reprobate, but I know in his heart he truly loves you."

Distressed by Elizabeth's tears, Jon sought to change the subject; it was time to leave the past behind. "I'm sure you have some questions you would like to ask of me. I know all women suffer from the same malady of terminal curiosity."

Elizabeth's mood brightened, and she smiled tremulously. "You're quite right, Father. I admit to being rather curious about several things."

Settling himself back in the chair, he crossed his arms over his chest. "Well then, fire away."

Chewing her lower lip, uncertain of how to phrase her question, Elizabeth finally blurted out, "Are you married?" She held her breath, waiting for the answer, and was quite surprised when her father threw his head back and roared.

"Heavens, no! Is that why you look so worried?"

She felt her cheeks warm. "Your home is so nicely decorated. I just thought—"

A warm smile touched Jon's lips. "The house is Abigail's doing."

"Abigail?"

"Abigail MacAlister . . . Cole's sister. I thought I had mentioned her."

"No . . . you didn't," Elizabeth replied. Questions she dared not ask darted around in her mind. Cole had a sister. Did she live here, too? Was she as awful as he was? No. She couldn't be. No one was as terrible as Cole Mac-Alister.

"Abigail and Cole were on the wagon train with your mother and me. Their parents died of the same cholera epidemic that took Kathryn. I adopted them—not legally—but they're family just the same."

"I see," Elizabeth said, pondering his words. "Where is Abigail? Why haven't I met her?"

"For some reason I have never quite been able to figure out, Abigail prefers to live on their ranch in Santa Clara. That's where Cole has gone. He spends as much time with Abby as he can. He's very protective of her."

"Is she so young that he needs to worry about her?"

Jon snorted. "Abby's five years older than Cole. I've told him at thirty-five she can take care of herself, but Cole hovers over her like a mother hen."

It was hard to imagine Cole mothering anyone. He was too cold, too nasty to be genuinely kind. "Cole doesn't strike me as a kind man," Elizabeth said.

Jon lit another cigar, puffing repeatedly until the tip glowed a flaming red. "Cole MacAlister is one of the kindest men I know, though he would kill me for saying so. He takes clients nobody else wants. They usually can't afford to pay his fee, so he tries their cases for free. He is quite the champion of the underdog."

Elizabeth snickered in disbelief. "You make him sound like a saint."

Jon smiled. "He's anything but. Cole has his faults, just like the rest of us. Maybe more. But he's a fine man; I'm proud to call him my son."

Elizabeth was at a loss for words. Her father certainly held a high opinion of Cole. Could she have misjudged him?

"Why all the interest in Cole? You don't have any romantic notions about him, do you?" her father asked.

Elizabeth turned crimson. "Certainly not! Why . . . I don't even like him."

"I thought as much. Just as well. Cole's not the marrying kind. He takes his pleasure where he finds it . . . if you get my meaning. I wouldn't want him toying with your affections."

"Father, really!" Elizabeth protested, covering her cheeks to still the burning.

"I'm sorry, Elizabeth," Jon apologized, looking quite contrite. "It's just that now that you've finally come back to me, I feel all my protective instincts rising to the forefront. Forgive me?"

Leaning forward, she placed a kiss on her father's cheek. "You've nothing to apologize for. I'm happy you're concerned for my welfare, but you needn't worry. I'm not the least bit interested in Cole."

Jon sat staring into the empty hearth long after Elizabeth had gone up to bed. He smiled to himself. Forbidden fruit was always so much more tempting. Would Elizabeth fall for his ploy where Cole was concerned? He certainly hoped so. Cole and Elizabeth would make a perfect couple. He had decided that the moment he saw them together.

If Cole married Elizabeth, she would have to remain in San Francisco. He was selfish enough to want that. He would be able to be near his grandchildren. Jon laughed aloud. First things first. He was getting ahead of himself. Cole and Elizabeth had to like each other before they could begin to fall in love. How could he help bring that about? There was definitely something between them. But what? He was damned if he knew, but he sure as hell was going to find out.

Chapter Five

"A party! For heaven's sake, why do you want to have a party?" Elizabeth asked her father, who was seated at the long mahogany dining room table finishing his lunch. The sun streamed in through the bow-shaped window, glittering off the crystal water glasses on the table.

"Why, to introduce you to San Francisco society, of course," Jon replied, wiping the last bit of apple pie from his lips.

"I think it's a wonderful idea, Elizabeth," Violet chimed in. "I'll be leaving in a few days, and this will give you a chance to make some new acquaintances."

"There . . . you see, even Mrs. Baxter thinks it's a good idea," Jon said, pushing away from the table.

Regarding the pair with no small amount of skepticism, Elizabeth fought the urge to grimace. She wasn't sure she wanted to meet the crème de la crème of San Francisco. The society functions she had attended in New York had been bad enough. They were tedious affairs, hosted by a lot of pompous individuals. Her grandfather had always insisted she go, stating, ". . . one had to be well connected if one was to marry well." How many times

48

had she heard him utter that sentiment? As if she cared at all about getting married, she thought.

Observing the hopeful expression on her father's face, she sighed deeply. "I guess that would be fine."

"Splendid! I'll make all the arrangements."

"I will be happy to assist in whatever way I can, Mr. Forrester," Violet offered. "I won't be leaving until next week."

"Then it's settled," Jon said, smiling. "We'll set San Francisco on its ear with the liveliest gala of the season. Shall we say the last Saturday of June? That should give us plenty of time to make all the arrangements."

The invitations were sent out three days later. Jon Forrester was, without a doubt, the most organized man Elizabeth had ever encountered. With Mrs. Baxter's eye for detail, all the pieces for the party were coming together like a well-constructed building.

An orchestra had been hired as well as extra staff. Marlow's Catering had been engaged to prepare the food and drink. The decorations were to be left in the capable hands of a charming Frenchman by the name of Marcel, who had informed Elizabeth, without batting an eyelash, that "No party of any consequence was given without floral arrangements by Marcel Du Pré." She smiled as she recalled the funny little man with the pencil-thin mustache.

The party was all anyone could talk about. It had dominated every breakfast, lunch, and dinner conversation for the past week. Elizabeth thought she would go mad if she had to listen to one more detail about it.

Slipping away to the rear of the house, she had seated herself on the wooden porch swing, stealing a few minutes of solitude before her next meeting with Mrs. Truesdale; she wrinkled her nose in disgust.

Mrs. Baxter had relinquished control of the party to Hetty Truesdale yesterday, before departing for Sacramento. It had been a tearful farewell for both Violet and Elizabeth, an occurrence that Elizabeth was certain had been a surprise to both of them. Violet had promised to return in two months time to bid Elizabeth good-bye before returning to New York.

Hetty Truesdale had been given the awesome responsibility of arranging the Forresters' party. Not wanting to burden Elizabeth with all the tiresome details, Jon had asked Hetty, who was one of San Francisco's pillars of society and a client of Cole's, to assist with the arrangements.

Elizabeth had found Hetty Truesdale to be an overweight, overbearing know-it-all, who had blown into the house like a hurricane, issuing orders as if born to command. If she had been on General Robert E. Lee's staff during the Civil War, the South would surely have been victorious, Elizabeth thought.

Hetty had driven Elizabeth so crazy that there were some days she was almost desperate enough to wish Cole would return from his ranch. At least fighting with him had offered her a bit of a diversion. She wondered if he would come to the party. Her father had already told her it was unlikely that Abigail would attend. Elizabeth thought it strange that a woman of marriageable age would not look forward to the opportunity of meeting men. Although, on second thought, maybe it wasn't so strange after all. Maybe Abigail was smarter than she was giving her credit for.

Cole had been conspicuously absent since the night of her arrival. She assumed he had stayed away to avoid seeing her. Funny, but she didn't quite relish his absence as much as she thought she would. Elizabeth, you are just being contrary, she chided herself silently. When he's here, you can't stand the sight of him, and now that he's gone, you wish he were here. What a ninny you are!

Still, it was hard not to remember the way his lips felt pressed against her mouth or the feel of his hands on her breasts. Her cheeks warmed at the memory. Pressing her hands against her face, she tried to halt the rising blush. "Stop thinking about him, you fool!" she shouted.

"What was that, dear? Did you say something?"

Elizabeth looked up to find the full-blown form of Mrs. Truesdale coming toward her. Her eyes widened. What had she done to her hair? She had never before seen hair that color. It was red—no, not red . . . orange. A dreadful orange color that made Elizabeth think of a large, ugly pumpkin. She fought the urge to giggle.

Hetty was peering at her through a lorgnette that hung around her neck from a gold chain. "It was nothing, Mrs. Truesdale. I was just muttering to myself," Elizabeth confessed.

"Tsk, tsk. You really should be careful about doing that, Elizabeth dear. I had a cousin . . . Myrtle Figg was her name. Poor thing was always talking to herself. Why, don't you know, she was finally locked up in one of those hospitals for the insane. Of course, she was only distantly related. Why, the Truesdales have always been of sound mind, don't you know."

Elizabeth smiled weakly, rising from her seat to follow Hetty into the house. It was going to be a long day . . . a very long day.

Later that same evening, Elizabeth was gathering up

the remainder of her belongings from Cole's room, preparing to move into the bedroom vacated by Mrs. Baxter, when a scraping sound from behind startled her. Picking up her silver-handled hairbrush, she turned, ready to strike down whoever had intruded on her domain. Her mouth fell open at the sight of the man who had occupied most of her thoughts during the past week. "Cole!" she whispered.

"Whoa, Sunshine, I give up. Don't hit me. I'm too damn saddle-weary after the long ride I've just made."

Swallowing her surprise, Elizabeth bit back a smile at the sight of Cole, arms raised above his head in surrender, a lopsided grin on his face. How could any man look so good after riding several hours on horseback? He was dirty and unshaven, and by the look of his red-rimmed eyes, he hadn't slept in a while. Just the same, he looked awfully appealing to her.

"You look like somebody has already beat you," she said, sniffing the air. "And you smell awful."

Cole's grin widened, his dimples becoming quite pronounced. "Why thanks, ma'am. Much obliged for your kind words," he replied, affecting a drawl for her benefit.

Elizabeth's smile quickly turned upside down when she realized the scandalous situation Cole had placed her in. "You shouldn't be in here. What if somebody were to find you? My reputation would be ruined."

Cole hadn't remembered seeing Elizabeth smile before. The sight of that smile, however brief, took his breath away. He stared at her for a moment before replying, "It is perfectly acceptable for an older brother to pay a visit to his little sister, and besides, no one knows I'm home. I came in through the wall." He motioned with his thumb toward the secret panel behind him.

"I do not consider you my brother," Elizabeth said, suddenly very aware that she was dressed in only her nightclothes.

Cole's look was frankly appraising. "I can't say I'm sorry. I don't need another sister; I already have one," he said, taking several steps toward her.

Elizabeth trembled, whether in fear or anticipation she wasn't certain. She stepped backward, not trusting the fervent look she saw in Cole's eyes, which burned hot like molten steel. When her leg came in contact with the bed, she realized she was trapped. Swallowing nervously, she lowered her eyes to avoid the lascivious look Cole was directing at her.

"I must say you look awfully tempting in that white virginal nightgown you're wearing, although I think I much prefer you in your chemise and stockings."

Her eyes flew open at his remark. "You're disgusting! And you're certainly no gentleman!"

"That's what attracts you to me, isn't it?"

He took another step forward until he was so close that she could feel his hot breath upon her face.

"I'm not like all those fancy-pants suitors you're used to back east, Sunshine. Why, they probably ask permission before they kiss you."

"They do not! They—" She clamped her mouth shut, then replied, "That is none of your business, and I am not attracted to you. Your conceit astounds me, Mr. MacAlister."

"Don't deny it, Elizabeth. You're hoping I'll kiss you. Admit it. You like my kisses."

"No, I—" But before Elizabeth could reply, Cole pulled her up against him, placing his mouth gently but firmly over hers. His let his tongue travel enticingly over her lips before thrusting it into her mouth.

Consumed with a burning fire she was sure would incinerate her, Elizabeth matched Cole's kiss with an ardor that surprised her, reveling in the musky scent of his skin, the brandy taste of his lips.

Sliding her hands up his chest, she gripped the front of his shirt, tearing two of the buttons off in the process. Her fingers tingled when they came in contact with the hard muscled planes of Cole's chest. Brushing the thickly matted hairs, she caressed his warm, naked flesh, smiling inwardly when she felt him tense beneath her fingertips. It was a heady feeling knowing she had the same power over him that he had over her. She listened as their hearts thudded in unison.

Easing Elizabeth back onto the bed, Cole was astounded at how excited he had become. The little baggage had effectively turned the tables on him. He felt like an untried youth in the throes of his first passion. He had only wanted to teach her a lesson, never intending for it to go so far. But Christ! He couldn't stop now; he wanted her. And he meant to have her!

Elizabeth became mindless with wanting at the feel of Cole's hands upon her breasts; her nipples hardened instantly as he massaged the aching globes gently, pulling her gown apart to take first one nipple then the other between his teeth. He nipped playfully, drawing the ruched nipple in, caressing the sensitive, swollen bud with his tongue.

An unbearable ache began to form between her legs. She was unable to resist when Cole's hand came up under her gown to lightly caress the inside of her thighs. Slowly, it moved up to massage the soft mound of her abdomen, lightly skimming over the silky patch of curls.

Burning with a desire totally alien to her, she arched her body upward, searching for release.

Suddenly, a great emptiness assailed her; Cole was no longer touching her. She opened her eyes to see Cole's fingers covering his lips to silence her. It was then she heard the pounding on the door.

"Elizabeth, are you in there?" Her father's voice sounded through the door.

Her eyes widening in panic, she cast a horrified glance at Cole before leaping off the bed. Hastily arranging her gown, she retied the ribbons with nervous fingers. "Yes," she replied, her voice choked and hoarse.

"May I come in? I want to talk to you about the party."

"Just a moment. I won't be a minute," she replied, turning her head in time to see Cole dive under the bed.

Oh, this was really too comical for words, she thought. She, Elizabeth Forrester, actually hiding a man under her bed—or, more correctly, *his* bed. Hysterical laughter bubbled up in her throat. Calm yourself, Elizabeth, she told herself. You're a grown woman. Taking a deep breath, she walked slowly to the door and opened it.

Smiling innocently, she inquired, "Did you wish to speak to me, Father?"

Jon stared at his daughter strangely, his brows drawing together in a frown. "You're not ill, are you, dear?"

"Why, no, of course not. I was just finishing my packing."

Stepping into the room, Jon looked about, taking in the valise that rested on the floor. It was then he noticed the two buttons lying next to it. Elizabeth watched in horror as her father bent over to retrieve them. She held her breath. Please, she prayed, don't let him look under the bed.

55

"Are these yours, Elizabeth?" he asked, holding out the buttons for her inspection.

Releasing the breath she was holding, she replied, "Why, yes. I believe they belong to an old riding skirt of mine." Jon smiled, seemingly satisfied with her explanation.

"Your face is flushed, and your gown is soaking wet. Are you sure you don't have a fever?"

Elizabeth chanced a look in the mirror, horrified at her reflection. Her cheeks were glowing, her lips red and swollen. Her nightgown was wrinkled and clung to her damp skin. She looked like a harlot after a night on the town.

She didn't have time to think about her disgusting behavior with Cole. Placating her father was much more important at the moment. "I'm fine, really. What is it you wish to speak to me about?"

"I just wanted to let you know that the Crockers have accepted our invitation to the party. They are one of the most prominent families in town."

"That's nice. Are they friends of yours?"

"Business acquaintances, really. Cole and Daniel Crocker went to law school together. It's Daniel who I'm anxious for you to meet. He's very good-looking and rich as Croesus." He didn't add that Cole hated Daniel on sight and was certain to put in an appearance at the party if he knew Daniel was going to be there.

"Well, I must say, that is certainly an irresistible combination. I look forward to meeting him," Elizabeth said, smiling up at her father. His attempt at matchmaking was terribly transparent but very sweet.

"Splendid. I'll leave you to finish your packing. Good night, my dear. Sleep tight." Giving Elizabeth a kiss on the cheek, he closed the door behind him.

Elizabeth had almost forgotten Cole was under the bed until she saw his sinewy form slowly inching its way out from underneath. She was startled by the nasty expression he wore on his face.

"So . . . you've got your sights set on Daniel Crocker, huh? I might have guessed as much."

"What are you talking about? I don't even know the man."

"That shouldn't take much. Just give him the same kind of reception you gave me, and I'm sure you'll be on intimate terms in no time."

Elizabeth gasped, her eyes filling with tears at the hurtful remark Cole flung at her. How could he be so passionate and loving one minute and such a hateful beast the next? "Please leave," she said softly.

Cole snickered. "Not likely. This is my room, remember?" He proceeded to take off his shirt and boots. "You're welcome to join me in my bed, if you'd care to stay. I'm not nearly as inhospitable as you."

Elizabeth's eyes narrowed into chips of blue ice. "You are, without a doubt, the biggest bastard I have ever met. I don't know how you've fooled my father all these years, but you don't fool me. I hate you!"

A humorless smile twisted Cole's lips. "Run along, little girl, before I make you eat those words."

"Oooh! You are contemptible!" she screamed, slamming out the door.

Reclining against the headboard, his hands cupped firmly behind his head, Cole smiled thoughtfully, staring at the closed door. Behind Elizabeth's icy reserve was a wild, exciting woman. He had come so close to having her tonight. Despite all her maidenly protests, he would bet his last dollar she was no virgin. Christ! No virgin kissed like that! He was growing hard just thinking about her. She was a woman ripe for the taking, and take her he would. He would take her and use her, and when he was through, he would ship her back to New York and out of Jon's life.

Elizabeth lay staring at the white plaster ceiling overhead. She had been awake for hours, unable to get to sleep after her humiliating encounter with Cole. Her face grew warm just thinking about it. Why did she turn into a shameless hussy every time the man chose to take her in his arms? She couldn't understand it. She didn't even like him.

Her father had been right to warn her against him. He was an experienced womanizer. What was it he had said? ". . . *he takes his pleasure where he finds it.*"

Elizabeth sat straight up in bed, hugging her arms tight about her. An intense anger began building in her breast at Cole's cavalier treatment of her. He probably thinks I'm a naive little fool who would jump at the chance to be in his bed, she thought. Well, why shouldn't he? You've certainly given him every indication that is exactly where you want to be, she told herself.

Lying back down, she pulled the covers up to her chin. "Well, Cole MacAlister," Elizabeth whispered to the ceiling, "you'll not find your pleasure with me. From now on, I intend to resist your masculine charms." Her lips tingled, and her breasts ached at the memory of his touch. "No matter if it kills me!"

Chapter Six

It was the morning of the party and Elizabeth felt wretched. Ever since that dreadful episode with Cole over a week ago, she had been unable to rest or relax. Every time she turned around it seemed Cole was behind her. His snide remarks and knowing looks were driving her crazy. The only respite she'd had from his taunts was while he was at work. Even then, she'd had the misfortune of running into him several times at the various shops and restaurants her father had taken her to.

Peering into the dining room to see if it was safe to enter, Elizabeth was relieved to find only Ah Sing clearing away some of the breakfast dishes. "Has my father already eaten, Ah Sing?" Elizabeth asked, strolling into the sunlit room.

The Chinaman bowed, smiling to display rotting, yellow teeth. "Yes, missy. Mista Jon and Mista Mac gone long time now."

Elizabeth heaved a sigh of relief. As much as she enjoyed her father's company, she was happy to be alone with her thoughts. Soon the caterer would arrive, and

Monsieur Du Pré would bring the flowers, and of course, Hetty would be there to supervise. But for now she was alone, and she would use the opportunity to sit down and relax over a cup of hot tea. She waited while Ah Sing pulled the blue upholstered chair out for her before taking her seat.

"You want me to bring food now, missy?"

"No, thank you, Ah Sing. I'm not very hungry this morning. I'll just have some tea."

Carrying the steaming pot of tea over, the servant poured Elizabeth a cup. "Maybe missy would like Ah Sing to tell her fortune with the tea leaves."

Elizabeth smiled brightly at the wizened little man. "What an intriguing idea. I'd love for you to read my fortune."

Ah Sing nodded, scurrying around to take a seat at the opposite side of the table. Picking up the cup of tea that he had just poured, he sloshed it around and around, pouring off the liquid until only the tea leaves remained in the bottom of the cup. He seemed quite adept at what he was doing, as if he had performed the ritual many times before.

She watched in fascination as Ah Sing studied the dark brown leaves, nodding his head excitedly, his long pigtail bobbing up and down. Finally, he smiled a mysterious little smile.

"What does it say, Ah Sing? Am I to have fame and fortune?" Elizabeth asked, a teasing note to her voice.

Staring at the leaves and then at Elizabeth, the old man replied, "The leaves say you will marry soon."

"Marry!" Elizabeth exclaimed, ready to protest, until Ah Sing motioned her to silence.

"The leaves point to a dark-haired man. You will leave

this city, but you will return."

Her eyes were wide and questioning. "Where will I go?"

Ah Sing shook his head. "I do not know."

"What else do they tell you?"

"You will have much heartache but also much happiness. There will be children."

A feeling of elation soared through her breast. Children. She had always wanted children. She just never thought she would marry. "How many?"

He studied the leaves more closely. "The leaves say you will have five children."

"Five! My goodness!" she exclaimed, clasping her hand to her breast. "Can you tell me anything else about the dark-haired man?" An image of Cole's ebony hair flashed through her mind.

"He rides a golden horse; that is all I know." Rising to stand, Ah Sing bowed. "I must go now, missy. You have good fortune. You like?"

Elizabeth's smile was thoughtful. "Yes. Thank you, Ah Sing," she replied, watching the little man disappear into the kitchen.

After Ah Sing departed, Elizabeth picked up the cup containing the leaves. There didn't seem to be anything unusual about their appearance. She laughed. Ah Sing was probably just jesting with her. Funny though, he had seemed awfully serious while he was reading her fortune.

Chewing her lower lip, she decided it wouldn't hurt to keep her eyes open for a dark-haired man with a golden horse. Who knows? Perhaps she would meet the man of her destiny tonight.

Suddenly, a chill swept over her body; the cup she was holding slipped from her fingers. The dream. She'd had a dream about a dark-haired man upon a golden horse. Could that have been a premonition? she wondered.

Don't be silly, Elizabeth, she chided herself silently. You don't believe in all this hocus-pocus, or do you?

The party was in full swing by the time Elizabeth entered the ballroom. She hadn't meant to oversleep, only to take a short nap before the festivities began. Thank goodness, Sally, Ah Sing's niece, had come to waken her, or she would have slept through the entire affair. That would have been disastrous, considering that she was the guest of honor.

Scanning the crowded room, she searched for some sign of her father. The room looked splendid. The Waterford chandeliers sparkled like gems, their crystal prisms reflecting the light from the candles they held. The black and white marble dance floor was polished to a sheen. One could almost see the reflection of the dancers who skimmed across its high-gloss surface.

Elizabeth had to admit that Hetty Truesdale had done herself proud, and Monsieur Du Pré had indeed proven himself to be a genius. The floral arrangements were stunning. Red and white roses, accompanied by baby's breath and white carnations, were proudly displayed in Oriental vases of blue and white. There were touches of color everywhere, reminding Elizabeth of a kaleidoscope she had treasured as a child.

"Elizabeth, there you are." Her father's voice intruded into her silent observations.

Elizabeth smiled brightly at her father's handsome appearance. He looked wonderful in his black formal evening attire. "I am sorry I'm late. I'm embarrassed to say that I overslept."

A look of admiration entered Jon's eyes. Scanning his daughter's appearance from top to bottom, he smiled in approval. "It was well worth the wait, I assure you. You look like a princess. I will be the envy of every man here tonight when I introduce you as my daughter."

"You're very kind to say so." She did feel especially pretty tonight. She had taken extra pains with her appearance just in case her mystery man were to show up. The blue satin of her dress was the exact color of her eyes. She had swept her hair up off her neck, leaving only a few curls to frame her face. The Worthington sapphires rested majestically against her throat, making her feel a little bit like the princess her father had called her.

"Come and meet our guests, my dear. Everyone is eager to make your acquaintance," Jon urged.

In the short span of an hour, Elizabeth had met most of the influential and powerful people of San Francisco society. The crème de la crème had consisted of the Athertons, who owned the largest newspaper in the city; the Crockers, from the prosperous banking family; the Sinclairs, who controlled much of the real estate in the area; and last but not least, the Truesdales, who had made their fortune during the Gold Rush.

It appeared that Hetty and Walter Truesdale, for all their airs and pomposity, were nothing more than middle class merchants who had prospered by gouging poor miners with outrageous prices for food and supplies. Her father had related some of the details of their avarice, with no small amount of animosity on his part. He revealed how the Truesdales had charged up to four hundred dollars for a barrel of flour and four dollars for one pound of coffee. It was clear he found Walter Truesdale's business practices distasteful.

Hetty had made her usual dramatic entrance dressed in a frothy white lace concoction that made her look like a ship under full sail. Elizabeth smiled to herself at the unkind comparison. Unkind, she thought, but nonetheless accurate.

Deciding to fortify herself with a glass of champagne punch before the next round of partners appeared, Elizabeth made her way to the refreshment table. Her feet were killing her; she wiggled her toes, grimacing when she thought of how the poor things had been trod upon by her overzealous companions.

Sipping slowly on her drink, the bubbles gently teasing her nose, she witnessed a myriad of color sweep by her as elegantly gowned ladies and gentlemen waltzed across the floor in front of her. Absorbed in her observations, she didn't notice the handsome stranger who sidled up next to her.

"However did I miss making your acquaintance? You're Jon's daughter, are you not?" A well-modulated voice sounded in her ear.

Elizabeth turned to find an attractive brown-haired man standing next to her. He was good-looking in a classical sort of way. He had a straight patrician nose and compelling brown eyes, and although he lacked the ruggedly handsome face of Cole and his build was not as muscular, he definitely had a pleasing countenance.

Elizabeth allowed a small smile to cross her lips. "I'm Elizabeth Forrester. And you are?" She looked questioningly at him.

Grasping Elizabeth's hand, he brought it up to his lips for a gentle kiss. "Daniel Crocker, Miss Forrester. I am delighted to finally meet you. Your father has been singing your praises for the past hour." Daniel was captivated by the beauty before him. Who would have thought Jonathan Forrester could have spawned such a glorious creature?

Elizabeth blushed charmingly. "I'm afraid my father can get a bit carried away at times," she said softly, lowering her lashes demurely.

"On the contrary, Miss Forrester. His description of your beauty did not do you justice."

Elizabeth's gentle laughter rippled through the air. "How very gallant you are, Mr. Crocker. Thank you for the compliment."

"You're quite welcome, and please . . . call me Daniel."

"And you must call me Elizabeth."

Daniel smiled, displaying even white teeth. "Would you care to dance, Elizabeth?"

Inclining her head, she took the arm that he proffered and let him lead her out onto the dance floor. Twirling about in the arms of Daniel Crocker, Elizabeth did not see the vehement gaze directed at her by the tall, dark-haired man who had just entered the room.

Cole's eyes became hard as gunmetal when they settled upon the laughing couple twirling about on the dance floor. Elizabeth looked like she was actually enjoying herself, he thought, a look of disgust crossing his face. She certainly had never smiled at him that way. Didn't the little fool know what she was letting herself in for? And what about Jon. How could he be taken in by Daniel's suave demeanor?

As if conjured up by his thoughts, Jon appeared at Cole's side, smiling warmly. "Cole . . . I'm glad you decided to come," he said, slapping him firmly on the back.

Cole shot Jon a disgusted look. "What can you be thinking of, allowing Elizabeth to associate with Daniel Crocker? You know what a degenerate the man is."

Jon was surprised by Cole's vehemence. He knew Cole disliked Dan, but he hadn't realized to what extent. "Aren't you being a bit harsh, my boy? Daniel may have sewn a few too many wild oats, but I'd hardly call him degenerate."

Cole sneered. "I certainly wouldn't want him practicing his charms on my daughter. Christ, Jon! Don't you remember the last time you defended him in court?"

"You mean that ugly paternity suit?"

Cole nodded emphatically. "Exactly!"

Rubbing his chin, Jon pondered Cole's remarks. The man sounded like a jealous lover or a protective brother. But which one? he wondered.

"What would you have me do?" he finally asked. "If I tell Elizabeth not to see Daniel, she will only find him that much more appealing."

"Maybe you shouldn't have painted such a glowing picture of him to begin with."

Jon's eyes narrowed suspiciously. "How do you know about that?"

Cole was momentarily at a loss for words. He certainly wasn't about to admit that he had been hiding under his bed during Jon and Elizabeth's conversation. After a moment, he replied, "I believe Elizabeth must have mentioned it to me."

"That's odd. You two don't seem to get along all that well."

Cole shrugged, fidgeting with his shirt studs. "That's true. I guess it was just one of those times when Elizabeth needed someone to talk to, and I was convenient."

"Perhaps you could talk to Elizabeth about Daniel, since she has confided in you," Jon suggested.

"Now wait a minute!"

Jon put up his hand to forestall Cole's argument. "Since you know Daniel better than most and Elizabeth seems to trust you, I think it would be wise for you to counsel her. You know? Like a big brother would," Jon said, laughing inwardly at the expression of chagrin on Cole's face.

"Of course, if that is your wish," Cole replied, sorry he hadn't kept his big mouth shut in the first place.

"Splendid. Here comes Elizabeth now. Why don't you ask her to dance, then take her out for a stroll in the garden? It will give you a chance to talk to her."

Before Cole could utter a protest, Jon turned his back, engaging Henry Atherton in conversation on the merits of domestic versus imported wines, leaving Cole to his own devices.

Elizabeth caught sight of Cole immediately. He towered over most of the other men in the room. His dark good looks were emphasized by the fine cut of his black dinner jacket and silver waistcoat. She was surprised to find him walking in her direction. Fortunately, the look of disdain he wore did not seem to be directed at her but rather at her companion, Daniel Crocker.

"Good evening, Elizabeth," Cole said, before looking over at Daniel. "You'll excuse us, won't you, Crocker? I have family business to discuss with Elizabeth."

Elizabeth's mouth dropped open, but she quickly clamped it shut. How dare he infer that we're related? she fumed.

Daniel's smile faded a bit at Cole's remark. "Of course. I didn't know the two of you were kin."

Elizabeth opened her mouth to protest, but the look of warning in Cole's eyes made her think better of contradicting him. She felt Cole's hand glide possessively around her waist, pulling her toward him.

"We're not actually blood relations, more like kissing cousins, wouldn't you say, Elizabeth?" Cole asked, smiling down at her, his eyes sparkling with mischief.

Elizabeth's face flamed. As the pressure on her waist increased, she could only nod in agreement. Taking a deep breath to calm herself, she said, "If you gentlemen will excuse me, I am in need of some fresh air."

Daniel bowed over her hand, placing a kiss upon it. "Until later," he said, tossing Cole a smug smile.

"Thank you for the dance, Daniel," Elizabeth replied, flashing him a brilliant smile. She felt Cole tense at her gesture and was pleased that she'd been able to annoy him.

Cole watched the exchange with suppressed fury. Pulling Elizabeth by the wrist, he guided her out into the cool night air. Reaching a secluded area of the garden, he stopped, the huge limbs of the live oak tree providing an effective cover from the occupants on the patio.

"Just what do you think you are doing?" Elizabeth demanded through gritted teeth. "I do not appreciate being hauled around like a piece of excess baggage." Her face reddened in anger as she rubbed her wrist where Cole had grabbed it.

"I should be asking you the same question. What do you think you're doing with the likes of Daniel Crocker?"

"I don't believe that is any of your business," she said, folding her arms across her chest. She refused to be intimidated by Cole's heavy-handed tactics.

68

"I'm making it my business."

"I don't have to listen to this," Elizabeth ground out. "You're crazy. Insane. Just leave me alone. I'm going back to the party." She turned to leave, but Cole stepped in her path, blocking her escape.

Placing his finger under Elizabeth's chin, he searched her upturned face. Her blue eyes smoldered like a banked fire ready to burst into flame. "Daniel Crocker is a rogue and a despoiler of women. He uses women, then throws them away."

"Like you?" she asked, her words laced with sarcasm.

Cole's eyes hardened into two bits of granite. "I'm nothing like Crocker. He's bad news, Elizabeth. I'm warning you, stay away from him."

"Oh, and I suppose I'd be safer with you?" she asked, disbelief clearly evident on her face. "You forget, Cole, I've already experienced how honorable your attentions are toward me."

Cole shot Elizabeth a twisted smile. "I never did anything you didn't want me to. You're just too damn proud and stubborn to admit it."

Elizabeth swallowed hard, trying to conceal her anger. "Your conceit continues to astound me. It just so happens that I find Daniel to be quite charming and quite a gentleman. Unlike yourself!"

Clenching his hands into fists, he tried to keep his temper under control. He had never struck a woman before, but he sure as hell felt like it now. "Don't push me, Elizabeth. I'm only trying to keep you from making a big mistake."

Elizabeth hadn't really been that interested in Daniel. She had found him to be too shallow, too caught up in himself. But having Cole warn her off him was like waving a red flag in front of her face; it was a challenge she wasn't likely to resist.

"I think you had better mind your own business, Mr. MacAlister. I don't need your interference or your concern. I am a grown woman, in case you hadn't noticed. I can take care of myself."

"Don't say I didn't warn you. You may be a grown woman, but when it comes to men, you're nothing but a child. I should know; I've experienced you firsthand."

Elizabeth gasped aloud. In one quick, fluid motion she raised her hand, slapping Cole soundly across the face. Turning on her heel, she hurried back to the party.

Rubbing his cheek, Cole observed Elizabeth fly up the path toward the house. Anger and admiration sparked in his eyes. Damn, but she was an irritating creature! She had provoked him into saying things he hadn't really meant. He hated being cruel. The look of hurt lighting her eyes had twisted his gut. Why wouldn't she listen? His brutal words were nothing compared to what she was going to experience at the hands of Daniel Crocker. He shook his head in disgust. Damn troublesome woman!

Chapter Seven

Elizabeth stared morosely out the window of her upstairs bedroom. The fog hung heavily over the trees, obscuring her view of the hills beyond. The gloomy atmosphere did little to revive her already sagging spirits. She had been summoned home.

A telegram from Josiah Worthington had arrived early this morning, demanding her return to New York. Elizabeth had told no one. She was not about to let her grandfather dictate his wishes to her again. If her father found out, he might decide to send her away; she couldn't let that happen.

She had finally found her father and with him a love and contentment that had been missing from her life. She didn't want to leave him just yet. There were still many things they needed to discover about each other. They had twenty years to make up for, and six weeks just hadn't been enough time.

There was also Cole to consider. Elizabeth had not been able to sort out her feelings where he was concerned. They had seen little of each other since the night of the party. Cole had kept his distance, only speaking to her when spoken to. She sighed deeply. She couldn't help the undeniable attraction she felt for him; she knew he felt it, too. Sparks would fly whenever they were in the same room together. Cole infuriated her beyond belief, but there were times when just the sight of his smile could send her heart dancing.

Elizabeth wrinkled her nose in disgust. Men. They were all such a bother; even Daniel was beginning to annoy her. She glanced up at the banjo clock hanging on the wall. She was going to be late for the picnic if she didn't hurry. Daniel would be here at any moment to pick her up.

They had seen each other almost every day since their first meeting. Elizabeth had found Daniel to be a charming and witty companion, but his self-absorption grated on her nerves.

Checking her appearance in the brass cheval mirror one last time, she adjusted her straw bonnet, straightened the skirts of her yellow dimity dress, and proceeded down the stairs to meet her escort.

Daniel had not yet arrived when she entered the library. She found, instead, her father, head bent over his desk, engrossed in a pile of legal-looking documents.

"Father," Elizabeth said, her eyes widening in surprise, "I didn't know you were staying home today." Although it was Saturday, Elizabeth knew her father always made it his practice to spend a few hours at his law office.

Jon looked up at the sound of his daughter's voice and smiled. Elizabeth looked fetching in her lemon-colored gown. "Good morning, my dear. You're a sight to brighten this dreary day. Am I to presume you have another date with Daniel?"

Flashing him a brilliant smile, she nodded. "Yes. We're to go on a picnic," she replied, "although I'm not too sure the weather is going to cooperate."

"You've been seeing quite a bit of Dan lately. It's not getting serious, is it?" Jon asked, quirking his eyebrow.

The look of genuine concern on her father's face almost made Elizabeth laugh. Walking over to the desk, she perched herself on top of his lap and gave him a hug.

"Why, Father! You know I don't have time for any man but you."

Patting her cheek, Jon replied, "Not even Cole?"

Jumping up, Elizabeth felt a warm blush creep up her neck, and her eyes widened innocently. "Cole? Now why would you ask that? You know how I feel about him."

Jon didn't miss the heightened color that came to Elizabeth's cheeks at the mention of Cole. And what about Cole? He had been as prickly as a pear on a cactus plant every time the subject of Elizabeth and Daniel had come up.

Jon had seen enough of Elizabeth and Daniel's relationship to know there was no romance brewing. He had only questioned Elizabeth about it to gauge her response. But Elizabeth and Cole . . . now that was an entirely different story. Just their reaction to each other the other night at dinner had been enough to make him suspicious.

The longing looks Elizabeth had shot in Cole's direction had been hot enough to ignite the candles on the table. And Cole had looked as if he would devour Elizabeth rather than his plate of Dungeness crab every time he chanced a look at her. There was definitely something between them . . . a certain chemistry.

It was time for a little fatherly interference, that was

for certain. The problem was, how was he going to go about playing Cupid with two such blind, stubborn children?

Jon's mouth curved with tenderness as he looked upon his daughter. "I guess I was mistaken, my dear. Where did you say you were going today?"

Before Elizabeth could reply, the door knocker sounded. Grateful for the reprieve, she excused herself and hurried to answer it.

Daniel stood waiting, hat in hand, looking very dashing in his tan trousers and brown jacket. "Daniel, how nice to see you. Come in," Elizabeth said.

Daniel entered, stopping short at the sight of Elizabeth's father in the hallway. "Mr. Forrester, I wasn't expecting to see you today."

Jon glanced at Daniel and then at Elizabeth, a look of annoyance crossing his face. "Why is it everyone seems to think it is so unusual to find me home in my own house?" he barked. Turning his back on the couple, he retreated back to the library, closing the door.

"What was that all about?" Daniel inquired, puzzled by Jon Forrester's uncharacteristic rudeness.

Elizabeth reddened, surprised by her father's behavior. "You must excuse my father. He's a bit harried this morning," she replied, shaking her head in disbelief. She had no idea what had gotten into him today.

Daniel stared at Elizabeth, a smile ruffling his mouth. "Are you ready to go? The sun has finally appeared, and I think it is going to be a glorious day."

Laughing gaily, Elizabeth teased, "Are you always so unequivocally optimistic about everything?"

"Of course. I always get my own way. It's what makes life so pleasant. Don't you agree?"

Choosing to ignore Daniel's question, Elizabeth grabbed the wicker basket resting near the hall tree and escaped out the door.

The horses' hooves clattered noisily over the basalt paving stones as the carriage rolled down California Street toward the downtown area. Elizabeth stared in wonder as they passed the impressive Fairmont Hotel and the prestigious Bohemian Club, where people of artistic and literary consequence gathered to meet and share ideas. The more she compared San Francisco to New York, the more similarities she discovered.

San Francisco was becoming a powerful city in its own right. The architecture was impressive, handsome, and substantial. The buildings, constructed from brick, granite, and stone, were tall and narrow; many possessed iron doors and shutters for protection.

Everywhere she looked there were dozens of hotels and restaurants of every nationality. She had counted three French, four Chinese, and two Spanish in the last two blocks they had traveled. As they passed Delmonico's, Elizabeth was reminded of the wonderful lunch she had shared with her father there only last week; it had rivaled some of the better restaurants New York had to offer.

The sun shone brightly, its warmth a welcoming addition after the drizzly morning they had experienced. If she lived here a dozen years, she would never get used to the cold, chilly dampness that seemed to pervade her very soul. It wasn't the freezing, biting temperature of the East, but it seeped under your skin, making you miserable just the same.

"Are you cold, Elizabeth?" Daniel asked, noticing how she huddled within her shawl.

Elizabeth smiled bleakly, embarrassed to have been caught shivering. "I'm fine. It's just that the weather here is so different from New York. I'm not sure I will ever get used to it."

Daniel laughed. "I know what you mean. I lived in Boston when I was in law school. I never thought I would survive my first winter there. I couldn't wait to get back to California."

Daniel's comment prompted Elizabeth's memory. "You and Cole attended law school together, didn't you?"

Turning away, Daniel stared straight ahead. He became quiet, almost introspective. After a few moments, he answered, "Yes, that's correct. I'm ashamed to admit it, but I never finished out my term."

"Why is that . . . if you don't mind my asking?"

"I might as well tell you. I'm sure Cole would be only too happy to let you in on all the scandalous details. I was booted out . . . for cheating."

Elizabeth stared down at her lap. "I see. I'm sorry if I have been the cause of dredging up unhappy memories."

Daniel shot her a side-long glance of utter disbelief. "You're not shocked? Disgusted with me?"

Elizabeth was neither shocked nor the least bit surprised by Daniel's revelations that he had cheated and been kicked out of law school. It fit in perfectly with what she had already observed about his character. "No, I'm not shocked; and as for being disgusted, I really try not to judge people too harshly. Everyone makes mistakes."

"You're a real wonder, Elizabeth. I can't imagine why some man hasn't snapped you up."

Bristling at his comment, she parried, "Perhaps it's because I don't wish to be snapped up."

"Now don't go getting your dander up. I'm not much for the state of matrimony myself. It's so much more pleasant to enjoy each other's company without getting all wrapped up in the overrated emotion of love. Don't you agree?"

Elizabeth was not sure how to answer. Gazing about at the unfamiliar scenery, she was nervous to find that they had traveled a good distance and were now in an isolated area in the hills above the city. Swallowing, she took a deep breath. She didn't want Daniel to think she was interested in a permanent alliance, nor did she want to give him the impression that she would consent to an illicit affair. Just as she was about to offer what she thought would be an acceptable response, a horse and rider came bearing down on them with unrelenting speed.

As the rider approached, Daniel pulled the carriage to a halt. Squinting because she was staring directly into the sun, Elizabeth was unable to ascertain exactly who the rider was. The horse slowed down to a trot, prancing and picking its way forward.

As the horse and rider came into view, Elizabeth gasped, clutching her throat. There, on top of a golden palomino, was none other than Cole MacAlister—dark-haired Cole MacAlister.

Dismounting, Cole strode forward. As he came around the side of the carriage to talk with Elizabeth, he noticed her swaying strangely in her seat. He approached just in time to catch her limp body as it fell toward the ground.

"Elizabeth, my God!" Daniel cried out, jumping down and rushing forward. He stopped in his tracks at the deadly look Cole directed at him.

"Stay where you are. Give her some breathing space,"

he ordered. Cradling Elizabeth gently in his arms, Cole carried her over to a shady spot under a stand of pine trees, carefully lying her down. Unbuttoning the two top buttons of her gown, he ordered Daniel to bring over his canteen. Soaking his neckerchief with the cooling water, he tenderly sponged Elizabeth's face. A moment later, her eyelids fluttered open.

"What happened?" she asked, horrified to find Cole leaning over her.

"You fainted, Elizabeth. You gave us such a fright," Daniel explained.

Relief flooded through her when she discovered that Daniel was still nearby. She did not want to be left alone with Cole for any length of time. "I'm so embarrassed. Please forgive me, Daniel." She purposely refused to include Cole in her apology.

Staring suspiciously at Elizabeth, Cole's eyes narrowed. Why had she suddenly fainted? He looked over at Daniel, then back at Elizabeth. Could she be pregnant? No. There hadn't been enough time for that occurrence. Placing his hand on her forehead, he remarked, "You don't appear to be feverish, but I think it would be a good idea for me to take you home."

"No . . . really. I'm fine," she protested, struggling to sit up.

"Perhaps Cole is correct in this case, Elizabeth. Your father was not in a good mood this morning. If he sees that you've become ill while in my care, he may refuse to let me see you again."

"That would be a blessing," Cole muttered under his breath. "That's very sensible of you, Crocker," he said aloud. "You can ride Equalizer back to town; I'll bring Elizabeth home in the carriage."

Helping Elizabeth to her feet, Cole watched in disgust as Daniel came forward to clutch her hand in his own.

"I will see you soon, Elizabeth. Perhaps we can finish that interesting discussion of love and matrimony we were having."

Elizabeth blushed, mortified that Cole would jump to the wrong conclusion. "Good-bye, Daniel. Thank you for the outing," she said softly. As she watched Daniel ride off on Cole's golden stallion, she couldn't help feeling abandoned.

Cole could barely keep his anger in check as he helped Elizabeth into the carriage. How dare she discuss matrimony with Daniel Crocker? Hadn't he warned her to stay away from that licentious bastard?

The carriage felt smaller with Cole's presence in it. Elizabeth's thigh burned where Cole's denim-clad leg pressed against it. Her close proximity to him filled her with nervous excitement. As she observed his lean, tanned fingers pick up the reins, those same fingers that had traveled over her breasts and thighs in exquisite exploration, her heart began to pound erratically in her chest. She shifted uncomfortably in her seat.

Glancing over at Elizabeth, Cole became alarmed at the redness of her complexion. "Are you sure you're all right? You look feverish to me."

Unable to meet Cole's probing gaze, she kept her face averted, staring down at her hands folded primly in her lap. "I'm fine," she replied in a small, tired voice. Satisfied with her answer, Cole cracked the reins and started the journey homeward.

The awkwardness of the situation was becoming increasingly unbearable with every mile that passed. Neither Cole nor Elizabeth spoke, each engrossed in their own tortured thoughts.

Elizabeth had been stunned to discover that Cole was the man of her dreams. The man the tea leaves foretold. He had to be the one, she thought. He possessed the dark hair and rode the golden horse. What other explanation could there be? Unless Ah Sing had misread the leaves. Yes, she decided, that must be the answer. He had said she would marry the dark-haired man who rode the golden horse, but that was impossible. She would never marry Cole; they didn't even like each other. Oh, she found him attractive and utterly masculine, but she couldn't conceive of spending the rest of her life with the overbearing brute. No. Ah Sing had definitely made a mistake.

Cole was anguished by his own disquieting thoughts. How far had Elizabeth and Daniel's relationship gone? If they were speaking of love and marriage, could they have already dispensed with the formalities and consummated their relationship? The thought of Daniel possessing Elizabeth filled him with raw fury. His fingers tightened unconsciously on the reins, causing the horses to rear.

Suddenly, the carriage lurched, and Elizabeth was thrown against him. He reached out with one hand to assist her, accidentally brushing her breast in the process. He heard her sharp intake of breath.

Spying a grassy area a short distance away, Cole pulled the carriage to a halt. In the aggravated state he was in, he wasn't fit to walk, let alone drive a carriage.

"Why are we stopping?" Elizabeth questioned. She didn't feel up to sparring with Cole right now. She was confused and frightened, and just wanted to go home and bury her head under the covers.

"The horses need to rest," he lied. "We can sit under the shade of that oak tree while they graze for a while."

Cole stepped around to help Elizabeth alight. Grasping her firmly about the waist, he let her slide slowly down the long length of his body.

Elizabeth's body tingled as it came in contact with Cole's. She looked up at him; their eyes locked and she was lost, mesmerized by the silver orbs that glowed with a savage inner fire.

Cole untied the ribbons of her bonnet, tossing it onto the carriage seat. Their mouths fused together hungrily, his kiss urgent, demanding. Elizabeth kissed him back with all the pent-up frustration she had experienced over the last few weeks. Her blood pounded in her brain, making her feel faint again.

When she was in Cole's arms, nothing else seemed to matter. Their differences and dislikes evaporated like the morning fog. Her need for Cole drove all rational thought from her head.

Sensing her surrender, Cole pulled reluctantly away, holding Elizabeth at arm's length. He was losing control, and he didn't like the feeling one bit. Staring into her passion-filled eyes, he knew he could take her right here and now if he wanted. She was willing, even eager. Did she respond this way when Daniel kissed her? he wondered, surprised by the feeling of jealousy that overtook him.

Elizabeth watched a multitude of emotions flicker across Cole's face as he distanced himself from her. She didn't want him to stop kissing her. She desired his kisses, his caresses. Didn't he realize that? She brought her arms up to circle his neck, pulling his head down to hers, pressing herself into him.

81

Cole took hold of Elizabeth's hands and gently but firmly put them back at her sides. He could see the confusion and hurt in her eyes, but if they were to continue on their present course, there would be no turning back. What an inconvenient time for him to have an attack of conscience, he thought ruefully. As much as he desired her, there was no getting around the fact that she was Jon's only daughter.

"You'll thank me tomorrow, Sunshine."

Her face burning in humiliation, Elizabeth's eyes glittered dangerously. Cole had rejected her, had scorned her advances. She wanted to lash out at him, to hurt him as he had hurt her. Lifting her chin, she stared directly into his eyes. "I should have known you would be a poor substitute for Daniel. You're not half the man he is," she said.

Cole's face turned dark and menacing. An unfathomable light shone in his strange silver eyes. Elizabeth knew real fear for the first time in her life. As quick as a flash of lightning, he lashed out, pulling her hard up against him.

"If you're so intent on playing the whore, Sunshine, I see no reason why I shouldn't accommodate you."

Elizabeth whitened. "No, please! I'm sorry," she cried, a tremor of fear lacing her voice.

Ignoring her pleas, Cole grasped the neckline of her gown, ripping the thin material to expose Elizabeth's milky white skin to his gaze.

Panic welled up inside her throat. She struggled wildly, trying to break free of Cole's embrace. When she finally managed to free her arms, she crossed them over her scantily clad breasts.

Cole laughed, a cold, derisive sound that chilled her soul. "What's the matter, Sunshine? You're not getting modest on me, are you? You forget . . . I've seen you in your underwear before." Grabbing her wrists in an iron grip, he imprisoned both in his left hand.

"Please stop!" Elizabeth begged, her voice hoarse from pleading.

With his free hand, Cole untied the ribbons of Elizabeth's chemise; her full ripe breasts spilled forth from their confinement. His breathing quickened as he stared at the lush mounds before him. The dusky nipples jutted forth proudly, begging for his attention. Slowly, he circled each hardened tip with his finger, running it over and over the stiffened peaks.

Gasping in sweet agony, Elizabeth's tears streamed down her face at the shame Cole was inflicting upon her. As much as she hated him at this moment, she couldn't deny her body's traitorous response. "Please don't!" she choked out.

Cole smiled mockingly. "What's the matter, sweetheart? Don't I do it as well as Daniel?" He lowered his head to lap at the rosy tips with his tongue, suckling each breast until Elizabeth's heart-wrenching sobs penetrated his passion-drugged mind.

Disgusted with himself as well as with Elizabeth, he released her immediately, causing her to stumble backward. She lay on her back, staring up at him, a wounded expression in her eyes.

Taking deep, calming breaths, he tried to restore his sanity. "If I thought you had bedded Crocker, I'd take you here and now . . . in the dirt like a whore," Cole said, his voice thick and unsteady.

Shaking her head, her eyes wide with fright, Elizabeth replied, "No . . . I didn't. I swear. I only lied to make you angry."

"Well, you certainly succeeded, Sunshine. I told you once not to push me too far. You should have heeded my warning."

"I—I—I hate you," she sobbed, wiping her nose with the back of her hand.

Cole almost smiled at the childlike gesture. Bending over, he pulled Elizabeth to her feet, wiping the tears from her eyes with his neckerchief. "Cover yourself," he demanded, "or I won't be responsible for my actions."

Quickly fastening the ribbons of her chemise, she stared in dismay at her once-lovely gown, which now hung in tatters about her. Pulling the torn edges together, she held them closed.

Handing Elizabeth her shawl, Cole said, "Here, tie this around you. We wouldn't want your father to guess what you had been up to."

Elizabeth reeled back as if struck, her eyes narrowing in hatred. "He would kill you if he knew what you had done," she said.

"Don't be too sure, Sunshine. You may have been Jon's daughter these past six weeks, but I have been his son for the past twenty years. When I tell him how I found you and Crocker, who do you think he'll believe?"

Elizabeth gasped, her face turning ashen. "You're despicable. You would lie to my father to save your own neck?"

Cole shrugged. "We all do what we must. Didn't you just tell me that you had lied to me?" he asked, helping Elizabeth into the carriage.

Elizabeth's blue eyes flashed angrily. Oh, how she would love to tell Cole that she and Daniel had been lovers. It just might be worth the price she would have to pay to shatter his inflated ego. Meeting his menacing stare as he waited for her answer, she decided this was not the time to press her luck. She nodded back at him without speaking.

"Enough said. Once we are home, I will do all the talking. Do you understand?" His tone left no room for argument.

"Yes, but what will you say?"

"Leave everything to me. If luck is on our side, we may not have to say anything."

Providence was clearly on Cole and Elizabeth's side as they approached the three-story house. Alighting from the carriage, Cole noted immediately that only a few lights had been left burning. Thank God, he thought, Jonathan had gone out for the evening. Dusk was beginning to descend as the nervous couple edged toward the side of the building. The cool night air was laced with the distinctive smell of the bay.

Glancing about to make sure no one had seen them, Cole took hold of Elizabeth's hand, guiding her to an opening concealed behind a large oleander bush. "Keep quiet, and don't say a word until we're safely inside," he whispered.

Elizabeth inclined her head. She was terrified her father was going to discover what had happened today. He would surely send her back to her grandfather if he knew of her shameless behavior with Cole.

It was pitch-black in the passageway. Elizabeth could barely see her hand in front of her face. Something furry scurried across her foot. Stifling the scream that rose in her throat, she lunged forward, grabbing blindly for Cole's waist. Relief poured through her when she connected with the solid wall of his body, hugging him to her.

"What's the matter?"

"There's a creature in here," she whispered.

Cole's teeth flashed bright against the dark. Turning, he embraced Elizabeth against his chest. The feel of her pressed so trustingly against him did queer things to his insides. Stroking the silky strands of her hair, he whispered, "There's nothing to be afraid of, Sunshine. I'm here, remember?" He could feel her nod, but she still held tight to his waist. "It's only a little bit further, then we'll be in my bedroom."

Somehow, Cole's words were not comforting. She was either going to be ravaged by furry rodents if she remained in the passageway or consumed by Cole's lustful advances when she entered his room. It was hard to decide which was the lesser of the two evils.

A moment later, light spilled into the tunnel and Elizabeth found herself back in Cole's bedroom, among familiar surroundings. She breathed a sigh of relief.

Relaxing a little when Cole made no move to attack her, she watched him glide about the room, lighting the lamps and candles. Soon a comforting golden hue illuminated his bedroom.

"Why don't you sit down for a minute. I want to check to make sure no one is about before you leave," he suggested, pointing to the chair by the fireplace.

Grateful for the chance to rest, Elizabeth did as she was told. She felt drained, both physically and emotionally. Her bout with Cole today had left her more confused than ever. She had seen a side of him that made her tremble in remembrance. He had been harsh, even brutal, but she had also seen a gentler side to his nature. She remembered how he had bathed her face after she had fainted and hugged her gently when she was afraid. Would she ever be able to figure out the real Cole? she wondered.

"The hall is clear," Cole said, entering the room. "You had better go back to your bedroom and change." He looked at Elizabeth and shook his head. She looked so damn small and vulnerable sitting in the large leather chair. Her snarled hair hung down in her face, and her dress was wrapped about her in shreds.

He felt ashamed at what he had done to her. He didn't know what had come over him. He had reacted like a man possessed by an inner demon. Elizabeth seemed to bring out the worst of his temper. "I'm sorry about your dress. I will buy you a new one," he said.

Elizabeth glanced up to find Cole's words matched by a contrite expression. Despite her reservations, she found herself responding to the entreaty in his voice. She felt confused by his apology. Sighing deeply, she replied, "I suppose I am as much to blame as you. It was my lie that perpetrated your actions."

Helping Elizabeth to her feet, Cole clasped her soft hands gently between his two roughened ones. "I want to make this up to you," he said, noting the shocked expression that crossed her face. "I have to leave town for a few days. When I return, would you consider having dinner with me?"

Elizabeth's face brightened instantly. She flashed him an uncertain smile, unable to believe that he actually wanted to be friends. "I would be honored."

Bringing her hands up to his lips, he kissed them tenderly, then followed her out the door until she crossed the threshold to her room. "Good night, Sunshine," he said, and then he was gone.

Closing the door, Elizabeth leaned heavily against it. She stared dreamily into space, like a schoolgirl who had just been given her first kiss. Hugging herself tightly, she twirled about, happy at the sudden turn of events that had taken place between Cole and herself.

Ah Sing had been right, she thought happily. Cole was her destiny . . . her shadowed dream.

Chapter Eight

The next few days passed by with agonizing slowness for Elizabeth. She missed Cole dreadfully. It had been seven days since his departure and still no word from him. Obviously, he had not missed her in the least, she thought dejectedly, pushing the eggs around her plate in a distracted fashion. Glancing up at the clock, she noted the time: nine-thirty. She sighed. She had the whole day ahead of her with nothing to do, and the prospect was decidedly dim. Elizabeth was bored. She had no friends in San Francisco except for Daniel Crocker.

Disappointed by Cole's apparent change of heart, she had accepted Daniel's invitation to the Athertons' party this evening, jumping at the chance for a little excitement. Now, however, she wasn't sure she had made the right decision. Cole would not be pleased to learn that she was going out with Daniel. Their newly made truce was sure to be shattered.

Heaving a sigh, she decided that she would not sit around another day waiting for Cole to make an appearance. If he arrived home today, he would be vastly disappointed, for she was going out with Daniel Crocker tonight—with or without Cole's blessing.

At the sound of approaching footsteps, she looked up, her heart jumping to her throat as she cast a nervous glance toward the door. Cole, she thought hopefully. It was hard to conceal the disappointment on her face when her father entered the room.

"What is it, Elizabeth?" Jon asked, his face a mask of worry. "You look so unhappy. You're not sorry you've stayed here so long, are you?"

Elizabeth's expression grew contrite. She never meant to hurt her father, but from the anxious expression on his face, she could see she already had. "It has nothing to do with leaving here," she admitted. "I'm enjoying my stay very much."

A look of relief smoothed Jon's features. "Well, what is it, then? What's happened to put such a dour look on your beautiful face?"

Elizabeth smiled tentatively. "It's just that—" She paused, unsure of how to explain her feelings to her father. Should she tell him about Cole, or would he jump to the wrong conclusion?

"Yes?" Jon prompted, his eyebrows raised in question as he took the seat opposite her.

"You remember me telling you about the carriage accident Cole and I had, and how my dress was torn?" she asked, hating herself for the falsehood she uttered. There was no escaping the whopping lie she had manufactured after Sally discovered the torn dress in her room the morning after the carriage ride.

"Of course, I remember. I was so relieved you weren't hurt."

Elizabeth had the grace to blush. "Well," she continued, "Cole promised to take me out to dinner to make amends for the dress, but it's been over a week since he asked me, and he hasn't returned."

"Is that what's bothering you?" Jon asked, noting the look of misery in his daughter's eyes. At her nod, he continued, "Cole sent a message two days ago, informing me of his delay. He probably assumed I would tell you. I'm sorry, Elizabeth. I've been so tied up with that damn Parker versus Peabody case, I completely forgot."

Elizabeth's heart sang with joy at her father's revelation. Cole hadn't forgotten her after all.

"I see my news has made you feel better," Jon remarked, noting the unconcealed happiness on Elizabeth's face. He smiled, praying his suspicions were correct.

"Much."

"Does this mean that you and Cole are getting along better?"

Refusing to meet her father's eyes lest she betray herself, Elizabeth made a great pretense of studying the napkin on her lap. "Yes," she replied.

"I can't tell you how happy I am to hear that two of my favorite people have decided to become friends."

At the memory of just how friendly Cole and she had become, Elizabeth shifted uncomfortably in her chair. She wondered how happy her father would be if he were to find out just how far their relationship had progressed. Keeping her face impassive and her voice neutrally calm, she replied, "Cole and I have called a truce of sorts."

"Splendid!" Jon exclaimed. "Let's go to Delmonico's this afternoon for lunch and celebrate."

Giggling at her father's enthusiasm, Elizabeth nodded. "That would be lovely."

Elizabeth, Jon added silently, you don't know how lovely it will be when you and Cole are truly more than friends.

Seated at the dressing table later that evening, Elizabeth fastened the diamond and emerald necklace around her throat, casting a critical eye at her hair, which had been curled and pulled close to her head with ringlets of gold hanging down her back.

She felt especially pretty tonight in her gown of green satin trimmed with Valenciennes lace. If only Cole were here to see her, she thought wistfully. It seemed like such a waste to have gone to all this trouble for Daniel. She knew by his leering looks and ardent expression that Daniel was enamored of her. But Daniel did not make her heart race or set her blood boiling the way Cole did.

Two light taps on the door announced Sally's arrival. "Mista Crocker arrive, missy."

Smiling at Ah Sing's ebony-haired niece, Elizabeth thanked her, rising from the bench. "Tell Mr. Crocker I will be right down." She watched the diminutive woman bow and scamper out the door, her delicate features and mannerisms reminding Elizabeth of a fragile tiger lily.

At the sight of Elizabeth floating down the stairs, Daniel's eyes lit up brighter than a Fourth of July sparkler. "Elizabeth, you look enchanting this evening."

"Thank you, Daniel. You look very nice yourself."

Puffing out his chest, Daniel adjusted the ruffle on his cuff. "I do try to keep up with the latest fashions from Europe, although it's damned difficult getting these

Chinese tailors to understand what I'm talking about."

Elizabeth bit back a smile. It was awfully hard not to laugh in Daniel's pompous face. She had decided earlier that this would be her last date with him.

"Are you up to doing something really daring tonight?" he asked.

"Whatever are you talking about? You told me we were going to attend a party this evening," Elizabeth said, unable to mask the annoyance she felt at Daniel's last minute change of plans.

"Now don't get your feathers ruffled. We are going to the party. But afterward, my chums and I decided it would be a lark to head over to Chinatown and visit some of the opium dens."

Before Elizabeth could respond, a loud crash sounded from behind, causing her to turn. Sally was bent over a porcelain vase, picking up the pieces, her eyes round with fright.

"Stupid coolie," Daniel sneered.

Elizabeth shot him a quelling glance. Turning back to Sally, she offered an encouraging smile. "It's all right, Sally. Don't worry about it. I hated that ugly monstrosity the moment I laid eyes on it."

"Come on, Elizabeth. We're going to be late," Daniel urged. He couldn't conceal his distaste over Elizabeth's concern for a Chinese. They were an incredibly stupid race of people, one step above a Negro as far as he was concerned. Although he had to admit, the women were awfully skilled in the art of lovemaking.

Staring at the horrified expression on Sally's face, Elizabeth was almost tempted not to go. What had upset the woman so? she wondered. Surely not the vase.

"Are you ready to leave?" Daniel asked, placing the

satin cloak about her shoulders.

Giving Sally one last reassuring smile, Elizabeth inclined her head and headed out the door.

The gas lamps were lit along Stockton Street as the revelers made their way through Chinatown. The fog had settled over the city like a blanket, its fingers reaching out to cloak the night in dampness.

Elizabeth huddled inside her cloak, shivering violently, whether from the cold or her nervousness at being here she didn't know. She was increasingly doubtful of the wisdom of accompanying Daniel and his cohorts on their journey into the area known as Chinatown.

From her position inside the carriage, she was able to view the natives of the Celestial Empire firsthand. There were dozens of people milling about the dimly lit streets. Chinamen dressed in strange-looking pantaloon-type pants and loose-fitting blouses, much the same type of garments Ah Sing wore, scurried about, darting in and out of sinister-looking alleys. Upon their heads they wore strange little straw hats that resembled upside-down soup bowls, their long black queues dangling freely below them.

The crowds grew thicker as the carriage pulled onto Grant Avenue. They had to stop several times to allow Daniel's friends, who rode in the conveyance behind, to catch up with them. Elizabeth covered her nose with her white lace handkerchief against the malodorous stench that drifted up from the dirty streets and narrow alleyways.

"We're almost there, darling. Sorry about the smell. These filthy Chinese are no better than animals," Daniel remarked, pulling the carriage to a halt in front of a group of flimsy-looking shacks.

As Elizabeth alighted and made to enter the building, she grew fearful of the hungry looks directed at her from its inhabitants. Whatever had possessed her to go along with Daniel's ridiculous scheme? she wondered, hurrying to catch up with the others.

The evening had started off fine. Daniel had taken her to the Athertons' party as promised. There had been hundreds of elegantly dressed people, all who behaved in a socially correct manner and all who talked of the most inane subjects Elizabeth had ever encountered. After being subjected to an hour of Patricia Atherton's piano concerto, she had been more than ready to leave. When Daniel suggested they depart, she had eagerly agreed; she wished now that she hadn't been so impetuous.

Daniel and his six friends had decided that a visit to Chinatown for a little gambling would be just the ticket to liven up the evening. Glancing about the room at the group of hostile faces staring back at her, Elizabeth wasn't so sure they were right. The smoke-filled room was filled to capacity. An orchestra of five men, grouped in the corner, played a strange, exotic tune, a noisy, grating sound, quite unlike anything she had ever heard.

A long mat-covered table stood in the center of the room. Strange brass objects, which appeared to be some type of gambling devices, rested on top. Elizabeth had absolutely no idea what type of game they were playing, and she had no desire to learn.

Staring wide-eyed at the scantily clad woman approaching her party, Elizabeth's mouth dropped open. The girl, who couldn't have been more than fifteen, came to stand before Daniel and herself. She was dressed in a black silk shirt, which had been embroidered with turquoise birds, and nothing else. The outfit, revealing most of the lower half of her body, left little to the imagination.

"You like China girl?" the black-haired girl asked Daniel, smiling seductively at him.

Taking another drink, one of many he had already imbibed that evening, Daniel looked the girl over, pausing to consider the question. "How much?"

Elizabeth gasped in horror, embarrassed by the snickers and crude remarks from Daniel's companions. As she turned to walk away, Daniel grabbed onto her waist, holding her firmly by his side. The Chinese girl gave her a triumphant smile.

"Two bits for you. Four bits if you want to bring the lady," she said.

Burning with embarrassment and anger, Elizabeth brought her booted foot down on Daniel's instep as hard as she could, relieved and gratified when he yelled, releasing his hold on her arm. Taking advantage of the opportunity, she ran out the building, past the startled faces of her companions and into the waiting carriage.

Moments later, a very drunk Daniel arrived, apologizing profusely. "I was only teasing, Elizabeth. Please don't be cross," he said, slurring his words as he spoke.

Elizabeth's eyes narrowed into chips of blue ice. "Take me home this instant," she shouted, unable to control her trembling rage.

"Sure . . . sure. I only have one more stop to make."

"Daniel, I'm warning you . . ." she threatened, clenching her fists. If she had a weapon in her hands at this very moment, Daniel Crocker would be past history.

Daniel laughed aloud, hiccuping in the process. "You don't scare me, darling. Now sit back and relax. I need to visit the *Den of Delights* before I take you home."

Sitting back against the cushion of her seat, arms folded across her chest, Elizabeth fumed in silence at the drunken lout next to her. Why, oh, why had she been stupid enough to come? she asked herself for the hundredth time.

"Here we are, darling," Daniel said, pulling the horses to a halt in front of a dilapidated wooden building. He came around to assist her down.

"I'm staying here," Elizabeth said, staring mutinously at her companion.

Daniel shrugged. "Have it your way. But don't blame me if you're murdered. Those trinkets you're wearing around your neck offer a very big temptation to these yellow devils."

Elizabeth clutched her throat—the Worthington jewels. Daniel was right, though she hated to admit it. She would be a sitting duck, a Peking duck, if she were to remain behind. "Very well," she seethed, "but you had better conclude your business quickly."

As the couple stepped down from the carriage, they did not see a pair of steely gray eyes following their every move.

Chapter Nine

Cole's eyes narrowed menacingly as he observed Elizabeth and Daniel enter one of Chinatown's most notorious opium dens. Clenching his fists, he swore under his breath; he would kill Daniel if anything happened to Elizabeth.

Damn her for her naivete! She had as much common sense as a mule. Maybe less. But what more could he expect? These society women were always looking for a few cheap thrills, new experiences. He thought she had learned her lesson; apparently, he was wrong.

When a quarter of an hour had passed and there was still no sign of Elizabeth, Cole began to worry. Checking his revolver, he pulled his Stetson low on his head and crossed the street.

The opium dens were open to the public. They were operated for the use of white and Chinese addicts alike, who could afford to indulge their habit in private. With the protection of several powerful politicians, the dens flourished. They were havens for all types of criminal activity and unsavory conduct; murder was not an unlikely occurrence.

Entering the building, Cole scanned the crowded room, searching for Daniel and Elizabeth. Studying the glazed expressions of the men and women who lounged in chairs and beds smoking their pipes of dreams, he felt disgust well up inside of him. These were not the hopeless and downtrodden who came to forget their troubles, but rather the educated leisure class who came merely for the perverse pleasures they could find.

Shaking his head, he was about to quit the room when he noticed Daniel propped up against the wall in the far corner. He approached, fearful of what he would find. Daniel was alone; Elizabeth was nowhere in sight. Panic gripped him. Where was she? Why had Daniel left her alone? Shaking the sleeping man repeatedly produced no results. Daniel was in a drug-induced slumber and would remain that way for hours. Damn the man and the seed of the poppy that these idiots craved! he cursed.

Darting out of the room, Cole ran down a narrow hallway, opening every door to peer into hazy, smoke-filled cubicles. Men and women, of dubious reputation, were engaged in all sorts of sexual perversities. Prostitution was a way of life in the dens and cribs of Chinatown.

Cole's anxiety for Elizabeth increased. Beautiful women brought a high price at the slave market. A white woman was a rare commodity that would fetch an even greater amount. Most of the prostitutes plying their trade were slaves, owned by wealthy Celestials who saw a chance to turn a profit and took it.

Coming to the end of the hallway, he was just about to give up when he spied a set of stairs leading to an attic. Drawing his gun, he took the steps two at a time, making his way to the door at the top.

The knob turned easily under his hand. Thank God! he

prayed silently. He wouldn't have to break the door down and draw attention to himself.

Engrossed in some type of business transaction, the occupants of the room, two corpulent Chinamen, did not see Cole enter and take cover behind a bamboo screen. He could make little sense out of what they were saying; the entire conversation was in Chinese.

After a few moments, the two men made ready to leave. Peering out from behind the screen, Cole noticed the larger of the two men gesturing wildly toward a door that was concealed in the floor beneath a straw mat. Both men laughed, their high-pitched giggles grating on Cole's already-taut nerves.

He heard the door close and then the key turn in the lock. Venturing quietly toward the trap door, he kicked away the mat, lifting the hatch. It was dark in the compartment. Lighting a match, he carefully descended the small set of stairs.

"Damn," Cole swore as the match burnt down to his finger, plunging him into darkness once again. Lighting another, he found a candle lying at the bottom of the stairs, which someone had obviously dropped in his haste to depart. Holding the candle out in front of him, he entered the musty-smelling room.

Glancing at the mats scattered over the floor and the chains fastened into the sides of the wall, he assumed that he had entered some type of holding area, probably for slaves.

Walking farther into the room, a small whimpering noise drew his attention. Cautiously, he approached the direction of the sound, fearful of what he would discover. He stopped dead in his tracks. Elizabeth, totally nude, lay on the mat at his feet.

"Thank God!" he said softly, a feeling of intense relief spilling over him at the sight of her. Kneeling down beside her, he discovered that she was unconscious. Opening her eyelids, he found her pupils dilated to twice their normal size; her wrist felt as limp as a rag doll's. She had been drugged.

As he knelt beside her, caressing her cheek with his fingertips, a cold fury settled over him. Daniel Crocker was a dead man.

Looking about for something to wrap her in, Cole spotted a blanket on the far side of the room. As he went to pick it up, he jumped back when a menacing-looking rat scurried out from beneath it. He smiled, grateful that Elizabeth had not witnessed his fright.

The blanket was filthy, but there was nothing else he could do. Gently, he lifted Elizabeth off the mat, wrapping her still body in the blanket and pulling it over her face to protect her identity. Slowly, he carried her up the stairs; she whimpered softly but did not awaken.

When Cole reached the top of the stairs, he looked about, making sure that the room was still empty. Satisfied that they had not been discovered, he climbed out, placing his precious burden on the floor. Walking over to the locked door, he withdrew his pocket knife, picking at the lock to pry it open.

Pushing the door open a crack, he peered down the second set of steps. No one was around. Hoisting Elizabeth over his shoulder, he stealthily made his way down the stairs, into the hallway, and out the door without being observed.

Equalizer waited across the street. Climbing up into the saddle with Elizabeth positioned across his lap, he urged the horse into a trot, heading in the direction of home.

Once they had ridden a safe distance, Cole slowed his pace, taking the time to think the situation through. Shaking his head, he cursed his stupidity. He couldn't take Elizabeth home; if she was seen in this condition, her reputation would be a shambles. He would bring her to the Fairmont, he decided. He kept a room there for entertaining; no one would be the wiser when he entered with his intoxicated companion. It wouldn't be the first time he had done so.

Just as Cole suspected, he was virtually ignored by the night clerk at the desk. Reaching into the front pocket of his jeans, he was relieved to feel the cold brass of his room key. Thank God he had remembered to bring it with him tonight; there would be no need to disturb anyone.

Unlocking the door, Cole dumped Elizabeth unceremoniously onto the bed. Removing the filthy blanket, he placed her head gently on the pillow, fanning her hair out away from her face. It felt soft as satin beneath his fingers; he tenderly kissed her cheek. Lighting the lamp, he stared in awe at the beauty before him. His breath caught in his throat; he couldn't control the tightening of his crotch. "Damn!" he muttered. This was going to be harder than he thought.

Elizabeth's nude body lay spread out before him like an offering from the heavens. Although he had seen her in various stages of undress, he was unprepared for the sight of such flawless perfection. Wiping the sweat from his brow with the back of his hand, he took a deep breath, trying to remain objective about what he must do.

Taking a washcloth and towel from the nightstand, Cole gently washed the grime from Elizabeth's body. He couldn't stand the thought of anything sordid and dirty touching her. Running the wet cloth over her breasts and arms, he forced himself to remain cool and detached. His hand trembled as he brought the cloth down over her stomach, inching closer and closer to the blond nest of curls between her thighs. Get hold of yourself, man, he told himself. You're doing this for her own good.

Lifting first one leg and then the other, Cole felt the moisture bead up on his upper lip. As hard as he tried, he couldn't keep his eyes from wandering back again and again to the soft mound of her womanhood. The soft yellow curls beckoned to him, drawing his hand like a magnet. Giving in to his lust, he let his fingers gently massage the area between her thighs. At the sound of her sigh, he pulled his hand away as if burned, disgusted by his actions. It was small satisfaction to know he had pleasured an unconscious woman.

The bath complete, Cole placed Elizabeth beneath the sheets and away from his view. Pulling out the bottle of whiskey he kept in the bottom drawer of the dresser, he proceeded to get rip-roaring drunk. If he was going to spend the night in the same bed as Elizabeth Forrester, he sure as hell wasn't going to do it sober.

Elizabeth regained consciousness slowly. Her mouth felt dry; her head pounded like a bass drum. The last thing she remembered was walking into the opium den and being attacked by two burly men. After that, everything had been a blur. She had no idea what had happened to Daniel.

Sheer fright swept through her as she realized that she might still be in the custody of her captors. Looking about the darkened room, she searched for some kind of

103

weapon. Spying the lamp on the table, she leaned over to light it, her hand coming in contact with a warm body. She gasped. A warm *male* body, if she wasn't mistaken.

Oh, God! What had happened? she wondered. She couldn't remember anything. Clutching her head, she rocked back and forth.

The man stirred, muttering under his breath. "Elizabeth . . . Elizabeth."

He knew her name! Whoever it was knew her name. Daniel. The sobering thought came to mind. Was Daniel evil enough to have had her drugged so he could take advantage of her? She thought of all the warnings Cole had given her and trembled.

"Cole," she mouthed his name softly. He would hate her when he discovered what had happened. Tears filled her eyes, but she brushed them away. Be strong, Elizabeth, she told herself. You have more important things to contend with right now.

Groping for the matches that she hoped were on the nightstand, she lit the lamp. The room became suffused with beams of amber light. Holding her breath, she looked down at the face of the man in her bed. Intense astonishment touched her pale face. Cole! She stared, mouth agape. How had he found her? And what was she doing naked in his bed?

Suddenly a pain so intense it threatened to explode rushed through her head. All other thoughts fled her mind as she tried to deal with the excruciating torment. Grabbing the sides of her head, she moaned loudly.

Cole came slowly to his senses. Cocking open his left eye, he grew alarmed at the sight of Elizabeth bent over him, holding the sides of her head. He sat up, holding his own head at the sudden dizziness he felt. Blasted whiskey! he cursed silently. "Elizabeth, are you all right?"

"Help me," she choked out. "My head hurts."

Helping Elizabeth back into bed, Cole ignored her shocked expression when she discovered his nakedness. "Lie down. I'll put a cool cloth on your forehead. It will make you feel better."

Rolling her head from side to side, Elizabeth tried to escape the throbbing torture. She babbled incoherently, the pain rendering her senseless.

"Shh. It's all right, Sunshine. Just relax," Cole crooned. "The drug they gave you is wearing off. That's why you feel the way you do." He bathed her brow repeatedly, whispering words of encouragement.

A few minutes later, Elizabeth's breathing deepened as she fell into a restful slumber. Cole heaved a sigh of relief, pulling the sheet up to cover her, grateful that she would be spared further pain. He lay down beside her, drawing her into his embrace.

Tomorrow would be plenty of time to sort everything out. Tonight they would get a good night's sleep, and tomorrow would take care of itself.

Elizabeth was having the most delightful dream. Cole was kissing the back of her neck, running his hands over her breasts and down between her legs. God! It seemed so real. She could almost feel the moistness at the center of her womanhood. She had never experienced anything like it before.

Suddenly, she opened her eyes, becoming instantly awake. This was no dream! Looking over her shoulder, she stared wide-eyed at Cole, who was grinning wickedly

105

at her. "Good morning, Sunshine. Did you sleep well?"

Elizabeth blushed to the roots of her hair. "Let go of me! How dare you touch me so intimately!" She struggled to free herself of Cole's embrace, but he held her fast.

"I confess I was overcome by your charms. It's not every day that I wake up with two such lovely melons resting so comfortably in the palms of my hands." He squeezed her breasts gently.

"Let go!" she hissed.

"Only if you give me a kiss," he taunted.

She shook her head violently. "Never!"

"Then I shall have to continue my tender ministrations." He continued to hold her breasts, rubbing them with slow, circular motions.

Elizabeth's breathing became shallow. The stroking of Cole's fingers sent jolts of desire surging through her. She didn't know how long she could hold out against the torture he was inflicting. "Very well," she choked out, "you win."

Leaning over, Cole took Elizabeth's head between his hands. "That's better, Sunshine." Ever so gently, he covered her mouth with his own, his tongue gently tracing the soft fullness of her lower lip.

Elizabeth was caught in a trap of her own device as soon as Cole's lips touched hers. She knew she didn't want him to stop. She was floating on a wave of ecstasy and wanted his kiss to go on forever.

Engrossed in their lovemaking, Cole and Elizabeth failed to hear the door open.

Two men, one dressed in the uniform of a police officer and the other in a dark brown suit, stared incredulously at the scene being carried out before them.

106

Chapter Ten

"Cole, for Christ's sake!" Jon bellowed. "Get the hell out of bed and send that streetside doxy home. I need your help. Elizabeth is mis—" Jon's face whitened. He stared in stunned silence as the woman in Cole's bed sat up, clutching the sheet to her chest.

"Elizabeth! My God!" Jon shouted, his face paling when he recognized his daughter. The shock of discovery hit him like a ton of bricks; he stared in disbelief.

Noting the disappointed look on her father's face, Elizabeth shuddered in humiliation. "Father, I can explain. I—"

"For God's sake, Jon," Cole interrupted. "Send that policeman on his way. We don't need any outside interference. This is a family matter."

Jon, realizing the wisdom of Cole's suggestion, turned back to the red-faced officer standing by the door. "I guess we won't be needing your assistance, Sean. It seems my impetuous daughter went and eloped." Jon heard Elizabeth's sharp intake of breath and Cole's crude profanity as he escorted Sean Michaels to the door. "I trust I can rely on your discretion, Sean?"

The Irishman gave Jon a commiserating pat on the back. "Don't you be worrying none about that, Mr. Forrester. Sean Michaels knows how to keep his mouth shut," he said.

Jon shut the door, staring blankly at it. Slowly he turned, his face revealing none of the raw emotion he was feeling at the moment. Cole was sitting on the edge of the bed, his pants firmly in place. Elizabeth, having donned Cole's shirt, which was ridiculously too large for her, sat behind him in the middle of the bed, her cheeks crimson with embarrassment.

Cole stood as Jon approached. He couldn't remember ever seeing Jon this angry before. Jon was always the even-tempered diplomat, never raising his voice or his hand to anyone.

Jon shook from the anger that had suddenly surfaced. His son, whom he had trusted, had betrayed him—and with his own daughter. Raising his arm back, he slapped Cole full across the face.

"Father, don't," Elizabeth cried out, scrambling off the bed, her face suddenly white. She stopped short at her father's menacing glare.

"Stay out of this, Elizabeth. I will deal with you later," Jon commanded. Turning his attention back to Cole, he said, "I trusted you. How could you do this to me?"

Elizabeth opened her mouth to speak, but Cole raised his hand to silence her. "Let me handle this, Elizabeth."

Jon crossed his arms over his chest. "I'm waiting, Cole."

Positioning herself at Cole's side, Elizabeth was ready to defend him if necessary; she was, therefore, grateful when he looked down at her and winked, smiling reassuringly.

Cole was stunned by Jon's reaction. He knew he was upset at finding Elizabeth in his bed, but he never realized Jon wouldn't give him the chance to explain what had happened. An odd twinge of disappointment ripped through his chest at Jon's apparent lack of trust. Staring him directly in the eye, he proceeded with his story.

"When I returned home late last night, I was met at the door by Sally. She was hysterical. Fearful that something had happened to Elizabeth. It seems she had overheard Daniel's plan to take Elizabeth to Chinatown . . . to the opium dens."

Startled by Cole's revelation, Jon's fists clenched in anger. "I can certainly understand why Sally would be upset after what happened to her there." He would never forget the night Ah Sing had discovered Sally prostituting herself in one of the dens; she had been sold there by her parents at the tender age of twelve.

Cole continued, ignoring Jon's interruption. "I went to Chinatown to search for Elizabeth. I found her in the *Den of Delights*. She had been stripped naked, drugged, and readied for transport to the slave market."

Elizabeth reeled, clutching Cole's arm for support. She didn't remember any of the incidents Cole was describing. To think how close she had come to being sold off to who knows where; she trembled violently.

"My God!" Jon shouted, the pulse at his temple throbbing wildly. "Where is Crocker? When I get my hands on him . . ."

"The last time I saw him, he was sleeping it off at the Den. Don't worry about finding him. There won't be enough of Daniel Crocker to bother with when I get through with him," Cole spat out.

"Why did you bring Elizabeth here to your room?"

Jon asked, eyeing the couple suspiciously.

"I couldn't risk the chance that someone near the house would recognize her. She was unconscious. I wrapped her in a blanket and carried her here."

"That doesn't explain what you were doing in bed together."

Elizabeth prayed the floor would open up and swallow her. The way her father was frowning at her and Cole, she felt like a woman of the streets.

Cole rubbed the back of his neck in aggravation. Why in hell did Jon have to play the outraged father now? Taking a deep breath, he explained, "I got drunk. I lay down to sleep it off."

"And you didn't lay a hand on her?"

Cole's face reddened. "I gave her a bath. She was filthy from the blanket I used to wrap her in."

It was Elizabeth's turn to blush. Filled with humiliation and shame, she released Cole's arm and dropped down on the edge of the bed. Holding her face between her hands, she tried to hide from her father's accusing stare.

Walking to the window, Jon pulled back the blue brocade drapery. The sun was just coming up over the horizon. There was no fog this morning to impede his view of the bay.

He tried to look at the problem objectively. As terrible as it was, the situation did have certain redeeming qualities. Cole and Elizabeth would have to wed. Under the circumstances, even Cole would not dare to refuse his request. It really couldn't have worked out better had he planned the whole thing himself. Rubbing his hands together, he anticipated the couple's reaction.

The room was silent except for the early morning sounds of a city awakening, which floated in through the open window. Padding back and forth across the dark pine floor on bare feet, Cole paced nervously. Elizabeth, on the other hand, sat perfectly still, not moving a muscle, while she stared wordlessly at the hands resting in her lap. A few moments later Jon broke the silence.

"Due to the unusual predicament we now find ourselves in, I find that the only recourse left to us is marriage."

At her father's words, Elizabeth jumped up, coming out of her trancelike state. Placing her hands firmly on her hips, she faced him. "No!" she screamed. "I will not be forced into marriage. Nothing has happened. There is no need."

Grabbing hold of Elizabeth's shoulders, Jon tried to reason with the stubborn woman. "Be reasonable. Your reputation will be ruined if word of last night's escapade leaks out. You spent last night naked in a man's bed. Who is going to believe that nothing happened? How do you know for a fact that nothing did? You were unconscious, for Christ's sake! Remember?"

Elizabeth blanched at the truth of her father's words, focusing her attention on Cole.

"Now wait just a minute," Cole shouted, grabbing onto Jon's arm. He hadn't missed the accusing glare both Elizabeth and her father directed at him.

Jon shrugged out of Cole's grip. "I am not naive enough to think that the two of you were not engaged in some type of hanky-panky. However much you protest, you forget . . . I witnessed your passionate embrace first-hand."

Elizabeth latched onto her father's sleeve. "Why would you want me to marry a man you took the trouble to warn me about? I thought you said Cole was not the marrying kind."

111

Jon had the grace to blush at the truth Elizabeth threw at him. He looked at Cole, who regarded him with an expression of confusion and dismay. Turning to his daughter, he replied, "Things have changed. I am certain Cole realizes his responsibility in this matter and will act accordingly."

Cole brushed back his hair and sighed. Christ! What a mess. He had known from the moment he laid eyes on Elizabeth that she was going to be nothing but trouble. He couldn't even deny Jon's allegations. Although they had not actually consummated their relationship, they had come pretty damn close on more than one occasion. He was trapped, and Jon knew it. He stared at Elizabeth and shook his head. She was never going to agree to her father's demands. The stubborn set of her jaw told him that much.

"I would like to have a few minutes alone with Elizabeth. There are some things we need to discuss in private," Cole said.

"Very well," Jon said. "I will drive home and fetch some clothing for you and Elizabeth to wear." His gaze slid insultingly over the scantily clad couple. "When I return, I expect to have your decision."

Walking over to Elizabeth, whose face was pale and full of pain, he put his arm around her shoulder, giving her a hug. "I know you will do the right thing, Elizabeth. You would never intentionally bring dishonor upon the name of Forrester." At the wounded look she gave him, he almost felt guilty about using that line on her; but desperate situations required desperate measures, and this was definitely a desperate situation. Kissing her cheek, he quit the room.

Cole and Elizabeth stared wordlessly at each other for several minutes. Finally, Cole shattered the silence.

"Your father is right, Sunshine. As much as it grieves me to say it, there is no other recourse but for us to get married."

Elizabeth's eyes narrowed. Folding her arms over her chest, she stuck her chin defiantly in the air. "I won't do it. It would never work. You just made your feelings quite clear on the subject. I would never want to be the cause of your," she paused, spitting out the last word, ". . . grief."

Cole grinned. "Perhaps I used the wrong choice of words. It's just that . . . I never planned to marry. This has taken me by surprise. But the fates have decreed that we marry, and so we shall."

Elizabeth shivered at Cole's statement. He didn't know how close his words hit home. The tea leaves had foretold of their marriage. She was being guided by forces that she had no control over. How could she fight against what she already knew to be her destiny?

Cole observed the conflicting emotions crossing Elizabeth's face. He thought she looked utterly charming and immensely desirable, standing in the middle of the room wearing only his shirt. It came to the top of her thighs, exposing her long, lovely legs to his view. Perhaps marriage to this stubborn minx wouldn't be half so bad, he decided. He already knew the depth of her passion; she would be an exciting, provocative bed partner. So what if she wasn't a virgin? They were nothing but a passel of trouble, anyway. Virgins always looked for love and commitment. A woman versed in the ways of the world, such as Elizabeth, wouldn't expect those types of things in a husband. Yes, the more he thought about it, marriage to Elizabeth would definitely have its advantages.

Elizabeth was having very similar thoughts of her own. Chewing her lower lip, she studied the man that would soon become her husband. He was very handsome; her heart raced every time she looked at him. He was also a very passionate lover. She had already experienced a preview of what their love life would be like. She blushed at the thought. There was definitely chemistry between them. That was important in a marriage. But was that enough to base a lifetime commitment on?

Although Cole had his good points, he also had plenty of faults. He had a terrible temper. She had witnessed that firsthand on more than one occasion. He could be mean and vindictive when the mood struck him, but there was also a gentler side to his nature. He could be tender, even kind, when he wanted to.

Cole was a man she could grow to love. Love was important to her. She had missed not having the love of a family when she was growing up. She wanted her own family; she wanted children. The leaves had foretold she would have five. She stared at Cole's virile form and smiled. Yes. He had a lot to recommend him for a husband, she decided.

Elizabeth's silence was starting to worry Cole. He knew she was going to be difficult to convince, and for some reason he couldn't quite fathom, he wanted to convince her. Stepping forward, he grabbed her about the waist, pulling her lithe form into his solid one. "Kiss me, Elizabeth," he said. "Let me convince you of my sincerity in wanting this marriage."

Any thought of protest died on her lips when she looked into Cole's compelling eyes. They held passion and tenderness unlike anything she had witnessed before. Giving herself into the warmth of his embrace, she kissed him back with a hunger that matched his own. The kiss seemed to go on forever, blocking out everything else but their own need for each other.

"It appears the two of you have made your decision," Jon said, entering the room. "So be it. The wedding will take place a week from today."

Cole and Elizabeth broke apart guiltily. They looked at each other and then at Jon, nodding their heads in unison.

The two men stood on the sidewalk, looking up at the three-story house. The front window on the first floor was illuminated by the glow of an oil lamp. As they peered through the denseness of the fog, they could barely discern the outline of a figure there.

The shorter of the two turned to face the taller one. "Are you sure this is the right house, Willy? I don't want no screwups. This guy Worthington has paid us a lot of money to kidnap his granddaughter and bring her home."

Willy spit his wad of tobacco onto the street, wiping his mouth with the back of his sleeve. "I've been casing this place for over a week. The woman in the house matches this here picture the old man sent us." He patted the breast pocket of his coat. "Don't worry, Jake, nothing's going to go wrong. You worry too much. The first chance we get, we grab the broad and bring her back to the old man, then we collect our money and make the big skedaddle."

Scratching his chin, Jake looked skeptically at his friend. Willy was usually right about things, but Jake had an uneasy feeling about this job. These rich folks could cause a lot of trouble for Willy and him if they were caught. And to make matters worse, both the girl's father and boyfriend were lawyers. He shook his head. Nope. He didn't like the feel of this at all.

Willy knocked Jake's arm. "Come on. We don't want to be caught loitering around this place, raising suspicions. We got plans to make if we're going to pull this job off without a hitch."

The two men scurried away, disappearing into the thick fog that shrouded the night.

Pacing nervously across the floor of the library, Elizabeth thought about the wedding that would take place in two days time. Two days and she would become Mrs. Cole MacAlister; her heart constricted at the thought.

Wringing her hands, she wondered how she had gotten herself into this predicament. If she had listened to Cole in the first place, she would never have gone out with Daniel Crocker. She shook her head.

Poor Daniel. She had seen him briefly yesterday. Her father had taken her downtown to pick up her gown for the wedding. As the carriage pulled in front of *Mimette's House of Fashion*, Daniel walked by sporting a cane and two blackened eyes. Elizabeth was shocked at the sight of him. He had been beaten to a bloody pulp, his face a mass of cuts and bruises. She didn't need to be told who had done the beating; Cole's visage popped into her mind.

Sighing deeply, Elizabeth slowed her steps as she pondered her plight. She hoped she was doing the right thing by marrying Cole. Of course, what choice did she have in the matter? None. Her father had seen to that. He was almost as dictatorial as her grandfather.

Cole didn't seem to be experiencing the same reservations about this marriage as she was. Could it be possible that he really cared for her? Her heart skipped a beat. Don't be a ninny, Elizabeth, she told herself. It was too

116

soon to tell. Perhaps, given time, he would grow to care for her . . . even love her. She hugged herself tightly.

Pausing to stop before the window, she gazed out, barely able to distinguish the shapes of two men hurrying away from the yard. That's odd, she thought, pressing her face closer to the glass, trying to peer through the thick fog. No one was there. Blinking several times, she rubbed her eyes. She must be imagining things, she thought.

"Hello, Sunshine."

Elizabeth spun around at the sound of Cole's voice. Her heart started to pound. He looked rakishly handsome in his tight blue jeans and denim shirt. The shadow of his beard made him appear even more manly. She felt a warm glow flow through her. "Good evening," she replied a little breathlessly.

Cole's eyes traveled suggestively over Elizabeth's body. Only two more days and he would have that lovely creature in his bed. Striding forward, he reached out, cupping her chin in his hand. "How about a kiss for your fiancé?"

A delicious shudder of anticipation heated Elizabeth's blood as Cole lowered his head for a kiss. His lips were incredibly tender, like the fluttering of butterfly wings, as they caressed her own. "I am very anxious for our wedding night, are you?" Cole whispered, his breath hot against her ear.

Blushing shyly, Elizabeth turned away. Taking a deep gulp of air, she ignored Cole's arousing question. His hands lingered possessively on her waist, while his lips nibbled at the nape of her neck. "Everything seems to be just about ready," she blurted out, scarcely recognizing her own voice. God! What was he doing to her? She couldn't think straight when his lips traveled over her neck like that.

Spinning Elizabeth about, Cole grinned wickedly. "I'll let you off the hook for now, Sunshine, but be forewarned: I won't be put off this easily two nights from now. I intend to kiss every inch of your body. My hands will know your body better than you do yourself." He rubbed her buttocks suggestively, cupping the firm mounds in his hands.

"This will not be a marriage in name only. I intend to exercise my marital rights to the fullest," he promised, before kissing her breathless and walking away.

Elizabeth experienced a gamut of conflicting emotions as she watched Cole walk out the door. A flicker of apprehension coursed through her when she thought of her wedding night. She had no idea what to expect. She was a virgin, untried in the ways of the flesh. No one, including Mrs. Baxter, had ever counseled her on her marital obligations.

Would it be divine and glorious, as the romance novels suggested? Or disgusting and repulsive, as some of the society matrons hinted?

Clutching her arms tightly about her, Elizabeth felt the painful hardening of her nipples—her body's burgeoning response to Cole's kisses. A thrill of anticipation surged through her and she smiled. There would be no fear in Cole's marriage bed, she decided. Of that, she was certain!

Chapter Eleven

The warmth of the hot July day did nothing to lessen the anxiety and distress Elizabeth felt the morning of her wedding. Droplets of perspiration dotted her forehead and upper lip as she stared nervously out her bedroom window at the preparations taking place in the yard below.

In just a few short hours, she would be Mrs. Cole Mac-Alister. The thought sent shards of fear rushing through her. She hadn't seen Cole since their meeting in the library, but she could recall word for word the promise he had made her. She knew her fears were silly and that Cole would be gentle with her, but still the dread of the unknown gnawed at her composure.

Perspiration covered her chest and arms. Dabbing at it with a towel, she wiped the beads of moisture off her skin. She hadn't bothered to dress yet. It was too hot, and it was too early. She wore only her chemise and pantaloons, in deference to the unusually warm weather.

Elizabeth caught sight of Violet Baxter shouting orders to one of the workmen her father had hired to construct the arch and altar for the ceremony. Mrs. Baxter had returned late last evening, expressing only moderate surprise at the news that Elizabeth was getting married.

Staring at the tiny woman who had entered her life so unexpectedly again, Elizabeth smiled. She felt so much closer to her now that she knew about her past. Violet had revealed a part of herself that Elizabeth had never realized existed. She thought back to their conversation of last evening.

They were seated in the parlor, discussing the plans for the wedding over a cup of hot tea, when Violet had taken Elizabeth's hands in her own.

"Be happy, Elizabeth. When Cupid strikes the heart, there is no escaping his arrow," she said.

"Thank you, Mrs. Baxter. I will try to remember your kind words."

Violet's brows furrowed together in consternation. "Your grandfather is going to have a fit when I inform him of your marriage. It serves him right, the stubborn, autocratic old fool."

Elizabeth couldn't control her sharp intake of breath.

"Don't look so shocked, my dear. I have worked for Josiah Worthington longer than you have lived. I know him better than you think. I have never told anyone this, but I think it's time you knew the whole story about Josiah and me."

Elizabeth's eyes widened. Mrs. Baxter and her grandfather? That was impossible! Mrs. Baxter was an employee . . . a housekeeper.

"I know what you're thinking, Elizabeth. I can see it written clearly on your face. How could a mere housekeeper have designs on a man as wealthy and well connected as Josiah Worthington?" Ignoring Elizabeth's blush, she continued. "I wasn't always a housekeeper. I came from a very wealthy family myself. Unfortunately, my father lost his wealth through several misplaced investments, and he committed suicide. My mother died shortly after, and I was left penniless.

"Your grandmother, Sarah, was my best friend. When my parents died, she took me in. Unfortunately, I was unable to hide the attraction that I felt for your grandfather." Violet paused, patting her hair nervously before continuing. "Sarah noticed my infatuation with Josiah and became jealous. Although she didn't force me to leave, I was relegated to the role of housekeeper. Our friendship waned, and I learned to accept my new lot in life."

"But what about Mr. Baxter? When did you marry him?"

"There was no Mr. Baxter, Elizabeth. I merely took the title of Mrs. to avoid the gossipmongers."

"I see," Elizabeth said, her brows wrinkling in confusion. "But if you cared for my grandfather, why didn't you pursue him after my grandmother died?"

"It wasn't quite as simple as all that," Violet said, coloring slightly as she spoke. "Your grandfather and I had a brief affair before your grandmother died. He never truly loved Sarah, but that did not excuse our dishonorable behavior. We became ridden with guilt and were unable to derive any real pleasure out of our relationship. The affair soon died a natural death, as it should have. Fortunately for everyone concerned, Sarah never found out."

Staring intently at Violet Baxter's face, Elizabeth was having a difficult time retaining her composure. She had so many questions she wanted to ask, but she didn't want to embarrass Mrs. Baxter in any way. She took a calming breath, relaxing against the cushion, waiting for her to

121

continue her narrative.

"After our affair ended, Josiah buried himself in his work. When Kathryn was born, he transferred whatever love he possessed to her. I stayed on after Sarah died, to help with Kathryn. Even though I would never be anything more to Josiah than a housekeeper, I was able to live with him, share his life, and help raise his daughter and granddaughter."

"You must have loved my grandfather a great deal."

Violet's expression grew wistful. "I still do, I'm afraid."

Wiping the tears that streamed down her face, Elizabeth fought to regain her composure. It was all so very sad, but yet so touching. Mrs. Baxter had given up her whole life for the love of one man.

Elizabeth thought of her grandfather, of how hard and unyielding he was. She shook her head sadly. He had thrown away a chance at happiness with a woman who loved him, and he didn't even realize it.

"Don't throw away your chance at happiness, Elizabeth. You may not get another. I'm telling you this because I have always looked upon you as the granddaughter I never had."

Violet saw the stunned look crossing Elizabeth's face and she sighed. "I was not able to express my love for you openly because of my position in the household. Josiah had very definite ideas about servants maintaining their rank. He would never have countenanced my trying to rise above my position."

"Well, then, he was a fool," Elizabeth said, throwing her arms around Violet and hugging her fiercely. "I've always abided a deep affection for you, Violet." Elizabeth decided it was time to break down the barriers between them, starting with the use of first names. "I would be deeply honored if you would consent to be my matron of honor tomorrow."

Violet blubbered loudly into her handkerchief.

"I know this is short notice, but I'm sure we can find something appropriate for you to wear. What do you say?"

Blowing her nose and dabbing at the tears that ran down her face, Violet smiled tremulously. "Thank you, my dear. There is nothing I would rather do."

The chiming of the clock on the wall brought Elizabeth quickly out of her reverie. She stared at the time: Ten o'clock. In only two short hours, she would be married to a man she barely knew.

A knock sounded at the door. "Elizabeth, may I come in?" Her father's voice floated through the door.

Quickly donning her wrapper, she opened the door. Her father stood in the hallway, an apologetic look on his face. "May I come in?"

"Of course," Elizabeth replied, stepping aside so he could enter. They had not really had a chance to talk of the circumstances that had brought them to this day. Perhaps he had decided it was time. Crossing to the dressing table, Elizabeth took a seat on the embroidered stool.

Jon paced nervously across the blue and gold Brussels carpet, unsure of what he was going to say. He had faced hundreds of angry clients and jurors in his career, but he suddenly felt oddly tongue-tied as he turned to face his daughter.

"I have done a lot of thinking over the past few days. I realize that I may have come down a bit hard on you. I—I hope you can forgive me," he stammered.

Elizabeth was touched by her father's humbling apology. Rushing forward, she threw her arms around him. "There is nothing to forgive. You acted out of love and concern; I realize that."

Setting Elizabeth from him, Jon looked into her tear-filled eyes, suddenly realizing that he might have done her a grave injustice. "Are you terribly unhappy about marrying Cole?"

Wiping her eyes on the edge of her sleeve, Elizabeth contemplated her answer for several moments. "This will probably sound foolish, but I believe our marriage was destined to be." At the look of bewilderment on her father's face, she smiled and continued. "A wise man told me I would marry a dark-haired man who rode a golden horse. I believe that man to be Cole."

Rubbing the back of his neck, a look of consternation on his face, Jon asked, "And would the wise man that told you this happen to be Ah Sing?"

Elizabeth's eyes rounded. "Why, yes! How did you know?"

"Just a guess. Ah Sing fancies himself a soothsayer of sorts. He is very well-known for his unusual predictions." What he didn't say was that most of Ah Sing's prophecies were too farfetched to be believable. After the ridiculous prediction he had made about how the earth was going to shake and all the buildings would fall down, Jon had ceased listening to him. He guessed that in Elizabeth's case, however, Ah Sing had probably done more good than not. At least he had convinced her to wed.

"Do you think he could be right about what he told me?" Elizabeth asked, a hopeful expression on her face.

"I think there is every possibility that he could be correct," Jon assured her. "But it's not important what I think. If you believe that Cole is the man he foresaw, then he is."

"Well, if that's the case, then you have nothing to feel guilty about," Elizabeth replied, trying to sound confident to ease her father's fears.

"I want you to be happy, Elizabeth. I know it may be selfish of me to say so, but I'm happy you'll be staying on here rather than returning to New York."

Elizabeth felt a measure of guilt at her father's words. They brought to mind the telegram she had received from her grandfather, now resting in the bottom of her dresser drawer. Well, at least now she had a good excuse to stay. She couldn't very well run back to New York and leave her husband behind. Surely, her grandfather would realize that when she wrote him of her marriage.

Smiling at her father, who was staring at her expectantly, she replied, "I'm happy to be staying. I never wanted to leave, so perhaps my marrying Cole was the best thing that could have happened."

"That's my girl," Jon said, kissing her cheek. "Now I'll leave you to prepare for your wedding. I shall return when it's time to escort you to the altar."

Watching her father depart, Elizabeth wondered why she didn't feel quite as optimistic about her marriage as she sounded. Plopping down on the blue velvet counterpane, she hugged her knees tightly to her chest. She was suddenly reminded of a line in a poem she had once read by Johann von Schiller: *"The dictates of the heart are the voice of fate."*

She sighed in resignation.

Cole stood nervously at the makeshift altar, resplendent in his suit of black superfine. The white of his shirt gleamed bright in the hot afternoon sunlight.

In a few minutes the ceremony would begin and he

125

would relinquish his freedom forever. A sudden chill passed through his body at the thought. He had seriously considered packing his bags last night and taking flight, but honor demanded that he face his responsibility—not to mention Jon. His sister would not even be there to offer support. Abigail's wire had arrived late last evening informing them that she would be unable to attend the wedding due to complications with the birth of a new foal. He would have to tie the nuptial knot alone.

Pulling his collar out, which suddenly felt two sizes too small, Cole had the sinking suspicion that the so-called nuptial knot was going to be tightened around his neck. Looking up, he found the Reverend Parker eyeing him strangely. He smiled sheepishly, turning his attention toward the patio door that had just opened; his stomach knotted anxiously.

Violet Baxter floated forward wearing a very becoming blue floral silk gown. Cole thought she actually looked somewhat attractive for an old biddy. In her hands she held a small bouquet of white daisies and cornflowers, the cobalt-blue color of the cornflowers reminding Cole of Elizabeth's beautiful eyes.

As Mrs. Baxter approached, she presented him with a friendly smile and a reassuring wink. Cole was taken aback by her gesture but returned the smile wholeheartedly. It seemed Violet Baxter had softened toward him a bit.

A moment later, Elizabeth appeared on the arm of her father. Cole's heart raced at the sight of such loveliness coming toward him. She was dressed simply in a long gown of white voile over satin. The arms and upper bodice were sheer enough to reveal just a hint of the delights beneath.

On her head she wore a crown of white daisies and

baby's breath. Her long blond hair flowed down her back in a mass of curls intertwined with more daisies. The bouquet she held was fashioned of the same simple arrangement of flowers.

Cole couldn't remember when he had seen a more glorious sight. She was like the Greek goddess Aphrodite, who had come to weave a spell over him, a mere mortal.

As Jon placed Elizabeth's hand in his, Cole realized why he hadn't objected to this marriage. He wanted Elizabeth . . . had wanted her from the moment he had set eyes on her down at the railroad station. And now he would possess her—every delectable inch of her.

The ceremony was finally over. Elizabeth stood alone in the center of the ballroom surveying Violet's handiwork. The woman was truly amazing. In just a few short hours she had literally transformed the room into an elegant reception area, complete with elaborate floral arrangements and long white linen-covered tables, which held platters of every type of food imaginable.

Although no guests had been present at the actual ceremony, a full reception, complete with orchestra, would commence within the hour.

Elizabeth glanced down at the plain gold band on her finger. She still couldn't believe she was married. When the minister had pronounced them man and wife, and Cole's lips had covered hers for a heart-stopping kiss, Elizabeth felt as if she were acting out a fantasy. It couldn't be real, she had thought. But here was the proof of her marriage for all the world to see.

The commotion at the front door signaled the arrival of the musicians. Where was Cole? she wondered. He had disappeared with her father shortly after the ceremony.

She didn't relish greeting a room full of well-wishers by herself.

Deciding to freshen up a bit before the reception, Elizabeth headed up the stairs to her room. As she passed Cole's room, she could hear voices raised in anger. Her father and Cole appeared to be having some type of disagreement. Knowing it was terribly rude but not being able to resist, she pressed her ear against the door.

"The money is yours, Cole. Why won't you take it?" Jon shouted.

"I won't be paid off like some kept man for marrying your daughter."

Gasping aloud at Cole's words, she covered her mouth.

"I don't want Elizabeth's money, nor do I need it. Keep it in trust for her in case something happens to me," he said. "Or better yet, put it in the bank for all those grandchildren you're always talking about."

Elizabeth's joy was boundless. Cole wasn't marrying her for her money. For the first time in her life, she truly felt like she was worth something, not just an extension of the Worthington fortune. Tears filled her eyes as she rushed across the hall to enter her bedroom.

A few minutes later the bedroom door opened and Cole entered, frowning at the sight of Elizabeth's tears. "You're not having second thoughts, are you, Sunshine?"

"Oh, Cole," Elizabeth sobbed, throwing herself into his arms.

"Sweetheart, what's the matter?" he asked, genuinely concerned. He had seen Elizabeth cry in anger as well as in fear, but never had he seen the heart-wrenching sobs that were racking her body at the moment. He held her gently, patting her head as best he could without disturbing the flowers that adorned it.

128

Elizabeth looked up, tears shining in her eyes. "Nothing's the matter. I'm just . . . happy," she cried, weeping loudly into his shirtfront.

For the first time in his life, Cole didn't know what to do. He wasn't used to the temperamental displays of women. His sister Abigail seldom displayed any type of emotion. Setting Elizabeth from him, he took his handkerchief and gently wiped the tears from her eyes. "If this is how you act when you're happy, remind me never to make you upset," he teased.

Elizabeth smiled tremulously. "I'm sorry for being such a baby. I've never been married before; I guess the whole thing just sort of got to me."

Cole could understand that. He had felt like crying on more than one occasion since this whole business began. Smiling down at her, he lifted her chin. "You had better go make yourself presentable before the guests arrive. We wouldn't want Hetty Truesdale spreading rumors that I beat you right after the ceremony."

Elizabeth giggled, hiccuping in the process. "I really don't care what that overstuffed pumpkin thinks. She's terribly pretentious, don't you think?"

Cole threw back his head and roared. "I've heard Hetty called many things, but never an overstuffed pumpkin. That's wonderful." Marriage to Elizabeth might be many things, but it was never going to be dull, he thought.

Cole stared at Elizabeth intently. It was as if he were seeing her for the very first time. She blushed under his scrutiny, unaware that her eyes bespoke an invitation too blatant for Cole to refuse. "Elizabeth."

The sound of her name on Cole's lips sent a delicious shudder throughout her body. Moving closer to him, she wrapped her arms about his neck, impelled by her own passion. Cole clasped her tightly to him, pulling her into

129

his male hardness—the evidence of his desire for her. He kissed her eyelids, her nose, her mouth, his lips leaving a trail of fire wherever they touched.

The feel of his tongue as it entered her mouth filled her with uncontrollable desire. She pressed into him, running her hands over his back and thighs, loving the feel of his muscles as they rippled beneath her fingertips. Emboldened by his response, Elizabeth trailed her hand down the front of Cole's thigh, caressing his hardened member. At the sound of his gasp, she drew it quickly away.

Raising his mouth from hers, Cole gazed into the blue depths of Elizabeth's eyes, clouded with passion. When his breathing returned to normal, he said, "Though it pains me to say it, I think we had better stop before we are unable to." Elizabeth felt her cheeks warm, mortified that she had gotten so carried away by her own passion. She took a deep breath. "Of course, you're right. We wouldn't want to disappoint the guests."

"I don't know how I'm supposed to enjoy our wedding reception when all I'll be thinking about is stripping you naked and taking you to my bed," Cole said, brushing back the hair that hung in his eyes.

Elizabeth blushed scarlet. "I'm sorry . . . I . . ."

Cole laughed. "It's not your fault that you're so damn desirable. I feel like a greenhorn with my first woman."

Grabbing her glowing cheeks between her hands, Elizabeth tried to stifle the blush threatening to rise again. How was she supposed to answer such an outrageous comment? My goodness! He made her sound like some femme fatale. "I think we had better go. I'm sure Violet and my father are wondering what happened to us."

Gazing at Elizabeth's flushed cheeks and reddened lips,

130

Cole smiled. She looked like a woman who had just been made love to. "I think you might want to do something about your appearance before you go downstairs," he suggested.

Seeing her reflection in the mirror, Elizabeth gasped, her hand going to her cheek. Cole's grinning face was clearly reflected, causing her temper to flare. "This is all your fault, you know. If you hadn't come in here and started . . . well, you know, none of this would have happened."

Cole's grin became even wider. "Do you know how incredibly sexy you are when you're mad? Why I could come over there right now and—"

"Don't you dare!" Elizabeth said, trying to bite back the smile that came to her lips. "You are depraved. If we're to have any type of wedding reception, you had better leave right now."

"Very well, but just remember, every time you see me looking at you today, I will be envisioning you without your clothes on," Cole teased, rushing out the door before the hairbrush Elizabeth hurled at him had a chance to find its mark.

Elizabeth stared at the door, a bemused expression on her face. If she wasn't careful, she was going to commit society's most shocking crime—that of falling in love with her own husband.

Chapter Twelve

Standing at the refreshment table sipping her glass of champagne, Elizabeth listened with half an ear to the monotonous tones of Florence Weatherby as she regaled her with all the latest gossip.

Florence was a stout woman with mousy brown hair and fleshy cheeks, which sported the most disgusting mole Elizabeth had ever seen. It was dark and round, with a long brown hair growing out of it. She stared at it with revulsion, trying to concentrate on what Florence was saying, which was becoming increasingly more difficult. Elizabeth was quite bored.

She had been standing in the same spot listening to Florence's inane chatter for the past forty-five minutes. She was positive she would go crazy if she had to listen for even one more minute.

"Are you listening to me, Elizabeth?" She heard Florence's nasal whine, the tone grating on her nerves.

Refocusing her attention on the obnoxious woman, Elizabeth's smile was bleak and tight-lipped. "I'm sorry. I was looking for Cole," she said. Actually, she was looking for any excuse to escape this harridan.

A smug expression crossed Florence's face. "That's what I've been trying to tell you. He's over there by the French doors. See." She pointed with her fan.

Elizabeth's eyes followed the direction of the ivory sticks. They fell upon her husband, who was engaged in conversation with an attractive red-haired woman.

"That woman your husband is with happens to be his mistress," Florence remarked. At the sharp look Elizabeth directed at her, she corrected, "His former mistress, I mean. Why, I can't believe he would actually invite—"

"Excuse me, Florence," Elizabeth interrupted. "I have to mingle with my other guests now." She flashed the older woman a disdainful smirk before lifting her skirts and walking to the other side of the room. Florence gaped openmouthed, too astonished to speak.

Stupid, interfering old busybody, Elizabeth fumed. How dare she make implications concerning Cole and that woman? Seething inwardly, she took several deep breaths to calm herself. As hard as she tried to ignore the innuendos Florence had made, Elizabeth couldn't keep her gaze from straying over to the other side of the room where Cole was standing. He looked very relaxed as he laughed over something the red-haired woman said. Feelings of jealousy, totally alien to her before, began to take root and grow as she watched the easy camaraderie between the two.

"Hello, dear, are you enjoying yourself?" Violet asked, approaching from behind.

Glancing over her right shoulder, Elizabeth smiled warmly at the older woman. She had never seen her former housekeeper looking so radiant. Violet's hair had

133

been curled in an attractive style that softened her features, making her look years younger. She had observed Violet dancing with Peter Maxwell, owner of the largest shipping company in the city, and Elizabeth wondered if perhaps Mr. Maxwell wasn't responsible for putting the roses in Violet's cheeks.

"It's a wonderful reception. Thank you so much for all the trouble you went to on my behalf," Elizabeth finally replied, giving Violet's waist a gentle squeeze.

Beaming as brightly as a lighthouse beacon, Violet replied, "I'm so happy for you, dear. Cole is going to make you a wonderful husband."

Elizabeth's eyes narrowed a fraction. "Is he? What makes you so sure?"

Frowning at Elizabeth's skepticism, Violet followed the direction of her stare, spotting the source of her uncertainty. "I see someone has informed you about Cole's former mistress." Her voice was laced with indignation. "I bet it was Florence Weatherby. Am I right?"

At Elizabeth's nod, Violet's face flamed in anger. "That woman is a menace to society. She ought to have a muzzle put over her mouth."

"But she was right. Cole does have a mistress."

"Did have," Violet corrected. "Amber Montoya is past history . . . has been for over a year. They're only friends now."

"How do you know so much about this woman?" Elizabeth questioned. She appreciated Violet's attempt at placating her, but she didn't want to have a rose-colored outlook where Cole was concerned. If he was the womanizer her father had said he was, then she wanted to know.

Patting Elizabeth's hand, Violet chuckled, "My dear,

everything that goes on in a household becomes common knowledge. I have found the kitchen to be the best-informed room in the house. It was true in the Worthington house and it's true here. You can't keep secrets from the staff."

There was a slight lifting of Elizabeth's brows before she replied, "I'll be sure to keep that in mind in the future." A small smile touched her lips. "What else did you learn about Amber Montoya?"

"She owns a ranch not far from Cole's. That's how they met. She's the widow of Alberto Montoya, who was one of the wealthiest ranchers in the state. After her husband died, Cole sought to comfort her. Apparently, he was quite good at it for a time."

Elizabeth's head jerked up. Shaking it from side to side, she giggled. "You're outrageous, Violet. I always thought you were such a proper, staid New Englander, and now I find that you're really quite a wicked woman," Elizabeth teased.

"Thank you, my dear. It's been dreadfully hard stifling my natural inclinations all these years. And now I must go. I see the charming Mr. Maxwell over by the buffet table. If you want some advice, don't stand here and brood about Cole and his lady friend. Go over there and meet her. You may discover that you'll like her."

Watching Violet depart, Elizabeth mulled over her suggestion. She deemed it highly unlikely that she was going to like a former mistress of Cole's, but she wasn't about to let the woman get her hooks in him again.

Feeling somewhat appeased by Violet's explanation of Cole's former lover, Elizabeth smoothed back her hair, adjusted her train, and strode forward to greet her competition.

Cole's eyes lit with pleasure as he watched his new bride glide across the room in his direction. He marveled at her grace and beauty, and could see by the appreciative stares she received from the other men in the room that they noticed it, too.

Noting Elizabeth's troubled expression, he assumed Florence had wasted no time in giving her an earful about Amber. Florence was, without a doubt, the most notorious gossip in San Francisco.

"Hello, Sunshine," Cole said, holding out his hand. "Come and meet a good friend of mine."

Taking Cole's hand, which felt warm and comforting to her at the moment, Elizabeth swallowed her nervousness, pasting on an affable smile.

"May I present Amber Montoya, a close friend and neighbor."

Elizabeth tried to appear calm and nonchalant while the introductions were made, as if meeting a former mistress were an everyday occurrence for her. She couldn't help the feelings of inadequacy she felt while gazing upon Amber's honey-gold complexion and thick auburn hair. She could certainly see why Cole would be attracted to her.

"Congratulations, Elizabeth. You are a very lucky woman to have caught such a handsome husband," Amber said, a lilting Spanish accent coating her words.

Linking her arm through Cole's, Elizabeth's smile widened. "Thank you. I do indeed consider myself to be a very fortunate woman." *It remains to be seen just how lucky I am when it comes to the choice of husbands, however,* she added silently.

"I must confess to feeling rather slighted," Elizabeth continued. "Cole vowed earlier that he wouldn't take his eyes off of me all evening, and now I find him enjoying the attentions of a very beautiful woman."

Amber threw back her head and laughed, a thick throaty sound that drew the attention of several people standing close by. She squeezed Elizabeth's arm affectionately. "You and I will be friends, I think."

Turning to Cole, Amber said, "You have made a good choice in a wife, *amigo*. See that you treat her well, or you will answer to me; and you know what a dreadful temper I have. Now, if you will both excuse me, I shall go and indulge myself at the buffet table. *Adios*." With a wave of her hand, she disappeared.

What an unusual woman, Elizabeth thought. I do believe Amber Montoya and I will be friends after all.

"Have I been slighting you, sweetheart?" Cole asked, rubbing the hand that rested possessively on his arm.

"Well, it is our wedding reception, and people may think it a bit odd if the bride and groom don't share a dance together," she replied, smiling up at him.

"Never let it be said that Cole MacAlister doesn't fulfill his marital obligations to the fullest." His eyes twinkled in merriment as he pulled Elizabeth toward the dance floor. "I am most eager to fulfill all of my marital obligations, Sunshine. When do you think we can leave this shindig?"

Elizabeth colored fiercely as Cole whirled her about the black and white marble dance floor. "I don't really know," she replied a bit breathlessly. "We wouldn't want to appear rude."

Cole nibbled her ear, running his tongue in and out of the orifice. "I really don't give a damn about being rude to these society snobs, do you?" he asked, breathing the words into her ear.

Gooseflesh broke out over Elizabeth's arms and neck. Her breathing became rapid and she began to feel light-headed. "Perhaps if we just slipped away, no one would notice," she said, her cheeks warming at her boldness.

Pleased by her response, Cole smiled inwardly. Guiding Elizabeth off the floor, he ushered her into the kitchen, past the startled faces of Ah Sing, Sally, and the rest of the staff, and up the servant's stairs to their rooms.

Opening the door, he stepped aside, allowing Elizabeth to enter first. Nervous apprehension gripped Elizabeth as tightly as a vise when her gaze fell upon the bed. Oh, God! What have I done? she asked herself, chewing her lower lip anxiously.

"I'll leave you to pack a bag while I do the same. I've reserved a room at the hotel. It will be much more private that way," Cole said, winking broadly.

Elizabeth heaved a sigh of relief, which she was certain could be heard all the way downstairs. She hadn't realized it, but she had been holding her breath the entire time Cole was speaking. She had been granted a small reprieve, and she was eternally grateful. Bestowing a nervous smile upon him, she replied, "I'll only be a minute."

"I'm glad you're as anxious as I am, Sunshine. I'll be back before you know it." The smile he gave her was as intimate as a kiss.

As the door closed and Cole disappeared, Elizabeth suddenly realized that the moment of truth was upon her. A mixture of anticipation and dread coursed through her. She would soon know the answers to all of her girlish fantasies and fears. There would be nothing to hide behind—no haughty demeanor, no grandfather's wealth—when she was stripped naked in Cole Mac-Alister's bed.

The escape from the house took place without incident, the guests too wrapped up in their own amusements to notice the disappearance of the newlyweds. Elizabeth marveled at how easy it had been to stroll out the front door and into the night air without so much as a raised eyebrow.

When the carriage finally came to a halt in front of the Fairmont Hotel, she shuddered, trying to hide the dismay that she felt. She had hoped they wouldn't be coming back to the scene of her recent humiliation; the hotel held too many memories of the awful night of her abduction.

"Are you cold, Sunshine?" Cole asked, coming around to help her alight.

Shaking her head, Elizabeth swallowed her anxiety. "I'm fine," she replied in a small, tight voice. She didn't want Cole to know how scared she was of being here, but most of all, she didn't want him to know how naive and inexperienced she was; he would find out soon enough.

Upon entering the hotel, Elizabeth surveyed her surroundings, surprised by the ornateness of the furnishings and decor. The furniture was of the rococo period, each chair covered by an antimacassar to protect the delicate red velvet upholstery. It was much nicer than she had remembered. The last time she'd been here she had been so anxious to depart that she had failed to notice anything about the place.

She waited while Cole strode to the front desk to confer with a bald man, who seemed to recognize him.

139

"Good evening, Mr. MacAlister. Everything is ready just as you ordered," the desk clerk said.

"Fine, Sam. I just wanted to double-check," Cole replied. "And, Sam, we don't wish to be disturbed tonight for any reason. Do I make myself clear?"

Feeling her cheeks warm, Elizabeth looked up in time to catch the knowing smirk of the desk clerk as Cole bent over to pick up the bags. Not about to let the awful little man get the best of her, she presented him with the iciest look she could muster, gratified when his bald spot reddened as he quickly bent over his ledger. Smiling in satisfaction, she hurried after Cole.

Pausing before the door while Cole hunted for the key, Elizabeth felt the knot in her stomach tighten. When he finally threw open the door and she caught her first glimpse of the room, she began to relax, comforted by the fact that this was a different room than the one they had previously shared.

Examining the suite, she found it contained beautiful white and gold Louis XIV furnishings. The drapes and carpeting were done in a lovely blue and rose floral design. She was just about to comment on the exquisite decor when her gaze focused on the huge four-poster bed at the far end of the room. She gulped, taking in a deep breath of air as she tried to steady her composure.

"This is the bridal suite," Cole said. "I hope you like it."

Elizabeth turned to find Cole smiling down at her with an incredibly erotic grin on his face. Her heart fluttered madly. "It's beautiful," she replied softly.

"Not nearly as beautiful as you," he said, coming forward to untie her cloak. His brow wrinkled in confusion at the hint of fear he detected in her eyes. Why

140

would she be afraid of him after all they had been through together? he wondered. Christ! They had already lain naked in each other's arms. All that was left for them to perform was the final act of consummation, and they had come damn close to that on several occasions. He would never understand the woman. One minute she was so hot she couldn't keep her hands off him, and now she was staring at him as if he were going to rape her.

"Would you like me to help you with your buttons?" he finally asked.

Staring wide-eyed, Elizabeth nodded, presenting Cole with her back. She quivered uncontrollably when his hands came in contact with the bare flesh of her back, his warm breath on her neck turning her insides to mush.

"There . . . all done. You may use the bathing room first. I'll just sit here and relax with a brandy while you bathe."

Elizabeth spotted the door to the bathing chamber immediately. Holding her dress tightly to her chest, she bent over to retrieve her bag.

"Let me know if you want me to come in and scrub your back for you," Cole teased.

Fear lodged thickly in Elizabeth's throat, rendering her incapable of answering. Hurrying into the bathing room, she locked the door behind her, listening to Cole's rich laughter as she collapsed in a heap upon the chair. Waiting a few moments for her nervousness to subside, she rose to prepare herself for the inevitable.

Cole stared thoughtfully at the amber contents of his glass. If he lived to be a hundred, he would never have thought he would find himself regally ensconced in the bridal chamber of the Fairmont Hotel. Shaking his head, he took a sip of the brandy.

He certainly hoped his new bride appreciated the sacrifice he had made for her. For thirty years he had prided himself on his bachelorhood, on his cleverness at eluding the marital trap.

Abigail was probably having a good laugh over it right now, he thought. She had always said that one day he would marry, and that she would laugh when he marched down the aisle with his intended. She hadn't said it out of meanness, for Abigail was never mean, but rather out of love for a younger brother, who was too stubborn to believe an older and wiser sister.

How would Abigail react to having another woman in the house? he wondered. For years, it had just been she and their housekeeper, Consuelo. Would she feel threatened by Elizabeth's presence? He drank the last of his brandy. There was no sense in worrying about it now. He would know soon enough; Cole planned to leave for the ranch first thing in the morning.

At the sound of the bathroom door opening, Cole looked up, sucking in his breath at the sight of his new bride floating through the doorway. Elizabeth was wearing a deep blue satin negligee that displayed every hill and valley of her body. His eyes riveted on the deep vee of her neckline, which revealed the full lushness of the mounds beneath it.

"You look enchanting, sweetheart," he said, rising to stand as she came forward.

Approaching her husband with a great deal of trepidation, Elizabeth felt naked in the gown Violet had insisted she wear. It was a wedding gift, and one she was hardly in a position to refuse. In her haste to prepare for the wedding, the one article of clothing she had forgotten to purchase was a nightgown. The look of admiration in

142

Cole's eyes made her suddenly grateful for Violet's thoughtfulness.

Cole was enraptured by the beautiful woman before him. Elizabeth's flaxen hair surrounded her face like a halo. She looked ethereal standing in the golden light of the candles he had lit. He felt himself harden as his eyes wandered over the perfection of her body. He remembered every detail of what lay beneath the gown. The way her skin felt beneath his hands as they . . .

"Christ!" he muttered, taking a deep breath. "Perhaps I had better use the facilities while you ready yourself for bed," Cole said.

Smiling tentatively, Elizabeth waited until he departed before climbing into the soft feather mattress. Stretching contentedly, she pulled the covers up over her. It felt wonderful to relax after the exhausting day she had just spent.

Running her hands down her sides, she touched the smooth, satiny material of her nightgown; it felt deliciously wanton beneath her fingertips. Recalling Cole's lustful gaze, Elizabeth smiled; he made her feel desirable.

She had come to terms with her fears while she bathed, deciding it was foolish to be frightened of something she knew was going to provide her with a great deal of pleasure. Each time she and Cole had come together, she had wanted more than just his kisses. Now that she was his wife, she could take all that he had to offer. Her skin grew hot at the thought.

With her eyes clenched tightly shut, Elizabeth didn't realize Cole had reentered the room until she felt his side of the bed sag. Slowly, she opened them. The candles were still lit. Hopefully, he would extinguish them before . . . Her thoughts fled as Cole turned to face her.

Elizabeth's eyes wandered over his body, widening at the realization that he was totally naked. Her cheeks warmed. Cole hadn't bothered to cover himself. In fact, he was removing the covers that hid her from his view.

"Let's dispense with these for now, sweetheart. We can cover up later when we're through enjoying ourselves." Cole's voice was soft and persuasive; the underlying meaning of his words captivated her.

Rolling Elizabeth gently onto her side to face him, Cole slid his hands teasingly over her back, legs, and hips in gentle massage. Covering her mouth with his own, his hands began a lust-arousing exploration of her flesh.

Elizabeth clung to Cole in mindless torment. Her hands journeyed over the hard-muscled planes of his body while he deftly explored the soft curves of her own. The spicy scent of his cologne, mingling with the musky odor of his body, sent torrents of desire rushing through her as she gave in to the hunger of his kiss.

She could feel Cole's driving need as his tongue darted in and out of her mouth in sensuous pursuit, the rhythmic movement driving her wild as she reciprocated the action.

Cole's hands slid magically over her naked flesh, pulling her nightgown up and over her head, baring her body to his view. He leaned over her, staring into her passion-drugged eyes. "You're the most beautiful creature I have ever seen," he whispered.

The candles glimmered, illuminating the sheen of perspiration covering Cole's body. Sticking out her tongue, she licked the sweat off his chest, hearing his sharp intake of breath, pleased at the effect she was having on him.

"You're a witch, sweetheart. You've driven me crazy with want of you," he said, covering her mouth once more.

The feel of Cole's hands on her breasts sent shivers of delight to the very center of her being. Her nipples grew taut with desire as his tongue brought the rosy tips to crested peaks. Slowly, his hands slid downward, skimming over her silken belly and thighs. Her body tensed in reflex to his touch; she moaned in exquisite agony.

Cole was pleased by Elizabeth's initial reaction to his lovemaking. Her uninhibited response further confirmed his suspicion that she was no virgin. He couldn't help the twinge of disappointment that tugged at his heart at the knowledge.

Cole's caress was light but painfully teasing as he ran his hands over her burning flesh. Elizabeth arched her body upward, searching for release, needing to end the torment he was inflicting upon her. "Please, Cole," she cried out.

Slowly, Cole parted her woman's flesh as he tenderly flicked the tiny bud of her being. "Is this what you desire, sweetheart?" At her groan of pleasure, he increased the motion, satisfied that Elizabeth was wet and ready for him; he couldn't wait much longer.

Thrashing wildly beneath him, Elizabeth attempted to assuage the burning hunger centering in her womanhood. When at last Cole's body covered hers and she felt his hardened member seeking entry, she experienced a moment of panic.

Elizabeth wasn't prepared for the tearing, burning sensation she felt deep inside when Cole's body penetrated the barrier of her virginity, and her eyes filled with

145

tears. She bit her lip to keep from crying out.

Cole stilled his movements immediately, his eyes widening in shock. Christ! She was a virgin! His feeling of surprise was overshadowed by one of great elation. Beads of perspiration covered his forehead and upper lip as he tried to withhold his own pleasure, wanting Elizabeth's first time to be memorable.

As the tempo of Cole's rhythmic movements increased, Elizabeth felt herself tighten like a bow drawn taut. "Now, now," she cried before drowning in wave after wave of glorious ecstasy. Tears filled her eyes at the deep and wondrous contentment she felt.

Cole finished a moment later, sighing in pleasant exhaustion. He felt sated, completely and utterly relaxed. He had never experienced such satisfaction before. Elizabeth truly was a witch, he thought, smiling happily to himself.

Rising up on his elbows, he gazed into her eyes. His heart thudded at the look of joy he saw reflected there. She smiled up at him, her eyes wide with wonder, and for just a moment, he thought he saw the light of love shining in them.

"You were wonderful, sweetheart. I'm sorry I didn't know this was your first time," Cole said, brushing away the damp hairs clinging to her cheek.

Elizabeth's mouth dropped open as Cole's words penetrated her passion-fogged brain, her cheeks pinkening. "You mean, you thought I had done this before?"

At her look of astonishment, Cole chuckled. "I confess, after experiencing your kisses and caresses in the past, I just naturally assumed you were not a virgin."

"Oh!" she cried, trying to hide her head in the pillow.

"Don't look away, Sunshine. I'm happy as hell you

were a virgin. I didn't think it would matter, but it did. I realize now, I wanted to be your first."

A small smile crossed Elizabeth's lips. "And I'm terribly happy that I wasn't yours. It would have been dreadful if neither one of us knew what we were doing," she replied.

Cole grinned, kissing the tip of her nose. "You are the most difficult woman to figure out. Just when I think I know who you are, you turn the tables on me."

"Well," she said, a coquettish smile on her lips, "I wouldn't want you to grow bored with me."

"Sweetheart, I have a feeling that you're going to lead me on a merry chase."

Trailing her fingers up and down Cole's back, Elizabeth licked her lips seductively. "Do you intend to talk for the rest of the night, or are we going to make love again?"

Cole didn't answer with words; he didn't have to. The proof of his desire resting between her legs was all the answer she needed.

Chapter Thirteen

Cole had been awake since dawn. Lying on his side, hand propped under his head, he watched Elizabeth sleep. He smiled softly, his chest tightening as he thought of their previous night's lovemaking.

His little virgin was definitely all woman. He had lost track of how many times they had made love. Elizabeth had been willing and responsive, and each time had been better than the one before.

Gazing upon her finely sculpted features, Cole was reminded of a lovely porcelain doll. Her incredibly long lashes rested softly against her cheek, while her long blond hair fanned out over the pillow like a satin coverlet. She was his, and he considered himself damn lucky.

He was grateful for whatever hand of fate had dealt Elizabeth to him. He smiled ruefully, thinking back to how he had chafed at the idea of matrimony. Of course, that was before he had fallen in love.

Christ! Had he actually said that? Even silently? He shook his head. It was bound to have happened sooner or later. Feeling like a schoolboy with a newly found secret, he leaned over, gently brushing Elizabeth's lips with his own.

"Cole," she murmured, still asleep.

His heart leapt with joy when he realized Elizabeth was dreaming about him. Lying back down, he closed his eyes. He loved her. When had it happened? How did that little piece of baggage worm her way into his heart? He mulled the questions over in his mind until at last, finding no suitable answers, he drifted back to sleep.

It was nearly noon when Elizabeth popped her eyes open. Gazing out the window of the hotel room, she could see the sun directly overhead. She stretched contentedly, her arm coming in contact with Cole's hairy chest. Withdrawing it quickly, she chanced a peek in his direction; he was still asleep. How boyish he appeared in slumber, she thought, smiling to herself.

Love flowed through her veins like warm honey as she recalled her wonderful initiation into the act of love. Cole had been gentle . . . caring. If only he loved her, then everything would be perfect, she thought. But this was an arranged marriage, one that he had been forced into. She sighed deeply. Oh, he lusted for her. Last night was certainly proof of that. But love. She shook her head. No. There was no reason to believe he would ever love her. Most of the time, he didn't even seem to like her.

Determination strengthened her resolve as she realized what she must do. What was it grandfather had always told her: *If you want something bad enough, go after it, let nothing stand in your way.* Well, by God, she wanted Cole to love her, and if she had her way, it was exactly what he was going to do. Slipping out of bed, she quietly tiptoed to the bathing chamber to perform her morning ablutions.

A half hour later, Elizabeth emerged fully dressed, ready and eager to start the day. She stopped short at the sight of Cole staring out the window dressed only in his trousers. There was something terribly intimate about seeing a man with his shirt off and his feet bare. Her heart gave a queer little lurch. The sight of his chest, thickly matted with hair, caused a lump to rise in her throat.

"Good morning," she choked out.

Cole turned, disappointed to find Elizabeth fully clothed; he smiled suggestively. "Although you look utterly charming this morning, I must confess, I like you better with a few less clothes on."

Feeling a blush steal over her cheeks, Elizabeth smiled shyly. "I thought you were anxious to make an early start this morning."

Circling her waist with his hands, Cole drew her into his chest. "That was before I discovered how much I enjoyed making love to my wife." He ran his tongue lightly over her neck.

Goose bumps broke out over Elizabeth's arms, her eyes rounding as big as silver dollars. "You can't mean you want to—"

Cole nodded, patting her buttocks suggestively.

"But it's broad daylight!"

"So?"

Elizabeth opened her mouth to protest, but Cole effectively silenced her with a kiss.

It was much later when the newly wedded couple

arrived back at the mansion on Nob Hill. They were greeted at the door by a bleary-eyed Jonathan, who had celebrated his daughter's wedding a bit too boisterously.

"Father!" Elizabeth exclaimed. "You look awful." His hair was tousled and his clothes were a mess; he had two different color shoes on.

Grabbing the sides of his head, Jon cried in abject misery, "Please, don't shout."

Cole and Elizabeth exchanged amused glances.

"It looks to me as if you could use a dose of the hair of the dog that bit you," Cole said.

"A splendid idea, my boy. Shall we go into the dining room? I'll have Ah Sing fix me one of his heathen remedies."

Seating themselves at the table, Jon reached for the coffee and one of the biscuits that Ah Sing had thoughtfully provided.

"Father," Elizabeth questioned, "where is Violet this morning? I wish to bid her farewell before Cole and I depart for his ranch."

Jon stopped buttering his biscuit and looked up. "She's gone. Left early this morning." He popped the flaky morsel into his mouth.

"Gone. But why?"

"Her sister was taken ill suddenly. She received a telegram late last evening. She left on the morning stage."

Seeing a look of dismay on Elizabeth's face, Cole patted her hand. "Don't look so downhearted, Sunshine. When Mrs. Baxter returns, we'll have her out to the ranch for a visit."

Jon watched the exchange with interest. He would bet his last dollar that Cole was head over heels in love with Elizabeth. The look of concern and love he saw reflected in Cole's eyes could not be disguised.

Jon's heart lightened at the prospect. He had been right all along, he thought smugly. Elizabeth wore her heart on her sleeve. Any fool would be able to see how she felt. But Cole was an expert at hiding his true feelings.

He remembered once, when Cole was fourteen, he had a dog who was killed by a hay wagon. Cole hadn't shed a tear when he found the dog. He carried her into the backyard and buried her beneath the oak tree. Jon had worried about his lack of feeling, until he had opened the door to his bedroom that night to find Cole crying his heart out over that dog. Jon shook his head. Why was it some men fought their feelings so hard? he wondered.

"We'd best be on our way," Cole remarked, "if we're going to make Rancho del Oro before dark."

"I don't imagine Elizabeth has had much experience sleeping out under the stars," Jon teased.

A disconcerted look passed over Elizabeth's face as she listened quietly to the exchange. "Perhaps we should wait until morning, Cole. Something might happen if we leave so late."

Cole and Jon shared an amused chuckle.

"Don't be such a tenderfoot, Sunshine. Nothing's going to happen."

The buckboard bounced along El Camino Real, heading south toward Santa Clara. Elizabeth sat primly in her seat, trying to maintain her balance as she was jostled about by the motion of the wagon.

Her eyes wandered over the countryside, taking in the sights and smells that surrounded her. The land was toasted brown by the unrelenting heat of the sun, relieved in spots by clumps of green that sporadically dotted the landscape.

The sky was clear blue for as far as the eye could see, save for an occasional white, fluffy cloud drifting by overhead. The air was still warm, and it was likely to remain that way until well into October, Cole had explained. The rainy season didn't begin until November, and then there was only enough rain to keep the rivers from drying up and the land from becoming too parched.

Inhaling deeply, Elizabeth noticed an unusual pungent fragrance in the air. "What's that strange odor?" she inquired.

Glancing over, Cole noticed Elizabeth wrinkling her nose at the smell. "You'll get used to it. It's the eucalyptus that you're smelling. And the yellow color you see over there on the hills is yellow mustard," he pointed out.

Cole's face became animated as he talked of the land that he loved. It was hard for Elizabeth to understand what attracted him to this ugly, barren land. The lush green hills of the East, with their towering maples and elms, was much prettier than what she had seen here thus far.

"You really love it here, don't you?" she asked.

"It grows on you. I hardly have any memory of what Missouri was like. I left there when I was ten."

"Tell me what it was like growing up with Jon for a father. Was he very strict?"

Cole caught a glimpse of Elizabeth's wistful expression and thought it strange that someone who had never wanted for anything seemed envious of his childhood.

"Jon was very good to both Abby and myself. He

153

treated us as if we were his own children. He was strict at times, more so with Abby, because she was a girl. But he was always fair."

A strange silence followed Cole's remarks. He glanced over to find Elizabeth wiping her eyes. "Why didn't you ever try to contact your father all those years he wrote to you?" His tone was harsher than he had intended.

"My grandfather kept his letters from me. I thought my father had abandoned me; it's what I had been told."

Cole's eyes widened. "Why didn't you tell me? Why did you let me go on thinking the worst of you?"

Smiling ruefully, Elizabeth shrugged. "You are not the only stubborn member of this family; I, too, have my pride."

"Your grandfather sounds like an old bastard. I'd like to get my hands on him and—"

"He's a tortured individual," Elizabeth interrupted. "He never got over the death of my mother. I pity him."

"Well, I wouldn't waste any of your sympathy on the likes of him. He's a mean old coot, and if you ask me—"

Suddenly, before Cole could finish his sentence, a bullet whirred past their heads, slamming into the back of the buckboard.

Elizabeth screamed, her eyes widening with fright as Cole snapped the reins, urging the horses to go faster. "Duck down," he ordered. "I'm going to try and outrun them."

The two riders were bearing down on them with incredible speed. The buckboard wasn't built to maintain the kind of pace necessary to outdistance them.

Several more shots were fired, causing the horses to rear. Cole made one last-ditch effort to bring them under control before losing hold of the reins. The last thing he saw before hitting the tree was Elizabeth being thrown from the wagon. Then everything went black.

The two men stared in satisfaction at the scene before them. "I told you my plan would work, Jake," Willy said, pulling the red bandanna down off his face.

"Yeah. But what about the girl? The old man is not going to pay us if she's dead."

Willy, seeing the wisdom of Jake's words, rushed over to Elizabeth's still form. "She's still breathing, but she's got a bump on her head the size of a goose egg."

"Whooey! Look at them tits," Jake said, rubbing his crotch.

"Knock it off, Jake. We don't touch the girl. Now get me a blanket and give me that letter the old man had forged," Willy ordered.

"How do you suppose he knew about their marriage?"

"I don't know. When you have as much money as that old man, you have powerful connections, spies everywhere. I expect one of his informants wired him. He's had the girl watched the whole time she's been here."

Shaking his head, Jake spit a stream of tobacco juice. "It must be something having all that money."

"Yeah . . . well, if we don't hurry and get the hell out of here, we're not going to make the train."

Nodding, Jake hurried over to where Cole lay. "This one's still alive, but his leg's busted. Looks like it snapped right in two."

"Just leave the letter in his coat pocket where he'll be sure to find it," Willy said impatiently. "Let's go."

Lying Elizabeth's limp body across the saddle in front of him, Willy turned his horse in the direction of San

Francisco and the railroad station.

They were going to be traveling in style this trip—a private railcar, no less. There would be no questions asked when they carried their sick sister on board the train. Yup, everything was going according to plan thanks to Josiah Worthington.

Opening his eyes slowly, Cole tried to focus on his surroundings. His head hurt like hell. And his leg. . . . Christ! He couldn't believe the pain.

A blurred vision of a woman's form came into focus. "Elizabeth," he choked out. But as his vision cleared, he could see it wasn't Elizabeth but Abigail who stood at the side of his bed, wearing a worried look on her face.

"Abby," he whispered.

"Shh. Lie still. You've had an accident," Abigail said, fearful for her brother's life as she gazed down upon his pale complexion.

Cole had been unconscious for over a week. Doc Willis wasn't sure his leg was ever going to heal properly. It had been touch and go since the night Buck Henry had ridden up in the buckboard with Cole's body in the back.

Buck had found Cole lying unconscious beneath a tree about twenty-five miles south of San Francisco. He had loaded him into the wagon and carted him the rest of the way to Rancho del Oro. Thank God Buck had been on his way to Santa Clara to shoe the horses at the Silvera ranch, or who knows how long Cole would have remained under that tree? Abby thought.

"Where's Elizabeth?" Cole asked. "Is she all right?" The vision of Elizabeth flying from the wagon was indelibly etched in his mind. He would never forgive himself if something had happened to her. His heart twisted painfully at the thought.

Abigail blanched. What could she possibly tell him? That Elizabeth was gone . . . disappeared? Or should she tell him the truth? That his new bride had decided marriage wasn't for her. She felt for the letter in her apron pocket, the one she had found in Cole's coat. No. She would wait until he was stronger.

"Elizabeth is fine; she's in San Francisco with Jon. Now you rest, and we'll talk some more later."

At Cole's sigh of relief, Abby blinked back her tears. Tiptoeing to the door, she glanced back to find that he was once again sleeping peacefully. The laudanum she had given him would keep him quiet for several hours.

Trudging wearily into the kitchen, Abigail plopped down at the old wooden table. Consuelo spun about, shaking her head at the young woman before her. Abby's eyes were shadowed from lack of sleep; she looked as if she had lost weight this past week.

"*Señorita* Abby, you will make yourself ill. Go and lie down. It will do you good."

Abigail rested her head on the table, too weary to make the trek to her room. "I'll be fine. I'm just upset about what that woman did to Cole."

"*Sí.* It is a terrible thing what she do to the *señor*. What will you tell him?"

Looking up, she shook her head. "I don't know. Perhaps Jon will be able to talk to him when he gets back from Sacramento. He went to see a Mrs. Baxter. He thought, perhaps, Elizabeth had taken refuge with her," Abby said, rising from the chair.

"Where do you go?" Consuelo's question was full of censure.

157

"I have to check on Star's filly. She's still weak and needs to be fed."

Pushing Abby back down in her chair, Consuelo replied, "You will do no such thing." She slapped her forehead with her hand. "*Madre de Dios.* Pedro and I can look after the *rancho.* You will look after yourself and your *hermano.* Now go and rest. A *siesta* will do you good."

Giving Consuelo an affectionate peck on the cheek, Abby smiled. For as long as she could remember, Consuelo had been bossing her around. Consuelo and Pedro had been hired by Jon shortly after the purchase of the ranch. Consuelo was an amply proportioned woman, standing a full head taller than her husband, Pedro. Where he was thin and wiry, Consuelo was pleasingly plump.

They made an incongruous sight standing next to each other at mass every Sunday. Cole had remarked once that the two reminded him of a heifer with a calf. Abby grinned in remembrance of Cole's impertinent remark.

Both she and Cole had been blessed the day the Gonzaleses had entered their lives. They were warm and loving people who had no children of their own. They were just the balm for two misplaced youngsters looking for a family. Not that Jon wasn't a good guardian. But he had his life and law practice in the city, and Abby and Cole preferred life at the ranch.

"*Sí, mi madre,*" Abby finally replied, noting the pleased expression that always came into Consuelo's eyes whenever Abby or Cole called her mother. "I will go. Arguing with you is like talking to the wind."

Consuelo observed Abigail's departure with pride. *Señorita* Abby had grown into such a lovely woman over the years. A woman any man would be proud to call wife. But no. Abigail wanted no man. No man she could have, anyway. And so she had thrown herself into her *rancho* and her family.

Consuelo shook her head in disgust. For twenty years, she had watched the *señorita* pine for the love of one man. *Dios!* Was he so blind he couldn't see the love shining in her eyes each time she looked at him?

And now *Señor* Mac will have big trouble because of this woman he married. She knew the kind of temper the *señor* had when he was mad. Consuelo crossed herself. I pray that he never finds this woman, Elizabeth, for if he does, he will make her very sorry she was ever born.

Chapter Fourteen

Watching Cole eat his bowl of *albóndigas* soup, Abigail was amazed at his recuperative powers. A week had passed and he was already much stronger. He was able to sit up in bed and take his meals, no longer needing to be fed like a baby—even though at times he certainly acted like one, she thought. Weary of staying in bed, he had chased Consuelo out of his room on two different occasions when she had tried to give him his medicine. Cole was definitely on the mend.

"When did you say Jon was coming with Elizabeth?" Cole asked between bites of his tortilla.

Abigail fidgeted nervously with the needlework on her lap, purposely avoiding Cole's question.

Noting his sister's reluctance to answer, a feeling of unease swept over him. "What is it, Abby? I know you're keeping something from me." He couldn't miss the drawn look she wore whenever he spoke of Elizabeth.

Abigail's face paled. How could she explain to Cole what had happened to his wife? She didn't want to hurt

160

him. "Cole . . ." She paused, unsure of what to say. "I haven't told you everything."

His chest felt as if it would burst. "It's Elizabeth. . . . She's dead, isn't she?" He held his breath, waiting for the answer. The fall from the wagon had killed her. Why else wouldn't she have come to be with him?

Sitting down on the bed next to her brother, Abigail removed the bowl from his lap, placing it on the nightstand. Reaching out, she took Cole's hands, holding them gently in her own. Taking a deep breath, she replied, "Elizabeth isn't dead."

At the look of relief spreading over Cole's face, she wished she could spare him the hurt that she knew was forthcoming. "She's gone, Cole; Elizabeth has left you."

Cole's brows creased together in confusion. "What do you mean, she's left me? I saw her thrown from the buckboard. I don't understand." But he was afraid that he did. The nagging suspicions hovering at the back of his mind crept steadily forward.

"I don't profess to understand everything that has happened. I only know that I found a letter addressed to you; it was stuck in the pocket of your coat the day of the accident."

Reaching into the pocket of her apron, Abigail extracted the letter. She had made it a habit to carry it with her for this eventuality. "I will leave you to read this in private," she said, handing him the note.

Waiting until Abby shut the door, Cole opened the envelope. His hands shook as he read the words so neatly penned on the paper: "*My dearest Cole, I have decided that our marriage was a mistake. Please forgive me, but I miss my life back in New York. One day you will thank me for letting*

161

you go. Fondly, Elizabeth. "

A small shiny object dropped into his lap. Picking it up, he examined it in the light. It was the gold wedding ring he had so recently placed on Elizabeth's finger.

He stared at the letter, the words suddenly clarifying the doubts he had refused to acknowledge. "*. . . our marriage was a mistake.*" The words drummed through his brain, keeping time to the violent beating of his heart. The accident had been staged. It was all an act . . . all a lie—the men . . . the holdup . . . their marriage . . . his love.

Suddenly, a raw and primitive grief overwhelmed him. "No!" he shouted, crushing the letter in his hand and with it the newfound love he had felt for his wife. Damn her fickle heart! She missed her life back in New York. He shook his head. "Once a society bitch, always a society bitch," he roared.

A deep burning rage welled up inside of him at Elizabeth's treachery. Clenching the ring tightly, he shook his fist in the air. "Elizabeth!" he screamed.

What a fool he had been. A stupid, lovesick fool. He had no doubt that Elizabeth and her grandfather had planned the whole abduction together. Thank God he had never told her of his feelings for her. She probably would have thrown the words right back in his face.

Taking in huge gulps of air, he tried to calm himself so he could think rationally. He recalled Elizabeth's fear right before the start of their journey and the words she had spoken: "*Perhaps we should wait until morning, Cole. Something might happen if we leave so late.*" Had she had a change of heart? Had she been trying to warn him?

Christ! There was no place on this earth the bitch

162

could hide. He would have his revenge on both Elizabeth and her grandfather, if it was the last thing he ever did.

The lights of the Worthington mansion were ablaze this last day of August. Josiah Worthington lay dying in his bed.

Seated at her grandfather's side, tears blurring her vision, Elizabeth watched him struggle for each breath he took. His face was pinched in pain, his complexion deathly white. The doctor had said it was his heart. Apparently, her grandfather had been ill for some time but had chosen to hide it from everyone. The Lion of Wall Street would roar no more, Elizabeth thought sadly.

Suddenly, an intense pain flashed through her head. Grabbing the sides of her skull, she tried to hold back the excruciating torment. The pains were occurring more frequently now; they had started upon her return from California. She could remember nothing about her trip there except for what her grandfather had told her.

He had explained that it had been a telegram from her that had prompted him to hire two detectives to bring her back home. She vaguely remembered being escorted by two disreputable-looking men, but other than that, there was no recollection.

What had prompted her sudden return home? she wondered. If only Mrs. Baxter were here to help sort out the pieces of the puzzle. She had sent a wire to her in California in care of her sister at the address Stevens had given her, but there had been no reply. Surely, she would want to bid farewell to her employer, Elizabeth thought.

"Elizabeth," Josiah called, barely above a whisper.

She leaned closer to hear his frail words. "I'm here, Grandfather."

Feebly, he reached for her hand, taking her soft fingers into his gnarled ones. "Forgive an old man for his selfishness," he said. "Tell Violet I love her." There was a long pause before he spoke again. "Be happy, Elizabeth. Find the love I never could. I love you." And then he was gone.

With tears streaming down her face, Elizabeth stared at the lifeless form of her grandfather. Patting his hand before placing it on his chest, she said softly, "Good-bye, Grandfather. May you find the contentment in your next life you never could find in this one."

Staring morosely at the portrait of her grandfather that hung over the fireplace in the drawing room, Elizabeth reflected upon his words. What had he meant by some of his deathbed utterances? she wondered. Why would he want Violet Baxter to know he had loved her? She shook her head. It didn't make any sense. But she was too tired to try and sort it out now. It had been an exhausting day. Her grandfather's death had drained her.

Lying her head back against the cushion of the wing chair, she closed her eyes. A vague form floated through her mind. Struggling, she tried to bring the form into focus. Slowly, the image cleared until she could see a tall man seated upon a golden horse. She clutched her head at the intense pain that suddenly surfaced. Squeezing her eyes tighter, she tried to see the face of the rider, but the pain became too unbearable.

Please, God! she prayed. What does it mean? Why

can't I remember?

At the sound of the door opening, Cole looked up from the pile of ledgers scattered over his desk. Jon walked into the study looking tired and defeated. Another one of Elizabeth's victims to suffer, Cole thought bitterly.

"I've struck out with Violet Baxter. It seems she's returned to New York," Jon said, reaching for the brandy.

"Why are you wasting your time? I told you, she isn't worth it." They'd had this same discussion over and over again since Elizabeth's disappearance, with Jon insisting on Elizabeth's innocence and Cole refusing to believe him.

Jon's face flushed in anger. "I tell you something has happened to her. I know her. She would never have gone back home to her grandfather."

The radiance of the kerosene lamps revealed the look of skepticism covering Cole's face. "And what about the wire you found hidden in her dresser drawer? That indicates collusion to me."

"Will you stop talking like a damn lawyer and listen to me? I tell you, Elizabeth is in trouble. I can feel it. We have to go to New York to look for her," Jon shouted.

"I don't give a damn if she's up to her ears in trouble. She's been nothing but trouble since I first laid eyes on her." He had thought of finding her and exacting his revenge, but now he decided she just wasn't worth it. He fingered the ring suspended on the chain around his neck—a constant reminder of Elizabeth's perfidy.

Walking dejectedly to the window, Jon pulled back the

heavy red velvet drapery, gazing out at the hills beyond. Rancho del Oro lay spread out before him like amber honey on a biscuit. The setting sun had turned the land a golden hue. A fitting color for the ranch of gold, he thought.

Gold . . . like the color of his daughter's hair. Damn! Why did Cole have to be so stubborn? Abby had told him about the letter Elizabeth had supposedly written. He shook his head, clenching his fists. By God, the old man was clever! He didn't doubt for a moment that Josiah was behind all this trouble.

He was more determined than ever to travel to New York in search of his daughter. Once there, he was sure Violet Baxter would be willing to help him.

He turned back to find Cole leaning heavily on his crutches. Doc Willis had said Cole's leg would be healed in a few more weeks. Damn it! He didn't want to wait any longer. Cole's leg would just have to heal on the train ride east.

"Cole, I'm begging you one last time. Come with me to New York. I need your help to find Elizabeth."

Cole's resolve hardened. It wasn't easy to refuse Jon's request, but he had to. Christ! Didn't Jon realize what he was asking of him? He had licked his wounds these past few weeks; they were just beginning to heal. He would not lay himself open to that kind of hurt again. Taking a few painful steps forward, he faced his surrogate father. "I'm sorry, Jon; I can't."

"You mean, you won't, don't you?" Jon said, his eyes narrowing in anger and disappointment.

"All right, have it your way; I won't."

"Haven't you overlooked something—or should I say someone—in all this confusion?"

Cole's eyebrows arched in question. "What are you getting at?"

"Have you considered the possibility that your wife might be pregnant with your child?"

Cole reeled, grabbing the wing chair just in time to break his fall. His face whitened. A baby. Christ! It was entirely possible. He had planted his seed inside of Elizabeth on more than one occasion.

Running his fingers through his hair, he looked up at Jon. "Get me a drink, will you?"

Pouring a generous amount of brandy into the snifter, Jon handed it to Cole. "I see you had overlooked that possibility." Jon's expression was triumphant.

Cole shot Jon a contemptuous look. He couldn't take the chance that Elizabeth might be pregnant with his child. The smug look on Jon's face told him that he knew that. "When do we leave?" Cole said, sighing in resignation.

Jon and Abigail faced each other across the darkness of the patio. They had come outside directly after dinner so Jon could have a smoke without "stinking up the house," as Consuelo had put it.

"What do you mean, you're taking Cole to New York?" Abigail shouted, her hands braced on her hips. "He's in no condition to travel. Do you want him to end up a cripple like me?"

Jon's eyes widened at Abigail's vehemence. He had never seen her so upset before. She was always so calm, so composed, whenever he was around her. His expression softened. "You're not a cripple, Abby. Your limp is hardly noticeable. Why do you hide behind it?"

Abigail's face flamed, the nutmeg color of her eyes darkening in anger. "I do not wish to discuss my lameness. I want to talk about Cole."

"I'll take good care of him. Haven't I always taken care of both of you . . . given you everything that you've wanted?"

The words she wanted to scream stuck in her throat. Everything—the only thing—she had ever wanted was Jonathan. Why couldn't he see her as a woman instead of as the fifteen-year-old girl he had rescued?

"Abby," Jon beseeched, placing his hand on her arm, "I would never do anything to hurt Cole or you."

Pulling out of Jon's grasp, she turned away from him. She couldn't bear to have him touch her. It was torture to be near him and not be able to hold him. "You have hurt me more than you will ever know," she said, hurrying back into the house.

"Abby, wait!" Jon stared at her retreating back, confused by her behavior.

"Is there a problem?" Cole asked, coming forward out of the darkness. He had witnessed the whole exchange between Jon and his sister; he almost felt pity for Jon's dilemma.

"It's Abby. She's angry with me for taking you to New York."

Cole shrugged. "She'll get over it."

"I'm not so sure. She seems to be upset about something else. Do you have any idea what it could be?"

Smiling enigmatically, Cole replied, "I have my suspicions."

"Well, for God's sake, tell me what it is," Jon demanded, irritated that Cole was keeping something from him.

168

"I'm sure you'll find out in due time. In the meantime, we all have our crosses to bear. I have Elizabeth; you have Abigail."

Observing Cole disappear into the darkness, Jon felt more confused than ever. Sitting beside the fountain, he listened to the uneven gait of Cole's crutches hitting the ground as he made his way back to the house. The water next to him gurgled and splashed soothingly, but offered no comfort.

In a few days they would leave for New York to solve the mystery of Elizabeth's disappearance, but who would solve the mystery that was unfolding here at home?

Putting the finishing touches on an arrangement of marigolds and white chrysanthemums, Elizabeth stepped back to admire her handiwork. Staring at the pretty flowers, a feeling of sadness swept over her. It was the same kind of arrangement that had adorned her grandfather's casket.

There had not been many mourners attending the funeral of Josiah Worthington, but he would have understood. Grandfather had always said that powerful men had many enemies but few friends.

The opening of the dining room door diverted Elizabeth's attention. Turning, her face split into a smile at the sight of Violet Baxter's familiar countenance. Dropping the remaining flowers on the table, she rushed forward to greet her housekeeper. "Mrs. Baxter, I'm so happy to see you; I wasn't sure you were coming."

Violet's brow wrinkled in confusion. "Not come? After everything that I told you."

Now it was Elizabeth's turn to look puzzled. Smiling,

she shook her head. "I'm sorry; I don't understand."

Staring at Elizabeth strangely, Violet removed her cloak and gloves. "Don't tell me you've forgotten that nice long chat we had in San Francisco?"

Seating herself on one of the mahogany Chippendale chairs, Elizabeth replied, "I'm sorry, but I can't seem to remember anything about my trip to California." She smiled apologetically.

Violet gasped, clutching her throat. Gracious me, what could all this mean? "My dear," she said, taking the seat next to Elizabeth, "do you mean to tell me that you can't recall one thing that transpired the entire two months you lived with your father?"

Elizabeth's eyes filled with tears. "I've tried . . . really, I have. But whenever I start to remember anything, I get these terrible headaches that block out all my memories."

"You poor dear. What does the doctor say?" Violet asked, concerned that Elizabeth might be seriously ill.

"I haven't seen him."

Violet's mouth gaped open. "Not seen him! For heaven's sake, why not?"

"It's been so terrible here, what with grandfather dying and you being gone. I just couldn't face any more bad news."

Standing, Violet helped Elizabeth to her feet. Taking the frightened girl into her arms, she held her close. "I'm here now, and we're going to straighten everything out. First thing tomorrow, I'll send for Dr. Edwards."

Pacing nervously across the green Aubusson carpet of Elizabeth's room, Violet waited for Dr. Edwards to conclude his examination. For the past thirty minutes, his snow-white head had been bent in concentration over Elizabeth, but he had made no diagnosis yet. Violet didn't want to rush him, but she was anxious to learn what he had to say about Elizabeth's condition. She prayed that it wasn't serious.

"Mrs. Baxter?"

Violet turned at Doctor Edwards's summons. Giving Elizabeth a reassuring smile, she approached, taking a seat next to her on the bed, waiting anxiously for the doctor to speak.

"It is my professional opinion that Elizabeth is suffering from hysterical amnesia," he said.

"Amnesia!" Elizabeth shouted, paling at the diagnosis.

"From what Elizabeth has told me, she has totally blocked out her entire trip to California, while remembering everything else. Most likely, she has been traumatized by something that happened to her there."

A shadow of alarm touched Violet's face. "But will her memory ever return?" she asked, patting Elizabeth's hand in a comforting gesture.

"In most of these cases, the memory is triggered by an emotional shock of some sort. If she receives the proper stimulus, there is every indication that her memory will return in full."

"When will I stop having these awful headaches?" Elizabeth questioned, pressing her fingers against her temples to lessen the persistent throb.

"I'm afraid that until your mind is ready to release the terrible episode you are blocking out, the headaches will continue."

"But I can't remember any terrible episode," she protested.

171

"Nevertheless, it is in your subconscious mind. You may have periods where you will start to remember brief glimpses of things. Someday, when you're least expecting it, everything will come flooding back to you," Dr. Edwards explained.

Staring forlornly out her bedroom window, Elizabeth watched Dr. Edwards depart in his carriage. The rain beat heavily against the glass, making it difficult to see clearly. Pressing her forehead against the cool pane, she prayed for her memory to return.

Noting the misery on Elizabeth's face, Violet shook her head. She was unsure about what she should do concerning Elizabeth's condition. She was torn by conflicting emotions. She wanted to protect Elizabeth from whatever it was that had robbed her of her memory. If she wired her father or husband, informing them of her illness, how did she know she wouldn't be endangering Elizabeth's life?

On the other hand, both Elizabeth's husband and father had the right to know of her whereabouts. What if they were frantically looking for her? What if they thought she was dead?

Wringing her hands, she marched nervously about the bedroom, unable to consult Elizabeth about her predicament. The doctor had felt it best that Elizabeth not be told of her marriage. The shock might be too much for her, he had explained.

"Elizabeth, dear," Violet said softly, "would you care to join me in a cup of hot tea? Mrs. Thomas has just brought up a pot of chamomile tea and a plate of scones." Whenever anyone in the household was ill, Mrs. Thomas could always be counted on to provide them with a pot of her medicinal remedy.

Wiping the tears from her face, Elizabeth spun about, forcing a smile to her lips. "That would be lovely."

"It's such a gloomy day, let's sit here by the window and watch the rain," Violet suggested, seating herself on the green cushion of the window seat. "I have always liked the rain. It makes me think that all the inhabitants of the heavens are crying over their loved ones that they had to leave behind."

"That's a beautiful sentiment, Mrs. Baxter."

"Why don't you call me Violet, dear? Mrs. Baxter sounds so formal. And now that Josiah . . . I mean, your grandfather is gone, there's really no need for us to stand on such ceremony."

Pouring the tea into the dainty china cups, Elizabeth handed one to Violet. "I've been meaning to tell you something, but in all the commotion, I completely forgot."

Taking a sip of the bitter tea, Violet pursed her lips before looking up. "What is it, dear? You know you can confide in me."

"Well, it's really very strange, but perhaps you'll know the answer. Before my grandfather died, he told me to tell you something."

Violet's heart pounded; her throat went dry. Her hands trembled nervously as she set the cup down on the teakwood table. "What was it?"

"Grandfather said, 'Tell Violet I love her.'" Elizabeth's forehead creased in puzzlement. "Isn't that strange? I mean, after all, you were only his housekeeper."

"Yes, dear, very strange," Violet said absently, gazing out at the rain. Were Josiah's tears falling down from the heavens over her? She sniffed, wiping her nose on her white lace handkerchief.

Leaning over, Elizabeth placed her arms about Violet's shoulders. "What is it, Violet? I'm sorry if I upset you."

"I'm just a sentimental old fool, dear," Violet replied, patting her hand. "I worked for your grandfather quite a long time. I haven't really allowed myself time to grieve. I guess hearing his words took me by surprise."

"I'm sure he must have cared for you very much. He was never one to bandy his words about lightly."

"Let's talk of something else, shall we?" Violet suggested, picking up her cup again. "Tell me, Elizabeth, have you had any episodes of memory that you haven't told me about?"

Elizabeth's stomach growled. Excusing herself, she reached for a scone. She hadn't eaten a thing all day, and she was starved. "Well, actually, I did have one strange flash of memory. It was the night my grandfather died."

Violet leaned forward. "What was it? Do you remember?"

"The only thing I can remember is seeing a man—a tall man riding a golden horse."

"Are you sure that's all?" Violet asked, staring intently into Elizabeth's eyes.

"Yes. I'm afraid so," she said, chewing on the rich bread. "Wait, there is one more thing. I remember being escorted back here by two men."

"Who were these two men? Did you know them?"

"No. Grandfather told me that they were detectives he had hired to bring me home. They were unkempt and slovenly; I remember that much. Grandfather said that I wanted to return." She frowned. "I don't know why, but I feel that he wasn't telling me the truth."

An uneasy feeling of suspicion crept steadily forward

from the recesses of Violet's mind. Leaning back in her seat, she assimilated the information. She was fairly certain that the man on the horse was Elizabeth's husband, Cole. But the two men who had escorted Elizabeth home were a complete mystery.

If Josiah had hired them to bring Elizabeth back, was it possible that she had been brought back against her will? Knowing Josiah as well as she did, that possibility was entirely plausible. She decided to wire Jonathan Forrester.

Chapter Fifteen

The train moved swiftly down the track, inching its way closer to the city of New York. Cole stared thoughtfully out the window, observing the golden color of the leaves that hung so precariously from the trees. The first touch of fall had spread its fingers over the hills and valleys of the Empire State. The ground was covered in a rich green velvet, so different from the tawny clay of California. He had forgotten how different the atmosphere was back here in the East; it had been a long time since his law school days in Boston.

Shifting his weight to take the pressure off his right leg, Cole positioned himself more comfortably. His leg still pained him at times, but according to Doc Willis, it was healing nicely.

At least he'd been able to convince Doc to take him off those damned crutches he had been using for weeks. The cane he relied on was bad enough, making him feel as old as Methuselah.

The trip had not proven as strenuous as he had originally feared. Jon had arranged for all of their meals to be taken in their private compartment, to lessen the strain on his leg. He didn't relish the idea of walking around with a limp for the rest of his life, which is exactly what Doc Willis had said was going to happen if his leg didn't heal properly.

Thank God they had been able to borrow Henry Crocker's private railcar. It would have been a damned nuisance trying to maneuver around a bunch of young children and their overprotective mamas.

The railcar had been Abigail's idea. She was still furious with Jon for insisting that Cole accompany him. Smiling to himself, Cole thought of how Abigail had lit into Jon again right before they had departed. She must have put the fear of God into him, for Jon had literally been waiting on him hand and foot. A fitting punishment, Cole thought spitefully, for Jon's clever manipulation of his conscience.

He tried not to think about tomorrow and their arrival in New York City. Their plan was to go directly to the Worthington mansion and confront Josiah Worthington.

Jon was certain that something dreadful had befallen Elizabeth. Cole's gut twisted at the thought; he cursed himself inwardly at the uncontrollable emotion that he felt. "She's probably living it up with all her pasty-faced dandies," he said, his eyes narrowing, his voice edged in anger. "Women like that always land on their feet."

The compartment door opened, allowing a cool blast of autumn air to enter. Jon approached, carrying a tray loaded with sandwiches and milk.

"You're not exactly my idea of a suitable handmaiden," Cole teased, pleased at the look of annoyance Jon directed at him. It was hard to stay mad at Jon. But damn it! Jon had placed him in one hell of a difficult situation over his concern about Elizabeth.

"You had better wipe that smug smile off your face," Jon threatened, "unless you want me to take that cane of yours and beat you with it; I don't think I punished you enough as a child."

They stared at each other for a second, then burst out laughing. The tension that had been building between them the past few weeks dissipated like the steam from the train engine.

Taking a seat across from Cole, Jon handed him a sandwich, staring thoughtfully at his foster son. "I want you to know how much I appreciate what you're doing for me. I know I coerced you into coming with me, but once we find Elizabeth, I'm sure my faith in her will be vindicated."

"I've had a lot of time to think things over, Jon, and I've come to the conclusion that perhaps Elizabeth was correct in leaving."

Jon opened his mouth to protest, but Cole raised his hand to silence him. "Let me finish. We come from two different worlds. Your daughter is a socialite—an heiress. I'm just a lawyer that happens to love ranching. Our marriage would never have worked."

"You're not exactly destitute, Cole. You're a wealthy individual in your own right, not some country bumpkin."

"Elizabeth has had everything given to her on a silver platter; she's been waited on hand and foot all her life. She would never have adapted to being the wife of a rancher."

"I think you're wrong," Jon said. "Elizabeth was raised in luxury, that's true, but her values are the same as mine. She's not adverse to working for what she wants,

178

and she's not a snob. She has never held herself up to be better than anyone else."

Digesting Jon's words, Cole smiled poignantly as he remembered back to his conversation with Elizabeth about Hettie Truesdale's pretentiousness. "Perhaps you're right about some of the things you say," he admitted, "but only time will bear out the truth of your words. We will just have to wait until tomorrow and see what the future holds in store for us."

Elizabeth lay in her bed staring up at the ceiling. It was still too early to rise, and she had nothing particularly important to do today, anyway. Violet had resumed her role of housekeeper, and under her excellent supervision, the Worthington mansion was running like clockwork again.

Frowning, she thought of how useless her life really was. She didn't know anything about cooking or cleaning or any of the other things involved in running a household. She had been raised to be an ornament—a pretty, useless ornament.

Her life had never bothered her before; she had never really given it much thought. Why should she be feeling so introspective toward it now? she wondered. She felt empty, incomplete, as if some large part of her was missing. "Why can't I remember anything?" she moaned, grabbing her head in frustration.

Rising from the bed, she tiptoed over to the fireplace, sitting cross-legged in front of it. It was unusual for the weather to be so chilly this early in the autumn season. The temperature had hovered near the freezing point the last three nights. She shivered, rubbing her arms to warm herself.

Staring into the golden color of the flames, she was reminded of the dream she had experienced last night: the man on the golden horse. Who was he? Why did he always appear to her in her dreams? His face had emerged more distinct last night. He was handsome in a rugged sort of way, with unusual light eyes, very compelling eyes that seemed to beckon to her.

Could he be part of the traumatic episode Dr. Edwards had talked to her about? Or was he just a figment of her imagination? Someone she had conjured up . . . her perfect dream man from the romantic novels she had read.

Deciding to take some decisive action, Elizabeth stood, crossing the room to her wardrobe. She would dress and go downstairs to the library. There she would peruse some of the old Jane Austen novels she was so fond of reading. Perhaps a clue to the identity of her dream man could be found between the pages of a book.

Several hours passed and Elizabeth was no closer to finding the answer to her dilemma than she had been before she started. Books of every color, size, and thickness were spread out before her on the red and gold Aubusson carpet of the library.

Hunched over a particularly ribald one, *The History Of Tom Jones*, she couldn't help the giggles that escaped her as she poured over some of the more scandalous passages.

"Whatever is going on here, my dear?" Violet asked, her brows drawing together in a frown, her mouth puckering in distaste as she observed the source of Elizabeth's amusement. Shaking her head, she scolded, "Elizabeth, shame on you. That is truly a bawdy book. I'm shocked to find you are reading it."

At the look of horror on Violet's face, Elizabeth burst out laughing. "You really should read this, Violet. I think it would do you some good."

Violet swallowed her smile. "Well, to be perfectly honest, I already have, but that doesn't mean I approve of you littering up your mind with such trash," she retorted, a mock look of disapproval on her face.

Assuming a look of innocence, Elizabeth explained, "I am only trying to find the answer to my puzzle. Perhaps the man I've been dreaming about is really just a hero out of one of my romance novels."

Violet colored slightly, patting her hair nervously. "Well . . . yes, that is entirely possible, but it is more likely that he is someone from your past."

Elizabeth's eyes widened. "Do you really think so? I would deem myself extremely fortunate to have made the acquaintance of such a handsome gentleman."

Violet smiled knowingly. Elizabeth was certainly going to be in for a big surprise when her memory returned. Thinking of Cole brought Elizabeth's father to mind. Violet was puzzled that she hadn't received a reply to her telegram. She was so sure Jonathan Forrester would be anxious to learn of his daughter's whereabouts. Wiping the frown from her face, she said, "While you're absorbed in your pursuit, I'll go fetch us a hot pot of chocolate and some of Cook's flaky pastries."

"That would be nice," Elizabeth said distractedly, resuming her search with renewed vigor. Picking through several more of the morocco-bound editions that lay on the pile in front of her, her interest was piqued by a book that must have belonged to her grandfather.

181

Picking it up, she stared intently at the title: *The Fortune Teller's Tale*. How odd that it should sound so familiar, she thought, quite certain that she had never read it.

"Here we are, dear," Violet chimed, entering the room with a silver tray. "Has anything jarred your memory yet?" she asked, setting the tray down on the tea table in front of the sofa.

Looking up, Elizabeth frowned thoughtfully. "I'm not sure. This book I found seems familiar to me." She handed it to Violet.

Violet glanced at the gilt-embossed lettering and nodded, handing it back to Elizabeth. "That's because Ah Sing, your father's servant, read your fortune for you. I remember you telling me about it."

A hopeful glint entered Elizabeth's eyes. "Do you remember what the fortune was?"

Violet hesitated, patting her cheek as she concentrated on the question. "Why, yes, I believe I do. Ah Sing told you . . ." She stopped, clamping her mouth shut tight. She couldn't tell Elizabeth what she knew of her fortune—that the man of her dreams was actually her husband.

Elizabeth's eyes widened in alarm at Violet's strange behavior. "What is it? What's wrong?"

Groping for the words to placate Elizabeth's curiosity, Violet fidgeted nervously with the strings of her apron. It wouldn't do any good to upset her needlessly about the man of her dreams. It would only lead to more questions that she wasn't at liberty to answer right now. "It was just some silly notion Ah Sing had that you would meet a mysterious stranger and marry."

"But who is the mysterious stranger? Could he be the man on the golden horse?"

Fearful that she had already said too much, Violet stammered, "I—I'm afraid that is all I can remember, dear. Perhaps I'll think of something more later."

Elizabeth listened with rising dismay to the finality of Violet's words. A look of frustration crossed her face. The short burst of hope that had bloomed so suddenly in her breast faded like last summer's roses. Nodding in resignation, she returned Violet's smile.

Was she destined to remain forever in the dark about the mysterious man on the golden horse? she wondered sadly. A single tear trickled down her face, falling dejectedly onto the leather volume she held in her lap.

The late afternoon sun was a welcoming presence to the two men alighting from the hired hack. Cole and Jon stood in the middle of the large circular drive that fronted the Worthington mansion, waiting for the driver to throw down their bags.

"Didn't think the Worthingtons would be getting much company now that old man Worthington's dead," the driver remarked, throwing the last bag down to the ground.

Cole and Jon exchanged startled glances.

"Did I hear you correctly? Did you say Worthington is dead?" Jon asked.

"That's right, sir," the driver replied. "He died several weeks back. They say it was his heart. Though from what I hear, the old man didn't have much of one."

"Do you know if his granddaughter is still living here?" Jon asked, distressed that he might have been wrong about Elizabeth's whereabouts.

"That I couldn't say, sir. I don't take many fares out

183

this way."

Jon paid the driver and watched him depart. Turning to Cole, who seemed to be preoccupied with disquieting thoughts of his own, he asked, "What do you make of it, Cole? Do you think Elizabeth might be here?"

"What I think, aside from what we discussed earlier, is that we should go up to the door and find out for ourselves."

Picking up their bags, the two men walked the short distance to the entry gate. Massive wrought iron railings separated the drive from the actual entrance to the mansion. Above the gate, scrolled in black iron, was an impressive letter *W*, the head of a lion surrounding the letter on each side.

"It's been a long time since I've set foot on this estate," Jon said. "I can't tell you how many memories of Kathryn have come rushing back to me in the short time that we've been here." Smiling wistfully, he pushed the heavy gate open.

Cole was filled with memories of his own. Not of the estate—he had never been here before—but of Elizabeth. He could feel her presence as strongly as if she were standing right next to him. He remembered how she had looked on the day of their wedding . . . the look of wonder she had worn the first time he made love to her. He shook himself. He didn't need to get wrapped up in a bunch of sentimental claptrap right now. Jon was doing a good enough job of that.

The huge brass knocker, again bearing the distinctive symbol of the lion, sounded ominous as it clanged against the heavy oak door. Cole's stomach tightened as he waited for the door to open.

"May I help you," an imperious-sounding voice

answered through the crack in the door.

"We are here to see Elizabeth Forrester," Jon replied.

The door opened wider to exhibit a tall, stately-looking gentleman dressed in the livery of a butler. "I'm afraid Miss Forrester is not receiving visitors, sir. She is indisposed," the servant replied.

Trying to hide his excitement at the news that Elizabeth was in residence, Jon assumed a condescending look of authority. "I am Jonathan Forrester, Elizabeth's father. I believe she will receive me."

Stevens's bushy eyebrow arched in surprise at the name so familiar to him. For years he had hidden the letters from the man known as Jonathan Forrester. Recovering his aplomb, he stepped aside to allow the visitors to enter. "If you will take a seat in the drawing room, I will see if Miss Forrester is available." He indicated the door to his immediate left.

"Pompous old coot," Jon muttered under his breath. He glanced over at Cole, who was taking in the splendor and opulence of the room with unconcealed surprise. "It's something, isn't it? The old man spent a fortune on this place. Some of the antique pieces are priceless, not to mention the artwork that adorns the walls. He always called this room the gold room. I guess you can see why."

Scanning the room, Cole noted that the gold velvet drapery at the window was the perfect complement for the gold Aubusson carpet beneath his feet. Everywhere he looked the color gold was in evidence, from the gilt-edged frames that bordered the portraits of Worthington and his daughter, to the solid gold andirons that stood majestically by the fireplace. Cole looked back at Jon and shook his head. "I can see why you wanted to leave here; this place looks like a mausoleum."

185

"Maybe now you can understand why I have tried so hard all these years to get my daughter out of here. She grew up in an atmosphere devoid of warmth. I never should have left her in the care of that manipulative old man."

"Elizabeth doesn't seem any worse for her upbringing. She's a survivor. These type of women know what they want out of life," Cole replied, a cynical smile twisting his lips.

"How can—" Jon paused when Violet Baxter entered the room.

"Mr. Forrester! Mr. MacAlister! How—how nice to see you," Violet stammered, shocked to find Elizabeth's father and husband standing before her.

"Thank God you're here, Violet. At least I know Elizabeth has been in good hands," Jon replied. "We've been worried sick about her. We didn't know if she was living here or not."

"*You* have been worried sick. I couldn't care less where she is," Cole corrected.

Violet shot Cole an indignant look before asking Jon, "Didn't you receive my telegram?"

"No. I'm afraid not."

Violet stared at the two men whose expressions were so totally different from each other. Jonathan Forrester's face was a mixture of concern and relief; Cole MacAlister's was as cold and remote as a winter's day. What could have prompted this reaction from Elizabeth's husband? she wondered. Perhaps he really was responsible for her present state of mind.

"If you would both care to have a seat, I think there are some things we need to discuss before I bring

Elizabeth down to see you."

Doing as requested, both men took a seat on the gold brocade sofa, waiting patiently for Violet to continue.

"Elizabeth has been ill," Violet stated.

Jon jumped up. "Ill! What's the matter with her? Is it serious?" Turning to Cole, he blurted out, "I told you something terrible had happened, but you wouldn't listen." His look was accusatory.

Violet held up her hands, trying to calm the distraught gentleman. "Please, Mr. Forrester, there is nothing to get so alarmed about. It is not a life-threatening situation," she said, noting the cocky look Cole directed at his foster father. It seemed to say, "I told you so."

Resuming his seat, Jon glared angrily at Cole, who smiled snidely in response. "Please continue, Mrs. Baxter," Cole urged.

"Elizabeth has been suffering from what the doctor calls hysterical amnesia." She went on to explain what Dr. Edwards had told her about Elizabeth's condition, relating what Elizabeth had told her about her grandfather's story and how she had come to return to New York.

"How very convenient for her," Cole sneered. "And I suppose both of you buy this story?" Shaking his head, he snickered.

"Mr. MacAlister," Violet retorted, her face flaming in anger, "Elizabeth has experienced a traumatic episode that has caused her to lose her memory. I am not entirely convinced that you did not have something to do with that loss."

"The only thing Elizabeth has lost is her desire to be wed. I don't believe all this amnesia business for a minute," Cole replied, crossing his arms over his chest.

"Well, really!" Violet exclaimed, parroting his gesture.

"Let's all calm down," Jon bellowed, the tone of his voice allowing no room for refusal. "There were some very mysterious circumstances surrounding Elizabeth's disappearance. Cole has reason to believe that Elizabeth left him of her own free will . . . that Worthington and she conspired to stage an abduction, injuring Cole in the process."

Violet gasped, noting for the first time the cane that Cole was using to assist him. "That's preposterous. Why, Elizabeth would never—"

"Violet," Elizabeth's voice sounded from the other side of the drawing room door, "are you in there?"

All eyes turned to stare at the young woman who entered the room. Cole's heart twisted painfully at the sight of the woman he had almost given his love to.

Elizabeth's blue eyes widened in astonishment, her face turning deathly white as she stared at the faces before her. "Cole!" she whispered, grabbing her head before collapsing to the floor in a faint heap.

Chapter Sixteen

"So much for Elizabeth's amnesia," Cole said, glancing over at the two stunned people before rising. Limping over to his wife's still form, he picked her up, carrying her over to the sofa. He gritted his teeth at the pain the extra weight caused him.

Jon jumped up from the sofa, allowing Cole to place his burden down.

Bending over Elizabeth's still form, Violet placed her hand on her forehead; her skin felt clammy beneath her fingertips. "I'm afraid she may be suffering from shock. The doctor told me this could happen."

"She's quite a good actress, I'll give her that much. If you will both excuse me, I feel the need for some fresh air," Cole said, stalking out of the room.

Shaking his head as he watched Cole depart, Jon muttered, "Stubborn to the last." Leaning over his daughter's form, he took her hand gently in his while Violet sponged her brow with a damp cloth, trying to revive her. They shared concerned glances before Elizabeth's moan drew their attention.

Elizabeth's eyes opened slowly, to find Violet and her father bending over her, concerned expressions on their faces. The sight of her father filled her with joy. She remembered him; she remembered everything. Just as the doctor had predicted, the shock of seeing Cole alive had stimulated the return of her memory. Clutching her father's hand, she asked, "Where is Cole?"

Jon and Violet exchanged worried glances.

"He went outside for some air, my dear. The anxiety of witnessing your fainting spell was too much for him," Violet lied.

"He'll be back shortly, then we'll be able to sort out everything that has happened to you," Jon replied, caressing her cheek.

Walking down the gravel path leading to the small pond at the back of the house, Cole turned his collar up against the chill of the afternoon. The sun had taken refuge behind a mass of clouds, producing a marked decrease in temperature.

Picking up a handful of pebbles, he tossed them into the water, watching the concentric swirls radiate out. How complicated his life had become since Elizabeth had entered it, he thought dismally. He had been so sure divorce was what he wanted, but now, seeing her again, he didn't know if he would be able to go through with it. And there was still the possibility of a child to consider. He kicked the dirt at his feet, disgusted with his ambivalent thoughts on the matter.

Stuffing his hands into the pockets of his coat, he turned back toward the house. Divorce was not the answer; he realized that now. The punishment was not severe enough for Elizabeth's deception. No. He needed to come up with a suitable revenge for his darling bride. One that she would have to endure, day after day, month after month, for the rest of her life.

Entering the house, Cole returned quickly to the drawing room. He knew what his course of action would be. Elizabeth wasn't the only one that could play a role to perfection.

Spying the prostrate body of his wife lying so still on the sofa, he rushed over to her. "Sweetheart, you had me so worried. I was afraid something dreadful had happened to you," he said, kissing her brow.

Jon and Violet stared openmouthed at the scene before them. Jon could not believe the abrupt change of heart that Cole was exhibiting.

Unaware of the intrigue going on around her, Elizabeth only knew a deep and abiding love as she stared into the face of the man she never thought to see again. Reaching up, she placed her hand tenderly on Cole's cheek. "I thought you were lost to me forever."

Cole stared into the guileless blue eyes brimming with unshed tears. She was a better actress than he had given her credit for. Smiling down at her, he kissed her cheek. "I believe we have a lot of time to make up for."

Their intimate exchange brought tears to Violet's eyes. Excusing herself, she rushed off to prepare the guest rooms.

Casting a suspicious glance at Cole, Jon said, "I will leave you two to get reacquainted." He smiled down at his daughter. "I will see you both at dinner." Shooting Cole one last look of distrust, he departed.

Once they were alone, Elizabeth felt shy in Cole's presence. Staring at the handsome visage of her husband, she wondered how she could have questioned who the man on the golden horse was. Sitting upright, she made room beside her on the sofa, noting how slow and awkward his movements were as he came to sit beside her. "You've been hurt," she said, a shadow of alarm threading her voice.

Biting the inside of his cheek, Cole tried to keep his anger in check at Elizabeth's artificial show of concern. "I broke my leg when the buckboard overturned."

"I thought you had been killed. I remember the wagon hitting the tree before I passed out," she said, her voice quivering slightly.

Wishful thinking on your part, I'm sure, Cole thought angrily. Picking up her hand, he rubbed it gently between his fingers. "Where is your wedding ring?" he asked, knowing full well that it rested against the base of his throat.

Looking down, Elizabeth was dismayed to find her ring was missing. "I don't know. Perhaps the two men that abducted me stole it." Tears came to her eyes when she thought of all the horror and uncertainty she had been forced to endure these past few weeks. Her grandfather's words echoed through her mind: ". . . *forgive an old man for his selfishness.*" She now understood, only too well, the meaning of his deathbed confession.

Cole stared in fascination at the fragile beauty of his wife. The black of her mourning attire only enhanced the delicate planes of her pale face. His brows drew together in an agonized expression; his heart became leaden. If only things had been different. If only she hadn't run away. If only . . . "Damn!" he said, not realizing he had spoken aloud until he noticed the confused look on Elizabeth's face.

4 FREE BOOKS

TO GET YOUR 4 FREE BOOKS WORTH $18.00 — MAIL IN THE FREE BOOK CERTIFICATE T O D A Y

Fill in the Free Book Certificate below, and we'll send your FREE BOOKS to you as soon as we receive it.

If the certificate is missing below, write to: Zebra Home Subscription Service, Inc., P.O. Box 5214, 120 Brighton Road, Clifton, New Jersey 07015-5214.

ZEBRA HOME SUBSCRIPTION
SERVICE, INC.
P.O. Box 5214
120 BRIGHTON ROAD
CLIFTON, NEW JERSEY 07015-5214

"Is something wrong?" she asked, stirring uneasily in her seat, puzzled by his abrupt change of mood.

A satanic smile crossed Cole's lips; a satisfied light entered his eyes. "Nothing is wrong," he said, patting her hand reassuringly. "As soon as we return to California, everything will be right once again."

Chapter Seventeen

California. Elizabeth had never thought to set eyes on the strange beauty of the land again. Waves of golden grass billowed in the wind over hills of sun-baked brown. The small window of the train could not contain the immense vista spreading out in all directions.

"San Jose," the conductor called out as the train slowly pulled into the station. Unimposing squat adobe structures with red tile roofs and whitewashed exteriors came into view as the engine finally ground to a halt.

"This is where we get off, Sunshine," Cole said, grabbing her hand to assist her up.

"We're getting off here?" Elizabeth questioned, puzzled by the sudden change of plans.

"What's the meaning of this, Cole?" Jon asked, flashing Cole an annoyed look.

Smiling, Cole answered smoothly, "I'm taking my bride home to Rancho del Oro. Did you think otherwise?"

Jon's face flushed red. "You led me to believe that you and Elizabeth would be living in San Francisco."

194

"Did I?" Cole said, shrugging his shoulders. "I don't remember."

"You know perfectly well that you did. You told me that you and Elizabeth would be setting up housekeeping on Nob Hill. What am I supposed to tell Mrs. Baxter when she arrives, expecting to find Elizabeth?"

"Tell her that Elizabeth is going to learn to become a rancher's wife," Cole advised, pulling out his pocket watch to check the time. He chose to ignore Elizabeth's startled gasp and the vulgar expletive her father uttered as Cole pulled her toward the door.

Elizabeth watched the entire exchange between her father and her husband in stunned silence, unable to believe the total metamorphosis Cole had undergone since their arrival a few minutes ago. The concerned, doting husband she had come to know had been replaced by the domineering, dictatorial bully she had met so many months before in San Francisco.

Stepping forward, Jon put a restraining hand on Cole's shoulder. "I'm not sure what you're up to, son, but no harm had better come to my daughter."

A feeling of unease settled over Elizabeth. Why would her father have reason to believe Cole would harm her? she wondered.

"It was you who assured me that Elizabeth would be able to assume the role of rancher's wife. Are you telling me now that she's only fit to be a social butterfly? Was I right all along?" Cole challenged.

The angry look Jon directed at Cole would have reduced lesser men to their knees, but Cole stood fast, determined to have the last word when it came to Elizabeth Forrester MacAlister. Ushering his wife off the train, he felt Jon's penetrating anger boring into his back.

195

Staring down at Cole and Elizabeth as they stepped onto the wooden planks of the walkway, Jon gripped the rail of the platform, holding himself back from following them. "I'll expect to see you both soon," he said.

Smiling, Cole grasped Elizabeth about the waist in a proprietary gesture. "I'll be into the city soon, but don't expect to see Elizabeth; she won't be joining me. She'll be staying at the ranch with Abby."

"All aboard," the conductor shouted, trying to make himself heard above the noise of the steam engine.

"Take care, Elizabeth. I'll see you soon," Jon shouted, waving as the train pulled out of the station.

Waving her handkerchief, Elizabeth blinked back the tears that threatened to spill at her father's departure. She glanced over at Cole, startled by the look of blatant hostility on his face. The nasty smile he cast her way made her blood run cold.

"Well now, Sunshine," he said, "there's no one else to come to your rescue—no interfering father, no conniving grandpa. You're all mine to do with as I please. You're bought and paid for; I have the bill of sale to prove it." Reaching into his pocket, he extracted an official-looking document, handing it to her.

Elizabeth blanched, her hands trembling as she unfolded the paper. It was their marriage certificate.

Cole grabbed the paper out of her hands, shoving it back into his pocket. "It's time to go home, Mrs. MacAlister." He didn't try to conceal the animosity in his voice.

Home. The prospect sounded like a threat rather than a haven, Elizabeth thought. Home to what? A house full of strangers in a land totally alien to her? She hugged herself tightly, a feeling of déjà vu coming over her as she

196

watched Cole load the luggage onto the carriage. It was as if the last four months hadn't happened. They were regressing back to their former relationship of animosity and dislike. Why? she wondered. Why?

The silence became a deafening sound stretching out between them, minute after minute, mile after mile, as they made their way to the ranch. The confining space of the carriage closed in around them, making it feel smaller than it actually was.

Elizabeth could hear every breath Cole took, every beat her heart made. She didn't smell the pungent odor of the manzanita and eucalyptus, only the musky scent of Cole's skin. She didn't see the blackbird swooping down from the branches overhead, only the black curls that fell riotously over Cole's brow.

It was times like these when they were so close, yet so distant, that she wished she had never gotten her memory back. At least then she'd been ignorant of the way Cole's lips felt against her skin or the way his hands felt when they tenderly caressed her most private places. Her palms became moist, her breathing labored at the painful memories her mind conjured up.

Would she ever experience Cole's lovemaking again? He hadn't touched her save for that one small peck on the cheek the day of their reunion. She thought he was only being considerate of her health, but she could see now it was more than that. He had lost interest in her as a woman. The thought ripped through her heart like a knife.

How different this trip to the ranch was compared to the one right after their wedding night. Then the glow of their lovemaking had been bright in their hearts and minds. Now it was dull, tarnished by the selfish actions of her grandfather. She shook her head sadly. She had been so sure that day that she could make Cole love her, so filled with determination. Glancing at the stubborn set of Cole's jaw, the tightness of his mouth, her heart ached. No amount of determination could erase the look of hatred he now wore on his face whenever he looked at her. What had happened to make him change so?

"We're almost there," Cole announced.

Elizabeth jumped, startled out of her musing.

"You're as skittish as a newborn colt," he said.

Cole's smug smile grated on her nerves. A slow anger started to build within Elizabeth, simmering just below the surface. Flashing Cole an annoyed look, she replied, "Maybe if you had spoken more than three words to me this entire trip, I wouldn't have been so surprised to hear the sound of your voice."

"I didn't have anything to say."

Elizabeth smiled sweetly. "You don't have anything to say even when you do speak, *Mr. MacAlister.*" She raised her voice, enunciating the last two words.

She felt no small amount of satisfaction at the red flush covering Cole's face. She'd had just about enough of his sarcasm and biting remarks; she wasn't about to take his abuse lying down. She had too much Worthington in her to be brought to heel that easily. If Cole thought to intimidate and humiliate her, then he just didn't know with whom he was dealing.

Cole's hands clenched the reins; a muscle flicked angrily at his jaw. "You had better learn to curb your viper's tongue and give your husband the proper respect that is due him," he demanded.

Fury almost choked her. She swallowed her nasty retort, saying instead, "If you wish to silence me, husband dear, there are far better ways to curb my tongue." She ran her tongue suggestively over her lips. "If you get my meaning . . ." she added, surprised by her own boldness.

Elizabeth bit the inside of her mouth to keep from laughing at Cole's shocked expression. His face had turned bright red, and he looked as if he were going to have an apoplectic fit. She smiled, feeling better than she had in weeks.

Her elation was short lived, however, as Cole pulled the carriage to a halt, glaring menacingly at her. "We shall see how bold you are, sweetheart, when you find yourself firmly entrenched in the enemy camp. Welcome to Rancho del Oro."

Her eyes widened, sliding past Cole's mocking face to land upon the noble structure of Rancho del Oro's main house, visible in the distance. It gleamed white like a beacon against the purple-hued sky of the setting sun. Her heart thudded loudly, her palms starting to sweat as the reality of Cole's words hit home.

In a short while, she would arrive in Cole's home, an unwelcome stranger amidst his family and friends. A shiver of unease gusted through her, like the sudden wind breathing life into the still branches of the live oaks lining the dusty, rut-filled road they traveled upon.

As the distance lessened, she could hear the barking of the dogs as they welcomed them in their own characteristic way. They had no sooner stopped when they were surrounded by an assembly of children.

"*Señor* Mac! *Señor* Mac!" they shouted. "What did you bring us?"

Elizabeth smiled at the children's antics, surprised to find Cole's expression filled with warmth and caring as he gazed into the four eager faces below him.

"You *niños* take the bags into the house, then I will see if there is a treat in store for you."

Amidst squeals of delight, the children did as they were told. Cole came around to help Elizabeth alight from the carriage. For just a moment their eyes met, and she caught a glimpse of tenderness and something else she could not fathom before he turned away.

He led her through the outer courtyard and through a walled structure, then into another smaller courtyard, past a multi-tiered fountain whose water gurgled and spurted against the blue of its tiles.

"Are you nervous yet, Sunshine?" he asked, his voice a velvet murmur as it cut through the night.

Staring at the maliciousness of his smile, Elizabeth experienced a feeling of dread as they approached the front door. Refusing to rise to his bait, she said nothing.

"I see the cat's got your tongue. I guess it won't be necessary for me to pull it out after all." His laughter was triumphant.

Elizabeth shook, not from fear, but from the uncontrollable anger coursing through her body. Clenching her fists, she gritted her teeth to keep from speaking what was on her mind. There was no torture bad enough, no punishment vile enough that she could think of to . . . Her thoughts were interrupted by the opening of the door.

A petite brown-haired woman stood there, a welcoming smile lighting her face when she recognized her brother's familiar features. "Cole!" she exclaimed, rushing forward to hug him, "I wasn't expecting you."

"Abby, this is my wife, Elizabeth." The words were

cold, flat, utterly devoid of any feeling.

Abby's eyes widened momentarily as they gazed upon the woman at Cole's side. A smile spread across her face, becoming every bit as welcoming as the one she had bestowed upon Cole. She came forward, throwing her arms around Elizabeth. "Welcome to Rancho del Oro, Elizabeth. I'm so happy to meet you at last," she said, kissing her cheek.

Elizabeth returned the greeting, surprised by the effusive welcome she had received from Cole's sister. Judging from the look of annoyance on Cole's face, he was just as surprised that his sister would greet "the enemy" with open arms.

Abby directed her attention back to her brother once again. "I'm so relieved to see your leg has healed properly," she said, noting that Cole walked unassisted without a cane.

"It's healing," he said. No thanks to Elizabeth, he added bitterly to himself.

"Let's go into the parlor where we'll be more comfortable," Abby suggested. "Cole! Where are your manners? Take Elizabeth's cloak and get her a glass of wine. She looks exhausted."

Smiling warmly at Abby, Elizabeth gave Cole a tight-lipped smirk. "Yes, dear. Would you mind? I'm really quite worn out." Turning on her heel, she followed Abby into the parlor, observing her sister-in-law's uneven gait.

A moment later Cole entered, carrying a tray with three glasses and a decanter of dark red burgundy. He practically dropped it onto the table, almost spilling the wine in the process.

"Do be careful, Cole," Abby admonished. "That's the only heirloom of mother's that I possess." She ran her hand reverently over the mahogany tea table.

Elizabeth almost laughed aloud at the contrite expression on Cole's face. She remembered what her father had said about Cole doting on his older sister; it looked as if Abby had him firmly wrapped around her little finger. She felt a moment's jealousy at Abby's enviable position.

Observing the two siblings together, she could certainly see a definite family resemblance. They both possessed the same strong chin, the same full lips, their smiles evoking an identical set of dimples on either side of their mouths.

But not everything about them was the same. Where Abby's hair was a deep, rich brown, almost a chestnut color, Cole's was as black as Satan's heart. His eyes were the cold, forbidding gray of gunmetal, while Abby's were the warm brown of freshly grated nutmeg.

While Abby informed her brother about what had been going on at the ranch during his absence, Elizabeth took the time to familiarize herself with the layout of the room.

A huge adobe fireplace covered the wall at the far end of the parlor. There was a comfortable-looking sofa, covered in deep green velvet, sitting directly in front of the window, with a red crocheted afghan lying across its back. Most of the furnishings were rugged-looking walnut pieces. The occasional chairs, which were placed in various locations about the large room, were covered in red and green leather. There were two red gingham wing chairs flanking either side of the fireplace.

All about the room were needlepoint pillows, braided rugs, and cross-stitched pictures, adding warmth and color to the surroundings. If Abby was the creator of these works, she exhibited a great deal of talent,

202

Elizabeth thought, asking, "Are you responsible for the lovely needlework displayed here?"

Smiling, Abby nodded. "I'm afraid that it's all over the house. I get a bit carried away at times. Feel free to remove anything you don't like. You're the mistress here now."

"Oh, no!" Elizabeth said, shaking her head emphatically. "I wouldn't dream of it. Everything looks perfect. And as for being mistress . . . well, I'm afraid I don't know too much about running a household."

"That's right," Cole sneered. "Elizabeth has never dirtied her hands doing common labor like the rest of us. She's used to being waited on hand and foot."

Observing the stricken look on her sister-in-law's face, Abby's lips thinned. "Cole, why don't you go and see what's taking Consuelo so long with dinner, while I show Elizabeth up to your room."

"She won't be staying in my room," Cole replied. "Put her in the adjoining one."

Elizabeth's cheeks reddened. How could he humiliate her this way in front of his sister? she thought, blinking back the tears that suddenly surfaced.

Flashing her brother a heated glare, Abby said, "Come along, Elizabeth. You'll much prefer the room that I'm going to put you in. It smells much better than the one Cole uses," she said, pleased by her brother's enraged look.

Bless you, Abby, Elizabeth thought as she followed the tiny woman down the hall. She noted that Abby's limp had become more pronounced, her steps slow and uneven, and wondered if perhaps it became that way whenever she was angry.

"Here we are, Beth," Abby said, throwing open the

203

door. "May I call you Beth? Elizabeth seems so formal."

"Of course, I'd be honored. I've never had a nickname before, except for the one Cole uses sometimes."

"What's that?" Abby asked, pulling back the bed covers.

Elizabeth felt her cheeks warm. "Sunshine," she replied softly.

Abigail's eyebrows rose. "Close the door and come sit down here on the bed next to me. I've always wanted a sister, you know. I hope we can become good friends," she said, patting the space next to her.

"I think we already have," Elizabeth replied, sitting down next to her.

"Tell me, Beth, why is Cole so angry with you? Didn't you resolve the problems about the letter when he was back in New York?"

At Elizabeth's puzzled expression, Abby became so furious she could barely speak. "Cole didn't tell you about the letter? Didn't give you a chance to explain?"

"What letter? I'm afraid I don't know what you're talking about."

"Damn his stubborn hide! The least I expected was that Cole would have given you a chance to explain your side of the story concerning your abduction."

"Please," Elizabeth beseeched, "tell me about this letter that you keep referring to."

Abby sighed deeply. "The day you were abducted, Cole was brought back to the ranch gravely ill."

"I thought he was dead," Elizabeth interrupted, covering her face. "I saw him hit the tree."

Patting her hand, Abigail continued. "Cole's too mean to die. Anyway, I found a letter inside the pocket of his coat . . . a letter from you."

The wet lashes shadowing Elizabeth's cheeks flew up. "But I didn't write any letter!"

"That's what Jon kept insisting. I'm afraid even I was skeptical at first."

"What did the letter say?"

"That your marriage was a mistake. That you were returning to New York to the life that you missed."

Elizabeth blanched. "Grandfather," she said, shaking her head sadly.

"Jon said that, also. He said your grandfather was probably behind everything. Cole didn't believe him. He still thinks you wrote that letter."

"How could he? After our wedding night? After everything we—?" She stopped, too embarrassed to go on. All the pieces of Cole's puzzling attitude suddenly fit together. Observing the compassion in Abigail's eyes, she felt comforted that someone believed her.

"It gets worse, I'm afraid," Elizabeth confided. She went on to explain about her temporary amnesia and how the shock of seeing Cole alive had triggered her memory to return.

"If I know my brother, he doesn't believe any part of your story. He's a lawyer, through and through. Give him facts not supposition, he always rants."

"I believe you're right," Elizabeth said, biting her lower lip. "His attitude toward me changed the moment we stepped off the train in San Jose."

Abigail rose, helping Elizabeth to her feet. "Don't worry about it. We have plenty of time to sort everything out. In the meantime, you need to freshen up. There's the bathing chamber that connects your room to Cole's." She pointed to the door to her right, a mischievous glint coming into her eyes. "I need to check on dinner; come down when you're ready."

"Abby," Elizabeth called out, "thank you."

Abby winked, tossing her a smile. "There's more than one way to skin a cat."

Elizabeth stared at the door, a bemused expression on her face. Now that she had Abby on her side, things didn't seem quite so hopeless. "Watch out, Cole," she said, "I'm sharpening my knife."

Chapter Eighteen

Taking a deep breath as she stood in the arched doorway of the dining room, Elizabeth braced herself for the evening ahead. Abby and Cole were already seated at the long rectangular table. They looked up when she entered, their faces a study in contrast: Abby's smile was reassuring, Cole's expression cold and forbidding.

Thank goodness she had shed her mourning attire for something a little more feminine. The blue silk gown she wore emphasized the fullness of her breasts, making her feel a little more confident about herself. She didn't miss the furtive glances Cole aimed at her cleavage as he pulled the chair out for her. Maybe he wasn't quite as immune to her charms as he pretended to be, she thought smugly.

"You look lovely tonight, Beth. Doesn't she, Cole?" Abby prodded.

"Elizabeth always looks lovely," he said, gulping down his glass of wine.

Elizabeth smiled, about to offer her thanks, when Cole's next sentence lodged the words in her throat.

"It's her job to be beautiful. It's what she's been groomed for. Did you know the New York newspapers called her 'The Gilded Lily'? An apt description, wouldn't you say? Looks always were deceiving."

Elizabeth's face whitened.

Abby shot Cole a baleful glance. "Please excuse my brother tonight, Beth. He's had too much to drink."

"I'm just getting started, sister dear. I have good cause to celebrate. It's not every day a husband gets his wife back from the clutches of death. Isn't that right, Elizabeth?"

"If you say so," Elizabeth murmured, unwilling to be drawn into the fight Cole was obviously itching for.

"Consuelo," Abby called out, "serve the meal now, *por favor.*"

"*Sí, Señorita* Abby," Consuelo replied, bustling into the dining room carrying a tray burdened with steaming bowls of delicious-smelling food. It was quite obvious from Consuelo's quick response that the inquisitive cook had been eavesdropping on the conversation going on in the dining room.

"Elizabeth, this is our cook, confidante, and most important member of our family, Consuelo Gonzales," Abby said.

Noting the warm, friendly smile covering the older woman's face, Elizabeth heaved a sigh of relief. It seemed not all the members of Cole's family were as rude as he.

The introductions made, Elizabeth, who hadn't realized how hungry she was, attacked the impressive array of Mexican delicacies that Consuelo had laid out before them.

The chicken enchiladas were delectable, filled with lots of meat and cheese. They were accompanied by bowls

208

of rice, refried beans, and a stack of flour tortillas.

"I didn't think to ask if you liked Mexican food, Beth. I hope everything is to your liking," Abby said.

Swallowing a mouthful of chicken and washing it down with the sangria, Elizabeth replied, "I love it. I've never tasted anything quite so exotic before."

"Then you must try one of Consuelo's jalapeño chilies," Cole suggested. "She gets them from her sister in Mexico."

"I don't think that would be a good idea, Cole," Abby said, flashing her brother a warning look. "You know Beth isn't used to this type of food yet."

"Well, of course, if she's too delicate to eat the food we serve here, far be it from me to insist." He leaned back in his chair.

The challenge was too blatant to resist. Flashing Cole a confident smile, Elizabeth replied, "I'd love to try one."

Handing her the plate of ominous-looking green peppers, Cole said, "Be my guest."

Picking up one of the smaller-sized ones, Elizabeth bit into the dark, shiny plant. Immediately, her eyes filled with tears, her throat burning as if it were on fire. She gagged, covering her mouth, fearful that she would spit the offending object out all over the table. Grabbing for the water, she gulped it down in huge quantities.

"Are you all right?" Abby asked, a horrified expression on her face. She came around the table, patting Elizabeth gently on the back.

Nodding, Elizabeth looked up to find Cole doubled over with laughter. Her insides burned, but this time it wasn't the pepper that produced the affliction. After a few moments the rawness left her throat, and she was able to breathe normally again.

Taking a sip of wine punch, Elizabeth resumed eating, ignoring Cole's amused smile. "My, that certainly was an interesting experience," she said, barely above a whisper.

"Care for another?" he offered, a devilish grin on his face.

"Thank you, no. I think I have had quite enough," she replied. Particularly of you, she added silently.

They sat at the table for another hour, conversing on topics that Abigail chose for their noncontroversial subject matter—the weather, the cattle market, crime in the city. Occasionally, Cole would try to interrupt with a snide remark about his trip to New York or Elizabeth's wealth, but he was unsuccessful in provoking another confrontation.

At his failure to instigate another fight, Cole became sullen and withdrawn, drinking glass after glass of wine until he became thoroughly intoxicated.

Fatigued from her trip, as well as from the mental and verbal sparring she'd been engaging in with Cole all evening, Elizabeth decided that it was time to retire. Excusing herself, she pushed back her chair, quite surprised when Cole rose at the same time she did.

"I'll see you to your room," he said, his speech thick, his words slurred by the effects of the alcohol.

She felt a moment of panic before replying, "I'm sure I can find my own way, but thank you."

"I said, I will see you to your room." He grabbed her arm.

"Cole," Abigail shouted, "leave Elizabeth alone! You're drunk. Take your hands off of her."

Abigail made a move toward her brother, but Elizabeth, fearing an argument was forthcoming between the two, motioned her back. "It's all right, Abby. I can

210

handle this."

"You're sure?"

The look of concern on Abigail's face was touching, but this was her battle—hers and Cole's. Elizabeth didn't want to ruin a brother and sister relationship over it. She nodded.

Cole gave his wife a lopsided grin, his dimples making him look quite boyish and not as threatening. "Come along, Elizabesh," he slurred, positioning his arm around her shoulders, propelling her through the dimly lit corridor.

They made it to her room without mishap, although the burden of supporting Cole's weight created an ache right in the middle of her back between her shoulder blades. Pausing outside the door, she freed her hand from around Cole's waist to open the door. Light poured into the hall from the oil lamp she had left burning.

Dragging Cole over to the bed, she leaned him up against the brass bedpost. "There," she sighed, taking a deep breath. He was certainly heavier than he looked.

"Elizabeth, give me a kiss," he pleaded, grabbing onto her waist.

Elizabeth's eyes rounded, shocked to hear Cole utter the words she secretly longed for. She knew that if he had been sober, he never would have said such a thing. Suddenly, a delicious, absolutely wicked idea came to mind. She smiled at the fiendishness of it. Revenge was going to be sweet.

Wrapping her arms around Cole's waist, she kissed him passionately, guiding him over to the mattress. It took only a gentle nudge on her part to push him backward onto the bed. Cole returned her kiss with an ardor that surprised her. She had thought his lust for her spent,

211

but apparently, there was still some held in reserve.

They kissed for several minutes until Cole's lips grew slack, his arms falling away from her waist. Raising her head, she stared into the unconscious face of the man she loved. Cole had passed out. Brushing back the hair that had fallen over his brow, she gave thanks that he had cooperated so willingly in her plan for revenge.

Some revenge, she thought, aggravated with the whole turn of events. She hadn't counted on becoming so aroused by Cole's kisses, then being left to pass the night frustrated and unfulfilled. Sighing deeply, she shook her head.

Rising from the bed, she tugged off his boots, unbuttoning his pants. Lifting him up, she slid the tight Levi's off. She stared at his underclothing, unsure if she could go through with it. It seemed sordid somehow, as if she were taking advantage of him. Well, it couldn't be helped. Cole had certainly asked for it after that rotten trick he had pulled with the pepper. She started to unbutton his shirt.

She had saved this piece of clothing for last. She unbuttoned it, one button at a time, letting her eyes roam over his virile physique. Her breath caught in her throat. The sight of Cole's muscular chest had always been wildly erotic to her. Releasing the last button, she spread the calico material open, her eyes landing on a shiny object nestled at the base of his throat. Picking it up, she was shocked to discover her wedding ring suspended from the gold chain. Where had he found it? And why did he wear it around his neck? Tears filled her eyes as she remembered back to their wedding day, when he had placed the ring on her finger. "Oh, Cole," she cried, "why did my grandfather have to spoil everything?"

Staring at the ring, a tiny spark of hope ignited in her breast. Perhaps Cole really did care for her. Why else would he wear her ring so close to his heart?

Eyeing the totally naked body before her, Elizabeth wiped her eyes with the corner of the bed sheet. Climbing on top of the mattress, she positioned her hands under Cole's armpits, pulling him up until his head rested on the pillow. Wrenching the covers out from under him, she laid him on the smooth white sheets, drawing the comforter up around him. That done, she undressed herself.

Lying naked next to Cole evoked poignant memories of their wedding night. Their union had been so perfect, so fulfilling. Turning on her side, she caressed Cole's chest, loving the way the soft hair felt beneath her fingertips. Her heart pounded; an uncomfortable ache formed between her thighs. Quickly, she pulled her hand away. Lying back down, she closed her eyes; she needed to rest. Tomorrow morning when Cole awoke, she would need all her wits about her.

As the first light of dawn crept in through the window, Elizabeth met it with eyes heavy from lack of sleep. She had been awake all night, Cole's arms wrapped around her like a boa constrictor. She was still firmly enveloped within his embrace, his warm breath tickling her nose. She heaved a sigh. Which one of them was going to suffer the most over her impulsive little scheme? she wondered.

Cole came awake slowly, his head pounding ferociously. Opening his eyes, he blinked several times at the sight of Elizabeth smiling down at him. Surely, he was dreaming. She was caressing his chest with her fingertips, running her lips over his stomach and neck. Christ! What had happened last night? He couldn't remember a damned thing after all the wine he had drunk.

"Good morning," she whispered huskily, nibbling on his nipples. "Did you sleep well?"

Elizabeth wore the satisfied look of a woman who had been thoroughly loved. He swallowed nervously. He couldn't let her know that he remembered nothing. She would think he was a drunken fool. Smiling sheepishly, he was unable to stop the flush creeping over his face.

Elizabeth could hardly repress her elation at the sight of Cole's ajbect misery. He was suffering; she was certain of it. And she was loving every minute of it. "You were wonderful last night, so forceful, so insatiable." She kissed his chin, running her tongue over his lower lip.

He stiffened, extricating himself from her embrace. Brushing back the hair that fell across his brow, he said, "I didn't hurt you, did I? I had a little too much to drink last night." There was genuine concern in his eyes.

Elizabeth stretched in an exaggerated show of contentment. Throwing her arms back, she thrust her breasts impudently in Cole's face. "I must admit, you were very masterful. I never would have dreamed of doing some of the things—" She stopped, covering her mouth in a maidenly show of embarrassment.

Cole could scarce take his eyes off the two protruding nipples moving in dangerous proximity to his lips. He threw back the covers, jumping out of bed as if the curse of Satan were at his heels.

"Where are you going?" Elizabeth asked, sticking out her lower lip. "You promised you were going to show me something you had learned in Chinatown. Did you forget?"

Cole's face turned as red as a man who had just consumed a bowl full of Consuelo's jalapeños. He made a strangling sound, heading for the bathing room door. "I just remembered an important appointment I have in San Francisco. I need to get dressed."

"But, Cole," Elizabeth wailed, "how can you leave me after everything that happened last night?"

"Christ!" he cursed, slamming his foot into the door he had neglected to open.

Covering her mouth, Elizabeth tried to hold back the laughter that was bubbling to the surface.

"I will see you at breakfast, Elizabeth." With that, he stormed out of the room, slamming the door behind him.

Staring at the door, Elizabeth burst into hysterical laughter, tears running down her cheeks as she watched the comical departure of her husband. Pulling the pillow over her face, she tried to muffle the sound.

It was a much different Cole that Elizabeth was faced with at breakfast an hour later. Gone was the befuddled buffoon of early this morning, replaced by the stern visage of the lawyer she remembered only too well. Dressed neatly in a suit of blue serge, he looked quite handsome despite the scowl on his face.

They sat alone at opposite ends of the long oak table. Sipping slowly on her chocolate, Elizabeth tried to remain calm and collected while she waited for Cole to speak.

Staring at Elizabeth's reserved demeanor, Cole couldn't believe that the calm creature before him was the same wildly enticing siren of only an hour ago. Her hair was pulled back in a tight knot, secured at the base of her neck by a tortoiseshell comb. Her turquoise dress, with its white lace collar and long sleeves, was demure in the extreme. She looked every bit as prim and proper as a Sunday school teacher as she sat sipping her chocolate.

Her lips touched the rim of the cup, and he could clearly recall those same lips doing such tantalizing things to his chest and neck. Unconsciously, his hand rose to his throat. The ring. She must have noticed her wedding ring. Why hadn't she said anything about it? he wondered.

Disgusted at the direction his thoughts were taking, he banged the table in anger, pleased at the sight of Elizabeth leaping up from her chair in fright.

"Is something the matter?" she asked, her blue eyes widening in alarm.

Tipping his chair back, Cole rested his locked fingers across his stomach. "That depends on your point of view, I guess," he replied, a nasty smirk on his lips. "Nothing's the matter as far as I'm concerned. However, you may have a different opinion once I explain what is going to be expected of you from now on."

Dropping back down in her chair, a look of dismay written over her face, she replied, "I don't understand." A sinking feeling formed in the pit of her stomach. She didn't like the self-satisfied grin covering Cole's face as he contemplated her fate.

"I have come to a few decisions concerning our marriage."

Panic welled up inside of her. Cole was going to divorce her. Please God! Let it be anything but that, she prayed silently.

"Since you are no longer the reigning queen of New

York society, I think it's time you came down off your throne."

She stiffened, her eyes flashing fire. "I've never considered myself a queen."

Ignoring her objection, Cole continued as if she hadn't spoken. "As the wife of a rancher, I believe it is time that you assume the duties befitting your new station in life. From here on out, you will become Mrs. Cole MacAlister and all that the name implies."

Elizabeth's heart lightened. Cole was suggesting a real marriage. He wanted her to become a real wife. Her joy was boundless, and she flashed him a devastating smile.

Noting Elizabeth's happiness, Cole frowned. "I think you misunderstand me, Elizabeth. It is not my intention to have a so-called traditional marriage. If last night led you to believe that, then I'm sorry. Last night should never have happened; it was a regrettable mistake. One that I must apologize for due to my intoxicated state."

Elizabeth felt the burning indignation blanketing her cheeks. Clenching her hands tightly in her lap, she tried desperately to keep her temper in check. She would not give Cole the satisfaction of knowing how his words hurt and angered her. "A regrettable mistake," he had said. Why, of all the pompous, conceited . . . Oooh! She would love to tell him exactly what had happened last night, but instead, she merely nodded.

"As the new mistress of Rancho del Oro, you will begin immediately to learn all there is to know about running this ranch."

Elizabeth's mouth dropped open; she said nothing.

"Starting today, you will be instructed by Consuelo and Abigail in the proper execution of the household tasks. You will learn to cook, clean, make soap, manage a household budget, and whatever else they see fit to teach you. Do you understand?"

Elizabeth's eyes hardened into blue sapphires. Oh, she understood only too well. What a fitting revenge he had thought of for a wife he believed had betrayed him. Displaying none of the indignation his words had instilled, she bestowed a pleasant smile upon him. "Perfectly."

Cole was taken aback at how well Elizabeth had accepted his dictates. He had expected a full-fledged fight or at least an argument from her.

"I will be leaving today for San Francisco. I have neglected my law practice too long as it is. You will have one week to learn the necessary duties of running the household. After that, you will be, more or less, on your own. Consuelo and her husband will be traveling to Mexico to visit her sister. You will be required to take over the kitchen as well as the keeping of the house."

"One week!" Elizabeth exclaimed, rising from her chair, bracing her hands on the table. "How am I to learn everything there is to know in one week? I have never been instructed in domestic labors before."

"Perhaps you should have paid more attention to what Mrs. Baxter was doing all those years, instead of traipsing around New York going to parties and indulging yourself in purposeless pursuits," Cole replied, a cynical twist to his lips.

"How dare you! You conceited, ill-bred bastard!" she shouted.

"I assure you, my parentage is intact." His smile was feral.

"Whatever is going on here?" Abigail demanded, entering the room. "I can hear the two of you clear out by

218

the corrals." She removed her riding gloves, throwing them on the table. Smoothing down her skirt, which was damp with perspiration from her early morning ride, she impaled her brother with hard brown eyes. "Cole, what is the meaning of this?"

"Why don't you ask Elizabeth? I really have to leave," he replied, smiling smugly. "Pedro is driving me to San Jose to catch the train."

Both women stood, mouths agape, as Cole picked up the valise resting inconspicuously by the front door and exited the house.

"You . . . cur," Elizabeth cried, barely above a whisper. "I'll see you in hell for this."

Chapter Nineteen

Hell would have been a picnic compared to what she had endured these past two days, Elizabeth thought, tears running down her cheeks as she chopped the onions into tiny little pieces. Consuelo was very particular about how the onions should look that went into her pot of chili.

"Be sure to cut them small, *Señora* Beth. We must get all the flavor out of them. *Comprendo?*"

"*Sí*, Consuelo," she said, wiping her eyes with the back of her sleeve. Not only was she starting to look like a common laborer, but she was also starting to talk like one. It was difficult not to use the few words of Spanish that had already slipped into her vocabulary.

"You are a good girl. *Señor* Mac will be very proud of you."

"Ha! I don't care what that insensitive clod thinks of me. I should have stayed in New York. I never should have come here. I hate him. I—" The tears falling onto the table were not caused by the onions this time.

Setting down the big wooden spoon she was using to stir the chili, Consuelo crossed to where Elizabeth stood. Putting her ample arms around the girl's shoulder, she said, "You have a lot of . . . how do they say . . . spirit. *Sí*, spirit. You will not give up until you learn what there is to know. Am I right?"

Smiling tremulously, Elizabeth nodded.

"*Bueno.* You will show *Señor* Mac what you are made of. He think you are a spoiled good-for-nothing, but you will show him he is wrong."

"Yes," Elizabeth replied, squaring her chin. "I will show him."

Lying down in the tub of hot water, Elizabeth let the soothing warmth seep into her tired muscles. God! She had never realized how backbreaking housework could be. Lifting her leg, she sponged her calf with the soft white cloth. Every muscle in her body ached.

She had spent the day lifting heavy mattresses to make the beds and had helped Consuelo in the kitchen with the chili and the bread baking. Her lovely nails were torn and ragged from weeding the flower beds; she stared at the jagged edges in disgust.

She was doing all the things she had seen Violet and Mrs. Thomas do a hundred times, the things she had taken for granted the past twenty years. This must be God's way of punishing her, she thought dejectedly.

Cole was right. She had indulged herself in purposeless pursuits. Damn him! She slapped at the water, wishing it were his head. Well, she would show him. She was a Worthington, and Worthingtons didn't back down from a challenge. She had enough of her grandfather's blood in her veins to make her as inexhaustible and determined as she needed to be.

After their evening meal, Elizabeth and Abigail sat on the floor in front of the fire and sewed on the patchwork quilt that Abigail was determined Elizabeth was going to learn how to make.

"Abigail?"

"Yes," Abby replied, biting off the thread from the square she had just stitched.

"Why is it that you've never married?" Noting the stricken expression on her sister-in-law's face, Elizabeth wished she had kept her big mouth shut. "Never mind," she added quickly. "You don't have to tell me."

Abby's eyes filled with sadness; her smile was melancholy. "That's all right. I don't mind telling you." Setting down her sewing, she stared into the flames of the fire. "I fell in love with a man who didn't feel the same way about me. I've never been able to forget him. I've loved him for the past twenty years, and I'll probably go on loving him for the rest of my life."

"But how do you know he doesn't love you? Perhaps you have misjudged him."

"No . . . I haven't misjudged him. He still treats me like the same child I was when he found me at the age of fifteen."

Her eyes rounding, Elizabeth gasped, covering her mouth with her hand. "You're in love with my father, aren't you?"

A single tear trickled down Abigail's face. "I hope you don't hate me."

"Hate you!" Elizabeth said, her face breaking into a smile. "Don't be a ninny. I think it's wonderful. My father deserves someone like you to love him. He's a fine man. I think he would make you an excellent husband."

Abigail's face paled. "Elizabeth, you don't understand. Jon doesn't love me. He cares for me as a father would a child, but he doesn't love me as a man should love a woman."

Throwing down her sewing, Elizabeth put her arms around Abigail's waist. "I may not know much about sewing or cooking or the proper way to plant flowers, but I do know a little bit about men. They're silly, egotistical creatures who crave attention and adoration. If you want to capture my father's interest as a man, you have to start acting like a woman around him."

Blushing profusely, Abigail shook her head. "I couldn't. I wouldn't know what to do. And besides, what man wants a woman who is crippled?"

"Bah! Don't hide behind your lameness. It's hardly noticeable."

Abby smiled, recalling the same exact words Elizabeth's father had said to her. "You're more like your father than you realize."

"Well, if that's true, then it won't take any time at all for Jonathan Forrester to fall in love with you," Elizabeth replied, hugging Abby. "I love you, and it only took me a few days."

"Do you really think he could?"

Abigail's wistful expression touched Elizabeth's heart. "Do you believe in destiny?" Elizabeth asked.

"I guess so. I never really thought about it."

"I'm going to tell you a story about how fate has touched my life. After I'm finished, we are going to put our heads together and find a way to help each other. I'm going to help you ensnare my unsuspecting father, and you, in turn, are going to help me enslave your undeserving brother."

Applying the last coat of beeswax on the dining room table, Elizabeth looked up at the sound of the door knocker. She wondered who it could be. Cole wasn't due home until tomorrow.

Wiping her hands on her apron, she smoothed the blue calico dress, which Abby had sewn for her, and hurried to open the door. "I'll get it, Consuelo," she called out, knowing the housekeeper was in the kitchen up to her elbows in flour tortillas.

Opening the door, her mouth fell open at the sight of Amber Montoya, accompanied by a handsome, dark-haired gentleman she had never seen before.

"Elizabeth? Is that you?" Amber asked, scrutinizing the younger woman's features.

Elizabeth clamped her mouth shut. She could feel the beginning of a blush creeping up her neck and face. "I'm so sorry. Please come in. How rude you must think me."

Amber swept in, looking regal in a rose velvet riding costume. "May I introduce my cousin, Rodrigo Montoya."

Bowing, the raven-haired man took Elizabeth's soiled hand, pressing it to his lips. "Your beauty can only be compared to the setting of the sun or the brilliance of the dew upon the grass."

"Thank—thank you," Elizabeth stammered, casting Amber an embarrassed smile at her cousin's effusive comment.

Amber snorted, jabbing her cousin in the side with her elbow. "Really, Rod! The dew upon the grass! Don't you think that's a bit much?" She threw back her head and laughed that deep, throaty laugh. "Please forgive my cousin, Elizabeth. He gets a bit carried away at times."

Elizabeth smiled inwardly as Rodrigo shot Amber an affronted look. "Won't you have a seat? I'll have Consuelo bring some refreshments," she said.

Shaking her head, Amber replied, "We can only stay a moment. I came to invite you and Cole to a fiesta I am planning in two weeks time. It will be a wonderful opportunity for you to meet all of your neighbors."

Elizabeth's face lit up with pleasure. "That sounds lovely. Of course, I shall have to check with Cole, but I'm certain he'll be delighted to attend."

"I, of course, will be expecting to dance with you," Rodrigo said, clicking his heels together and smoothing down his black mustache.

The corners of Elizabeth's mouth tipped up into a smile at Rodrigo's pompous behavior. He was handsomely dressed in tight-fitting black pants, a white shirt, and a short black jacket that reached only to his waist, looking very much like a Spanish matador.

Dancing with Rodrigo at Amber's fiesta could prove to be very useful, especially if Cole were to become jealous. "I would be delighted to save a dance for you, *Señor* Montoya."

"Please, you must call me Rod; I insist."

"Very well . . . Rod."

Amber flashed her cousin an exasperated look. "Elizabeth, if you don't mind me asking, why is it that you are dressed like a servant? Are you short of help? I can send someone over if you are."

225

A faint blush stole over Elizabeth's cheeks. What could she say to Cole's former mistress? That her over-bearing, brute of a husband was taking out his revenge on her? That her sister-in-law, who did not want her to ruin all of her beautiful clothes, had sewn some dresses for her?

"Forgive my appearance," she finally replied, fidgeting self-consciously with the folds of her apron. "I was just helping out with some of the chores. I thought I should learn some of the household duties before Consuelo leaves to visit her sister. I wouldn't want Abby to shoulder all the responsibility by herself."

"How very kind of you," Amber said, pulling on her riding gloves. "Speaking of Abby, where is she? I didn't see her when I rode up."

"Abigail went into Santa Clara with Pedro. She's picking up supplies." A calculating look entered Elizabeth's eyes. "By the way, do you mind if we bring Abigail and my father along to the fiesta? Neither of them gets out too often. I think it might be good for them to socialize."

"But of course!" Amber replied, clapping her hands. "The more the merrier, as the saying goes. But do you think Abby will come? You know how self-conscious she is of her leg."

"Leave Abigail to me. I believe I will be able to convince her."

"*Bueno.* Now we must go, my friend. It was good to see you again. Give my regards to Abigail and Cole. I will see all of you on the first of November. *Hasta la vista.*" Lifting her skirt, she swept out the door.

Bowing, Rodrigo placed another kiss on Elizabeth's hand before he exited the room. Smiling, she watched the eccentric couple depart. The Montoyas certainly were a flamboyant family, she thought.

Adjusting the leather saddlebags over his shoulder, which contained many hours' worth of work that he needed to finish, Cole bid Pedro good night and exited the barn, making his way up to the house. He was tired, having just spent an exhausting week catching up on his caseload. All he wanted to do was soak in a nice hot tub, eat a good meal, and hit the sack.

Reclining in the tub after an exhausting day of canning applesauce, Elizabeth thought back to the piles of apples she had peeled and chopped. Ugh! She screwed up her face in disgust. If she never saw another apple again it wouldn't bother her in the least.

Rising from the tub, she leaned over to reach for a towel, when the bathroom door slammed open with a resounding thud. Her eyes widened, her mouth dropping open at the sight of Cole standing in the doorway. By the shocked expression on his face, she knew he hadn't expected to find her in here.

She swallowed her surprise and smiled. "Hello," she said.

Cole stared, transfixed, his eyes glazing over as they raked Elizabeth's body, devouring her naked flesh while she stood proudly before him. Droplets of water clung to her skin, glistening in the lamplight. Her hair was damp, hanging in golden strands to her waist. Beads of moisture covered her breasts. Her nipples, wet and puckered, protruded enticingly.

He lowered his eyes to the yellow nest of curls springing forth between her legs. He felt himself harden.

As if pulled by an invisible force, he stepped forward, reaching out to touch the curly mound. His fingers tingled in anticipation and desire.

Hearing Elizabeth's soft gasp, he stopped, remembering how it was between them. He breathed deeply, trying to still the throbbing in his loins. "I'm sorry to have intruded. Pedro told me you were canning apples."

Elizabeth smiled, taking the towel from the rack and wrapping it around herself in a seductive motion. "Welcome home. Did you just arrive?" Picking up another towel, she proceeded to wipe her hair with it.

"Yes," Cole replied absently, watching Elizabeth's breasts jiggle beneath the damp towel as she vigorously dried her hair.

"Did you see my father?" she asked, knowing Cole's eyes followed her every movement. It was such fun to torment him. She hadn't missed the hardened bulge beneath his tight-fitting pants. It was a small price he had to pay for all the torture she had endured this past week. She took a deep breath, expanding her chest, the movement causing the towel to fall to the floor.

Their eyes met and held. Hers glittered like brilliant blue sapphires; Cole's sparked intense as a silver flash of lightning. They bent over simultaneously to retrieve the fallen towel. She heard his sharp intake of breath as his mouth came in close proximity to her breast. She rose; he followed.

"I'll leave the bathing room for your use," she said, turning to leave.

"Elizabeth," Cole called out.

His voice had a husky quality to it, sending shivers up her spine. It was like warm brandy heating her blood to liquid fire. Her heart beat rapidly, her nipples aching with unfulfilled desire. "Yes," she replied, trying to act nonchalant.

"You forgot your brush."

His hand accidentally brushed hers, sending bolts of charged current running through her veins.

"You're very beautiful."

Her smile never reached her eyes. "It's what I was groomed for, remember?" she said, slamming the door in his face.

Staring at the door, Cole shook his head, wondering, not for the first time, how he was going to survive marriage to such an exasperating, provocative woman.

It was the morning of Consuelo's departure and Elizabeth had been up since dawn, assisting both Consuelo and Abby with the last minute preparations for the journey to Mexico. They were in the kitchen packing the wicker basket that the Gonzaleses would take with them.

"You are certain you will be able to manage without me?" Consuelo asked, looking skeptically at the two young women.

"*Sí, mi madre*," Abby said, giving Consuelo a hug. "You are not to worry about us. Go and have a nice visit with Carmen. We will be fine. Isn't that right, Beth?"

Smiling to reassure Consuelo as well as herself, Elizabeth nodded. "We will be just fine. Abby and I have everything under control." She threw Abby a conspiratorial wink.

"*Madre de Dios!* You two are up to something," Consuelo moaned, slapping her forehead and sighing in exasperation.

"Look!" Abby exclaimed, pointing out the window.

"There is Pedro with the buckboard." She gave Consuelo a naughty smile.

"*Si.* I will go, but I will be back. And I expect to find my house in order when I return." She gave each girl a hug and hurried out to meet her husband.

"I think Consuelo suspects something," Elizabeth said, seating herself at the kitchen table. She poured two cups of chocolate, sliding one over to Abby, who was seated across from her.

"She won't say anything, and by the time she returns, everything should be running smoothly."

"Who knows," Elizabeth teased, "she may have a wedding to prepare when she gets back."

"Elizabeth!" Abby said, her face as red as the gingham tablecloth.

Both girls were laughing so hard they did not hear the kitchen door open.

"Did I hear someone say something about a wedding?" Cole asked, strolling into the room. "Is some other unsuspecting sucker going to be encased in the velvet trap?"

Jumping up, Elizabeth turned to face him. With her hands on her hips and a mutinous expression on her face, she looked ready to march into battle. "You certainly didn't seem to mind the 'velvet trap,' as you so aptly call it, on several occasions that I can distinctly remember." At the sound of Abby's gasp, her face reddened; she was mortified that she had said such a vulgar thing in front of Cole's sister.

Cole stared coldly at his wife, his face a mask of granite. "Where is my breakfast?" he bellowed.

Taking a deep breath, Elizabeth turned toward the

230

cookstove, away from Cole's menacing stare. "If you care to have a seat in the dining room, I'll bring it right out." He stormed from the room, slamming the door behind him.

A muffled sound caught her attention. Turning, she found Abigail sitting at the table with her hand over her mouth, tears streaming down her face. Rushing over to her, she patted the distraught woman gently on the back. "I'm sorry if I offended you. Please forgive me."

At the sight of Elizabeth's contrite expression, Abby released the laughter she had been holding. Wiping her eyes on her napkin, she tried to compose herself. "You were wonderful, Beth."

An expression of chagrin crossed over Elizabeth's face. "I've probably only made things worse with my big mouth."

"Oh, pooh! Cole deserved it. It serves him right for butting into our conversation."

"Abby," Elizabeth said, her forehead creased in worry, "I don't want my problems with Cole to come between the two of you."

Abby brushed the comment off with a wave of her hand. "Don't be silly. I love Cole; nothing could ever come between us. But that doesn't mean I don't wish to take him down a few pegs. He'll be a better person for it; you'll see."

Observing Cole's scowling face as she placed the hot-cakes in front of him, Elizabeth was not so sure that he was going to agree with his sister's confident opinion.

Taking her seat, she placed her napkin in her lap, waiting for Abby to offer a blessing. She would need help from above once her husband had a sample of her

231

cooking, she thought.

Peeking over the rim of her coffee cup, Elizabeth observed Cole trying to cut the hotcakes with his fork. The rubbery disks seemed to have a mind of their own as they bounced around on his plate. Finally, he managed to loosen a piece, shoving it into his mouth, then spitting it out into his napkin just as quickly as he had put it in.

"Good Christ! What the hell are these supposed to be?" Cole shouted, looking up at Elizabeth.

"What's the matter? Don't you like them?" she asked, a wounded look on her face.

"Hell no! I don't like them. They're awful!"

Grabbing her napkin, Elizabeth covered her face. "I tried so hard," she sobbed, her voice muffled through the cloth. "You're just being mean." Jumping up, she ran for the safety of her room.

"Now look what you've done," Abby accused, pushing back her chair. "You can't expect Elizabeth's cooking to be as good as Consuelo's after only one week. I don't think you are being very nice at all." Rising, she exited the room, leaving Cole alone at the table.

Cole stared at the two empty chairs and then at the offensive concoction on his plate. He stabbed at them. The rubbery cakes closed in around the tines of his fork. Shaking his head in disgust, he pushed the plate away.

What had he done? His plan for revenge just might be the cause of his death due to starvation. How would he survive until Consuelo returned? he wondered.

Everything was a mess. Abby was mad at him; Elizabeth would probably never speak to him again. Why was his well-ordered life suddenly a shambles? Elizabeth . . . that's why, he told himself.

Well, he was stuck with her for now. He had better

232

make the best of it. Pushing himself away from the table, he vowed to keep his comments about Elizabeth's cooking to himself.

"Elizabeth," Cole shouted, barging into her bedroom two days later. "What has happened to my good white shirts? They have brown burns all over them." He held the shirt up for her inspection.

Setting her book down, Elizabeth turned to face her angry husband, smiling sweetly. "I'm terribly sorry. I haven't quite got the knack of using the iron yet. I'm sure in just a few more weeks, I'll be better."

"A few more weeks! How the hell am I supposed to greet my clients looking so ragged?"

"I've been trying, really I have," she said, tears brimming in her eyes.

Cole's expression softened. Walking over, he put his arm around her shoulder. "I know you have. You're doing pretty good, too. Why, that apricot pie you made the other night wasn't half bad."

Elizabeth smiled inwardly. It had been awful, and he knew it. How was she supposed to know that the dried apricots had to be soaked in water before being put into the crust? "It's kind of you to say so. Perhaps I'll bake you another since you liked it so much." She almost laughed at the horrified expression covering his face.

Patting his stomach, Cole replied, "I really should lay off the sweets for a while. I think I've been putting on a few pounds."

Elizabeth stared critically at him, nodding her head. "I do believe you're right." She patted his stomach, which was hard as a rock. "You are getting a little paunchy."

Rushing to the mirror, Cole examined his physique, turning this way and that to see what Elizabeth was talking about.

Elizabeth's heart ached as she watched her husband's antics. God, how she loved him. When was he going to realize how wrong he had been about her? How long did she have to go on playing his little game?

"Cole," Elizabeth said, "are you going to see my father today?"

"Yes. We're working on a case together. Why?" Shrugging into his shirt, he buttoned it up as he talked.

"I was wondering if you would invite him to come for dinner on Saturday. I've missed him."

"Dinner, huh?" A mischievous glint came into his eyes. "What a great idea. I think one of your dinners is a just reward for all of Jon's deeds," Cole said.

"You'll ask him, then?"

"Count on it," Cole replied, heading for the door. "Don't expect me home tonight; I'm staying overnight at the hotel."

At Cole's words, a warning bell sounded in Elizabeth's brain. "Why the hotel? Why aren't you staying with my father?"

"It's just business. I often stay at the Fairmont when I'm working."

"I see," Elizabeth said, biting her lower lip. And who will you be working with? she wondered. She wasn't innocent enough to think that a man with Cole's sexual prowess didn't crave the attentions of the opposite sex.

Following him to the door, she latched onto his arm. "I was hoping that you would give me a kiss before you leave."

"Elizabeth," Cole said, a warning note to his voice.

Ignoring him, she put her arms around his neck, standing on tiptoe to touch her lips to his. He resisted for a moment, then surrendered to the persuasive movement of her lips. She drank in the sweetness of his kiss, feeling intoxicated by it. His arms closed about her waist, drawing her into him. Her knees weakened as his tongue entered her mouth, taking it with a savage intensity that left her breathless. She moaned softly.

Raising his mouth from hers, Cole gazed into her eyes, the bottomless blue pools reminding him of a clear mountain lake. "I have to go," he said, his voice choked.

"Do you?" she asked, running her hands over his chest. "I don't want you to."

Pushing her away, he reached for the doorknob. The expression on his face was puzzling. She thought she saw a hint of regret mingled with fear. "Good-bye," she heard him say before pulling the door closed behind him.

Elizabeth stared at the door for several moments, a bemused expression on her face. Cole had responded to her kiss with an intensity that belied his outward behavior. Could it be he was softening toward her?

She heaved a sigh. Well, at least he would have something to think about while he was away from her. A few more meals and a few more kisses, and she would have Cole right where she wanted him. Staring meaningfully at the bed, she smiled.

Chapter Twenty

The flowers fluttered gently in the early afternoon breeze, their tall stems swaying like waltzing legs upon a dance floor. Surveying the vast variety of blooms before her, Elizabeth smiled in satisfaction, wanting the arrangement for tomorrow night's dinner party to be exquisite since her father would be there.

The gold chrysanthemums would be the perfect choice for the center of her table arrangement. Taking the scissors out of her apron pocket, she snipped the long green stems near the base. Proceeding down the next row of flowers, she added some cream-colored daisies, white anemones, and bright orange marigolds to the wicker basket on her arm. Absorbed in her task, she did not hear the approach of eight brown, bare feet coming toward her.

"You are *muy bonita, señora*," a child's voice declared.

Looking up, she was startled to find four shy faces smiling back at her. They were the same four faces she had seen the night of her arrival at Rancho del Oro. Standing, she brushed the dirt off her hands. "And who might you be?" she asked, smiling at the children.

The oldest of the group, a boy of about twelve, took off his straw hat. "My name is Juan Garcia. These are my brothers and sister," he said, pointing to the boy on his right. "This is Manuel, and the small, skinny one is José." The child named José smiled widely, displaying a large gap in his mouth where his two front teeth were missing.

Stepping forward, Elizabeth patted the head of the little girl who stood shyly next to José. "And what is your name?" The child smiled but did not answer.

"That is Maria. She does not speak English yet. *Señorita* Abby is still working with her."

Elizabeth's eyes widened. "Abby has taught you to speak English?"

"*Sí, señora.* We come once a week with our *padre.* He works for *Señor* Mac. We have our lessons then," Juan said proudly.

"Then you must be Esteban's children. Am I right?" She remembered Abby telling her of Esteban Garcia and of how his wife had died giving birth to their youngest child. She felt sorry for the poor, motherless children, especially for Maria, who had never had a chance to know her mother. Elizabeth felt a strong affinity with the child. She, too, had never known her mother.

"Would you like to carry these flowers into the house for me, Juan? I think I might have some cookies and milk lying about somewhere in the kitchen."

The children squealed with delight. Taking the basket Elizabeth handed him, Juan smiled, following Elizabeth back to the house.

*   *   *

Later that same evening, Abigail and Elizabeth sat in front of the hearth working on the patchwork quilt that never seemed to get finished.

"Abby?" Elizabeth said, pinning the six-inch squares together.

"Hmmm?" Abby responded, her mouth full of pins.

"I met the Garcia children today. They told me you were helping them with their English."

Taking the pins out of her mouth, Abby replied, "Yes, I am. I feel sorry for them. I know how it feels to lose a mother when you're just a child."

"I never knew my mother, either," Elizabeth said. "She died when I was just a baby."

"It must have been hard on you, having only your grandfather," Abby replied.

Thinking of her grandfather brought tears to Elizabeth's eyes. Even after everything he had done, she still missed him terribly. "He was good to me in his own way. And I did have Violet Baxter to help me over some of the rough spots." She would have to remember to ask her father about Violet when he arrived. According to the last letter she had received from her, she should have been here by now.

Noting Elizabeth's morose mood, Abigail thought it wise to change the topic. "Why do you want to know about the Garcia children? They haven't been bothering you, have they?"

"Oh, no! Nothing like that. I had an idea that I wanted to put to you."

Abby's eyebrow shot up. "What might that be?"

"There must be other children besides the Garcias who could benefit from some schooling. Juan told me that they live in the village of Santa Clara; that's not too far

238

from here."

"Are you thinking what I think you're thinking?" Abby asked, excitement lighting her eyes.

"I'm afraid so," Elizabeth replied, smiling eagerly. "I think it would be wonderful to open up a school for the children of the village. Juan informs me that there is none."

"That's a fabulous idea, Beth. I wish I had thought of it myself."

"Do you really think we could?" Elizabeth asked, putting her sewing down. "I've never done anything like this before, but I would be willing to try."

"First thing in the morning, we'll go out to the storage shed. It's been empty for almost a year now. With a little soap and water, we should be able to get it in some semblance of order."

Elizabeth stood up, throwing her sewing back in the basket.

"Beth, where are you going? Don't you want to talk about the school?"

"I have to go bake the pies for dinner tomorrow night. I know once I start working on the schoolhouse, I'm not going to want to stop and make dinner. The more I get done tonight, the less I have to do tomorrow."

"But it's nearly bedtime. Are you sure you want to do this now?"

Elizabeth nodded. "I wouldn't be able to sleep, anyway. I'm too excited. There's the school to think about, and my father coming. Aren't you excited, too?"

Staring into the fire, Abby avoided Elizabeth's probing eyes. "I'm scared, Beth. I don't know if I can go through with what we've talked about."

Seating herself beside Abby once again, Elizabeth

picked up the frightened woman's hand. It felt as cold as ice. "Nothing worth having ever comes easy. I don't know how many times my grandfather used to tell me that. He lived by those words, and I think we should, too. I know you're scared; I'm just as frightened about Cole. But we have to try. We would never forgive ourselves if we didn't fight for the men we love."

Reaching over, Abby gave Elizabeth a hug. "Thank you. I don't know what I would do without you. You're my strength . . . my courage."

"You've got plenty of that yourself. Didn't you tell me that you worked in the gold fields as a miner? I never could have done some of the things that you've admitted doing."

"But I was just a child; it was all a lark," Abby protested, shaking her head.

"You're still the same person you were, only older. The same courage and strength are still within you. When it's time to reach for it, you'll find it's still there."

"I wish I could be as certain as you are, Beth."

Elizabeth smiled enigmatically. If Abby only knew how terrified she was of so many things: of cooking dinner for company, of starting a school, of failing at the one thing that was so important to her—winning Cole's love.

The next day found Elizabeth up at dawn. Bending over the pile of bread dough on the table, she laughed aloud. Who would have ever thought that she, Elizabeth Forrester MacAlister, queen of New York society, would be kneading bread dough? She thought of Cole's calloused words and punched at the dough.

Kneading the satiny mass, she pushed down hard with

the heels of her hands. There was a lot of satisfaction in baking bread—watching the dough rise, smelling the fresh loaves of bread as they came out of the oven. It always made her feel as if she had performed a major feat. And the bread was getting better. It tasted light and fluffy, instead of hard and dry as sunbaked adobe. She was proud of herself.

"What's put that self-satisfied grin on your face?" Abby asked, striding into the kitchen. There were dark circles under her eyes, as if she had spent a restless night.

"You look awful," Elizabeth said, patting the dough into loaves. "I can see our talk last night did little good."

Feeling ashamed, Abby put forth a small smile. "I spent the night making up conversations in my head about what I was going to say to Jon. I know he's going to think something's strange when I start engaging him in meaningless banter. We've just never had that type of relationship before."

Stepping over to the sink, Elizabeth washed the dough off her hands. She wiped them on her apron, taking a seat next to Abby at the table. "Quit worrying so much. You're going to do just fine. Just remember what we discussed: Men like to talk about themselves. All you need do is ask him about his work; he'll do the rest."

"But Jon will think it's odd that I'm interested," Abby protested.

"Perhaps he will at first, but then he may find it very flattering that an attractive woman is interested in his work. Dressed in the gown we have fixed for your debut as a femme fatale, my father can't fail to notice you as a woman."

Abby's look was skeptical. "I don't know." She bit her lower lip.

241

"Just leave everything to me. I'll be there the whole time to assist you if the conversation bogs down. You forget . . . I am quite adept at the social graces. It's all your brother seems to think I'm good for."

Noting the forlorn expression on Elizabeth's face, Abigail grabbed her hand. "Cole's not going to know what hit him tonight. Between the gourmet meal that you're going to prepare and the scandalous dress you've chosen to wear, he won't have a chance. You'll be able to wear down his defenses in no time. I have a lot of faith in you."

"I hope you're right. I wouldn't want our plan for the fiesta to go awry."

"Has Cole said he will go?" Abby questioned.

"Once he hears it's for your benefit, both my father and Cole will eagerly agree," Elizabeth replied, smiling confidently. "The fiesta is just the catalyst we need to bring about a response from those two."

"Well, first things first. Let's get through this dinner party, then we'll talk about the Montoyas' party," Abby said.

"You're right. Help me get this bread in the oven, then we'll go out and take a look at the new schoolhouse. We've got lots of time before Cole and Jon are due to arrive."

Standing up, the girls locked arms in a mutual feeling of unity, walking happily out the door. Tonight was the first step in a long march to fulfilling a shared dream.

"Beth," Abby called, peeking out from behind the lace curtains in her bedroom, "they're here!"

Rushing to the window, Elizabeth peered out at the two figures who had just descended from the carriage.

Turning to face Abby, she smiled. "You look beautiful. My father will be spellbound by your loveliness."

"Do you really think so?" Abby asked, a hopeful note to her voice. Gazing at herself in the dresser mirror, she was stunned by her own reflection. She had never worn such a beautiful gown before. It was one of Beth's, which had been altered to fit her. She almost looked pretty, Abby thought.

"That copper satin dress never looked as good on me. I can tell you that with all honesty," Elizabeth said. "Now, I've got to hurry. Give me a few minutes to get the men settled in the parlor, then make your entrance."

"I can't!" Abby wailed, wringing her hands nervously.

Elizabeth frowned. "Nonsense! You'll be just fine. And don't forget, I'm counting on you to help me with Cole." Noting Abby's weak smile, she winked. "Courage. I'll see you downstairs in a few minutes."

Upon entering the house, Cole and Jon exchanged curious glances. Cole frowned, puzzled that neither Elizabeth nor Abigail appeared to be anywhere about. Suddenly, a flash of color to his left caught his eye. Turning his attention toward the stairs, his mouth fell open at the sight that greeted him.

Elizabeth, dressed in a bright red satin gown complemented by a diamond and ruby necklace, floated down the stairs toward him. He blinked, certain that the vision was merely a figment of his imagination. She was too beautiful to be real; he stared in awe at the sight of her.

As Elizabeth greeted her father with a kiss and an affectionate hug, Cole's eyes remained transfixed on the décolletage of her gown. He had never seen her display her charms quite so brazenly before. The gown was cut so low that a deep breath would cause her to fall right out

243

of it.

"Did you have a good trip?"

Pulling his eyes up forcibly, he stared into her face. His own face warmed when he realized that Elizabeth knew he had been staring at her bosom. "The—the trip?" he stammered, recovering himself. "Yes. It was fine."

Jon smiled at the exchange between the two young people. You'd think from the way Cole was staring at his wife that he had never seen her dressed up before.

"Shall we go into the parlor for some refreshment?" Elizabeth suggested, linking her arms through Cole's and her father's.

"Did you buy some new furniture?" Jon asked. "I don't remember seeing these pieces before." He pointed to the two end tables by the sofa.

"No," Elizabeth said, smiling. "I just applied a few coats of beeswax to them. It seems to restore their natural beauty."

Cole's eyes widened. The walnut tables did look new. In fact, he thought, glancing about, the whole room was cleaned and polished. The floor was newly waxed, and the brass light fixtures sparkled. Someone had been very busy, and he was shocked to discover that someone to be Elizabeth.

A moment later, he was again surprised when his sister entered the room. Abigail was wearing a copper-colored gown he had never seen before. It showed her diminutive figure off to perfection. Her hair had been arranged in an upward sweep, with a cascade of curls falling down her back. Around her neck she wore a cameo pinned on a black velvet ribbon.

His chest swelled with pride at the sight of her loveliness. She had always been afraid to show her femininity, worried that people would mock her as they had when she was a child. Her lameness, caused by a breech birth, had left her crippled in more ways than one.

"Good evening. I hope I'm not late," Abby said, her eyes resting on Jon. She felt elated by the admiration she saw reflected in the blue depths of his eyes.

"Abby, you look beautiful!" Jon said, rising from the sofa.

"Thank you," she murmured shyly, taking a seat next to him.

Elizabeth was ecstatic. Her father had shown a man's appreciation for Abby's beauty tonight, and Cole seemed a little stunned by her own appearance. Pouring four glasses of Bordeaux into the crystal stemware, she handed one to Abby and one to her father. Crossing to the other side of the room, she bent over the table in front of Cole's chair, placing his glass before him. Hearing his sharp intake of breath, she knew he was getting an eyeful as her breasts poured over the front of her gown, the dusky tops of her areolae clearly visible. Observing Cole's hand shake as he reached for his wine, she smiled in satisfaction.

As she straightened her stance, their eyes locked for a moment. His glowed with an eerie light that made her shiver. Taking a deep breath, she tried to return her breathing to normal.

"I hope everyone is hungry; I've prepared tonight's meal entirely by myself," Elizabeth announced, smiling inwardly at the pained expression on Cole's face. "I do hope everyone likes duck. It's my first time preparing it."

Drinking down his glass of wine in one gulp, Cole looked visibly ill.

"Shall we adjourn to the dining room?"

The first course of pumpkin soup wasn't half bad, Cole thought begrudgingly, wiping his lips on the white linen napkin while he waited for Elizabeth to bring out the promised ducks. He could just imagine what they would be like. She probably neglected to pull the feathers off before she cooked them, he thought smugly.

Staring down the long length of table, he couldn't believe how animated Abby was tonight. Gone was the reserved, quiet girl he was used to, replaced instead by a vivacious conversationalist. Jon appeared almost mesmerized as he laughed at something Abby whispered to him. Cole shook his head. You would think the man had never been around Abby before, the way he was clinging to her every word. Why . . . he seemed flattered by her attention. It was odd, very odd, Cole reflected, sipping thoughtfully on his wine.

"Here we are," Elizabeth announced, carrying a large ceramic platter laden with four succulent-looking ducks. Setting them down on the table in front of Cole, she smiled.

Cole stared at the ducks in amazement, then up at his wife. "They look nice," he said, clearly astounded that they did.

"Why, thank you," Elizabeth replied. "You didn't think I was going to leave the feathers on, did you?" she asked, smiling at the guilty look passing over Cole's face.

Cole was impressed by the incredible meal Elizabeth had laid out before them. The ducks, roasted to golden perfection, were topped with a cherry glaze. They were accompanied by bowls of wild rice, hot buttered peas, and the best bread he had ever sank his teeth into. It was truly a meal fit for a king. Had his society wife really done all this by herself? According to Abby, she had.

"Everything's quite delicious, my dear," Jon said. "I had no idea you were so proficient in the kitchen."

Laughing, Elizabeth caught Cole's eye. "It took a bit of practice," she admitted, warmed by the look of admiration on Cole's face.

"I propose a toast," Cole said, lifting his wine glass. "To Elizabeth, on her first truly gourmet meal."

Blushing as red as the wine, Elizabeth smiled happily as everyone raised their glasses in her honor. She had never felt such pride in anything she had ever done before, realizing that she owed that feeling to Cole. If it hadn't been for his perversity in making her work, she never would have recognized her own worth.

Once the meal was completed and they had finished their last bites of apple pie, Elizabeth suggested going outside for a walk. Regarding her father as he placed Abby's shawl around her shoulders, she smiled to herself. She just knew everything was going to work out between them.

"Cole," Elizabeth said, for his ears alone, "would you mind staying in the house and helping me clear the dishes?"

Cole's brow wrinkled in confusion. "But I thought you just said that you wanted to go for a walk."

"Don't you want to spend some time alone with me? Why, you didn't even kiss me hello," she said, rubbing her breasts against his arm.

Cole's crotch tightened. Pulling his collar out away from his neck, he turned to face Jon and Abby, who were waiting by the front door. "You two go on. We'll catch up in a few minutes."

While her father turned to open the door, Elizabeth gave Abby a wink of encouragement. "Good luck," she mouthed silently.

The brisk night air, coupled with Abby's nervousness, made her shiver as she followed Jon to the fountain.

"Are you cold, dear?" Jon asked.

"A little. Perhaps you could put your arm about me and share your warmth," Abby suggested, waiting for Jon to tell her that she must be out of her mind. When his arm came around her shoulders, she almost cried out in relief. This was all so awkward to her. How had she let Elizabeth talk her into this? Elizabeth's words came back to haunt her: *"Nothing worth having ever comes easy."* She snuggled closer to Jon's side.

The feel of Abby in his arms felt right, Jon thought. Tonight, as he had conversed with her at the table, it was as if he were seeing her for the very first time. She was warm, loving, beautiful . . . and she was practically his own daughter. Guilt riddled through him at the lascivious thoughts he was having about her; he pulled his arm away.

Noting Jon's reddening features, Abby asked, "Is something wrong?"

The hurt expression in Abby's eyes wounded him. Suddenly, unable to control himself, Jon pulled her into his embrace, planting his lips firmly but gently over hers. He kissed her thoroughly, shamefully, until he heard her moan of pleasure. Realizing what he had done, he thrust her from him. "I'm sorry, Abby. I don't know what came over me."

Before Abby could reply, he jumped up, hurrying back to the house. Abby wiped at the tears streaming down her face. She knew she had been foolish to think Jon could ever care for her. Why, he was practically repulsed by just one of her kisses. She shook her head. Elizabeth had been wrong. Jon would never grow to love her.

Elizabeth was having similar thoughts about Cole as she faced him across the formal expanse of the parlor. She was seated on the sofa, while he sat rigidly in the wing chair by the fireplace.

"Would you care for a brandy?" she offered, hoping a little alcohol might warm up his blood. She could certainly use a little fortification herself right about now.

Cole stood, pouring two generous portions of brandy for each of them. Walking over to the sofa, he sat down next to her. "Your expertise in the kitchen surprised me," he said, handing her the glass of amber liquid.

Her smile was openly provocative. "There are a lot of things about me that would surprise you," she said, sipping slowly on her brandy.

His eyebrows rose at her statement. "I like your dress. Is it new?" he asked, running his finger over the material that lay next to her breasts.

Elizabeth's nipples hardened instantly. "Why, no," she choked. "This old thing? I've had it for ages." Her voice sounded strange to her ears.

Moving closer, Cole dipped his finger between her breasts, picking up the ruby pendant that rested there. Bending over, he examined it more closely. "This is a rare and beautiful sight."

Cole's hot breath on her breasts was driving her wild with desire. Clearing her throat, she straightened her posture, the gesture causing her nipples to rise halfway out of her dress. "Thank you," she murmured, lowering her eyes demurely.

Captivated that his own wife was flirting with him, Cole smiled inwardly. He could see desire burning brightly in her eyes; it mirrored what he was feeling for her at the moment. Unable to stop himself, he leaned over, brushing her lips lightly with his own.

Wrapping her arms about Cole, Elizabeth deepened the kiss with a primitive ardor that surprised her. She wanted him; she couldn't stand not having him touch her. And if *she* had to ravish *him* instead of the other way around, then so be it.

Cole's hands roamed freely over Elizabeth's breasts. The feel of the milky white globes instilled a hunger in him that could not be appeased. Inserting his hand into the top of her gown, he freed the luscious mounds from their confinement, rubbing the tops of her nipples.

Plunging her tongue into Cole's mouth, Elizabeth darted it in and out in a frenzied mating motion. The touch of his hands on her breasts filled her with yearning.

"Elizabeth."

At the sound of Abby's voice, Cole and Elizabeth broke apart guiltily. At the sight of Abby's tear-stained face, Elizabeth adjusted her bodice. "What is it? What's happened?"

Observing the two lovers on the couch, Abby burst into tears. Covering her face with her hands, she hurried toward the stairs as quickly as her impairment would allow.

Elizabeth stared after her, clearly in a quandary about what she should do. She was torn between her desire for Cole and her friendship with Abby.

Turning back to face Cole, who was looking at her with a mixture of frustration and longing, she said, "I'm sorry. I have to go and see what's wrong with Abby." The smile she wore was filled with regret.

Staring after Elizabeth, Cole shook his head in consternation. "Damn!" he cursed, gulping down the brandy, praying it would burn away the lust he was feeling at the moment. It was getting increasingly difficult to ignore Elizabeth's blatant overtures. He couldn't allow himself to become entangled within her web of deceit again. He was through with her, he thought angrily, throwing the glass against the fireplace. He watched it shatter into a hundred pieces. The same way she had shattered his heart.

Chapter Twenty-One

As she stood facing the mirror, her face a mask of concern, Elizabeth wondered, not for the first time, how tonight's fiesta was going to unfold. She bit her lip, uncertain if her plan to make Cole jealous was foolish.

And Abigail! The poor thing was counting on her to make everything right with her father. Pacing nervously about the room, she was beginning to wonder if she had bitten off more than she could chew. What right did she have to assure Abby that everything would work out with Jon? Her own plans for Cole certainly had gone awry this past week.

She had actually believed that Cole was starting to weaken toward her. The night of the dinner party he had been so warm and responsive. She shook her head. She couldn't have been more wrong. Cole had treated her like a leper this past week, barely acknowledging her presence, refusing any and all advances, hardly speaking to her at all. What was she going to do? She couldn't arrange her own life, and here she was trying to advise Abby about hers.

Plopping down on the stool in front of the dressing table, she cupped her chin in her hands, staring into the mirror. Had she been wrong to tell Abby to stick it out with her father? she asked herself.

The night of the dinner party, when she and Cole had been interrupted by Abby's hysterics, had been an exercise in diplomacy on Elizabeth's part. Trying to convince Abby that she had not made a fool of herself where Jon was concerned had been no easy feat. She thought back to their conversation of that evening and sighed.

Entering Abby's room, she had found the distraught woman lying across her bed, sobbing pitifully into her pillow. Rushing in, she sat on the edge of the bed, drawing Abby into her arms. "Tell me what happened."

Looking up, her lashes wet with tears, Abby's expression was hopeless. "It's no use. I told you it was a mistake. Jon will never love me."

Taking a handkerchief off the nightstand, Elizabeth wiped the tears from her sister-in-law's face. "I passed my father on the stairs on my way up to your room. He looked ashamed . . . riddled with guilt. Why is that?" Elizabeth questioned. She had her own suspicions concerning what had happened, but she wanted to hear Abby's explanation first.

Taking the handkerchief from Elizabeth, Abby sniveled into it. "He kissed me."

Elizabeth's eyes widened. "But that's wonderful. Isn't that what you wanted?"

"Yes," Abby replied in a small voice. "But he was repulsed by me. After the kiss, he jumped up as if I was contaminated. I tell you, it's because of my lameness." She sobbed louder.

"That is pure and utter nonsense. Now stop your

253

crying this instant," Elizabeth demanded. From the shocked look on Abigail's face, she could tell her sister-in-law was clearly astounded at her sharp reprimand. Smiling, she tried to soften her words. "I don't ever want to hear you talk about yourself that way again. Your being lame has nothing to do with any of this. Goodness gracious! You're as blind as my father." Rising, Elizabeth paced the floor as she talked.

"If you would think about this rationally, you would see, as clearly as I do, that you have scared my father to death. He has feelings for you, Abby. He feels guilty about them. Don't you see? He's frightened of the way he feels about you."

"Do you really think so?" Abby asked, her eyes widening in wonder.

"Think back to the kiss. Was it the kiss of a man in the throes of passion, or one who was being forced against his will?"

Abby blushed scarlet. "I think he enjoyed it until he realized who he was kissing."

"See. That only confirms my suspicions. He hasn't been able to reconcile his feelings quite yet. But he will; just give him time. And for goodness sake, don't give up on him. His response to you is more than I could have hoped for."

Abby smiled. "You're right as usual; I won't give up."

The gong of the clock on the mantel brought Elizabeth quickly back to the present. It was seven o'clock. They would be leaving soon for the Montoyas' fiesta. She took a deep breath to calm the butterflies in her stomach. Staring at her reflection in the mirror, she smiled. Cole was going to be in for a big surprise tonight.

Standing, she twirled around and around. The long

cotton skirt swung freely about, coming to rest at the top of her ankles. It was a deep red color, almost a burgundy, signifying the passionate blood in her veins. She giggled. She was beginning to sound like Rodrigo. The blouse was white and loose fitting; it hung off her shoulders, exposing the tops of her breasts. She wore nothing under it. Abby had assured her that this was the way all the Mexican peasant girls dressed. She felt deliciously wanton without the restrictive undergarments to hamper her.

Grabbing her shawl, she secured it around her blouse. It wouldn't do for Cole to see her dressed like this. He might raise an objection, and she had no intention of changing her clothes tonight.

Descending the stairs with trepidation, Elizabeth took another deep breath. She wanted everything to go according to plan for Abigail, as well as for herself.

Entering the parlor, she discovered everyone was there ahead of her. Cole was standing near the fireplace, a wine glass in his hand. He looked dashing in his tight-fitting black pants and white silk shirt. The shirt had been left open, exposing his muscular chest. Abigail looked lovely in a rose-colored gown embroidered with tiny white flowers over the skirt and bodice.

"Good evening, everyone. I hope I'm not late," Elizabeth said, noting Abby's nervous smile.

"Not at all, my dear," Jon assured her. "And if you were, it would have been well worth the wait. Don't you agree, Cole?"

Glancing over at Cole, who was staring at her with an expression of unbridled lust on his face, Elizabeth smiled warmly.

"Yes," he replied. "Elizabeth looks beautiful." He

smiled briefly, turning away to look into the fire.

"Thank you, and I must say the men of the family certainly look dashing tonight." She patted her father's cheek.

"Shall we go?" Jon suggested. "I don't know about the rest of you, but I'm starved." Placing Abigail's shawl around her shoulders, he was rewarded with a captivating smile.

"I fear my appetite won't be easily sated tonight," Cole whispered into Elizabeth's ear, chuckling at the gasp that escaped from her throat. Why should she be surprised? he wondered. For weeks she had been flaunting herself at him, driving him crazy with desire. Well, she was his wife, by God, and tonight he would let her service his needs. After all, he rationalized, if he was going to be saddled with a wife, he might as well make some use out of her. Grabbing Elizabeth roughly about the waist, he propelled her outside to the waiting carriage.

Elizabeth was confused by Cole's behavior this evening. Chancing a peek at him beneath lowered lashes, she noted that his eyes were fixed firmly on the road ahead, his expression betraying no clue as to what he might be thinking.

What had come over him? All week long, he had seemed as if he couldn't stand the sight of her, and now that they were going to the fiesta, he was suddenly interested in her. Unless, of course, he wasn't really interested in her, but in his former mistress, Amber Montoya. Perhaps he wanted to make Amber jealous. Her eyes narrowed. She would make certain that Cole got a taste of his own medicine.

Dozens of brightly lit lanterns hung from the trees lining the drive to Casa Montoya. As they approached the adobe house, Elizabeth could hear the lively music of the band. Tapping her foot, she kept time to the spirited tune.

"I see you are anxious to dance," Cole remarked. "Pity, I don't like to dance."

Shrugging her shoulders, she smiled. "That's all right. I will find someone who does."

Before Cole could answer, she hopped down with the help of her father, who was waiting for them outside the front gate. Grabbing Abigail's arm, Elizabeth guided her forward toward the inner courtyard.

"How is everything going?" Elizabeth asked when they were far enough away from her father and Cole. They had traveled in separate carriages, and Elizabeth was anxious to know if there had been any further developments.

"Jon told me he liked my hair fixed this way," Abby said, smiling shyly.

"That's a good start. What else did you talk about?"

"Nothing much. Just about his work, mostly. I did tell him how handsome he looked. He seemed pleased by my compliment."

Squeezing her hand, Elizabeth smiled. "Excellent. Keep up the good work. And remember, if he asks you to dance, say yes."

They halted their conversation as the two men approached. Latching onto Elizabeth's arm in a proprietary fashion, Cole ushered her forward to meet their hostess.

"Elizabeth . . . Cole. Welcome to Casa Montoya," Amber said, giving them both a hug. "I would like to introduce you to my fiancé, Matthew Flores."

Elizabeth felt giddy with relief as the introductions were made. If Amber had a fiancé, then she couldn't be interested in Cole.

"And you remember my cousin, Rodrigo," Amber said, smiling at Elizabeth.

Elizabeth smiled up at Rodrigo as he took her hand and placed a kiss upon it. "Your beauty continues to captivate this mere mortal, Elizabeth. You haven't forgotten that you promised to dance with me, have you?"

Elizabeth felt Cole's fingers tighten on her arm. "I am looking forward to it, Rod."

As they made their way further into the courtyard, Cole pulled Elizabeth aside. "Where do you know Rodrigo Montoya from?"

"Don't you remember me telling you about their visit and subsequent invitation to the fiesta?" Elizabeth replied, smiling innocently up at him.

"I remember you telling me that Amber called, not about her cousin."

"He's really a very nice man and so terribly gallant. Those Mexican men certainly do have a way about them."

Cole stiffened. "I would prefer that you stay away from him."

"But why? I've already promised him a dance and you said that you don't like to dance, so it all works out for the best." She found perverse pleasure in the annoyed expression on Cole's face. "Oh, there is Abigail signaling to me. I'd better go and see what she wants. Have a good time," she said, rushing off before Cole had a chance to voice any more objections.

In less than an hour, Elizabeth had made the acquaintance of many of her neighbors, most of them wealthy Mexican landowners. The Montoyas owned the largest ranch, with approximately twenty-five thousand acres.

Next came the Silveras, with ten thousand. And the list went on and on. Elizabeth discovered that Cole's ranch was actually quite small in comparison to his neighbors. She had thought two thousand acres to be quite large, until hearing the acreage of some of the other ranches in the valley.

Observing the costumes of some of the other women, she was relieved to find that she was not the only woman dressed in peasant dress tonight. Lupe Silvera and Anna Delgado were both dressed similarly to her. Noting Cole's gaze following the two women about as they danced in front of him, her eyes narrowed into thin slits. He smiled as if he were enjoying the spectacle immensely. Deciding that it was time to remove her shawl, she tossed it carelessly aside.

"Are you having a good time, my friend?"

Glancing over to her right, she found Amber's speculative gaze upon her. "It's a wonderful party, Amber. Thank you for inviting us."

"Why are you not dancing with that handsome husband of yours? He is a very good dancer, you know."

"I don't believe he feels like dancing right now," Elizabeth replied.

"I don't know what is going on between the two of you, and I don't want to know. It is none of my business. But I just want to say that if Cole is being difficult with you, it is your duty as a woman to make his life miserable. Do you understand what I am saying?"

Squeezing Amber's hand, she smiled wickedly. "Oh, I understand perfectly, and believe me, I am doing everything in my power to do just that."

"Here comes my foolish cousin, Rodrigo. I'm sure he will be able to assist you in whatever misery you have

259

planned for your stubborn husband."

Staring across the yard, Elizabeth observed Rod's approach. "*Gracias, Señora* Montoya, you are very wise."

"Be happy, Elizabeth. I have waited a long time to find my Matthew. Now that I have, I want everyone to be as happy as me," she said, giving Elizabeth a brief hug before she departed.

"Are you ready to dance, Elizabeth?" Rodrigo asked, bowing before her.

Flashing him a brilliant smile, she replied, "I do believe I am."

Elizabeth lost herself in the frenzied rhythm of the music. Twirling about, she clapped her hands above her head, laughing gaily at Rodrigo's outrageous compliments. Had she observed the pair of steel-gray eyes glittering in anger at her every suggestive move, she would have undulated in fear rather than enjoyment.

Clenching his hands tightly at his sides, Cole observed Elizabeth's indecent display with distaste, the muscle in his jaw quivering angrily at her undulating movements. Good Christ! Did she have nothing on beneath that skimpy blouse she wore? The large milky white globes bounced and jiggled, unfettered by any undergarment he could discern. He looked with disgust upon Rodrigo Montoya, who was raping Elizabeth with his eyes.

Just as he was about to confront the laughing couple the music ended, and they disappeared into the darkness. Jealousy, raw and stark, ripped through his gut like a jagged blade. Glancing about the shadows of the courtyard, he was furious when he could find no trace of his wife or Montoya. Stalking off, with murder on his mind, he passed right by Jon and Abby, who had paused at the refreshment table for a glass of punch.

260

"I'm having a wonderful time," Abby said, smiling up at Jon.

"Would you care to go for a stroll? I understand the Montoyas' garden is quite a showplace."

Abby's heart pounded furiously within her breast. "I'd love to," she murmured, hoping she didn't sound too anxious. She didn't want to scare Jon away again.

They walked along the gravel path that followed the duck pond. The strains of the violins were barely discernible, becoming less distinct as they ventured deeper into the garden. The occasional splashing and quacking of the ducks was an unusual accompaniment to the music.

The night air was laced with the aromatic scent of anemone and marigold from the flower beds. Abigail breathed deeply, drawing in the fragrant odor.

"Would you care to have a seat?" Jon asked, indicating the wooden bench next to the pond.

Nodding, Abby seated herself, folding her hands primly in her lap, waiting for Jon to speak.

"Abby."

Jon's voice breathed softly in her ear. She turned to face him, their mouths scant inches apart.

"Abby, I—"

"Yes, Jon?" she prompted, placing her hand over his, praying that what he had to say was what she wanted to hear.

Looking down at the small white hand placed so trustingly over his larger one, he picked it up, kissing her fingers tenderly. "I don't know quite how to say this. You're going to think that I've lost my mind."

She squeezed his hand reassuringly. "I wouldn't be too sure of that."

Jon arched his brow. "We've known each other a long

261

time—almost twenty years. In that time, I've grown very fond of you. I had always thought of you as a daughter, but—"

"Please! Don't say any more," Abigail interrupted, her eyes misting with tears. All her hopes were going to be dashed by Jon's admission. "I know you care for me as a daughter," she choked out, "but God help me, I love you as a man!"

Jon's face lit up, his eyes widening in disbelief at Abby's confession.

Covering her face, Abby sobbed gently into her hands. She had shamed them both by her stupid admission of love.

Wrapping his arm around Abby, Jon enfolded her into his embrace. "Abby, my little Abby, what I've been trying so clumsily to tell you is that I no longer think of you as a daughter. I haven't for a long time. I love you, Abby."

Glancing up, her lashes wet with tears, Abigail asked, "You love me?" She was unable to believe her ears until Jon's lips closed over hers in tender avowal of his declaration.

After the kiss ended, Abigail sighed contentedly. "Oh, Jon, I've loved you for so long. I've despaired of ever hearing you say those words."

Tipping up her chin, he stared tenderly into her eyes. "Is that why you stayed away, never coming to San Francisco to visit with Cole?"

She nodded, smiling tremulously.

"Christ! What a stupid blind fool I've been. You were afraid to come to me because you loved me, and I stayed away from you because I felt guilty about my unfatherly feelings toward you."

"That's what Elizabeth said."

"Elizabeth?" Jon's brows furrowed in confusion. "What's she got to do with all this?"

"She's been helping me overcome my shyness where you are concerned. She thinks you would be an excellent husband for me." Abby lowered her eyes demurely.

"Oh, she does, does she?" Jon said, laughing loudly. He shook his head. "I don't suppose I had much of a chance against the two of you."

Abby's smile turned upside down as she thought of Cole and Elizabeth.

"What's wrong? Why are you so glum? I *will* make an excellent husband, you know."

Abby waved her hand. "I know that," she said absently. "It's just that I feel guilty about our happiness, when Elizabeth and Cole are still not reconciled."

Jon's mouth gaped open. After a few moments, he inquired, "You mean to tell me that those two are still having problems? I thought that they were acting a bit strange, but I thought surely, after all this time, Cole wouldn't be able to fight his feelings for Elizabeth."

"He can, and he does." Abby went on to explain what had been happening since the newly wedded couple had returned from New York.

Jon shook his head. "Cole always was as stubborn as a mule. Although, I think this time he's met his match in Elizabeth. She's as tenacious as a bulldog. I don't think she'll give up all that easily."

Elizabeth giggled as Rodrigo continued to regale her with hilarious anecdotes about some of the more flamboyant members of the Montoya family. She was hardpressed to believe that any of the other members of the family could be as outlandish as he was. She was just

263

about to tell him so, when the shadow of a man fell over her. Looking up, she discovered the agitated face of her husband.

"It's time to leave, Elizabeth," Cole said, his words edged in ice.

Taking a sip of her punch, she tossed back her head defiantly, her blond hair swirling about her in a cloud of gold dust. "But I don't want to leave. I'm having such a good time." Looking over at her partner, she said, "We're having a wonderful time, aren't we, Rod?"

At the menacing look Cole directed at him, Rodrigo Montoya paled. Bowing, he smiled apologetically. "I must bid you farewell, *Señora* MacAlister. I hear my cousin calling me."

Elizabeth covered her mouth, afraid she would burst into laughter at the sight of Rodrigo running off like a frightened rabbit. "You scared him away. Shame on you, Cole."

Grabbing Elizabeth's wrist, Cole's voice was chilling. "Put that damned drink down. You've had enough. I wasn't aware that I had married a woman who liked to overindulge in spirits."

"You're just jealous because I was having such a good time with Rod. He thinks I'm pretty. How come you never tell me I'm pretty? Don't you think I am?" She draped her arms about his waist.

"Elizabeth! You are making a spectacle of yourself in front of our neighbors. Have you no care for your reputation?"

"Oh, fudge! You're such an old stick-in-the-mud. Come on, let's dance." She tugged on his hand.

Cole raised an affronted eyebrow before replying, "Get your wrap; we are leaving."

"If you're nice to me, I will tell you a secret."

Taking Elizabeth's hand, he guided her to a darkened corner of the courtyard, away from prying eyes. "You have one minute, then we are leaving."

Wrapping her arms about Cole's neck, she placed her mouth next to his ear. "I don't have a stitch on under this blouse. Want to see?" She pulled the loose garment down, exposing her breasts.

Pulling her into his chest, he glanced about to make sure no one had seen. "Are you crazy? Do you want to expose yourself in public?" Swearing under his breath, he pulled her blouse back up.

Smiling seductively, Elizabeth held out her arms. "Give me a kiss."

"What I'm going to give you is a slap on your backside if you don't behave yourself. Now we are going to leave. If you say one more word, I shall throw you over my shoulder and carry you out of here like a sack of potatoes."

"You'll have to catch me first." She darted past him, taking off in the direction of the garden.

"Elizabeth, come back here. I'm warning you," Cole threatened, running after his errant wife. He was closing in on her; she was only a few yards ahead of him. Suddenly, as they neared the duck pond, he heard a loud splash.

"My God! Elizabeth!" he shouted. Pulling off his boots, he plunged into the water, grabbing frantically for his wife. "Elizabeth, can you hear me?"

"Of course I can hear you, silly. Do you think I'm deaf?" She swam next to him, just out of his reach.

Deciding to use a different tactic, Cole's voice softened. "Elizabeth, I was hoping to give you a kiss."

"You liar. You're just trying to catch me," she said, slapping at the water, splashing it up in his face. God, he was furious. She wasn't nearly as drunk as he thought her to be. The cold water had a sobering effect on her. If Cole realized that, he would kill her for sure. She swam toward the other side of the pond.

A moment later, Cole caught up to Elizabeth, his quick, sure strokes making up the distance between them. Reaching out, he grabbed her ankle, pulling her back toward him. "I've got you now."

Grabbing onto his waist, she pressed her wet body up against him. "And what are you going to do with me?" she taunted.

Dragging her up to the edge of the bank, he paused a moment to catch his breath. Seating himself on the ground, he pulled her swiftly over his lap. "This," he replied. Holding both of her hands in his, he flipped her skirt up over her head. Yanking down her drawers, he spanked her soundly on her bottom.

"Cole!" she screamed, tears streaming down her face. "Stop, please!"

A moment later the pain stopped, replaced by a tingling feeling in the lower portion of her body. Cole's hand was rubbing her bare flesh, his fingers gliding gently over her naked bottom. She squirmed, unable to withstand the torture he was imposing.

"I think I have just the punishment for your actions. I've been neglecting the base side of your nature for far too long." Pulling her skirts down, he hauled her up. Cole placed his hand behind her head, he ground his lips down over hers in a punishing kiss.

The force of Cole's mouth on hers took her breath away. Elizabeth started to sway.

266

"Perhaps I should always kiss you into submission," he said before releasing her.

Too startled to reply to Cole's conceited statement, Elizabeth pulled back her hand, intending to wipe the smug look off his face. But Cole was quicker. He grabbed her hand and, with one quick, fluid motion, hoisted her up over his shoulder.

"Put me down, you savage brute. How dare you treat a lady in such a fashion!" she cried, beating against his back with her fists. The sound of Cole's boisterous laughter incensed her.

"You're no lady, sweetheart. Ladies don't flirt with other men, and they don't expose themselves in public. Now be quiet, before I give your backside another paddling."

Thank God she would be spared the public humiliation of going out through the front courtyard. It seemed Cole knew another way of exiting through the garden. One of the many things he had learned while serving as Amber's lover, she supposed.

At the sight of the carriages, Elizabeth's head cleared. What was she going to say to her father and Abigail? How could she explain to them that she had drank too much and had made a perfect fool out of herself? Abby would probably never speak to her again. It was no more than she deserved after the way she had deserted her.

Cole deposited her, none too gently, on the leather seat of the carriage.

"Ouch," she yelled, rubbing her behind.

He chuckled. "Still smarts a bit, does it? Well, it's nothing compared to what you're going to get once we get home."

Pushing back against the seat, Elizabeth's eyes

267

widened in fear. My God! He was going to beat her. This time she had really messed everything up. She started to shiver; the wet clothes, combined with Cole's threats, produced shudders of misgiving throughout her body.

"Are you going to beat me?" she asked in a small voice.

Cole looked over at her, his smile wicked. "Your punishment will be no more than you deserve." His words were ominous and final as they fell against the quiet of the autumn evening.

Chapter Twenty-Two

As Cole pulled the carriage to a halt in front of the house, a knot the size of an orange took root in Elizabeth's stomach and started to grow. Her teeth chattered and she shook violently, whether from her wet clothes or the fear of the unknown, she didn't know.

Cole hadn't spoken a word to her the entire journey home. She had tried to broach several different topics, but he had kept his mouth shut as tightly as a lid upon a casket. She watched in trepidation as Cole walked around the side of the carriage, pausing by the step to help her down.

"Go to your room and get out of those wet clothes immediately. And take a hot bath. It wouldn't do for you to get sick," he ordered harshly. "I must see to the horses; Esteban is off tonight."

Too frightened to argue, Elizabeth ran into the house and up the stairs to the safety of her room. Once she reached her haven, she bolted the door, leaning heavily against it, trying to catch her breath. Moving cautiously about the darkened room, she made her way over to the nightstand, feeling for the matches she always kept there. She lit the lamp and the room was quickly bathed in a warm golden glow.

Disrobing as quickly as she could, she hurried into the bathing chamber, lighting the wall sconces and locking the door to Cole's room. She had to hurry before he returned.

Sinking down into the hot tub, she let the warm water seep into her chilled flesh. As the heat pierced her pores, her skin tingled like a thousand tiny pinpricks. It felt wonderful to be warm again. She wished she could lie there forever, but she wanted to get into bed before Cole arrived. Perhaps if he thought she were sleeping, he wouldn't want to punish her, she thought hopefully.

Pulling a warm flannel nightgown out of her dresser, she slipped it on over her head, climbing into the large brass bed. Clutching the covers up to her chin, she squeezed her eyes shut at the sound of Cole's footsteps on the stairs. She heard the rattling of the doorknob, then a loud banging.

"Elizabeth, open this door," Cole shouted.

Sinking down even further under the quilt, she pressed her hands over her ears, waiting for the door to come crashing in on her.

"It wasn't very wise of you to test my patience, Sunshine. I'm afraid that you've pushed me as far as I'm going to go." The voice was as cold as steel and unmistakably Cole's.

Popping her head out of the covers, she was surprised to find Cole standing by the side of the bed. She blanched. "How did you get in here?"

Cole's smile was sinister. Holding up a large brass key, he said, "I unlocked the bathing room door."

"Oh," she replied, biting her lower lip, her eyes widening in alarm at the sight of Cole unbuttoning his shirt. He stripped it off, throwing it carelessly on the floor. The mattress sagged as he sat on the edge of the bed, pulling off his boots. She tensed, holding her breath as each boot hit the floor with a resounding thud.

Rising to his feet, Cole unbuckled the thick black leather belt from around his waist.

Elizabeth's eyes widened in terror. "Please don't beat me," she begged, kneeling before him on the bed. "I'm sorry, truly I am."

Cole's gut tightened at the sight of Elizabeth kneeling before him, her hair falling down around her like a silken mantle, her eyes filled with tears. He hadn't meant to frighten her, but he had to admit, it did give him a small measure of satisfaction to see her humble herself so. Perhaps it was time she learned who was boss. Removing his belt, he held it in one hand. "Take off your nightgown, Elizabeth," he ordered, his voice absolutely emotionless.

"Please don't beat me."

"Take it off. Now!" he repeated, snapping the belt.

Elizabeth flinched, her heart thudding loudly in her chest as she hurried to do his bidding.

"Come here," he directed.

Moving forward, she inched her way across the mattress on her knees, her eyes never leaving Cole's face. Swallowing her fear, she tilted her chin up defiantly.

Wrapping his hand around her hair, Cole pulled her into him. His eyes smoldered with a burning desire. "Unbutton my pants," he ordered.

Her face flaming with humiliation and resentment, Elizabeth stared in disbelief. What kind of perverse

271

pleasure could Cole get from beating her while he was stark naked? she wondered. She wanted to refuse, to tell him no, but the cold, unyielding look on his face made her think otherwise. Her hands shaking, she fumbled with the buttons. When her fingers came in contact with the bare flesh below his waist, she heard his sharp intake of breath. Her heart thudded wildly when she realized he wore nothing beneath his pants.

"Now lie facedown on the bed."

Doing as she was told, Elizabeth held her breath, waiting for the first lash of the belt to strike her flesh. A moment later, she felt the bed sink beneath Cole's weight. She shivered uncontrollably as Cole's hands caressed her backside, his fingers running up and down the back of her legs, thighs, and buttocks. Lifting her head, she asked in a small voice, "Are you going to beat me now?"

"I have a more fitting punishment for you. One that is going to last most of the night. When I'm through with you, Sunshine, you'll be begging for mercy," he said, spreading her legs apart, tracing the crevice with his finger.

"Oh, God!" Elizabeth cried as his finger moved in rhythmic motion. She felt humiliated, angered at the debasing way he was using her, but she couldn't help the surging moistness that flooded between her legs at his touch. "Please!" she choked out.

Cole cupped her breasts, massaging the aching globes, pulling on the already-taut nipples. His mouth claimed a torturous path down her back and thighs, his tongue replacing his finger as it closed over the opening of her mound.

Elizabeth gasped, writhing uncontrollably as he flicked

the tiny bud of her being with quick, feathery strokes of his tongue. "Take me. Please, take me," she begged. She couldn't believe it was her own voice, so thick with longing and emotion, that cried out for release.

"Oh, no," he said, flipping her over. "We have a long way to go yet."

He covered her mouth with his own, thrusting his tongue between her lips. She could taste herself on him, the musky scent inflaming her already-heated senses. His kiss left her mouth burning with fire as his head moved down to capture first one rigid nipple, then the other between his lips, while his fingers manipulated the hardened nub of her womanhood.

Bucking under his assault, she tried to assuage the torment between her thighs. Tenderly, she caressed the strong tendons of his back, running her hands up and down his spine until she heard his low groan of pleasure.

"Please, Cole," she begged. "I can't take much more of this torture."

Raising his head, he gave her a calculating smile; beads of perspiration dotted his upper lip and brow. "This is your punishment, remember?" he said, grabbing a pillow and placing it under her hips.

"What are you doing?" she gasped, her eyes widening.

"Ssh!" he crooned, kissing her tenderly. "I am in charge now."

A warm blush suffused her body as Cole raised the lower part of her to explore her most intimate of places. His fingers massaged, plying her flesh with his thumb until she could no longer contain her cries of pleasure.

As her body was roused to the peak of desire, she felt the familiar tightening in her loins. "Cole! Cole!" she cried out. The tremor inside her began to build; her breathing grew shallow and rapid. When at last he plunged his hardened member into her waiting flesh, she wrapped her legs about him, taking him deep within her. Higher and higher they climbed the peak of their passion, reaching the summit of shuddering ecstasy.

"I love you," Elizabeth cried out, her declaration of love smothered by Cole's kiss.

When it was all over, they lay side by side, their breathing deep and ragged. After a few moments, Cole turned on his side, gazing at the sweat-covered body of his wife. Her eyes were closed, her long lashes fanning out over her cheeks. Their union had been exhilarating, overwhelming, stirring emotions within him that reached down into his very soul. Elizabeth had said she loved him. If only he could believe her. He wanted to. But something inside of him, fear perhaps, warned him against being hurt. He did not want to lay himself open to that kind of pain again. He felt for the ring that rested against his throat. No. He did not want to be hurt again.

The next morning, Elizabeth woke up with one of the worst headaches of her life. Grabbing the sides of her head, she moaned, vowing never to let another drop of alcohol pass by her lips again.

Reaching across the bed for Cole, she encountered only empty space. Turning over to face the day, a warm tingling sensation flooded over her as she recalled the previous night's episode. Hugging Cole's pillow to her, she inhaled the spicy scent of his cologne that lingered on the case.

A small smile crossed her lips. Everything was going to work out. She just knew it would. Jumping out of bed, she padded over to the wardrobe to dress herself for the day ahead, anxious to learn what news Abby had for her.

Upon entering the dining room, Elizabeth discovered that everyone was already seated at the table. Abby had prepared a breakfast of what appeared to be vegetable stew. How odd, she thought, taking her seat.

"Good morning, everyone," she said, feeling her cheeks warm as her eyes locked with Cole's.

"You mean, good afternoon, don't you? It's nearly half past noon. You must have really tired yourself out at the fiesta last night," Cole said.

Elizabeth's face turned beet-red. She cast her eyes down, hoping her father and Abby wouldn't comment on Cole's suggestive remark. "It was very nice," she muttered.

"What's that you say? Nice? Personally, I thought it was one of the best evenings I have ever experienced," Cole remarked, buttering his bread.

Elizabeth shot him a lethal look. God! He was an infuriating man, she thought, secretly delighting in the fact that he had enjoyed their lovemaking as much as she had. Trying to compose herself, she turned her attention to Abby. "Did you have a nice time last night, Abby?"

A dreamy look came over Abigail's face, and she blushed. "Yes. We had a wonderful time."

Cole's eyebrow shot up. "What do you mean, *we?*"

Before Abby could reply, Jon interrupted, "What Abby means is that she and I spent a good portion of the evening together. We had a lovely time."

"And just how good of a time did you have?" Cole sneered, staring angrily across the table at Jon.

"Cole!" Elizabeth said. "That is really none of your business."

"Like hell it isn't. Abby's my sister. It seems as if I'm the only one looking out for her best interests."

Abby stood, throwing her napkin on the table. "I am not a child, Cole. I am five years older than you. You seem to forget that fact. It is my business who I spend my time with, not yours," she said, rushing out of the room.

"Abby," Cole shouted, starting to rise.

"Stay where you are," Jon ordered. "Abby is my responsibility; I will see to her."

"Like hell you will!"

"Cole," Elizabeth intervened, "I would like to speak to you alone . . . in the library." Seeing the stubborn glint in Cole's eyes, she added, "Please, Cole."

Closing the door to the library, Elizabeth wasn't quite sure what she was going to say. She had never once considered the fact that Cole would be upset by Abby and Jon's relationship.

"Please don't be angry about Abby and my father," Elizabeth said, taking a seat next to Cole on the brown leather sofa. "They can't help it if they love each other."

"Love each other! For Christ's sake! He's practically her father!" Cole shouted.

"Abby's loved Jon for a very long time. She never thought anything would come of it. But I persuaded her—"

"You persuaded." He stared accusingly at her. "I should have known that you would have had something to do with this."

"And what's wrong with trying to help two people who love each other discover that fact? I'm not ashamed of it. I think it's wonderful that they will be able to spend the rest of their lives together. I only wish—" She clamped her mouth shut.

"Yes?" he said, his eyes searching her face.

"Nothing." She had said too much already. He knew how she felt about him. She wasn't about to lay her heart on the floor for him to stomp all over it.

"Love is too precious a commodity to waste. If Abigail and my father love each other, then you should be magnanimous enough to give them your blessing."

Cole stood, rubbing the back of his neck. For years he had protected and cosseted Abby. Now that he faced the threat of losing her, he didn't know what he should feel. Christ! First, his place in Jon's affections is usurped by a daughter the man hasn't laid eyes on in twenty years, and now, he was going to lose his sister to a man who was supposed to be a father figure to both of them.

Shit! What a mess. He couldn't take much more of this emotional teeter-totter he was on. Between Elizabeth, Jon, and Abigail, he was afraid he was losing his sanity.

A multitude of emotions crossed Cole's face as he paced nervously back and forth across the room. Elizabeth didn't know how she could help reconcile the loss she was sure he was feeling. She knew what a close relationship Abby and Cole shared.

"Cole," she said softly, crossing over to where he stood, "please talk to me. Let me help you." For just a moment, she glimpsed the raw pain that entered his eyes before he shuttered them closed.

Picking up her hand, he kissed it tenderly. "Love hurts, Elizabeth," he said, walking out of the room.

She stared at the closed door, Cole's words echoing over and over again in her brain. *"Love hurts, Elizabeth. . . . Love hurts, Elizabeth. . . ."* What did he mean by that? Was he referring to the love he felt for his sister? Or did the enigmatic words have a deeper, more personal meaning?

Tears stung her eyes at the realization that she might never truly know the feelings and emotions of the man she loved so desperately.

The first days of November flew by quickly. Jon had returned to the city, leaving behind a despondent Abigail who had still not reconciled with her despotic brother.

Cole, as secretive as ever about his feelings, had continued coming to Elizabeth's bed each night, making mad, passionate love to her, but making no avowals of love nor spending an entire night beside her. She could sense he was troubled by a great many things. There were times when he took her with an urgency and desperation that rocked them both to the very core of their existence. But he steadfastly refused to open up any part of himself to her. She would often catch him following her about with brooding eyes that made her feel as if he was waiting, biding his time for something. But what? Elizabeth shook her head; she didn't know.

Sitting at the makeshift desk inside the tiny schoolhouse, Elizabeth stared down at the letter she had just received from Violet. In it, Violet had apologized profusely for her delay in coming, promising to arrive in time for the Christmas holidays. She made no mention of why she had been delayed or what she had been doing.

"Honestly, I don't think I can stand another mystery. All of this melodrama is driving me crazy," she muttered to herself. Thank goodness she had the school to occupy some of her time. She and Abigail had been taking turns, alternating days, teaching some of the local children the basics of English and other fundamental skills.

Cole had balked at the idea at first, but then had shown up one afternoon carrying boxes full of books, slates, and a big wooden ruler that he told Elizabeth was sure to come in handy.

After one full week, she had yet to use the ruler and felt she was making some real progress with some of the children. Maria seemed especially receptive to the affectionate hugs and additional help she'd been giving her. She was a sweet, lovable child. Her big brown eyes sparkled with happiness whenever she entered the schoolroom.

"Here you are, Beth. I've been looking all over for you." Abby bustled into the room, hurrying to reach the wood stove that sat in the corner. She warmed her hands by the fire.

"I decided to stay out here for a while. I was reading Violet's letter, then I guess I just started woolgathering. Is something the matter?"

Abby shook her head. "Not really. I just needed someone to talk to."

"Well, you know I'm a good listener. Take a seat on one of the benches and tell the teacher what is troubling you," Elizabeth teased. A smile broke out on Abigail's face, the first one Elizabeth had seen her wear since Jon's departure.

"I got a letter from Jon today. He wants to announce our engagement."

Elizabeth jumped up, rushing over to embrace Abby. "That's wonderful! When is the wedding to take place?"

"That's what I wanted to talk to you about. You have much more experience in these types of affairs than I do. I thought maybe you could help me plan it." Abby's look was hopeful.

Clapping her hands together, Elizabeth giggled. "I'd love to. Let's go back to the house where it's warmer. That old wood stove your brother installed doesn't throw off much heat."

Grabbing hold of Elizabeth's arm, Abby stayed her departure. "That's another problem: Cole. What am I going to do about him? What if he won't come to my wedding?"

"Abigail Martha MacAlister! You are without a doubt the most negative person I know," Elizabeth scolded.

"But you should know better than anyone how stubborn and pigheaded Cole can be."

"There's a big difference between my relationship with Cole and yours. Cole loves you, Abby. You're his sister. He would never do anything to hurt you. Give him time; he'll come around."

"It wouldn't hurt you to take some of your own advice," Abby said. "I know deep down Cole loves you. He's been hurt by something he thinks you've done. But in time, he'll see how wrong he was about you. Anyone who knows you can't help but love you, Beth."

Elizabeth's smile was wistful. "Only time will tell. And right now, I have nothing but time to spare."

Chapter Twenty-Three

Lying on the floor of the parlor in front of the fire, Elizabeth and Abigail pored over their lists for the upcoming wedding. Christmas Eve had been set aside as the day for the ceremony, since the entire family would be together. Only this morning, they had received a wire from Consuelo and Pedro, telling of their impending arrival.

"I'm so excited Consuelo will be coming home. I was worried that she wouldn't arrive in time for Thanksgiving," Abby said, holding the silk swatches of material up to the light.

"I'm relieved that I won't have to cook dinner for everybody," Elizabeth said, adding another note to her list. At the sound of Cole's laughter, Elizabeth glanced over her shoulder to find her husband deeply engrossed in his newspaper. "You needn't sound so delighted. I think my cooking has improved a great deal."

Lowering the paper, Cole smiled wickedly. "There are a great many things you have improved at." He winked suggestively.

Elizabeth reddened, sticking her tongue out at him in a childlike fashion.

"You may give me ideas if you keep that sort of thing up, Sunshine," he threatened.

Elizabeth gasped, presenting him with her back. How could Cole be so crude in front of his own sister? Sometimes she could just strangle him.

"I'm going up to soak in the tub, so I'll bid you ladies good night," Cole said, standing. "Are you coming to bed, Elizabeth?" His look was frankly suggestive.

Smiling weakly, she felt her face growing warmer by the minute. She cast Abby an embarrassed glance, relieved to find she was still absorbed in her wedding plans. "I'll be up in a few moments," she replied. God, how she hated the way he could turn her insides to butter; it just wasn't fair.

After Cole had left the room, Abby turned to face her sister-in-law, a worried expression creasing her brow. "Beth, have you made any more progress where Cole is concerned?" At the shocked look on Beth's face, Abby amended, "I mean, about my wedding."

"Oh . . . well, actually, no. But that doesn't mean I'm not going to keep on trying."

Her mouth opened in dismay. "But the wedding is only a few weeks away!"

Patting Abby's hand reassuringly, Elizabeth replied, "I'll speak to him about it tonight." She sounded more confident than she actually felt, having no idea what she could say that would change Cole's stubborn mind.

Rising to her feet, she bid Abby good night, searching her brain for the best way to approach Cole about his sister. Suddenly, a slow, secret smile lit her face, and she hurried to her room.

"Elizabeth? Is that you?" Cole called out from the bathing chamber.

"Of course, it's me. Who else would it be?" She heard his low chuckle. Opening the wardrobe, she extracted the most provocative of all her nightgowns. Cole had never seen her in this one. She had ordered it from *Godey's Lady's Book*, and when it arrived, she had been too timid to wear it.

Stripping off her clothes, she settled the diaphanous black negligee over her body, staring openmouthed at her reflection in the mirror. Every part of her anatomy was clearly visible through the sheer material. Pulling the pins out of her hair, she brushed the silken strands until they shone. Rushing to the bed, she artfully arranged herself against the pillows and waited for Cole to make his entrance.

"Elizabeth, I—" Cole stopped, his eyes rounding, his mouth dropping open. Christ! Where had she gotten that nightgown? It looked like something out of a brothel. He felt himself harden beneath the towel that was wrapped around his waist.

"Yes," she replied innocently, smiling up at him.

Cole stepped toward the bed, pulled by the magnetism of his wife's sexual allure. "Where did you get that gown? I don't remember it."

"Do you like it? Let me get up and model it for you." Jumping off the bed, she paraded this way and that, the sheer material floating around her like wrapping on a present.

The gray eyes flashed like quicksilver. "Let's get into bed," he suggested, hopping onto the mattress, propping himself up against the brass headboard.

"I'm not very tired. Do you think we could talk?"

Elizabeth asked, sitting down next to him.

"Talk?"

Running her fingers up and down his chest, she played with the chain around his neck.

He grabbed her hand. "What do you want to talk about?"

"I was wondering if you would do me a favor." She nibbled his lips, running her tongue over them, her free hand running up and down the inside of his thigh.

Cole became as hard as a mountain of granite; beads of perspiration dotted his forehead and chest. "A favor?" he choked.

"Hmmm," she murmured, licking his nipples, letting her tongue stray almost to his waist.

"Anything! Anything!" he cried.

Elizabeth's triumphant smile was hidden behind her curtain of hair. Waving the silky strands back and forth across his abdomen, her hot breath coming within inches of his hardened shaft, she asked, "Do you mean it?" She flicked her tongue out over him.

Writhing beneath her, Cole moaned in agony. "Yes. Christ! Anything you want."

"Promise?" She circled the tip with her tongue.

"I promise. As God is my witness, I promise."

Smiling in satisfaction, she took him deep within her mouth, giving him the same pleasure he had given her on so many nights.

The sun streamed in through the window, landing on Cole's scowling face. "You tricked me!" Cole shouted, leaning over Elizabeth, his hands braced on either side of her head.

284

"You promised that you would do anything I wanted," she countered, running her finger over Cole's lower lip. She smiled smugly. Cole had spent the entire night in her bed, his lust deceiving him in more ways than one.

Throwing back the covers, he jumped out of bed, reaching for his pants. He stood, glaring down at his wife. "You're certainly dressed for the role of whore," he said, a nasty smirk on his face, "but I didn't think you would actually go so far as to become one."

Balling her hand into a fist, she drove it as hard as she could into Cole's midsection, pleased by the grunt he emitted. "You are disgusting!" she shrieked. "How dare you speak to me that way. I—I—" She burst into tears, covering her face with her hands.

Heaving a deep sigh, Cole sat back down on the bed, drawing Elizabeth into his chest. "I'm sorry; I never should have said what I did. I was just mad at being tricked," he said, patting her hair gently, relieved when, after a few moments, she quieted.

Looking up at him, her lashes wet with tears, she said, "I didn't mean to deceive you, but Abby was so hurt that you had refused to give her away at the wedding. I had to do something to try and help her."

"I've been a real ass where Abby is concerned, haven't I?"

She nodded. "I know you're afraid of losing her, but Abby and my father will be very happy together. And . . . you'll still have me." She looked beseechingly into his eyes.

"Will I?" he asked, more of himself than of her. He kissed the top of her head, wishing that he could believe her. Every time he attempted to trust someone, to give them his love, they abandoned him. First his parents, then Jon, now Abby. And most especially, his wife. That had been the cruelest desertion of all.

Seeing the hurt in his eyes, Elizabeth wrapped her arms around his waist. "I love you, Cole. I know you don't believe me, but I do."

Extricating himself, Cole stood. He couldn't let Elizabeth's lies weaken his will to resist her. "I will smooth everything over with Abby. Will that make you happy?"

Wiping her eyes on the edge of the sheet, she replied softly, "For now."

Leaning her head over the commode, Elizabeth spilled the entire contents of her breakfast into the pot. For the past six days, she had vomited every morning. This was more than the influenza that she had convinced herself she had.

"What an idiot I am," she admitted, wiping her face with a cool cloth. Pushing herself to her feet, she hastened to the long mirror that stood beside the dresser. Turning sideways, she pulled her dress tight around her abdomen. She couldn't see any difference, except perhaps in the fullness of her breasts. I'm pregnant, she thought, dropping down into the chair.

Covering her face, she gave in to the tears falling down her cheeks. She didn't want to be pregnant. Not now, anyway. Nothing had been resolved between her and Cole. She didn't want to be just the mother of his child; she wanted to be his wife.

The mother of his child. The words reverberated around her head, mingling with the words Ah Sing had spoken. She raised her head, wiping her eyes on the edge of her sleeve. What was it he had said? She would have much heartache, but also much happiness. How could she have forgotten that? And there was more. Yes, now she remembered: *"The leaves say you will have five children."*

Everything about her fortune had come to pass thus far: She had met a man on a golden horse, and she had married him; she had gone away, and she had returned; she was certainly having much heartache, so it only stood to reason that she would soon have much happiness.

And now she was pregnant. Her face brightened, and she hugged herself tightly. What would Cole think? she wondered. Should she tell him? She shook her head. No. She wouldn't tell him yet. Not until she was certain of his feelings. But how long would that take? She only had nine months, and part of that was already used up. Counting back to the night of the fiesta, she calculated that she must be nearly four weeks along. That still left eight months. Surely, in eight months she could make Cole love her. She had to. There was the baby to consider now.

"Consuelo, you have outdone yourself as usual," Cole remarked to the happy cook who was seated at the table along with the rest of the family.

"*Gracias, Señor* Mac. Pedro and I are happy to be home."

"Well, I know Cole is happy that you are. He made it quite clear on several occasions what he thought of my cooking," Elizabeth said.

The room filled with laughter. Everyone seated around the long dining room table was in good spirits on this day of Thanksgiving. Cole had finally reconciled with Abby, and Jon, Consuelo, and Pedro were excited to be home with "their children," and Elizabeth held the secret of her pregnancy close to her heart.

The rain splattered down on the tile roof overhead as the hungry diners dug into the festive meal Consuelo had prepared for the occasion. There was a large roasted turkey stuffed with a savory sage bread stuffing, tender green beans floating in butter, a large bowl of applesauce that Elizabeth had slaved over, candied sweet potatoes, and of course, bowls of refried beans, Mexican rice, and flour tortillas.

After the main meal ended and the dishes had been cleared, Consuelo hurried into the kitchen to bring out the pies. Waiting patiently, five eager faces lit up as she placed two sumptuous pumpkin pies in the center of the table. The scents of cinnamon and clove permeated the air with a spicy, mouth-watering aroma.

"I don't think there's anyone who can fix a pumpkin pie the way that you do, Consuelo," Cole remarked, savoring his first bite of filling.

"Gracias, Señor Mac, but I did not fix these pies."

Cole looked up from his plate in time to catch the smug smile plastered across Elizabeth's face. "You prepared the pies?" he said, his eyebrows raised in disbelief.

"Yes, and I even remembered to remove the seeds this time," she said. Her eyes locked with Cole's and they laughed, sharing a past memory of another pie with a much different taste.

"My compliments to the chef," Cole said, bowing his head in tribute.

Clearing his throat, Jon tapped the side of his water glass with his fork. "If everyone will be silent for a moment, there is an announcement I would like to make."

Observing the warm smile Elizabeth directed at Abigail, Cole's heart warmed. Elizabeth had been good for his sister. The change in Abby since her arrival had been remarkable, he thought, turning his attention back to Jon.

"I am pleased to announce that Abigail has done me the honor of consenting to be my wife."

As Jon uttered the last word, pandemonium broke out. Consuelo began blabbing loudly in Spanish, raising her hands in praise to the Lord. Even Pedro, who was usually silent, leaned over to bestow a kiss upon Abigail's cheek.

Cole stood, placing his hands upon the table.

Everyone quieted.

Elizabeth tensed, fearful of what Cole had to say. Although Cole had reconciled with both Jon and Abby, she was not certain he had truly accepted their impending marriage.

Raising his glass high in the air, Cole looked directly at the happy couple. "I propose a toast: To Jon and Abigail, may they find happiness in life and in each other."

Breathing a sigh of relief, Elizabeth flashed Cole a brilliant smile. There just might be hope for him after all, she thought happily.

Chapter Twenty-Four

The two men sat huddled in the cantina, a deck of cards spread out between them on the table. The strumming of the guitar across the room added a festive touch to an otherwise sinister conversation.

"What are we going to do, Willy? Our money is almost gone."

Willy downed the glass of whiskey, wiping his face on the filthy sleeve of his torn denim jacket. "We get more, that's what we do."

"But how, Willy?" Jake insisted. "You know we ain't never been no good at robbing banks or rustling cattle. We almost got hung last time we tried that."

Willy leaned back in his chair, a smug expression on his face. "There's a much easier way to get the money. One we've already been successful at." At the puzzled look crossing Jake's face, Willy frowned in annoyance. "Think, Jake. What have we done recently that made us plenty of money?"

"You don't mean killing that old prospector, do you? I don't want to get involved in no more killings, Willy."

Jake's look was apprehensive.

Grabbing Jake's arm, Willy whispered, "Keep your voice down, you idiot. Do you want to get us hung? What I'm talking about is that sweet deal we had with the old man. The one in New York." Picking the queen of hearts out of the deck, he flipped it faceup on the table.

"Yeah. But the old man's dead. Didn't you tell me that when you went back to blackmail him, you found out he had died?"

"He may be dead, but the granddaughter is very much alive. I know for a fact that she's living down near Santa Clara."

Jake's eyes widened. "How do you know that?"

"'Cause I make it my business to know. Now shut up and listen. I'm not going to spend the rest of my life living in this godforsaken greaser town. Once we get our hands on some money, we're blowing San Jose and heading back to Sacramento."

"I don't get it," Jake said, scratching his head. "If the old man's dead, how are we going to get money for the granddaughter?"

"Jesus! You're as dumb as a stump," Willy said, shaking his head. "The woman's married, ain't she? I hear tell her husband and father are both well-off."

"You mean for us to kidnap her again?" Jake didn't like the sound of that one bit. They were lucky the first time. But to chance kidnapping the same woman twice? That didn't sound too smart to him.

"We're going to grab the broad and ransom her off. Her husband or father will pay handsomely for her safe return."

Jake licked his lips. "She sure had nice tits. I remember that. Do you think this time we can have a

291

little fun with her before we send her back?" Spit dribbled down his face; his eyes burned with lust.

Watching Jake rub the front of his crotch, Willy shot him a disgusted look. "Why don't you go upstairs and buy yourself one of the whores. I got plans to make."

Pushing back his chair, Jake stood, leaning over the table. "What about the girl? Do we get to diddle her?"

"I'll think about it. Now go on upstairs before you make me lose my train of thought. We don't want any screwups. I don't relish dangling at the end of a rope."

"Sure, Willy. Sure."

Watching Jake climb the stairs, Willy spit his wad of tobacco out on the floor in disgust. How'd he ever get paired up with an idiot like Jake? he wondered. Just 'cause Jake had saved his life during the war didn't mean he needed to be saddled with him for the rest of his life. He shook his head. Nope. Something would have to be done about Jake, but for now, he had more important things to think about. Lots more important things.

The first day of December brought a storm the likes of which Elizabeth had never seen since her arrival in California. The rain pelted against the window of the schoolroom, making it difficult to see the main house. Wiping the glass with the palm of her hand, she stared out, observing that several of the branches had snapped off the oaks, littering the ground with debris.

Hopefully, the children would finish with their English test soon so she could dismiss them before the storm worsened, she thought, taking a seat back at her desk. She gazed out over the bent heads working so diligently at their desks.

The sturdy oak desks that filled the schoolroom had mysteriously appeared one Monday morning when she arrived. She had a sneaking suspicion who had provided them, but when questioned, Cole had merely smiled and shook his head denying any part in it.

Thinking of Cole brought a smile to her lips. He had been so thoughtful and considerate this past week. She felt that she was making some real progress with him. Perhaps it wouldn't be too much longer before she would be able to tell him about the baby.

"*Señora* Mac." A boy's voice interrupted her thoughts. Elizabeth looked up to see Juan calling out to her, his hand waving excitedly. She smiled. "Yes, Juan, do you need help?"

"No, *señora*, but I think you do."

Her brows drew together in puzzlement. "What do you mean?"

"The stove, *señora*. The wind . . . it is blowing the smoke back inside."

Glancing back to the corner where the wood stove sat, Elizabeth saw the black puffs of smoke coming out of the aging metal contraption. Some of the children started to cough, their eyes turning red and watery. Standing up, she clapped her hands. "Gather your things, children. We need to leave here immediately."

"But, *señora*," Juan protested, "our families will not be here for several more hours to pick us up."

Elizabeth stared at the concerned expressions on the children's faces. Maria's eyes were round with fright. Oh, God! Why had Cole and Abigail picked today to go into Santa Clara for supplies? she wondered. Consuelo was in bed with a cold. Not even Pedro was around to help, he and Esteban having gone to gather stray calves on the western border of the ranch. She would have to deal with this alone.

"Juan, do you know how to hitch up a wagon?"

"Sí, Señora Mac. My padre . . . he show me many times."

She heaved a sigh of relief. "Go out to the barn and hitch up the two plow horses to the old hay wagon."

"But, señora, that wagon is no good, and the horses they are old," Juan protested.

"They are all we have. Now go and do what you are told. The rest of us will come out to the barn in a few minutes."

Grabbing his hat and poncho, Juan hurried out into the rain to do her bidding. The señora may know a lot about English and history, he thought, frowning, but she doesn't know anything about horses and storms.

Piling the children into the rear of the wagon, Elizabeth covered their shaking bodies with the canvas tarps she had found in the barn. "Now stay under there and huddle together to keep warm," she ordered.

"Juan," she called, trying to make herself heard above the downpour, "I will need you to help me drive the wagon. I'm afraid I don't know too much about such things," she admitted.

Juan smiled, puffing out his chest. "I know everything about it, señora. Do not worry. I will get us safely back to Santa Clara."

Elizabeth prayed with every mile that passed that Juan's confident statement had not been an idle boast. She further prayed that Cole and Abigail would still be in the village so she could get a ride back to the ranch with them. It occurred to her that if they had already left and she had missed them, she was in serious trouble. She shivered, wet and miserable, within the confines of her cloak.

Twenty minutes later, Juan pulled the wagon to a halt in front of the old whitewashed church. Father Martinez rushed out, helping the smaller children off the wagon and into the shelter of the building. Wiping the rain off her face with the edge of her cloak, Elizabeth said, "Juan, please run over to the mercantile and find out if *Señor* Mac is still there. I need him to take me home."

"*Sí*, I will go," Juan replied, jumping down off the seat. "Wait inside the church, *señora*. I will only be a minute."

True to his word, Juan returned a moment later with the distressing news that Cole and Abigail, not finding what they needed in Santa Clara, had left a little while ago for San Jose.

Elizabeth bit her lip, trying to decide what the best course of action would be. She hadn't told anyone about her departure. Consuelo would be out of her head with worry if she didn't return home today. Deciding that the best thing for her to do would be to drive the wagon home, she turned to face Juan, pulling him into her embrace. They huddled inside the doorway of the church, the rain beating down only inches from where they stood.

"I will drive myself home, Juan." At the look of fear on the boy's face, Elizabeth ruffled his wet hair. "Do not worry. I am twice as old as you, so I should be able to drive the horses twice as good." She smiled to reassure him. "*Gracias*, Juan, for all your help today. You were very brave."

"I will pray for your safe return, *señora*." Juan replied, looking up at the sky, which had darkened since their arrival. Watching Elizabeth climb onto the seat of the wagon, he crossed himself. *"Vaya con Dios,"* he said, waving at her retreating form, which soon became lost in the curtain of water.

An hour later, Cole and Abigail pulled the buckboard up in front of the mercantile store in Santa Clara. They had decided to return rather than risk becoming stuck in the mud that had made the roads impassable.

Both were drenched to the skin. Abigail shook pitifully in her cloak, which now reeked with the distinctive odor of wet wool. She sniffed distastefully at the offending garment. Both occupants of the wagon jumped down, hurrying into the cover of the store.

Upon entering, they were greeted by the anxious face of Juan Garcia, who rushed forward, grabbing onto Cole's hand. *"Señor* Mac! *Señorita* Abby! Thank God you have come back."

Taking off his hat, Cole shook the water onto the floor, adding more to the puddle that had already formed at his feet. "What's the matter? Why aren't you still in school?"

As Juan related the details of the afternoon's incident, Abigail covered her mouth, stifling the scream that rose in her throat.

Putting his arm around her shoulders, Cole said, "Don't worry. We'll find her."

Abby grabbed onto the front of Cole's leather jacket. "If something has happened to Elizabeth, I will never forgive myself. I was supposed to work at the school today. I—" She started to cry.

"For Christ's sake! Pull yourself together. Now is not the time for self-recriminations." Putting on his hat, he turned to face Juan. "Find Doc Willis. Send him out to

296

the ranch. I'll take the buckboard and search for Elizabeth."

"I'm going with you," Abigail said, a determined tilt to her chin. She knew Cole was going to argue the point, but this was one fight she was going to win.

Cole shook his head. "It's too dangerous, and you're too upset. You'll only slow me down."

"Be reasonable," she pleaded, grabbing onto his arm. "You will need my help if anything has happened to Beth. I insist that you take me along."

Staring into his sister's implacable features, Cole nodded. "Come along, then, but you must do everything that I tell you. Promise me."

"I promise," she replied, barely above a whisper.

"Give me some blankets and pillows," Cole shouted to Jasper Simmons, the storekeeper. "Put it on my bill."

"But, Mr. MacAlister, you can't go out in that storm. You'll both be blown away," the wide-eyed storekeeper replied.

"For Christ's sake! Do what you're told! I don't have time to argue. My wife is out in that storm."

Looking into Cole's eyes, Abigail saw the fear that she'd been too distracted to notice before. She trembled, stuffing her hands into the pockets of her cloak to keep them still.

They came upon the broken wagon about five miles from the village. One of the wheels had come off, and it was leaning to the left at an odd angle.

"Elizabeth," Cole shouted, pulling the buckboard to a halt. A sick feeling of dread centered in the pit of his stomach when he saw the motionless body of his wife lying facedown in the mud. Please God, he prayed silently, let her be alive. Jumping down, he pushed against the driving rain and wind, trying to move forward toward the front of the wagon.

Screaming, Abigail covered her mouth as she approached the still form of Elizabeth. "Is she dead?" she asked, covering her face, unable to face the truth of Cole's answer.

Kneeling down, Cole turned Elizabeth over, feeling for the pulse at the base of her neck. "She's still alive," he called out. "Quick. Bring me the blankets." He wiped her face with his handkerchief, removing the mud from her eyes and lips.

Wading through the muck that reached up to her ankles, Abigail brought Cole the items he requested. "She's so blue. She's going to die; I just know she is," she wailed.

"Shut up! For Christ's sake! She's not going to die. Now get back in the wagon before you injure yourself." He had never seen Abby so distraught; she was always the pillar of strength in a crisis.

Abby did as she was told, trying to regain her composure. Swallowing her anguish, she watched as Cole laid Elizabeth carefully in the back of the wagon, placing the pillows all around her body and under her head. He covered her with the blankets, laying the tarp down on top of them.

They made the trip back to the ranch in total silence. Cole drove slowly, moving the buckboard around several of the deeper ruts to avoid jarring Elizabeth. Abigail glanced over at her brother's ashen face. It was hard, rigid in his determination to get them safely back to the ranch. She thought she saw a tear slide down his cheek, but she could have been mistaken. The rain was beating down so hard that it was difficult to tell the teardrops from the raindrops.

The sight of the ranch house as it came into view was more welcoming than anything Cole could have ever imagined. Fear for Elizabeth's safety gnawed at him like a cancer, eating away at his composure. He wasn't sure how long he could hold on to the self-imposed control that he had placed on his emotions.

Jumping down from his perch, Cole hurried to the rear of the wagon, shouting to be heard above the wind that had picked up in intensity. "Abby, have Consuelo build up the fire in Elizabeth's room. Check to see if Pedro and Esteban have returned yet. I want Doc Willis brought up as soon as he arrives."

Abigail nodded, her skirts dragging like an anchor behind her as she hobbled through the mire to reach the house.

Picking Elizabeth up as gently as he could, Cole's heart twisted painfully as he cradled her lifeless form to his chest. "Please, don't die," he whispered, rushing her into the house and up the stairs to her room.

"*Señor* Mac, what has happened?" Consuelo asked, twisting her hands nervously as Cole placed Elizabeth on top of the bed.

"There's no time to explain now. Go heat up some water in case Doc needs it for something. Abby can fill you in on the details later."

Stripping off his leather jacket, Cole threw it on the chair. Bending over Elizabeth's still form, he carefully removed the sodden garments from her body, wiping the remaining dirt away from her face and hands. Taking a fluffy towel from the nightstand, he dried the dampness from her skin, rubbing her chilled feet and hands with his own to bring life back into her numbed extremities.

"Cole," Abby said, entering the room, "Doc Willis is here."

Sparing only the briefest of glances while he continued to work on Elizabeth, Cole nodded his head in greeting. He was grateful for the familiar presence of Doc Willis. With his peppered black hair, bushy beard, and rumpled brown suit, Doc looked more like a derelict than a doctor of medicine, but Cole knew differently. After twenty years of treatment at Doc's capable hands, he trusted him implicitly.

"Thanks for coming so quickly, Doc. My wife got caught out in the storm. Her skin is as cold as ice."

Approaching the bed, Doc Willis stared down at the frail form before him. She was a pretty thing, he thought. Placing the scuffed black leather bag on the floor, he took Elizabeth's hand, feeling for the pulse. It was weak but steady. Her skin was cold beneath his fingertips, tinged almost blue, indicating a subnormal temperature of an extreme nature.

"Get me some hot bricks. We need to get this girl's temperature back up. Bring more blankets and some hot water," he shouted.

Abigail scurried out of the room to do his bidding, calling for Consuelo to bring the necessary items. A few minutes later, Consuelo, armed with bricks, blankets, and hot water, climbed the stairs, her sides heaving in exhaustion.

Together the group worked tirelessly, taking turns at heating the bricks, warming the blankets, and much to Consuelo's annoyance, supplying Doc with cup after cup

300

of hot tea. It seemed Elizabeth wasn't the only one to suffer from exposure this wet day.

When Doc was satisfied that Elizabeth was starting to show signs of recovery, he set his teacup down, turning toward the anxious faces. "I want everyone but Cole to leave the room. I need to make my examination of this woman now."

Abby and Consuelo exchanged startled looks before gathering up the unneeded supplies and exiting the room.

Pacing nervously back and forth from one end of the room to the other, Cole glanced over at the bed from time to time, observing Doc at work. At the moment, he was listening to Elizabeth's chest with his stethoscope.

Rubbing his chin, Doc shook his head from side to side.

Cole's eyes widened in alarm. "What is it, Doc? What's wrong?"

Doc pulled the blankets up over Elizabeth MacAlister's body, relieved to find that her temperature had returned nearly to normal. Her face and hands felt warm, and she seemed to be resting in a natural slumber.

Turning to face Cole, he removed the stethoscope from around his neck, shoving it back into his bag. "Your wife seems to be on the mend. She's going to have to take it easy, however, seeing as how she's pregnant."

"Pregnant!" Cole shouted, before collapsing into the chair.

Chapter Twenty-Five

"How can she be pregnant?" Cole asked, holding his head between his hands.

Lighting his pipe, Doc glanced over at his patient to make sure that she was resting comfortably. "I assume you and your wife have engaged in the marital act. Pregnancy is quite a common occurrence of that endeavor."

Cole flashed him a look of annoyance. "I'm not stupid, Doc. I know how women get pregnant."

Smiling, Doc patted Cole on the back. "Congratulations for knowing how to do it and getting it done right."

Cole stood, gazing into the flames of the fire. The oak logs crackled and hissed as the raindrops splattered onto the hot embers. "When's the baby due?"

"Near as I can tell, Elizabeth's about four weeks along. The baby will probably be born sometime in August."

Cole thought back to the night of the fiesta and smiled. Why should he be so surprised? A night filled with as much passion as that one was bound to produce just such a result. Crossing to stand by the bed, Cole swept the hair away from Elizabeth's cheek, brushing it tenderly with his fingertips. "A baby. Did you hear that, Sunshine? We're going to have a baby," Cole whispered. Turning to face Doc, he said, "Please keep this news under your hat, Doc. I think Elizabeth was planning to surprise everyone with it."

Putting on his coat and picking up his bag, Doc smiled. "You know me, boy. My mouth's as tight as the widow Murphy's corset."

Cole grinned knowingly. Everyone for miles around knew that the two-hundred-pound widow, Constance Murphy, had her sights set on Doc. "She may surprise you one day, Doc. Never doubt a determined woman."

A hearty chuckle emanated from Doc's chest as he made his way to the door. "You may be right, boy. You may be right. I'm not getting any younger, and a fleshy woman like the widow could sure keep my skinny old bones warm on a blustery night such as this."

Cole laughed, shaking his head as he watched the crusty old codger make his way down the stairs. Closing the door quietly, he tiptoed over to Elizabeth's bed. She was still sleeping soundly.

Pulling back the covers, he placed his hand gently on her abdomen. Her skin felt warm beneath his touch. Cole breathed a sigh of relief. Caressing the flat contour where his child grew safely within her womb, he smiled wistfully, tears misting his eyes. He had planted his seed and it had taken root. Soon his son or daughter would be born, and he would have the responsibility of teaching it to grow up into a worthwhile human being . . . someone honorable and fair as Jon, good and kind as Abby, and strong and loving as Elizabeth.

How many times had Elizabeth professed her love to him, only to have it thrown back in her face? His gut

303

twisted. He had almost lost her today. She would have died never knowing how much he loved her. He was finally man enough to admit it. It was time to put his petty jealousies and hatreds aside. A child was on the way. A child for him to father . . . to raise . . . to love.

Reaching up, he unhooked the chain that had choked off his feelings for so long. The small gold ring rested comfortably in his hand. It still shone bright as his love for the woman before him. Taking Elizabeth's left hand, he placed the ring on her finger, kissing it tenderly before placing it under the covers.

He hadn't said the words, but the ring spoke volumes about what he felt for his wife. Surely, when she found it, she would know that he had forgiven her. Quietly, he exited the room, vowing that tomorrow would be a new beginning for them.

Elizabeth awoke the next morning to find Cole, unshaven and disheveled, sleeping in a chair right next to her bed, his booted feet propped up in front of him on the mattress. How had she gotten back to the house? she wondered. The last thing she remembered was the wagon wheel coming off and her body being thrown to the ground.

Her hands went quickly to her abdomen. If anything had happened to her baby because of her stupidity, she would never forgive herself. She stretched her legs out; there were no cramps, no discomfort. Everything seemed to be in good working order. Satisfied that the baby was fine, she turned her head to study her husband.

Cole's face looked haggard, as if he had spent a restless night. There were purplish shadows under his eyes and a

304

dark stubble of beard covering his face. He was dressed in Levi's and black leather boots. The rest of him was deliciously naked. Reaching out, she touched his chest, pulling her hand back when Cole's eyes flew open.

"Are you trying to take advantage of an innocent man while he sleeps, Sunshine?"

Blushing furiously, Elizabeth stammered, "I was just . . . I mean . . . How did you find me?"

Dropping his feet to the floor, Cole straightened, stretching the taut muscles of his back that had tightened from an uncomfortable night's rest. "If I wasn't so relieved that you are all right, I would take you over my knee and paddle the living daylights out of you. Do you have any idea of the stupidity of your actions?"

Elizabeth slunk down, pulling the covers up to her chin. Cole's face was red in anger. She watched nervously as he paced back and forth across the pine floor.

Crossing back to the bed, he sat down next to her on the mattress. "Do you know how scared we all were? How frightened I was of losing you?"

Elizabeth shook her head, tears running down her cheeks. He cared. Cole cared about her. It was worth all the pain and misery she had endured to hear that particular admission.

Gathering her into his arms, Cole wiped her tears away. "Elizabeth, don't ever do anything like that again."

"I won't. I promise," she choked out, grateful to be held so close to his heart. She could hear the steady beat, and it was comforting.

Straightening, Cole smiled. "Do you need any help with your morning ablutions?"

Elizabeth reddened, mortified that Cole would speak of

such things. "No! I'll be fine."

"Good. You can take care of that while I fetch your breakfast. After you're done, I want you to get right back into bed."

"But, Cole, I feel fine."

"No arguments. You had a close call, and Doc says you need to rest."

A shadow of alarm touched her face. "You had a doctor here?"

Cole didn't miss the way Elizabeth's hand went instinctively to her abdomen, covering it protectively. He nodded. "You were blue when I found you. Did you expect me to leave your recovery to chance?"

Not knowing what to say, she merely shook her head, dismay rising in her breast at the news she had just discovered. Waiting until Cole had left the room, she rose from the bed to perform the necessity she was too embarrassed to ask him for help with.

Grabbing the hairbrush from the dresser, she settled back down under the covers, brushing her tangled head of hair that had knotted and snarled overnight. Holding the strands with her left hand, she brushed vigorously with her right. Glancing down, a flash of color caught her eye; the sun reflected off the shiny object on her left hand. She paused, holding the silver hairbrush in midair to gaze upon the golden wedding ring that now adorned her finger.

Cole, she thought, giddy with happiness. Cole did love her. He did care for her. He . . . She groaned. He knows. He knows about the baby. The doctor had been there to examine her. Of course! Now she knew why he had suddenly become so attentive and concerned. The one thing she had feared had come to pass: Cole had discovered she was pregnant. How would she ever know if it was her he truly cared about or the child? She shook her head, tears brimming her lashes.

The door opened, admitting a cheerful Abigail, who was carrying a large silver tray. "Welcome back. You had me scared to—" At the sight of Elizabeth's tears, Abby paused. "What's wrong? Are you ill?" Setting the tray down on the dresser, she rushed forward.

"Oh, Abby, everything is such a mess."

Abby sat down, taking Elizabeth's hand in her own. "Tell me what's happened. Surely, nothing could be as bad as all that. Why, Cole is positively glowing. He's so relieved that you're all right."

"How do I know it's me he truly cares for? How will I ever know now?" Chewing her lower lip, she gazed forlornly out the window, her mind reeling in confusion as to how she would face this newest predicament in her relationship with Cole.

Abby listened, puzzled by Elizabeth's odd speech and morose behavior. "Perhaps if you tell me what it is that's troubling you, I can find a way to help."

"I'm pregnant."

Abby's face lit up with pleasure. "But that's wonderful! I'm so happy for you." She enfolded Elizabeth in her arms.

Shaking her head, Elizabeth said, "You don't understand. It's not wonderful at all. Cole knows. I'm sure of it."

"What do you mean, you're sure of it? Didn't you tell him?"

"I wanted to be sure of his feelings for me. I don't want a marriage without love."

"Beth," Abby chided, "Cole loves you. I know it *here*."

She placed Elizabeth's hand on her heart. "If you could have seen him yesterday like I did, there wouldn't be a doubt in your mind."

"I wish I could believe you."

Abby glanced down, noticing for the first time the ring on Elizabeth's finger. "I see you got your wedding ring back."

Gazing at it dejectedly, Elizabeth sighed. "He must have placed it on my finger after he learned about the baby. Don't you see, Abby? It's the baby he wants, not me."

"Pooh! Now, who's being negative? I can't believe that you're the same woman who told me to fight for the man I love . . . that nothing worth having ever came easy. What happened to the old Beth I knew and loved?"

"She got pregnant."

"Nothing's changed. You were determined to win Cole's love before the child, and now that you're pregnant, that should make it even easier. Besides, you don't know for certain that Cole knows about the baby. He didn't say anything to me."

"But how can I be sure?"

"Trust in yourself, in your woman's intuitiveness. And most of all, trust in your love. Wars have been fought over love. Love conquers all, remember? You only have one misguided man to conquer. It should be a snap," Abby said, snapping her fingers to make the point.

Before Elizabeth could reply, Cole entered, shaved and neatly dressed in black trousers and a white linen shirt. He frowned when he saw the tray of untouched food on the dresser.

"Why haven't you eaten? You need to keep up your strength."

"I'll leave you two alone," Abby said, rising from the bed. "Call me if you need anything. I'll be right downstairs."

Elizabeth sent Abby off with a warm smile. Turning, she faced her husband, who approached with the tray. "Just set it down on the nightstand. I'm not very hungry right now."

"Definitely not," he said, placing a napkin around her neck as if she were a child. "Consuelo would have my hide if she found out you hadn't eaten. You're not going to risk her wrath, are you?" he said, tweaking Elizabeth's nose. "Do you want sugar in your coffee?"

Cole, she screamed silently, tell me you love me. Tell me it's me you care about, not just the baby. But aloud she merely shook her head and replied, "Two lumps, please."

Elizabeth was up and about within two days of her accident. Other than a few scrapes and bruises and a couple of tender ribs, she felt fine.

Cole had taken up residence in his old bedroom. She guessed he was trying to be solicitous of her health, but it only made her feel more depressed.

Staring down at the blank piece of paper before her, Elizabeth didn't know how she was going to concentrate on her present task of planning Abigail's wedding. In only three more weeks, Abby and her father would be joined in matrimony. She was so happy for Abby; the woman literally floated around the house on a cloud of love. But Elizabeth had to admit that she was a little envious of her, too. At least Abby knew where she stood in Jon's affections.

309

"Beth, are you listening?" Abby repeated. "I said, do you think we need to order more champagne from the monastery in San Jose?"

Elizabeth looked up at the sound of Abby's voice. "What? The champagne?"

"Oh, never mind. I can see your heart is not into this right now."

Elizabeth blushed guiltily. "Don't be silly."

"It's Cole, isn't it? You're thinking about him again."

"Cole! Whatever are you talking—"

"Did I hear my name mentioned?"

All eyes turned toward the doorway as Cole strode casually into the room, his hands stuffed in his pockets, a smile on his face.

"What are you doing home? I thought you were going into the city today," Abby questioned.

"Can't a man change his mind? Or is that only a woman's prerogative?" He pulled a chair out from the table, straddling it with his legs. "I thought I'd stay home and take my lovely wife on a picnic."

"A picnic!" both women chorused, exchanging startled glances.

"Don't look so shocked. I've been known to do nice things once in a while." He focused his gaze on Elizabeth, who was twisting the pen nervously in her fingers. "How about it?"

She chewed her lower lip. "I don't know. I have Abby's wedding to plan, and it's December, in case you hadn't noticed."

"I noticed," he said, grinning. "I have the weather completely under control. Besides, it's not that cold out. In case you hadn't noticed," he mimicked.

"She'd love to go," Abigail butted in, helping

310

Elizabeth up from her chair.

"But!" Elizabeth protested.

"But nothing. Go up and change. Since Consuelo is outside in the washhouse doing the laundry, I'll fix the picnic lunch myself."

"Very well," Elizabeth said, smiling happily. "I'll be back in a minute."

The minute turned into thirty, and still Elizabeth had not appeared. Cooling his heels while he waited, Cole adjusted the blankets and basket for the tenth time. At the sound of footsteps, he turned, his eyes lighting in wonder at the sight of Elizabeth coming toward him dressed in a red wool dress with a white lace collar.

Elizabeth glowed under Cole's admiring gaze. Handing him her cloak, she waited patiently for him to assist her up onto the seat. "Where are we going?" she asked when they were finally settled inside the carriage.

"Somewhere I used to go as a kid. You'll see when we get there."

Intrigued but not wanting to spoil Cole's surprise, Elizabeth sat back, resting against the cushion of the seat. The temperature was brisk but not cold, the warm wool dress she wore offering adequate protection from the late morning breeze. They chatted as they drove, Cole pointing out various items of interest about the ranch.

"That's where we had our first house," Cole said, pointing to a building that was really just a dilapidated old shack.

"You lived there!" Elizabeth said, her mouth dropping open at the sight.

"You didn't think Rancho del Oro just sprang up from nowhere, did you? We had to live in something while we were building the house."

She felt stupid. There was so much about Cole's past that she didn't know. "You haven't told me very much about yourself," Elizabeth pressed. "Why?"

Cole shrugged. "There's not much to tell. We left Independence, and my parents died of cholera. You know the rest."

"But how did you feel when you lost your parents? Were you decimated by their deaths?"

"I was only ten. Naturally, I was upset."

"But how did you feel . . . deep inside, I mean." She didn't know why, but she felt it was important for her to understand how Cole felt about such things. Maybe it would give her a deeper understanding of him as a man.

"I was hurt . . . bitter. I couldn't understand why they had to die," he admitted. "But then I was only a kid."

"Thank you for telling me that. Sometimes I don't feel I know you very well."

Cole stared at her strangely. "Why would you say that? After all, we've lived as man and wife for quite some time."

"You won't let me get close to you. You keep your feelings hidden. I've seen many Cole MacAlisters in the last six months, but which one is the real you?"

Cole smiled. "I could say the same about you, Sunshine. When I met you, I thought you were nothing more than a shallow socialite."

"And now?" Elizabeth asked, anxious to hear if his opinion of her had altered.

"I can see that you're more than just a pretty face. You've adjusted well to your new life."

It was as close to an admission of respect as she was going to get. "Better than you thought I would, I take it."

She smiled smugly.

Cole grinned boyishly, displaying two charming dimples. "We're here, Sunshine."

Looking down, the two men who were hidden behind the rocks spotted the object of their surveillance. "Look, Willy, there she is. Ain't she something all decked out in that red dress. She looks like a cherry, ripe and ready to eat." Jake licked his lips.

"Yeah. And in case you hadn't noticed, she's got someone with her. We can't risk grabbing her when her husband's around. We'll have to wait until she's alone."

"Do you suppose that they're going to do it out there in the open? Shit! I want to stay and watch. You never did let me see the girl naked the last time we had her."

Willy knocked Jake across the back of the head. "Shut up, you imbecile. Is that all you can ever think about? I think you got more brains in your dick than you do in that soft head of yours."

Jake smiled, displaying a mouthful of rotted, tobacco-stained teeth. "At least I still got a dick. Too bad yours got shot off in the war." He cackled.

Willy's eyes narrowed. He had taken all the snide remarks he was going to from this perverted little runt. Clenching his fists, he took a step forward, halting at the frightened look on Jake's face. Calm yourself, Willy, he told himself. There'll be plenty of time for getting even once the plan is completed. They had been lucky today in spotting the girl. Next time, she might be alone. He would bide his time. Hadn't his ma always said that good things came to those who waited?

313

"Mount up," he sneered, spitting his wad of tobacco and hitting Jake's boot. "We're leaving."

"What is this place?" Elizabeth inquired, gazing at the wall of stone. "It looks like a cave."

Cole removed the brush from in front of the rock, revealing an entrance. "It is a cave. Come on, I'll show you inside." Grabbing her hand, he pulled her forward like a little boy eager to share a secret.

It was dark and musty inside the cave, reminding her of the secret passage they had taken once to get into Cole's room. She sniffed. "Is that water I smell?"

Lighting a torch that was fastened into the side of the rock, Cole replied, "There's an underground spring. It's what feeds the river that flows through our property."

"Are there creatures in here?" she asked, stopping to wait for Cole's answer.

"Only us," he replied, grabbing her about the waist. "Watch your step; it might be slippery up ahead."

As the cave widened out, Elizabeth's mouth opened up in surprise. Someone had taken a hole in the mountain and turned it into a comfortable abode. There were two small-sized cots, the kind a child would use, a scaled-down version of a table and chairs, and painted on the far wall in big red letters was Cole's name.

"This was yours!"

"I spent a lot of time here after we moved to the ranch. It was my place to come and think."

She noticed the crudely carved wooden soldiers that sat on the old crate and a primer that had once been read quite thoroughly. "Are those your things?" she asked.

Cole's eyes got a faraway look in them. He was silent

314

for a moment, as if remembering something from long ago. "That's all I have left of my old life before I moved here." He picked up one of the soldiers. "My father carved these himself. He wasn't very good at it, but at the time, I thought they were the best toys in the world."

A lump formed in Elizabeth's throat. She was catching a glimpse of Cole that was usually hidden. The Cole that had buried his parents' death deep inside, where it couldn't reach out and hurt him. She touched his arm. "Thank you for bringing me here."

Cole shrugged, his mask firmly back in place. "It's just an old hideout I thought you might enjoy seeing."

"I'm enjoying it very much," she said, running her fingers up the inside of his arm. "I would enjoy it even more if you would kiss me."

Scooping Elizabeth up in his arms, he carried her over to the narrow cot. Placing her down gently, he covered her lips as well as her body with his own. The lunch basket lay forgotten, time standing still for the two lovers who hungered only for each other.

Chapter Twenty-Six

Setting the plates down on the dining room table for dinner, Abigail stared in amazement at the two disheveled people walking toward her. "What on earth has happened to the two of you?" She had despaired of ever seeing Cole and Elizabeth again after they had disappeared for most of the afternoon. "You look like you've been rolling in the dirt," she continued, eyeing the couple suspiciously.

Glancing over at Cole, who was grinning from ear to ear, Elizabeth looked down at the dress she was wearing, which was covered with bits of mud and grass. She blushed, matching the color of her dress almost exactly. "I'd better go up and change," she said.

"Well, you had better hurry," Abby said, placing another fork on the table. "Jon will be here any minute, and he's bringing you a surprise. His wire just arrived."

Cole's eyebrow shot up. "What's that rascal up to now, I wonder?"

Abby's smile was secretive. "Why don't you go up and change as well. I'm sure Elizabeth could use some help with her buttons."

"Oh, no, that's all right. Why, I didn't have a bit of trouble earli—" She covered her mouth, horrified at what she had been about to admit. Turning, she fled to her bedroom, Cole's and Abigail's laughter following her up the stairs.

Quickly unfastening her gown, she fetched another dress from her wardrobe. What could Abby have meant about her father bringing her a surprise? she wondered. He doesn't even know about the baby yet. He's the one that's going to be surprised, she thought, giggling to herself.

She had come to a decision this afternoon: She was going to tell Cole about the baby. After all, there was still the possibility that he didn't know about her pregnancy.

They had shared a closeness today that had been missing from their marriage. Even though Cole didn't love her, they still had the baby to consider. If they were to make a go of their marriage, she didn't want any secrets to come between them.

Throwing the blue and red plaid taffeta gown onto the bed, Elizabeth swung about at the sound of the door closing, to find Cole entering the room. She swallowed. Now would be as good a time as any to tell him, she decided, anxiety turning her stomach queasy.

"Did I startle you?" Cole asked.

Fidgeting nervously with the ribbons of her chemise, she replied, "You might have knocked."

His brow creased. "What is it? Why are you so tense?" Placing his hands on her shoulders, he gently kneaded the taut muscles.

Chewing her lower lip, Elizabeth finally blurted out, "Cole, there is something I have to tell you."

317

Leading Elizabeth to the chair, he sat down, positioning her squarely on his lap. "I'm all yours," he replied. He had a good idea what she was going to tell him; he had sensed her anxiety all afternoon. Something had changed between them today. He couldn't quite put his finger on it, but something definitely was different.

"Cole," she began again, pulling and twisting at the gold ring on her finger.

"Hmmm," he answered, playing with the pink satin ribbons of her chemise.

"Have you ever thought about having a family?"

"I have a family," he replied. "I have you, and Abigail, and Jon, and—"

"No," she interrupted, "I mean a family of your own . . . a son or daughter to carry on your name."

Cole's eyes twinkled mischievously, and he shook his head. "Can't really say that I've given it much thought," he said, smiling inwardly at the two bright spots of color touching Elizabeth's cheeks. "Why do you ask?"

Twisting herself about, she stared intently into Cole's eyes, wanting to gauge his reaction when she told him about the baby. "I'd start thinking about it if I were you."

"We've got plenty of time to have children. Right now, I just want you all to myself." He kissed her shoulder, running his tongue under the satin straps.

Goose bumps broke out over Elizabeth's neck and arms. "Stop that," she scolded, crossing her arms firmly over her chest. "I'm trying to tell you something."

"What is so important that I can't even enjoy the taste of my wife's succulent skin?"

"I'm going to have a baby!" she blurted out, jumping up from his lap.

"Well, of course you are. In a year or two, we'll make plans to have a child."

She heaved a sigh, shaking her head in aggravation. "Are you listening to me?" Taking his hand, she placed it on her abdomen. "Your child grows within me; I'm pregnant."

Silence enveloped the room save for the popping of the logs in the fireplace. Cole sat motionless, a blank expression on his face.

Not able to stand it a moment longer, Elizabeth exclaimed, "Well, aren't you going to say something?"

Jumping up, Cole swept Elizabeth into his arms, lying her spread-eagle on the bed. "Hell, yes, I'm going to say something!"

Elizabeth tensed, waiting for the angry retort she was certain was coming.

Covering her body gently with his, he spread her arms out to her sides, staring into the brilliant blue depths of her eyes. "I love you, Sunshine."

Tears filled her eyes. "No . . . you don't," she said. "You're just being nice because of the baby."

Cole's head jerked up, his eyes widening. "You're wrong." Of all the reactions he had expected from Elizabeth, this wasn't one of them.

Shaking her head in disbelief, she insisted, "You don't!"

Cole's eyes narrowed. "The hell you say. Don't tell me I don't. I'm telling you I do." He got up, pulling her up with him.

Wringing her hands nervously, Elizabeth replied, "Please don't do this, Cole. For months I have told you that I love you, and you've said nothing. Now I tell you that I'm pregnant, and suddenly you love me. Even *I'm* not that naive."

Cole rubbed the back of his neck. He couldn't believe what he was hearing. Was this how Elizabeth had felt all the times she had confessed her love, only to have him throw it back in her face? He was such a fool. How could he make her understand?

Taking her hand in his, he said, "Elizabeth, I swear . . ."

She covered his mouth with her fingertips. "Say no more; it's not necessary. Perhaps someday you will grow to love me for myself, not just for the baby. Until then, I have enough love for both of us."

Grabbing her shoulders, he shook her. "Why won't you believe me?" he shouted.

"Cole, Abby told me about the letter you received . . . the one that you thought I wrote." She was surprised at how calm she felt now that the time had come to confront Cole.

"But I have forgiven you for that."

Elizabeth's eyes glittered angrily, her calmness suddenly evaporating at the one word that aroused her ire: *forgiven*. Placing her hands on her hips, she threw back her head to stare accusingly at Cole. "How can you forgive me for something I didn't do? When you love someone, you trust them. You thought I had deceived you . . . lied to you. You even kept my wedding ring from me." She held her finger up in front of his face. "Don't profess to love me now. I finally realize that you have too much hurt inside of you to really love anyone."

Cole's face whitened. "That's not true." Christ! Why wouldn't she listen. He had given her the ring. Didn't she understand it was a token of his love for her?

"Please leave. I need to dress for dinner." Turning,

she walked back to the bed.

"Elizabeth."

She refused to turn around. "Please!" she pleaded, relieved when she finally heard the door close behind him.

It would be better this way. She wanted no marriage based on deceit. She realized after today's outing that much of Cole's distrust was based on his feelings of abandonment as a child. When he came to grips with his real feelings, then maybe . . . just maybe, she would believe that he loved her.

The tension in the parlor was so thick it could have been cut with a knife. Seated on the sofa next to Cole, Abigail stared at him out of the corner of her eye, concern marring her smooth features. Whatever had happened this afternoon was having a devastating effect on her brother. She had never seen him so distraught, except perhaps when he thought Elizabeth had left him. And Elizabeth. She sat across the room staring pensively into the fire, looking as if she had just lost her best friend.

Abby sighed. Why couldn't those two work out their problems? she wondered. She wanted to shake some sense into them. It was obvious that they loved each other. Why did they fight so hard to recognize what others could see so clearly? She shook her head in disgust. She had never encountered two more obstinate people in her entire life. If only Jon would get here. At least then she would have someone to talk to.

As if on cue, the door knocker sounded. Abigail heard Consuelo bustling to the door. She rose from her seat, hurrying into the entry hall, her eyes lighting up at the sight of her fiancé. Standing next to him was Elizabeth's surprise, a woman of middle age whom Abigail surmised, from her sister-in-law's description, was Violet Baxter.

Smiling, she gave both Jon and Violet a hug. "Elizabeth is going to be so surprised," Abby whispered. "You couldn't have come at a better time."

Violet took off her hat, cloak, and gloves, handing them to Consuelo. "I take it nothing has improved since I've been gone," she inquired, noting the distressed look on Abigail's face.

At the sound of footsteps, Elizabeth looked up, her eyes clouding with tears. "Thank goodness you've finally come," she cried, rushing forward to throw her arms around Violet Baxter. "I've missed you." She gave her a tight squeeze, noting the new attractive hairdo Violet sported and the expensive cut of her dress.

"What about me?" Jon said. "Don't I get a kiss?"

Smiling up at her father, Elizabeth kissed him on the cheek.

"Cole, my boy," Jon said, entering the room, "I didn't see you sitting there. Why are you so quiet?"

Glancing over at Elizabeth, whose face was glowing, he shrugged. "No reason." He stood, coming forward to greet his guests.

"Hello, Violet, it's good to see you again," Cole said. He could see by the thin-lipped greeting Elizabeth's former housekeeper gave him that he was still on her list.

Crossing to Elizabeth's side, he put his arm protectively around her waist, smiling down at her. The look of pleasure she directed at him warmed his heart.

He had done a lot of thinking about Elizabeth and their relationship while he brooded over his brandy. Some of what she had said about his past had hit home. He didn't want to lose her. He had persuaded some pretty tough judges and jurists in his career. Surely, he would be able to convince one stubborn little blonde that the words he spoke were the truth. He pulled her to him tightly, kissing her cheek, amused by the startled expression on her face.

During a lull in the conversation, Cole cleared his throat. "Since we are all together once again," he said, staring meaningfully at Violet, who managed a small smile for him, "I would like to make an announcement. Elizabeth has informed me, only today, that we are to become parents." He kissed his wife soundly on the lips amidst a chorus of cheers.

Stepping back, Cole watched as the trio cavorted over his news. Elizabeth was passed back and forth, the recipient of dozens of hugs and kisses. He could feel his own eyes mist as he watched Jon weep with unconcealed joy.

"Congratulations, Cole, you've made me a happy man," Jon said, coming to stand before him.

Cole pumped his hand. "No happier than you've made me."

Jon's eyebrow shot up in surprise. "So, you've finally come to your senses, have you? Glad to hear it. I knew you couldn't hold out against Elizabeth forever."

Cole pulled Jon to the other side of the room. "It's not me who's holding out," Cole whispered. "Your daughter doesn't believe that I love her."

"Well, what did you expect, my boy? After the way you've treated her, I'm not the least bit surprised."

"But I told her that I had forgiven her . . . that I loved her."

Jon shook his head. "Cole, you may be a damned good

lawyer, but when it comes to women, you're not very smart."

"And I suppose you are," Cole countered. "Aren't you forgetting about my sister? You certainly didn't seem to be very smart where she was concerned."

Jon had the decency to look abashed. "You're right. Love is blind. It keeps us from seeing what is right under our noses. But we're not talking about me; we're talking about you and Elizabeth. You've treated her badly . . . convicted her without benefit of trial or jury."

"But the letter! I had evidence," Cole argued.

"Circumstantial at best. I told you from the beginning that Worthington was behind it. You were just too hard-headed to believe me."

"I'm still not entirely convinced that she wasn't involved."

"And Elizabeth is not entirely convinced that you love her. Is it an impasse, then?" Jon asked, noting the look of anguish on Cole's face. "Swallow your pride, my boy. Love isn't based on facts and logic. It's trusting someone when all the evidence points against them. You should know better than anyone that sometimes it becomes necessary to look below the surface to discover the truth. When you believe in your heart that Elizabeth is innocent of any wrongdoing, it will show through. It will be then—and only then—that Elizabeth will believe that you love her."

Jon walked away, leaving Cole to stare thoughtfully into the flames of the fire.

It was the week before Christmas, and the house was a flurry of excitement and activity. Violet had stayed to help with the preparations for the wedding. She and Elizabeth stood side by side in the kitchen, making tiny fruitcakes to pass out to all the wedding guests. The steam from the boiling water on the stove had fogged up the windows, making it difficult to tell the mist from the rain that beat against the windowpanes.

"Aren't you going to tell me why you took so long in getting here?" Elizabeth asked, licking the icing off her fingers.

"I've been terribly busy closing up the mansion in New York, finding employment for the staff. Mrs. Thomas was devastated by the news that you wouldn't be coming back to live there," Violet confided.

"Poor Mrs. Thomas. She's such a sweet lady. Did you find her another position?"

"Yes. I placed her with a very prominent family in Brooklyn by the name of Cutler. I think she'll be very happy there."

"And what about you? What are your plans?" Elizabeth asked, certain that Violet had something up her sleeve.

Blushing, Violet wiped the flour off her hands. "Do you remember that nice man I danced with at your wedding reception?

Elizabeth's eyes widened. "You mean Peter Maxwell?"

Violet nodded, smiling like a young girl. "Peter and I have grown very close since my return to San Francisco. He's been lonely since his wife died two years ago, and . . . he's asked me to marry him."

Elizabeth squealed with delight, throwing her arms around Violet and kissing her cheek. "I'm so happy for you. When is the wedding?"

325

"Not for a few months. We want to give his children time to get used to me."

"They'll love you. How can they not?"

The two joyful women did not notice how the water on the stove had boiled over onto the floor, until a very distraught Consuelo came barging into the kitchen with murder in her eyes.

"Are you two *loco*? What are you doing to my kitchen?" She ran to the stove, grabbing some towels to mop up the mess on the floor.

"Now, Consuelo, don't be a grouch. Mrs. Baxter just informed me that she is getting married," Elizabeth said.

Swinging about, Consuelo raised her hands in supplication. "Ayeee! She is getting married . . . *Señorita* Abby is getting married . . . you are having a baby . . . and I am doing all the work. Now get out, both of you!"

Elizabeth and Violet stared openmouthed at Consuelo's tirade. The laughter Elizabeth had tried so valiantly to contain suddenly burst forth, prompting Violet to cover her mouth in an uncharacteristic fit of giggling. Not wanting to increase Consuelo's wrath, both women ripped off their aprons and hurried out the door to escape the epithets that Consuelo hurled at them in Spanish.

Grabbing the last sack of grain off the wagon, Cole tossed it onto the wooden pallet. "That should do it, Pedro," he said, wiping the sweat off his face with his neckerchief.

"*Sí, Señor* Mac, we have finished in no time," the short, wiry Mexican answered. "Why don't you go back to the house, I can finish up here."

326

"Are you sure there is nothing more that I can do? I don't relish spending the afternoon locked up with a bunch of babbling females. All they can talk about is that blasted wedding."

"Well, there are always the stalls that need to be cleaned," Pedro offered. He knew how much *Señor* Mac hated to clean the stalls. Ever since he was a little boy, he would always look for ways to get out of that chore. Pedro smiled inwardly at the look of distaste that crossed Cole's face.

"Hand me a pitchfork," Cole said, holding out his hand.

The two worked side by side as they had so many times since Pedro had come to work as the foreman of Rancho del Oro. Suddenly, Pedro stopped, leaning on his pitchfork.

"*Señor* Mac, there is something I have been meaning to tell you."

"What is it?" Cole asked, throwing the dirty hay into the wheelbarrow.

"Yesterday, Esteban and I see two strange men when we are gathering up the strays."

"Do you think they were just passing through?" Cole asked, not breaking his stride.

"No, *señor*, I do not."

Cole paused, noting Pedro's concerned expression. "Why do you say that?"

"I have seen these men before. Once in Santa Clara when I went to pick up supplies, and once in the hills above our property. It was the day you took *Señora* Mac out to visit your cave."

Removing his gloves, Cole pushed the hair out of his eyes. "Do you think they could be rustlers?"

Pedro shook his head. "I do not know."

"I want you and Esteban to keep an eye out for these men. Tell the other vaqueros to do the same. If you see them again, I want to know immediately."

"*Sí, señor.* It will be done."

Cole walked over to the barn door, staring out at the rain that had all but stopped. Why would these men pick his cattle to rustle? There were much bigger ranches around to choose from. The risk of being spotted and getting caught would be considerably less on a larger ranch. Should he mention it to the women? he wondered. No. He would wait. He didn't want to alarm them unnecessarily, and besides, they might just be a couple of drifters who had happened by.

Chapter Twenty-Seven

"Where do you want the Christmas tree?" Cole snapped.

Elizabeth eyed the eight-foot fir and shook her head. "Is that the best one you could find? It's so scrawny." She wanted everything to be perfect for the wedding tomorrow evening, and the tree did not measure up.

Dragging in the gigantic conifer with the help of Esteban, Cole's smile was more of a smirk. "This is it, lady, so tell us where to put it."

Crossing her arms, Elizabeth's eyes glittered dangerously. She wasn't in any mood to put up with Cole's surliness when there were still a million and one things left to do. "I'll tell you where you can put it. You can just take it and—"

"Elizabeth!" Violet shouted, trying to head off what was quickly becoming an ugly disagreement. "I think perhaps you need a rest, dear. You've been working terribly hard. Why don't you go upstairs and take a nap."

"If you two females can make up your mind, we'd like to put this damn tree down. It's getting mighty heavy,"

Cole said, trying to keep his temper in check.

Elizabeth turned on him, her face a mask of fury. "Oh, be quiet. Can't you see we're having a discussion. Must you always—" Suddenly, she burst into tears. Picking up her skirts, she ran from the room.

Cole's mouth dropped open; he looked anxiously at Violet. "What did I say?"

Violet smiled knowingly. "Why don't you put the tree in front of the window. I think it will look just fine there."

The two men carried their heavy burden into the parlor, placing it down where Violet directed. Esteban made a hasty retreat, while Cole stared forlornly out the window. The sun shone brightly in the sky, contrasting markedly with his dark and dismal mood.

"You mustn't take what Elizabeth says to heart, Cole," Violet said. "She's just reacting like any pregnant woman would. She's overtired. I've tried to get her to rest, to delegate her responsibilities, but she insists on doing everything herself. She says it's expected of her as mistress here."

"Oh, Christ!" Cole muttered, looking genuinely distressed. "What a mess I've made of everything."

Placing her hand on Cole's arm, Violet said, "Why don't you go up and see if you can talk some sense into that wife of yours. Perhaps she will listen to you."

Cole shook his head. "That's not likely, but I'll try."

The room was dark when Cole entered, the curtains drawn against the late afternoon sun. Elizabeth lay huddled in the center of the bed, weeping pitifully into her pillow. Crossing to the bed, Cole gazed down at her distraught form.

"Sweetheart," he crooned, sitting down on the edge of

the mattress, drawing Elizabeth into his arms.

"Oh, Cole," Elizabeth sobbed, "I don't know what's come over me. I've turned into such a shrew." She clung to him, crying softly against his shoulder.

Smiling tenderly, he wiped her eyes with the edge of his shirt. "You're tired; you've been working too hard. Abby doesn't expect you to make yourself sick over her wedding. She'd be very upset to find out that you've been overdoing."

"Promise you won't tell her? I don't want to spoil anything for her."

He frowned. "I shouldn't have let her run off to San Francisco, leaving you here to do everything by yourself."

"She had to go. She wouldn't have been able to find any decent items for her trousseau in Santa Clara. And besides, it's good for her to get away. She's having a difficult time adjusting to the fact that she won't be able to live at the ranch anymore. Anyway, she said she'd be home in time for dinner."

Cole sighed sadly, thinking of Abby's move to the city. He would surely miss her. "I guess you're right," he admitted, kicking off his boots and leaning his head back against the headboard. It felt so good to lie here, holding Elizabeth in his arms, shutting out the problems they were faced with.

Cole was certain Elizabeth was beginning to soften toward him. He sensed a closeness between them that hadn't existed before. He had tried to show his love for her in countless little ways: rubbing her back at night, drawing her bath when she was too tired to do it herself, fixing her breakfast and serving it to her in bed. He smiled lasciviously, remembering back to that particular episode and the delightful things they had done to each other with the blackberry jam.

He had turned into a besotted, lovesick fool, the kind he had always laughed at scornfully. Well, he wasn't laughing anymore. He needed Elizabeth; she was as necessary to him as food and water . . . his sustenance for life. Without her, his life would have no meaning, no purpose.

Holding Elizabeth close to his heart made him realize how much he wanted her. They hadn't made love for quite a few days, but to him it seemed like years. "I've missed you, Sunshine," he whispered softly into her hair.

"I've missed you, too," Elizabeth replied, toying with the buttons on his shirt. Slowly, she undid them, running her hands over the corded muscles of his chest, following them with her lips.

Cole hardened instantly. Easing Elizabeth onto her back, he undid the hooks holding her dress together, sliding the garment off her shoulders and tossing it to the floor.

He drank in the sight of her. Her breasts had grown larger, spilling over the confinement of her chemise. Untying the ribbons, he revealed the satiny globes to his view, kissing her nipples, watching them harden into stiff peaks.

Elizabeth moaned, arching back her body.

Removing her garments slowly, Cole whispered his love for each part of her body that he uncovered. His mouth traveled over her breasts, up her neck, finally capturing her lips in urgent exploration.

Elizabeth savored the addictive pleasure of Cole's kisses. She writhed uncontrollably as his lips bathed her

332

body, his tongue gliding over her most intimate of places, tantalizing and teasing until she felt herself grow moist with her need of him. "Cole," she cried out, running her hands up under his shirt, digging her nails into the bare flesh of his back.

Unable to wait any longer, Cole stood, quickly discarding his clothes. Leaning over her, he parted her legs. Positioning himself, he entered her, pledging his love with every stroke. "I love you . . . I love you," he uttered over and over as he took her higher and higher.

They clung to each other, their hearts and souls becoming one as they climbed to the peak of their ecstasy. Elizabeth's heart filled with love, her body exploding with pleasure as she reached her climax of physical fulfillment.

Peace and contentment washed over their sweat-glistened bodies like a tidal wave drowning them in an ocean of love.

Still glowing from the aftermath of this afternoon's lovemaking, Elizabeth listened inattentively to Abigail's questions while she put the finishing touches on her gown. They had been sequestered in Abby's bedroom since dinner, putting the hem up on the voluminous skirts.

"Well, what do you think?" Abigail asked, spinning around and modeling her wedding gown for Elizabeth.

Elizabeth looked up, smiling with approval. She scrutinized the beautiful ivory satin gown embroidered with tiny seed pearls. She knew how many hours Abigail had spent stitching each and every one of them onto the bodice of her dress.

"You've done a beautiful job. It's the prettiest gown I've ever seen. Now hold still so I can finish pinning this hem."

"Really? I know you must have attended some awfully posh weddings back in New York."

Elizabeth nodded, her mouth full of pins. Sticking the last pin in place, she rose to her feet. "Let me see if it's even. You know I'm not very good at this sort of thing."

"Why are you so modest?" Abby scolded. "The quilt you made turned out beautiful, and the robe you've made for Cole's Christmas present looks splendid."

"Shh!" Elizabeth cautioned, turning quickly to gaze at the door. "He might hear you."

"Not likely. Cole's downstairs in the parlor with Jon. He's giving Jon advice about his duties as a husband."

Elizabeth burst out laughing. "Cole's giving my father advice?" At Abigail's nod, Elizabeth started laughing again. "Forgive me," she said, wiping the tears away from the back of her hand. "I just think that's terribly amusing."

"Well, it won't be very amusing if Jon decides to follow it," Abby replied, shaking her head. "I certainly don't relish having a husband as stubborn and opinionated as yours." Both girls broke out in laughter.

Stepping out of the dress, Abigail took a seat on the chair next to her bed, lying the gown over her lap. "Beth," Abby said, pausing a moment to thread her needle, "is tomorrow . . . I mean . . . am I going to know what to do when the time comes?" She felt her cheeks redden.

Glancing up, Elizabeth threw the last of the pins into her sewing basket, her brows furrowing in confusion. "What do you mean?"

Abigail's cheeks flamed red as the coals in the fireplace. Throwing the gown on the bed, she stood, approaching Elizabeth. "I've never been intimate with a man before. I'm not sure that I'll know what to do," she confessed.

Elizabeth smiled knowingly, patting Abigail's hand. "You'll do just fine. Just follow Jon's lead; he'll do everything else."

"Does it hurt?" Abby asked, embarrassed at having to ask Elizabeth such personal questions, never having been instructed on the intimate aspects of the marriage bed before.

Pulling Abigail over to the two rockers by the fireplace, Elizabeth motioned for her to sit down. "There is a small amount of pain at first. After that, it's the most wonderful experience in the world." A whimsical smile crossed her face.

"Judging from your expression, I guess I don't have any cause to be nervous," Abigail teased.

Elizabeth's cheeks turned a charming shade of pink. "I think we had better get downstairs and rescue my father from Cole's good intentions. He may just try to talk Jon out of getting married."

The wedding took place as scheduled. All the hours Elizabeth had spent planning and decorating paid off. It was the prettiest ceremony she had ever witnessed, even nicer than her own, she thought. Reflecting back upon the wedding, which had taken place the night before, Elizabeth smiled happily as she thought of Abby and her father. They had both been euphoric. The smiles they wore while exchanging their marriage vows had been as wide as the San Francisco Bay.

The sound of pots banging in the kitchen brought Elizabeth back to the present. Consuelo was making breakfast. Soon Cole would be up and they would share their first Christmas morning together. She hugged herself tightly. She had tiptoed out of their room early this morning, wanting to place Cole's present under the tree before he awoke. She hoped he would be pleased with her gift; she had spent many hours sewing it for him.

"Here you are, Sunshine," Cole said, strolling into the parlor. He was dressed in a suit of navy-blue wool. "I wondered where you had disappeared to." Walking across the room, he placed a large pile of brightly wrapped boxes beneath the tree. "Merry Christmas," he said, pulling Elizabeth into his embrace and planting a kiss on her lips.

Elizabeth felt as giddy as a schoolgirl when she saw all the presents with her name on them. She hadn't expected Cole to be so generous. "Are those all for me?" she asked, her eyes bright with pleasure.

"That depends," Cole said, his eyes twinkling. "Have you been a good little girl?"

Wrapping her arms about his neck, she pressed herself into him. "Santa says I'm very good." She kissed him ardently on the lips.

Cole grinned, tweaking her nose. "Well, in that case, I guess they're all for you."

Elizabeth's smile softened. "It's going to be a little lonely around here with just the two of us. I wish Abby and my father had stayed to open presents instead of leaving last night. Even Violet has deserted us."

Cole shook his head, lifting Elizabeth's chin. "I think Abby and your father had other things on their mind last night. We'll see them soon enough. Did you forget the New Year's Eve party they're planning to have?"

She shook her head.

"Well, then, let's get started with our own celebration. Soon I will have to start playing Santa for someone else besides you."

They seated themselves on the floor in front of the gaily decorated tree. The tiny white candles Elizabeth had lit twinkled prettily against the dark green background of the fir. The fire in the hearth sputtered loudly, the ancient oak logs giving off their glow to add warmth to the festive occasion.

Picking up a large package wrapped up with a red velvet bow, Elizabeth handed it to Cole. "Merry Christmas," she said shyly.

Cole's eyes widened in surprise. "You bought something for me? You shouldn't have." He lifted the lid, unable to hide his surprise at the beautiful silver satin robe that rested inside. Picking it up, he caressed the soft material between his fingers. "It's beautiful! Where did you get such a handsome robe? I know you haven't been to the city."

Elizabeth's smile was full of pride. "I made it myself."

Cole's eyebrows shot up. "You made this for me? All by yourself?"

Elizabeth's smile lit up her face as brightly as the candles on the tree.

"Thank you, sweetheart. I'll wear it proudly."

Elizabeth's expression was childlike as she opened the presents Cole handed her. The first box contained an exquisite pair of sapphire earrings. "Oh, Cole, they're just beautiful!" she exclaimed, holding them up to the light to admire their clarity and sparkle.

337

Handing her the next box, Cole's grin became devilish. "I have also purchased something for you to wear in the bedroom."

Elizabeth stared openmouthed at the flimsy creation nestled in the box. Picking it up, she felt her cheeks warm. Thank goodness no one else was here to see it, she thought. The gown—if you could call it that—was bright red. It was so transparent that Elizabeth could see Cole's handsome face clearly through the material. He was grinning wickedly. She held it up in front of her, giggling when she realized that the material only reached the tops of her thighs.

"Shame on you," she scolded. "Where did you find such a scandalous garment?"

"I seem to remember your penchant for wearing such items," he teased.

Elizabeth laughed, draping the garment over the top of Cole's head.

Throwing off the nightgown, Cole grabbed Elizabeth about the waist, tackling her to the floor. "I love you, Sunshine," he said, kissing her on the lips.

Reaching up, she tenderly caressed his cheek. "I know; I realize that now." She knew in her heart that Cole loved her. She wasn't sure when she had first realized it, but she knew with a certainty that it was true.

Cole's eyes lit up with pleasure at the words Elizabeth uttered. From now on, he would let nothing come between them. They would have each other, for now and for always.

Chapter Twenty-Eight

The cold winds of January brushed harshly against the faces of the two men who sat astride their horses watching the large white house below them. From their vantage point upon the hill, they were able to ascertain the movements of the occupants of Rancho del Oro.

"How much longer are we going to have to stay out here, Willy? I'm freezing my ass off," Jake said, shivering inside his sheepskin jacket. They had been surveying the ranch for weeks, waiting for the opportunity to grab the rich Mrs. MacAlister.

"Quit your griping. We'll stay until we find our opportunity, then we'll grab it."

"But we've been coming back here every day for two weeks without any luck."

Willy leaned forward on the pommel of his saddle, grabbing tightly on the horn. If only it were Jake's neck beneath his hands, he thought, squeezing hard. "The husband will have to return to work soon. He's a lawyer. I know he's got a practice in San Francisco."

"Why don't we just kill the husband and grab the

339

broad now?" Jake questioned. He shifted uncomfortably in his saddle; his crotch tightened painfully whenever he thought of the pretty blonde. If Willy thought he wasn't going to get a taste of that sweet meat this time, he was crazy. He aimed to plant his dick between those satiny thighs of hers before they let her go. On second thought, maybe he wouldn't let her go. Maybe he would just keep her for his woman.

"Use your head, for Christ's sake!" Willy shouted. "Who do you think is going to pay the ransom?"

Jake's eyes squinted at Willy's harsh tone. Willy was always yelling at him, always thinking he was so dumb. Well, he was smarter than Willy thought. Once they grabbed the woman, Willy would see just how smart he was.

Elizabeth snuggled closer to Cole, reluctant to release her hold on him. She knew the day would come when he would have to return to work, and she dreaded the thought of his being away from her for too long. "Are you sure you have to leave?" she asked.

"Now, Sunshine, we've been through this before. You know I have a law practice in San Francisco. I just can't walk away from it. I have clients who are counting on me." He kissed the tip of her nose.

"I know you must think it's terribly selfish of me, but I can't stand the thought of you leaving." She hugged him about the waist.

Extricating himself from Elizabeth's hold, Cole sighed. "I've got to get up and get ready for work. I'll only be gone a few days. You'll be so busy decorating the nursery, you probably won't even miss me."

"Well, it would serve you right if I didn't," Elizabeth teased, throwing back the covers. "But you're right. I'll find plenty to do while you're gone. Maybe I'll even iron some of your shirts." At the horrified look on Cole's face, she laughed.

"Please! Anything but that! I can't afford the expense your ironing efforts generate."

"Very well. I shall leave your shirts to Consuelo's capable hands," she said, shrugging into her robe. She would probably spend a considerable amount of time sewing some new dresses for herself. She felt the soft roundness of her stomach and smiled. The baby was finally starting to show.

"That's a good girl. There is one more thing I would like you to do for me." Cole's expression stilled and grew serious. "I don't want you venturing too far from the house. I don't want to worry about you while I'm gone."

"Oh, Cole, don't be silly. I'll be fine. Just because I had that one little accident with the wagon, you can't expect me to stay cooped up here like a prisoner. I have the school to run."

"Just promise me that you'll stay close to the house. No more running into Santa Clara by yourself." The strangers Pedro had spotted hadn't been seen again, but he wasn't going to take any chances with Elizabeth's safety.

"I promise," she said, giving his waist a squeeze before she went downstairs to fetch his breakfast.

The two days since Cole's departure had seemed like an eternity to Elizabeth. Thank goodness she'd had Consuelo to keep her company or she would have gone mad.

341

She'd been so used to having Abigail's company and before that Violet's, that now that she was all alone, she couldn't stand the solitude.

She sat at the kitchen table drinking her morning cup of coffee. Her grandfather would have been scandalized to know that she dined with the servants every morning and evening while Cole was away. It was much nicer having Consuelo's and Pedro's company in the kitchen than to eat in the big empty dining room by herself.

"What are you going to do today, Consuelo? Do you think, perhaps, we should bake more bread?"

Consuelo looked at *Señor* Mac's lovely wife and smiled. The *señora* had proven herself to be every bit as capable and productive as *Señorita* Abby. With *Señora* Mac as her replacement, it softened the blow of having her baby gone. "*Señora*, we do not need to bake any more bread this week. We have baked enough the past two days to last us the rest of the month."

Elizabeth smiled sheepishly. She knew Consuelo was right. She had to quit relying on the housekeeper to provide chores for her to do. Due to the unusually cold weather this week, the children who regularly attended her school had not been able to come. She had been at her wit's end trying to find things to occupy her time.

"You are right, Consuelo. I think I have had enough bread baking for one week. I've decided to pay a visit to *Señora* Montoya. I will have Pedro hitch up the buggy for me."

"Do you think that is wise, *señora*? *Señor* Mac did not want you to travel too far," Consuelo said, wringing her hands nervously.

Sipping her coffee, Elizabeth smiled. "I promised Cole that I would not drive into Santa Clara. Amber only lives a short distance away. I promised her I would come and visit after the holidays."

"But, *señora* . . ."

Elizabeth stood, grabbing onto Consuelo's arm. "I know you are worried about me because of what happened the last time I drove the wagon, but you needn't be. I'm going to take the buggy. It's brand-new, and I'll have Pedro hitch up Blossom. That horse wouldn't run if her life depended on it."

Consuelo smiled, kissing Elizabeth's cheek. "You will be careful. I don't want anything to happen to you or the baby."

"Don't worry. What could possibly happen?"

Elizabeth felt the sting of the wind lashing across her cheeks. She wished now that she had stayed at home in front of the fire sewing clothes for the baby instead of venturing out in this miserable weather to pay a visit to a woman who wasn't even expecting her.

She shivered within the confines of the new cloak Cole had given her for Christmas. Although it was lined with sable, there was little that could offer protection from the biting cold of the day. What had happened to sunny California? she wondered. This cold snap was going to have some devastating effects on the orange trees growing in the orchard she had just passed. Cole had explained that one of these unexpected cold spells could ruin an entire year's worth of produce.

"There she is," Willy shouted, knocking Jake on the arm.

343

Jake stood up in his stirrups to get a better view of what Willy was pointing at. Sure enough, the vision that had haunted his dreams these past weeks was driving the rig all by herself. "Looks like you were right after all. Our waiting has paid off."

"I don't leave things to chance, Jake. You should know that by now. That's why I'm in charge and you're not." Willy's look was condescending.

Jake nodded. "You're right, Willy," he agreed. You're always right, he added silently.

"Come on. Let's give our pretty little lady a real special greeting." Pulling up the red bandanna, he positioned it over the lower half of his face, watching as Jake did the same.

Riding down off the hill, it took them only a few moments to catch up with the buggy that had been traveling at a snail's pace. Splitting up, Jake and Willy surrounded it.

Elizabeth screamed at the sight of the two masked riders approaching. They grabbed onto the reins, pulling the horse to a halt. Fear surged through her as she looked upon her captors. "What do you want? I have no money if you've thought to rob me," she said.

"It's not your money we're after, little lady," the taller of the two men said. "Get down off that buggy. We need you to come with us."

Elizabeth's eyes widened in fear at the sight of the gun the bandit waved at her. Nodding, she stepped down carefully. "Please, don't shoot," she pleaded.

"Tie her up, Jake, and be quick about it. We don't have much time to waste."

"Please . . . why are you doing this? I told you I haven't any money. If you'll just let me go, I'm sure my

344

husband will pay you for my safe return."

Jake's laugh was sinister. "That's what we aim to do, pretty lady." Taking the rope from his saddle, he tied it securely around Elizabeth's wrists, fastening it around her waist. "Come on, honey, you can ride with me."

"I don't want no funny stuff, Jake. Do you understand?"

Positioning Elizabeth in front of him on the saddle, Jake smiled. "Sure, Willy, sure. Don't worry; the lady will be in good hands."

"I'm going to ride on ahead to make sure the coast is clear. Put a gag on the woman and follow. Don't dilly-dally or we won't reach the hideout before dark."

Raw terror surged through Elizabeth's breast. She didn't dare fight these animals; she had the baby to think of. God, why hadn't she stayed home today. Tears fell down her cheeks as the gag was shoved into her mouth.

"You and me are going to get better acquainted, pretty lady," Jake said, grinning as he watched Willy ride off. Holding the reins in one hand, he put his other arm about Elizabeth's waist, drawing her back against him. She squirmed, trying to break free. "Don't be so disagreeable, pretty lady. I wouldn't want you to accidentally fall off this horse. It's a long way down to the ground."

Elizabeth ceased her struggling. Bile rose up in her throat as the man called Jake let his hand travel up to cup her breast. He flicked her nipple back and forth, pinching it roughly between his fingers. Oh, God, Elizabeth prayed, please let this nightmare end.

Not satisfied with touching Elizabeth through her clothes, Jake untied her cloak. Reaching down, he pulled her shirt out from the waistband of her skirt. "I want to touch some skin, pretty lady. I remember you had some real big tits."

A glimmer of recollection darted through Elizabeth's brain. That voice. She knew she had heard that voice before. The feel of his fingers on her naked breast sent tears flooding down her. Be strong, Elizabeth, she told herself. You have the baby to think of.

Jake's craving increased a hundredfold at the feel of Elizabeth's ample breast in his hand. What a tasty morsel, he thought, licking his lips. He squeezed the nipple again, laughing when she squirmed. She loved it; he was really turning her on. He couldn't wait to get her drawers off and dive into that sweet nest of curls. He wiped the dribble off his chin, smiling to himself.

It wouldn't do for Willy to find out he had touched the woman. He didn't want no trouble until he was ready to make his move. "I wouldn't mention our fooling around when we catch up to Willy. He don't like women. He might kill you right on the spot."

Elizabeth gasped, her eyes widening in terror. What kind of animals were these men? To kill an innocent woman? What if they found out she was pregnant? Cole, she prayed silently, please find me.

"*Señor* Mac, thank God you have returned." Consuelo met Cole at the door, tears filling her eyes.

"What's happened? Where's Elizabeth?" Cole asked, searching about for some sign of his wife.

"She isn't here, *Señor* Mac. That is what I am trying to tell you."

"But it's dark out. Where would she be at this hour?"

"I do not know. She said she was going to visit *Señora* Montoya. She was supposed to be back this afternoon.

When she didn't arrive home, I sent Pedro over there to fetch her." Covering her face, Consuelo sobbed into her hands.

Grabbing the older woman's shoulders, he shook her gently. "Get hold of yourself, Consuelo. Tell me what has happened."

"Pedro went over to the Montoyas. *Señora* Mac never arrived."

Fear surged through Cole's body, tightening around his heart. Taking a deep breath, he asked, "Did any of the men see anything?"

Consuelo nodded. "*Sí*. Esteban found the buggy that *Señora* Mac had taken this morning. There was no sign of her. He said there were hoofprints in the dirt—two, maybe three, horses."

"Where are Pedro and Esteban now?"

"They have gone to search; they should be back soon. They will not be able to search in the dark."

He was certain that the two men Pedro had spotted some time back were responsible for Elizabeth's abduction. If they had kidnapped her, there would probably be a ransom note coming. "Send Pedro to me when he arrives. I will be in the study."

"Shall I bring your dinner in there?" Consuelo asked, frightened by the savage expression the *señor* wore on his face.

Shaking his head, Cole replied, "I'm not hungry. Just bring me a bottle of brandy and send Pedro in when he gets home." Turning on his heel, he walked away.

Slamming the door to his study, Cole paced deliberately back and forth across the room. Why? he thought. Why now, after everything was going so good for them? It was just like after the wedding, when he had first realized his love for Elizabeth. No sooner had he voiced his feelings than everything fell apart.

A feeling of déjà vu swept over him. Just like after the wedding, he thought again. The two men. He would bet his last dollar that the two men who had abducted Elizabeth the first time were the same men that had her now. Tears filled his eyes. Christ! To think he had ever doubted her. He cursed himself for the fool that he was.

Approaching the oak cabinet, he removed the rifle and bullets. There was no doubt in his mind anymore. He knew who had done the abduction, and this time they would pay with their lives. First thing tomorrow, he would take Pedro and Esteban. They would hunt the animals down, just like they had hunted so many others, so many times before. But this time it wouldn't be for sport; this time it would be for revenge.

Chapter Twenty-Nine

Elizabeth sat with her back pressed against the wall of the dilapidated shack. She had no idea how far they had traveled, but she knew it had taken several hours to reach their destination.

She was still tied up, although the gag had been removed from her mouth. The two men, whom she now knew as Willy and Jake, sat across the room from her at an old wooden table, their backs to her. She recognized them the moment they removed their masks. They were the same two men who had abducted her right after her wedding . . . the ones her grandfather had hired. She shook her head. If only her grandfather had realized how his selfishly motivated actions were still reaching out to harm her.

Observing her surroundings, she sought a means of escape. The house appeared to have only one room. There was a window and door at the front and rear. The only furnishings, other than the table, were four ladderback chairs and four filthy cots. It was on one of the cots that she rested.

Her throat felt parched, but she was too sacred to ask for water. She didn't want to draw attention to herself. Jake might try to put his hands on her again. She recoiled, thinking of what he had done to her. She wanted to bathe, to wash the feel of his hands off her breasts, but she feared no amount of scrubbing would ever erase the memory of Jake's touch from her mind. Resting her head back against the wall, she listened intently to the conversation going on across the room.

"When do you suppose MacAlister will receive the note?"

Leaning back in his chair, a self-satisfied smirk on his face, Willy replied, "I sent it with that old padre we passed on the road. I told him it was to be delivered tonight."

"How do you know he'll do it?" Jake asked, looking over his shoulder at Elizabeth.

Willy smiled, spitting a stream of tobacco juice into the fireplace. The logs hissed in response. "I told him it was a matter of life or death. Told him if the note didn't get delivered, a young woman would die."

Elizabeth couldn't control her gasp.

"What's the matter, little lady? Are we making you nervous?" Willy's laugh was like slime oozing out of his mouth.

Elizabeth tilted her chin up, her blue eyes flashing fire. "My husband will kill you both when he finds you," she said with more confidence than she felt.

Willy snickered. "You better hope he brings the money we've asked for. Twenty-five thousand dollars isn't a lot to pay for a pretty thing like you."

Turning her back on the disgusting pair, Elizabeth drew her knees up to her chin, hugging them tightly, praying fervently that Cole would come and rescue her.

"Where did you get this note, padre?" Cole asked the wrinkled old man who stood before his desk. It was well past midnight, but he was still up, trying to figure out a way to locate his wife.

"A man. He gave it to me. He say that a woman will die if I don't deliver this note," he said, fidgeting nervously with the hat he held in his hands.

Gripping the edge of his desk, Cole blanched, fear for Elizabeth's safety rushing through him like a raging river. "What did the man look like?"

The padre shrugged. "It was getting dark, *Señor* MacAlister. My eyes, they are not so good anymore." He hung his head, staring at the floor.

"Can you remember anything? Anything at all?"

After a few moments, the old man looked up. He nodded. His hair gleamed white in the glow of the lamp. "*Sí . . . sí*, I remember. When the man handed me the note, I noticed that two of his fingers were missing."

"Which hand?"

The padre scratched his head then smiled. "The left. It was the left. I am sure of it."

"Thank you, padre. Go to the kitchen; Consuelo will feed you. You may bed down in the bunkhouse if you like."

"*Gracias, señor.* You are too kind. May God be with you in finding your wife." The old man bowed, and Cole watched him exit.

Unfolding the note, Cole spread it out in front of him on the desk. He read the crudely scribbled missive once again: "*If you want your wife back, bring twenty-five*

351

*thousand dollars to the old mission in San Jose, Friday at
dusk. Come alone or the woman dies.*" His eyes narrowed at
the last sentence. If anything happened to Elizabeth,
there would be no place on the face of this earth they
could hide.

He read the note again. Friday. Today was only
Wednesday; he would have to wait two more days. He
couldn't take the risk of endangering Elizabeth's life with
some foolish heroics. They would leave at first light on
Friday. If they rode hard, they would make the mission
well before the appointed time. Once there, he would
send Esteban to search for tracks. He was a skilled hunter
and tracker. If anyone could find out where Elizabeth
was, it was Esteban. If they could reach the kidnappers'
hideout before dusk, they would have the element of
surprise on their side.

Wadding up the paper, he clenched it in his fist. The
bastards would pay for all the misery they had caused in
his life. His heart twisted painfully when he thought of
what Elizabeth might be suffering at their hands. God! If
they touched her . . . He slammed his fist down on top of
the desk. "I will kill them with my bare hands," he
shouted to the empty room.

The smell of coffee brewing brought Elizabeth out of
her miserable night's rest. She had slept fitfully, worried
that Jake would try something once Willy had gone to
sleep. Thank God they had both consumed a great deal of
whiskey and had left her alone. She screwed up her face
in disgust as she listened to Jake's loud snores from
across the room.

Her stomach growled; she was starving. They had not

352

seen fit to feed her last night. Were they planning on starving her to death? she wondered.

Willy looked over at her. "Care for some coffee, little lady? I guess you might be a bit hungry by now. My apologies. It seems we plumb forgot about dinner last night."

"Please, I need to relieve myself. Could you untie my hands?" She held up her bound wrists beseechingly.

"Not likely, little lady." Willy looked over at Jake and shook his head. The fool was still asleep. Well, it was probably for the best. He wouldn't want to send the woman out alone with him. "I'll take you outside; there's a privy out back. I'll hold on to your rope while you go inside. At least you'll have some privacy."

Elizabeth breathed a sigh of relief. Thank God Willy seemed to have a small amount of decency; he didn't seem to hate women, as Jake had indicated.

Willy helped her to her feet, guiding her out the door. How humiliating to be guided about on the end of a rope like an animal. Hopefully, these two monsters will know how it feels when they are dangling from the end of one, she thought bitterly.

Jake was awake when they returned. She saw the look of distrust and jealousy that entered his eyes when he looked at her and Willy together.

"Where have you two been? I hope you ain't been sneaking around my back."

Willy deposited Elizabeth at the table. "Shut up, Jake. I had to take the lady out to piss."

Elizabeth colored fiercely.

"Why didn't you let me do it? I wanted to pull down her drawers."

Tears blurred her vision. Oh, God, she thought, shaking her head. If she was left alone with Jake, something terrible was going to happen to her.

"Shut up, you pervert. Now you've upset the little lady. Go outside and cut some wood, while I fix us something to eat," Willy shouted.

Jake pulled on his boots. "I don't see why I have to do all the dirty work. Why do you get to stay inside with the woman?" His eyes narrowed suspiciously.

"Because I don't trust you, that's why. Now do what you're told."

Jake's glare was menacing, Elizabeth shivered at the intensity of it. He was dangerous. She hoped Willy could keep him in check until Cole had a chance to find her.

After Jake slammed out the door, Elizabeth turned to face Willy. "Thank you for protecting me," she said.

Willy scratched the front of his shirt. "Jake's crazy; he's getting worse all the time. I wouldn't leave his own mother alone with him," he said, pouring two cups of coffee into the battered tin cups.

The rising steam tickled her nose, making her stomach growl again. Picking up the cup with both of her hands tied was not an easy feat. Her fingers burned as they came in contact with the hot metal. Taking a sip, she carefully set the cup back down on the table. "Why are you doing this?" she asked.

Willy smiled, his teeth brown from years of chewing tobacco. "That's easy. I need the money."

"Didn't my grandfather pay you enough?" She saw the surprise that registered on his face.

"So . . . you remember, huh? I was wondering how long it would take you. The money the old man paid us is gone. We need more. We figure your husband has plenty to spare."

"He won't pay you; he probably won't even come. I

354

lied when I said he would come after me. We don't get along. He was planning to divorce me before you abducted me." She saw the look of skepticism on Willy's face, but she also saw the uncertainty in his eyes. If she could convince him that he had made a big mistake, maybe he would let her go.

"Well, if your husband won't deliver, we'll just have to send your father a note," Willy replied. "We'll find out soon enough. Friday is the deadline. By tomorrow, we'll know how much MacAlister wants you."

Thursday night found Cole, Pedro, and Esteban camped outside the village of Mission San Jose. Unable to wait any longer, Cole had departed the ranch early in the morning, hoping to find some clue as to the whereabouts of his wife. He sat facing the fire, digging absently at the burning embers with a stick he held like a dagger.

"Señor Mac," Esteban whispered, approaching the campfire. "I think I may have found out something important." The stocky Mexican looked pleased with himself, having just returned from the village where he had gone to search for information. Removing his sombrero, he hunched down by the fire.

Looking up, Cole's expression was intense as he gazed at his vaquero. "What is it? Did you find out where they've taken Elizabeth?"

Esteban shook his head. "No, señor, not that. But I did find out that two men matching the description Pedro gave me came through the village about two days ago."

"Anything else?"

"Sí. There was a woman with them. A woman with hair the color of gold."

Sitting up, Cole tossed the stick onto the fire. "Come morning, Pedro, I want you to go to the village and see what you can find out. Ask at the cantina. Those kind of scum usually hang out at places like that."

"Esteban," Cole turned to face the taller man, "I would like you to look for tracks in the hills above the village. They can't be too far away if they want us to meet them at the mission."

"*Sí, señor*, it will be done," Esteban said.

The three men sat staring into the fire. Cole took his revolver out, spinning the chamber. He checked one more time to make sure it was loaded properly. He would take no chances, make no mistakes. Tomorrow, he would shoot to kill.

Elizabeth held her breath, her heart pounding in her chest. The blackness of the cabin prevented her from seeing who was prowling about. As the figure approached her bed, she stifled the scream that rose in her throat, clenching her eyes tightly shut. Jake. Why was he standing over her? Where was Willy? Why didn't he protect her?

She felt Jake's hands run under her dress, up her calves to her knees. She could smell the whiskey as he bent over her body; her stomach roiled. Please, God, make him stop. She wanted to scream, to yell, but terror kept her voice silent. Her heart beat faster, her palms sweating profusely.

She heard Willy's snore and knew he was still inside the cabin. Relief flooded through her at this small consolation. When she felt Jake's hand inching up her thigh, bile replaced the scream in her throat. She flipped her-

356

self over, pretending to be sound asleep; she heard his disgruntled sound.

After a moment, Jake slunk back to his cot. When she finally heard his deep, even breathing, she released the breath she was holding. Tears slid slowly down her cheeks, soaking the cot that she lay upon. How much more of this degradation could she stand? she wondered, placing her hands against her swollen belly. Whatever she had to do to protect the baby, she would do. But she would not submit to that animal. The first chance she got, she would kill him . . . slaughter him like the pig he was.

Leaning over the front of his saddle, Cole peered down through the trees at the cabin below. Smoke rose from the chimney, indicating the place was inhabited. His eyes searched the yard; no horses were in sight. There was no sign of any activity.

"Are you certain this was where the tracks led you, Esteban?" Cole asked, turning to face the rider on his left.

"*Sí*, I am sure. There were no other tracks; they did not bother to cover their trail."

Cole snorted. "Probably thought I was some tenderfoot from the city." Turning to his right, he said, "Pedro, I want you to circle around back. If we are to make this work, we must use the element of surprise."

"*Sí*, I understand. They will not even know that I exist."

Cole slapped his friend on the back. Pedro was taking a risk. They all were. But if they were to find Elizabeth, then it was a risk well worth taking.

"Esteban, I think we should leave the horses here and go in on foot. There is less chance of being spotted that way. Good luck, my friends. May God be with us all."

Carefully and silently, Cole and Esteban crept down the hill, using the trees and rocks for cover. When they were within twenty yards of the house, they stopped. On closer inspection, the cabin was more of a flimsy shack. The shutters hung sideways off their hinges, and the window was cracked in several places.

Crawling across the small clearing on their bellies, their rifles held out in front of them, they were prepared to shoot anything that moved. Finally, reaching the side of the building, they stood. They could hear no sounds from inside.

Cole and Esteban exchanged puzzled glances. Motioning for Esteban to remain, Cole inched his way to the window and peeked in. The room appeared to be empty. Signaling to Esteban, the two men flanked each side of the door. With his booted foot, Cole kicked the rickety door in. There was no one about. Calling to Pedro, who entered from the rear, the men set about to search the premises. How could Elizabeth's abductors have known they were coming? Cole wondered.

Spying the cot on the far wall, Cole's interest was aroused by the sight of several long blond hairs lying on a filthy, stained pillow. Picking them up, he felt his stomach tighten. Clenching them in his hand, tears stung his eyes. "Elizabeth, where are you?" he whispered.

"*Señor* Mac, I think you had better come outside."

Following Esteban to the rear yard, Cole spotted Pedro standing by the outhouse, holding the door open.

"Take a look. It is not a pretty sight," Pedro said.

The horribly mutilated body of a man lay in a pile of

excrement. Cole gagged at the sight, wiping his brow with his neckerchief. What kind of animal had done this? Upon closer inspection, Cole noticed something that struck a chord in his memory: Two of the fingers of the man's left hand were missing. He remembered the description the padre had given him. This had to be one of the kidnappers.

If this man's partner had done this to him, what would he do to Elizabeth? Fear pierced his gut like a burning arrow.

Turning his back on the gruesome sight, Cole walked slowly back to the cabin. They had been so close to finding Elizabeth, he thought, clenching his fists. Judging from the warmth of the coals that remained in the hearth, the man couldn't have much of a lead on them.

"*Señor* Mac?"

He turned at the sound of Pedro's voice.

"What should we do now?"

A lethal calmness settled in the cold silver of Cole's eyes; his voice hardened ruthlessly. "We find them."

Chapter Thirty

Would the nightmare never end? Elizabeth wondered dismally as she watched Jake fix the campfire, wishing it were the fire of hell that would suddenly consume him.

As long as she lived, she would never forget what had happened this morning; the gruesome activity was still fresh in her mind. Poor Willy. Even though she hated him, no man deserved to die like that. What kind of demon lurked inside Jake's soul? What would he do to her now that they were alone? Trembling, she pulled her cloak tightly about her.

Cole. Would she ever see him again? And if she did, would he still want her? She was defiled . . . dirty. Even though Jake had not performed the ultimate act of dishonor, she knew her time was coming. He couldn't keep his eyes off of her. They were lifeless eyes . . . evil eyes. She hated him with every fiber of her being.

"I made us a nice cozy fire, Elizabeth."

Cringing at the sound of her name on his lips, she said nothing.

Grabbing Elizabeth's wrist, Jake hauled her to her feet.

"I hope you're not going to play hard to get, honey. I know you're hot for me; all women crave my body."

Throwing her head back, she gazed defiantly into his eyes. "You're disgusting; I can't stand the sight of you."

Pulling her roughly to his chest, he ground his lips down upon hers. Elizabeth gagged at the foul odor of his breath. She could feel the bile gurgle in her throat.

"I'm hot for you, baby," he whispered, his hands reaching under her cloak to claw at her breasts.

Elizabeth struggled wildly, trying to free herself from his embrace.

"Still playing hard to get? Well, you won't be so eager to run away once I plant my rod into that sweet little nest you've got hidden." He grabbed her crotch, squeezing painfully.

Tears streamed down her face. "Please," she begged, "don't touch me. I don't want you to touch me."

"That's too bad, honey, 'cause I want to touch you real bad. Once we finish eating some supper, you're going to strip out of them duds. I got me a hankering to see you naked. I know you're going to be all soft and white, your big tits rosy and sweet like candy." He pinched her nipples painfully. "Mmmm," he muttered, licking his lips. "Just like penny candies to suck on." He laughed.

Elizabeth clenched her stomach, fighting the nausea that rose to her throat as she watched Jake cross to the fire. Falling down to the ground, she placed her head between her knees, taking deep breaths. Oh, God, what was she going to do? How would she survive Jake's rape upon her body? If there is a God up in heaven, she prayed silently, please help me.

* * *

The riders pulled their horses to a stop beneath a stand of pine trees. Esteban dismounted, crouching down to inspect the ground. "They have passed this way. The tracks are still fresh. They cannot be much farther up ahead.

"Let's ride," Cole ordered. "I don't want to leave Elizabeth in the hands of that madman any longer than I have to."

Elizabeth ate slowly, the beans tasting like ashes in her mouth. She had to stall for time. The longer she could postpone the inevitable, the longer she had time to figure out a plan. She looked about the campsite, searching for something . . . anything that she could use for a weapon. Her eyes landed on a sharp, jagged rock. She was just about to close her hand around it when she heard Jake belch.

"I'm all done with my dinner, honey. How about you and me having a little fun now?"

She had to distract him . . . had to buy herself some time. Surely, she could outsmart this dim-witted clod, Elizabeth thought. Taking a deep breath, she smiled, tilting her head back coquettishly. "I've been doing a lot of thinking."

"Oh, yeah? Like what?" he asked, picking his teeth with the blade of his pocket knife.

"Since my husband doesn't want me and you do, I thought perhaps I would stay with you."

Desire lit Jake's eyes, and he started to rise.

Lifting her hand, she motioned him back down. "If you want me to be your woman, you're going to have to treat me nicer. I don't like it when you paw at me. I like to

362

make love slowly, so it takes all night . . . if you get my meaning."

Jake's eyes glazed over; he wiped the spittle from his chin. "I get it. But how do I know what you're saying is true?"

Forgive me, Cole, for what I'm about to do, she prayed silently. "You said you wanted to see me naked, didn't you?"

"Yeah. You got a real nice set of tits. I want to see the rest of you."

"I will undress for you, if you promise to stay where you are and not touch me."

"Hey, wait a minute. What kind of deal is that? I could rip your clothes off anytime I wanted to and look at your body all I wanted."

Elizabeth licked her lips seductively, untying her cloak. "You could do that, but then I wouldn't be willing. Wouldn't it be nicer to have me parade in front of you stark naked? Let you get your fill of me?" She jiggled provocatively.

Jake rubbed his crotch. "But when would I get to touch you?" he asked. "I don't just want to look."

Unbuttoning her blouse, Elizabeth's eyes never left Jake's face. "Know your enemy, Elizabeth," her grandfather had always said. "Watch his eyes." She watched Jake's eyes darken with unconcealed lust. When she finished with the last button, she said, "We have all night, Jake. There's no need to rush. You're too impatient. Women like to be wooed and courted." She saw him smile knowingly. "Do we have a deal?"

Nodding, he rubbed his hands together anxiously. "All right, but you have to take every stitch off. I want to see those springy curls between your legs. I bet they're blond just like your hair." He wiggled his fingers suggestively.

The knot in Elizabeth's stomach tightened. Taking off her blouse, she laid it down upon the jagged rock, remembering back to the many times she had undressed this way for Cole. Tears filled her eyes but she blinked them away. Then it had been for fun and games. Now it was for her life and that of her unborn child.

Rising to her feet, she stepped out of her skirt. One by one, she unrolled the tattered stockings from her legs, exposing her long limbs to his view. Jake seemed mesmerized by her actions. He just sat there, a dazed expression on his face. She removed her petticoats and pantaloons, leaving only her chemise. She could hear the gasping sounds he made, like the panting of an animal. She tried to swallow the fear that threatened her determination.

"You are one fine-looking woman," Jake said, rubbing his thighs with the palms of his hands. The light from the fire reflected in the dark of his eyes, making him appear demonic. "Hurry up and take the rest of it off. I want to see you jiggle them watermelons of yours around." He chuckled.

Elizabeth trembled, praying that she would be able to hold Jake to his part of the bargain. Stepping back toward the rock, she untied the ribbons of her chemise. When they were undone, she took a deep breath, sliding the garment off her shoulders, letting it glide down to the ground. She stood in front of Jake completely naked. The firelight illuminated the flawlessness of her body.

Jake started to rise; the determined glint in his eyes was unmistakable.

Elizabeth's eyes widened in fright. "Don't forget your promise. You want me to be willing when we finally make love, don't you?"

He came toward her, crawling on his knees to close the space between them.

Kneeling down on the ground, Elizabeth felt for the rock. Jake was upon her in an instant, grinding his pelvis into her naked flesh, the buckle of his belt cutting into her tender skin. She felt his mouth upon her breast. Where was the rock? her mind screamed, groping wildly for it.

Raising his head, Jake looked into her eyes, his smile feral. "I couldn't wait any longer, honey. I need to diddle you now. I'm hard as a rock," he said, reaching for the fastenings on the front of his britches.

Feeling the jagged edges of the rock beneath her fingers, Elizabeth took a deep breath. Taking it firmly in her hand, she brought it up as hard as she could, bashing it into the side of Jake's head. She saw his startled look before he collapsed to the ground. A feeling of relief rushed through her.

A moment later, all hell broke loose. Three men rode into camp, their guns drawn. The tallest of the group jumped down off his horse, rushing toward her. Elizabeth's eyes widened in fear and she screamed, a bloodcurdling sound that ripped through the night air. She couldn't stop . . . couldn't control the anguished cries that sprung from her throat.

"Elizabeth, it's me . . . Cole." He shook her gently, trying to shake her out of her hysteria.

Suddenly, his words penetrated her fear and her eyes cleared. "Cole! Oh, God, Cole!" She threw her arms around his neck, sobbing into the front of his shirt.

Gently, he cradled her. "It's all over now, Sunshine. Everything is going to be all right."

365

She looked up at him but said nothing. How could everything be all right? she wondered, hanging her head in shame.

Picking up Elizabeth's cloak, Cole draped it around her shoulders. He didn't want to ask what had happened; he didn't want to know. It wasn't her fault, he told himself. She was the victim; she might have been killed. He should be grateful that she was still alive, rather than worrying about what had happened between her and that piece of dead scum.

Esteban and Pedro tactfully disappeared while Cole helped Elizabeth dress. Silent rage tore through him at the sight of the teeth marks on Elizabeth's breasts and neck. He couldn't help the look of repugnance that entered his eyes when he gazed upon the marks of another man's passion.

Noting the look of distaste on Cole's face, Elizabeth's eyes filled with tears. Cole would grow to despise her now. She couldn't blame him. What man would want a woman who had been dirtied . . . fouled by a pig as rotten as Jake?

Tying the cloak about her, Cole drew Elizabeth into his arms. "You're not to worry about a thing. Everything will be just fine."

Elizabeth withdrew into herself the closer to home they traveled. She refused to stop anywhere for the night, insisting on the comfort and safety of her own bed. She spoke very little, only answering the inane questions Cole put to her. She knew he had other questions on his mind. Why didn't he ask them? What was he afraid of? That he would learn his wife was a slut, another man's whore? She swallowed the sob that rose in her throat.

Cole was concerned about Elizabeth's withdrawal. Her

face was white and haggard; she stared straight ahead as if in a trance. What had happened to put such a look of detachment on her face? If only he could have had the pleasure of killing that animal himself, he thought, his hands tightening unconsciously on the reins.

Suddenly, he felt ashamed about the way he had felt when he first came upon Elizabeth. She was his wife, his only love. It didn't matter if another man had touched her body. No one could ever touch what was inside of her. She was his. Now and for always.

When the weary group finally dismounted in the courtyard of Rancho del Oro, Elizabeth walked to the door, saying nothing. Cole watched her, concern reflecting in the depths of his eyes. She did not respond to Consuelo's greeting, merely nodding at the older woman and heading up the stairs.

"*Señor* Mac, what is wrong with the *señora?*" Consuelo asked, tears filling her eyes. She looked sadly in the direction of the stairs, crossing herself. "Something is very wrong."

Cole put his arm around the portly housekeeper. "I think she's in some sort of shock. First thing in the morning, I want you to send for Doc Willis. We need to make sure everything is all right with Elizabeth and with the baby."

"*Sí.* I will do this, *Señor* Mac. But I do not think it is the *señora's* body that is sick; I think it is her mind."

Cole was inclined to agree with Consuelo when he came upon Elizabeth stark naked, standing in the center of the empty tub. She held her hairbrush in a deathlike grip, scrubbing her body with it. He rushed forward, alarmed by the ugly red scratches she had inflicted all over herself. She screamed when he grabbed the brush out of her hand.

"I have to get clean . . . I have to get clean," she ranted.

Tears filled Cole's eyes. "Elizabeth, let me help you. I will draw a bath for you." When he reached out to touch her, she screamed.

"Don't touch me! I'm dirty. Don't soil your hands on me."

Picking her up bodily, Cole deposited her in the center of the bed. Wrapping her up in a blanket, he carried her over to the chair by the fire, holding her firmly on his lap, rocking her gently back and forth.

There was a light tapping on the door and then Consuelo entered. "I hear the screams. Is everything all right?"

"Please draw a bath for Elizabeth," Cole said. "And stoke up the fire in here. I need to help her bathe."

Staring at the couple, Consuelo shook her head sadly. They had conquered so many problems, only to be faced with this. *Madre de Dios*, haven't they suffered enough? she asked, raising her hands in supplication. She hurried into the bathing room.

Chapter Thirty-One

The weeks went by slowly and painfully for Elizabeth, who had not been able to put her bad experience behind her.

Cole had sent for Abby in the hope that the familiar presence of Elizabeth's best friend would have a soothing effect on her. Unfortunately, Abby had not been any more successful in reaching her than Cole.

Sitting behind his desk in the study, Cole observed his sister pacing back and forth in front of him. "What am I going to do, Abby? I don't know how to reach her." He held his head between his hands, shaking it back and forth.

Crossing to the window, Abigail peered out. The rain fell silently, lightly caressing the ground with its life-giving nourishment. If it were only that simple to give Elizabeth back her spirit, she thought sadly. She had been shocked by the sight of Elizabeth when she had first arrived two weeks ago. There was a vacancy behind the blue eyes that had never been there before. Although Elizabeth smiled and uttered all the correct responses, there was something missing. She had changed. Those monsters had robbed her of her vitality, of the inner strength that she had grown to rely on.

Slowly, she turned to face Cole, whose appearance these past weeks was becoming as gaunt as his wife's. There were dark circles under his eyes, a great unhappiness reflected in the depths of them. "What did Doc Willis say? I thought you had him out to check on Elizabeth this morning."

Placing the flat of his hands on the desk, he pushed himself to his feet. "He said that physically she's fine. She admitted to him that she hadn't been sexually violated." He couldn't help the feeling of relief that had surged through his body at the news. "Doc says that she's holding herself responsible for what's happened."

"But that's ridiculous! Why would she do that? She was an innocent victim. The target of two crazed criminals."

Cole shook his head. "Don't you think I know that? I admit, I was shocked when I first found her, but I soon realized that it wasn't her fault . . . that she was not accountable for what had happened to her."

Abby's face whitened, and she grabbed onto Cole's arm. "Cole, when you came upon Elizabeth, did you let your feelings show? Do you think, perhaps, she feels that you look upon her as soiled goods now?"

"I love her! I've tried to tell her that what happened doesn't matter, but she won't respond to me. She won't even let me touch her."

"But don't you see? She thinks because of what happened, she's not good enough for you. She feels your love for her is tarnished."

Cole's eyes filled with tears. "I love her, Abby. I swear

I do. If she had been raped, it wouldn't have made me feel any different. I admit, I was relieved to find out that she hadn't been violated, but that doesn't mean I don't love her."

"You're the only one that can reach her, Cole. She loves you more than you realize. Go to her. Make her believe that you love her beyond everything that has happened. You're her only salvation. If you want your wife back, you must reach her."

Cole sat, pondering Abby's words long after she had departed. Abby would be leaving in the morning; she needed to get back to care for Jon, who had been ill with influenza.

Perhaps he should send for Violet. He shook his head. No. She was on her honeymoon. Abby was right. He was the only one who could help his wife. But how? How could he make her believe that he still loved her despite everything that had happened? Well, he had done it once before, he told himself. There was no reason he couldn't do it again.

Feeling better than he had in weeks, he brushed back his hair, straightened his wrinkled clothing, and headed for Elizabeth's room.

Cole found Elizabeth staring morosely out the window, her forehead pressed against the glass. "Hello, Sunshine. How are you feeling today?"

Turning, Elizabeth presented Cole with a wan smile. She was still dressed in her nightclothes, even though it was the middle of the afternoon. "I'm fine."

"Good," Cole said, walking toward her. "I want you to get dressed. I need your help."

Elizabeth's eyebrows furrowed in confusion. "My help? I don't understand."

"It seems I've completely messed up my account books. I was wondering if you would help me straighten them out."

She shrugged. "If you like. It will take me a few minutes to get dressed."

"Fine," Cole said, taking a seat on the bed. "I'll wait for you."

"No!" she shouted, a wild expression lighting her eyes. At the look of hurt on Cole's face, she added, "I don't think you should waste your time watching me. Why don't you go back downstairs and start your work?"

"I don't consider it a waste of time to watch you. I love you. I want to see you . . . all of you."

Elizabeth took a deep breath. How could she undress in front of Cole after she had disrobed in front of that animal? She couldn't perform the same act for her husband. "I don't think—"

"Elizabeth," Cole interrupted, his voice firm, "I am not leaving. Take off your clothes and get dressed. I am your husband. I love you."

Tears filled her eyes as she untied the sash on her robe. She couldn't bear to look at Cole. She hung her head, staring down at the floor.

Unbuttoning her nightgown, she slipped it off her shoulders, letting it drop to the floor. A feeling of déjà vu came over her. Elizabeth felt the nausea rise in her throat. She ran into the bathing room and leaned over the chamber pot.

Rushing after his wife, Cole held her head gently, wiping the vomit from her face with a cool cloth. She was completely naked. It was the first time he had seen her like this since before her abduction. He felt her stiffen when he took her into his arms. "What is it, Sunshine?

Tell me why the idea of undressing in front of me makes you so ill."

She shook her head. "I can't; I'm too ashamed."

Leading her back to the bed, he sat down next to her on the mattress. "Look at me, Elizabeth. Take a good look. I am your husband . . . the man who loves you. I know that you've been hurt and degraded, and maybe you think that changes things between us, but it doesn't. I will love you no matter what. Those men might have been able to touch your body, but they could never touch you *here*." He placed his hand on her heart. "That belongs to me. Your heart, your soul, your love, are all mine. No one can ever change that. Do you understand?"

Tears streamed down Elizabeth's face, falling onto her bare chest. "But I saw your face; I saw the disgust there."

Grabbing Elizabeth, Cole drew her into his embrace. "Never for you. I've never felt disgust for you. It was for what those animals had done to you. When I saw those marks upon your body, I wanted to scream, to cry out my rage at how they had hurt you. I should have been able to protect you, to keep you from being harmed."

Elizabeth looked into Cole's eyes. They were filled with tears. She had never seen him cry before. Despite her own pain, she sought to comfort him. "It wasn't your fault. I should have listened to you. You told me to stay home . . . not to go far."

Stroking her head as if she were a small child, Cole replied, "What's done is done. Nothing can change what is in the past. We have our whole future ahead of us. We have a baby to look forward to." He patted the growing roundness of her stomach. "Will you tell me what happened to make you so withdrawn?"

Elizabeth stared at the hands in her lap. Her palms had

grown moist; her throat felt as dry as the desert sands. What if she told him and he hated her? She looked at his face once again. She saw only love and concern reflected there. She nodded.

Cole listened patiently while Elizabeth recounted the entire episode of her abduction. He tried to hide the anger that simmered inside his chest at the scenes that she described between her and Jake.

He could have killed the bastard a thousand times over for all the pain she'd had to endure at his hands. He could see in her eyes the fear and loathing she felt as she recounted each horrible incident. When she came to the night of her rescue, she paused, covering her face in her hands.

"I'm so ashamed to have done what I did. I needed to buy myself some time."

"Sweetheart, whatever it was that you did, I know it was done to protect yourself and the baby. You shouldn't feel ashamed about it."

"I disrobed for him," she blurted out. "I smiled and played the whore while I took off my clothes, watching his demented face drool with lust as he gazed upon my body."

"But don't you see? It worked. You outsmarted him. You used the only weapon you had in your defense—that of your body. I think you were very clever."

Elizabeth looked up, her eyelashes wet with tears. "You do? But I thought you would despise me."

"Sweetheart, it took a lot of courage to do what you did. I would rather see you parade naked down Market Street in San Francisco than to have one single hair on your head harmed."

A tremulous smile touched Elizabeth's lips. "Oh, Cole,

I love you so much."

Curling the strands of blond hair between his fingers, Cole stared intently into her eyes. "Prove it."

Elizabeth blanched. "You mean? . . ."

Taking her hand, he kissed her gently. "The only way you are going to erase what has happened from your memory is to replace it with much different memories." He placed his lips close to her ear and whispered, "We can make new memories, Sunshine."

Wrapping her arms cautiously around Cole's neck, she drew his head down. Placing her lips softly against his, she kissed him, waiting for the revulsion she was sure would follow. When nothing happened, she kissed him again, this time more passionately. She felt a burgeoning response stir within her breast; she felt her nipples harden. "Touch me," she breathed softly.

Cole placed his hands on her breasts, massaging the aching globes tenderly. He thrust his tongue into her mouth, feeling her tense for a moment before she relaxed again. Slowly and tenderly, he let his hands roam over her body, caressing each part with reverence, letting his fingers communicate the love that he felt for her. When he heard her sigh of pleasure, he eased her onto her back.

"Make love to me, Cole. I need you," she whispered.

"Are you sure? I don't want to rush you."

"I've never been more sure of anything in my entire life."

Chapter Thirty-Two

The ravages of winter slowly turned into the warm days of summer. Time had a healing effect on the land, which had shed its winter coat of green for the amber haze of gold.

Time also had a healing effect on Elizabeth. Gone were the shadows that clouded her mind, replaced by a love so intense that it sometimes frightened her.

Sitting on the porch swing, she gazed out at the brown hills beyond. Her stomach had grown large with the impending birth of her child. She felt the movement of the baby constantly now.

Doc Willis had said that in one more week she would be a new mother. She smiled happily into her glass of milk. She had been drinking a lot more milk lately. Consuelo had seen to that. The older woman had turned into an autocratic despot. *"You must drink more milk, señora; the baby needs to grow. You must take a nap, señora; the baby needs to rest."* Elizabeth giggled, thinking of the daily advice Consuelo dished out to her.

Cole, too, had felt the need to offer his opinions on

everything: the amount of work she was to do, how much rest she needed, the color of the nursery, the proper foods for her to eat. The list went on and on. Smiling wistfully, she shook her head. Some days she felt as if she was right back inside that gilded cage she had tried so hard to escape. Only this time, her jailer was a warm and loving husband who adored her.

"*Señora* Mac, you should come inside now and take a nap. Your father and *Señorita* Abby will be here soon and then you will have no time to rest," Consuelo said, folding her arms across her ample bosom, an indication that she felt the matter was settled.

Sighing, Elizabeth pushed herself to her feet. "*Sí*, Consuelo, I will rest, but first we need to discuss the plans for the cookout this afternoon."

"You are not to worry; I have everything arranged. Already, I have started to prepare the chili. It is going to be so hot it will burn the soles right off *Señor* Mac's feet." Her pendulous bosom shook when she laughed.

Elizabeth giggled at Consuelo's enthusiasm. "And the beef for the *carne asada*? Has Pedro prepared the pit?"

"*Sí . . . sí*," Consuelo nodded. "And your father is bringing the bananas from the city. If you are good, I will prepare the fried bananas for you."

Throwing her arms around Consuelo, she gave the older woman a hug. "You will wake me as soon as Cole arrives?" Cole had ridden into San Jose early this morning on some mysterious errand.

"*Sí*," Consuelo said, nodding her head. "Now go up and rest. We want the baby to grow big like his *padre*."

Cole arrived home an hour later, carrying a large bundle wrapped in brown paper. Hurrying into the kitchen, he found Consuelo standing over the cookstove, beads of perspiration dotting her brow as she stirred the large pot of chili. He snuck up behind her, grabbing her waist. "That's not chili I smell, is it?"

Consuelo spun around. "Ayeee! You scare me to death. Have you learned nothing since you were a small boy?" she chided, waving her wooden spoon at him.

Cole grinned. "Now, *mi madre*, don't be mad. I was only giving you a hug," he said, kissing her cheek. "Did you get Elizabeth to take a nap?"

Consuelo nodded. "*Sí*. She is asleep." Casting a curious eye at the large bundle Cole had set on the table, Consuelo asked, "What is that?"

"It's a surprise for Elizabeth. I am going to put it in the nursery and then wake her up."

Watching Cole depart, a cheerful smile lit her face. It was good to see the *señor* so happy; the *señora* had been good for him. After everything that had happened, they both deserved much happiness. A feeling of contentment welled up inside of her. All her children were happy. Soon there would be more babies to care for, she thought, wiping the tears from her eyes with her apron. *Sí*. She was truly blessed.

Walking quietly into the room, Cole deposited his parcel on the floor. They had converted his old room into the nursery, and it looked much different than when he had used it. The walls had been painted a pale lemon-yellow. Bright yellow and white gingham curtains hung at the window, and a big wooden rocker waited patiently by the hearth.

Crossing to the crib, he ran his hands over the quilt Elizabeth had fashioned. Pride welled up inside his breast at her accomplishments: the school, her sewing, even her cooking. He smiled to himself. Yes. Elizabeth had proven that she was no shallow society miss. She was a capable, caring, determined woman that he loved more than life itself.

Opening the door to their bedroom, he gazed longingly at his wife. She was even more beautiful in the last stages of her pregnancy than she had been when they first met. It was hard lying in bed beside her each night, not being able to make love to her. Tiptoeing over to the bed, he ran his finger over the flawless perfection of her cheek, and her eyes opened. They were as tender and soft as blue velvet; her love for him was reflected in their depths. The warmth of her smile took his breath away.

"Cole," Elizabeth said, sitting up. "When did you get back?"

"Just a little while ago." Bending over, he kissed the top of her head. "Get up. I have a surprise for you."

Bouncing out of bed as quickly as her cumbersome state would allow, Elizabeth grabbed on to his arm. "What is it?" she asked, her eyes sparkling with excitement.

Pulling her by the hand, Cole led her into the nursery. "Close your eyes and no peeking until I say so." He guided her to the center of the room, turning her to face the hearth. "Now you can look."

"Oh, Cole," Elizabeth exclaimed, rushing forward to touch the walnut cradle. "It's beautiful. Where did you get it?"

Cole smiled, pleased by her response. "A man by the name of Felipe Sanchez makes them in San Jose. I ordered this one about a month ago."

Throwing her arms about his neck, Elizabeth planted a passionate kiss on his lips. "I love you."

"Then why are you trying to torture me?" he teased,

tweaking her nose.

She looked down at the unmistakable bulge in his pants and smiled. "I'm sorry; I forgot. But you won't have to wait much longer."

Cole's expression was pained. "That baby had better come soon, so I'll be able to make love to my wife again."

"Cole!" Elizabeth scolded, covering his mouth. "Someone might hear you."

"The only person I want to hear me is that little one growing inside of your belly!"

"You're terrible!" Elizabeth said, smiling and patting Cole's cheek. "Come on. We need to get dressed before Abby and Jon arrive, or we'll be late for our own party."

"Oh, and I suppose you're going to parade around in front of me stark naked and inflict more torture on me?"

"Cole MacAlister!" Elizabeth shouted, holding her burning cheeks between her hands.

"I'm coming . . . I'm coming," Cole replied, a wide grin splitting his face. Damn, but she was cute when she was mad, he thought, following her into their bedroom.

Elizabeth and Cole walked about the courtyard, mingling with the friends and neighbors who had come to their first get-together. There were many of the same people who had attended Amber's fiesta last November, with the addition of several new faces.

Elizabeth had insisted that Doc Willis be invited, as well as Esteban and, of course, Pedro and Consuelo. There were to be no class distinctions of any kind at any of her gatherings.

Spotting Amber and her new husband, Matthew Flores, Elizabeth excused herself from Abby and Jon's company and crossed the courtyard to greet her friend. *"Buenas tardes, mis amigos."*

Amber laughed, giving Elizabeth a hug. "I see living with Consuelo has rubbed off on you, my friend."

"In more ways than one," Elizabeth replied, patting her protruding stomach.

"You are so lucky to be pregnant. Matthew and I are still hoping it will not be much longer for us," Amber said, smiling up at her handsome husband.

"It is not for a lack of trying on my part, I can assure you," he replied, kissing his wife on the cheek.

Elizabeth giggled, shaking her head at Matthew's outrageous comments. It seemed Amber had picked a good mate to complement her unconventional behavior, Elizabeth thought.

Speaking of unconventional behavior, Elizabeth eyed Rodrigo Montoya flirting with Maria Valdez. She couldn't contain the smile crossing her face as she watched Rodrigo's flamboyant tactics. She nodded her head in his direction.

"Elizabeth, you look lovelier than the roses in your garden!" Rodrigo exclaimed, coming forward to kiss her hand.

She smiled in greeting, nearly laughing aloud when she thought of how she had planned to use Rod to make Cole jealous. The thought was downright comical.

"I will expire on the spot if you don't consent to dance with me this very instant," Rod said.

"I am flattered, *Señor* Montoya, but as you can see, I am very pregnant. I don't think you would enjoy dancing with someone as clumsy as I am right now."

Rodrigo grabbed his chest. "How can you say that? I am wounded to the quick." He offered his hand, bowing dramatically.

How could she refuse such a gallant offer? she thought, smiling to herself. Latching onto Rod's hand, she followed him out to the area set aside for the dancing. They had just started a lively Mexican folk dance when Elizabeth felt a sharp pain in her lower abdomen. Feeling a gush of water between her legs, she looked down to find Rodrigo's calfskin boots soaking wet. The expression of dismay on Rod's face when he glanced down and saw what had happened would normally have put her into a fit of hysterics, but right then she was in too much pain to laugh. "Please, Rod, go and fetch Cole. I will wait here for you."

A few minutes later, Elizabeth found herself the object of everyone's attention as she stoically waited for her husband. Cole's expression of unadulterated fear was touching as he ran across the yard to where she stood. He looked positively ashen.

Consuelo was shouting at Pedro, in a mixture of Spanish and English, to find Doc Willis.

Even Abigail, who was usually calm, was hanging on to Jon's arm so tightly Elizabeth thought she would surely faint.

"You picked a damned inconvenient time to do this. You know that, don't you, Sunshine?" Cole said, scooping her up in his arms. Kissing her soundly on the lips, he carried her to their room.

She smiled through her pain. "But I only did what you requested," she said.

Elizabeth wasn't smiling a few minutes later when her labor began in earnest. Her abdomen contracted regularly like clockwork every three and one half minutes. Cole kept track on his pocket watch.

Doc finally arrived, ushering everyone out except for Cole. "Looks like your efforts are finally going to be rewarded, boy," Doc said, leaning over the bed to place his hands on Elizabeth's stomach. "Are you sure you want to stay and watch?" he added, noting Cole's pale face. "I don't want you fainting on me. I'd just as soon have one of the women in here to help if you think you might."

Sweat broke out over Elizabeth's brow; her breathing became labored as her contractions came closer together.

"Run and fetch me some hot water, boy, and have Consuelo bring me up some tea. Make sure the water is hot; let it boil for at least fifteen minutes."

Cole ran out of the room to do Doc's bidding. Hearing the door slam, Doc smiled down at Elizabeth, rolling up his shirtsleeves. "Now that he's out of the way, maybe we can get down to some serious birthing."

A half hour later, Cole walked into the room toting a large basin of steaming hot water. Consuelo trailed behind, carrying a tray laden with a china teapot and four cups. They were greeted by a smiling Elizabeth and a haggard-looking Doc.

"Congratulations, boy, you've got yourself a set of twins."

"Twins!" Cole shouted, his eyes widening in shock at the sight of the two small bundles nestled comfortably in the crook of Elizabeth's arms. Setting down the basin on the dresser, he hurried over to the bed.

The smile of wonder on Cole's face as he stared down at the two tiny babies brought tears to Elizabeth's eyes. "There appears to be one for each of us . . . a boy and a girl," she said.

Brushing the damp strands of hair back from

Elizabeth's face, Cole kissed her forehead. He couldn't control the tears coming into his eyes. "They're beautiful, just like you." He kissed each child on the cheek.

Doc and Consuelo waited quietly in the corner of the room while the happy parents shared their moment of joy. Consuelo's hands were raised in prayer as she thanked God for bringing two such beautiful babies into her care.

"Well, I guess since we've got two, we won't have to have any more children," Cole said, relieved that he wouldn't have to put Elizabeth through this again. His eyebrow raised in question at the secretive smile that crossed her lips.

"Remind me to tell you about the fortune Ah Sing read for me," she said, smiling. "I think you're going to be in for a big surprise."